THE STEALING

Mirador Publishing
10 Greenbrook Terrace
Taunton
Somerset
TA1 1UT
UK

The Stealing

Elisabeth Clare

~ *Foreword and Acknowledgements* ~

My thanks are due to Mirador Publishing, in particular Sarah Luddington and team, for their encouragement, courtesy and swift responses to my many enquiries, many of which, as an absolute novice, were probably laughable.

This first attempt at novel-writing, with all its flaws, has been many years in the hatching. The idea for the story dawned on me gradually whilst reflecting on my sighting of 'Ruth', as she became known to me, watching a little boy gazing into a shiny department store window, with utter absorption, in Wimbledon in July1990 when I was living and working in that area. There was in fact no swinging toy monkey in that window but swinging toy monkeys do exist in shop windows specifically in a well-known shoe shop in the Royal Arcade in Norwich, close to where I now live and work. The swinging toy monkey somehow made its insistent way into my story.

My thanks are due in this respect to George Wilson, now aged 19. He it was who, then aged 12, noticed that this much-loved icon of shopping with children in Norwich had disappeared from the window. On enquiring he was told that the monkey was broken whereupon he politely asked whether he could take it home to repair it. This he did, painstakingly and meticulously, thus restoring the monkey to full 'health' and back on to its swing where it continues to delight generations of children and provide some respite for the accompanying adults whose children are not keen on shopping and need urgent distraction.[1]

I would also like to acknowledge the influence and expertise of one of my university teachers, Professor Tony Davenport, who taught the *Special Author: Henry James* module in the final year of my English degree at Royal Holloway, University of London, (1988 to 1991). My story took shape and, I hope, substance in my mind as I read and studied James' *What Maisie Knew*. I came to understand the layers of damage adults can cause children and deepen my

---

[1] The full account of George's undertaking can be found at http://www.eveningnews24.co.uk/news/no-monkeying-around-as-george-finds-new-norwich-shop-icon-1-917224

understanding of the nature and scope of knowing at the same time as appreciating James' ability skilfully to manipulate his readers and characters using the: 'I know that you know that she knows' technique with consummate artistry.

My thanks are due also to my brother, Andrew, who gave me permission to put a short extract from his prose poem, *Bored Summer,* written when he was about 17, into my story, attributing it here, with his permission, to the fictional Louise. It is printed in full at the back of the book.

I owe a particular debt of thanks too to Professor Dame Hermione Lee for her biography of Penelope Fitzgerald:

Hermione Lee: (2013) *Penelope Fitzgerald, a life* p278 Vintage, UK, 2014 Knopf, US

As an award-winning writer and acclaimed biographer Lee needs no accolades from me, but just to note here that this was for me a wonderfully multi-faceted, 'world within a world', experience of understanding through Lee's vivid portrayal of Penelope Fitzgerald's own development as a writer, relatively late in life, something more of the craft of novel-writing, a skill which I hope to develop as I tentatively take my next steps with my second novel which is about the contemporary lifeboat community.

~ *Chapter 1* ~

The reflection startled her at first, as she scuttled quickly into the shop's doorway to shelter from the short, sharp summer shower. It was not just that the curve of the shop window appeared to distort his body, but that the boy's face seemed to be floating, disembodied, next to the naked mannequin.

The rain splattered against the summer-shiny windows of the old-fashioned looking haberdashery shop, *Hardcastle's*, which stood at the entrance to an arcade of several similarly iconic shops, in striking and pleasing contrast to the large, newly-refurbished, independently owned, department store immediately opposite. The gusts of wind, heralding autumn, blew a discarded plastic fast-food carton into the confined space in the doorway of *Hardcastle's* to jostle for position with chocolate bar papers, chewing gum wrappers and, oddly, a battered shoebox lid. It was to be remembered though that this was only the second week in July.

Ruth Forster decided to make her way across the road to the third floor for a cup of coffee in the department store's restaurant, relishing the hours of Saturday leisure stretching out ahead of her. For once she had no commitments and nobody waiting for her. She frequently used the department store in this way, as a rest stop, enjoying the slightly old-fashioned, faded luxury of the décor and the salubrious toilets. She rarely actually bought anything in the store, apart from scarves, purses and wallets for work colleagues at Christmas, the odd 'toiletry' – as the store called them – and the occasional greetings card and wrapping paper.

As she glided up the escalator she glanced down the stairwell towards the main entrance and was again startled to see the boy still gazing in the rain streaked window opposite. The water running down the glass was now performing its own distorting, disembodying act like a mirror in a fairground. He could not have been more than about 4 years old, she thought; no doubt his mother – or whoever he was with – would catch up with him soon.

Ruth selected her favourite two seat corner table from where she could idly 'people-watch' as she sipped her coffee, effortlessly entering into the tensions and nuances of the groups around her, while at the same time enjoying the fact that *her* script was not yet written. She had already, aged only 22, endured long loneliness, a sense of being on the periphery, of being peripheral, extraneous even, to the teeming humanity around her. She found herself at times glancing in at lighted windows, Moley-like, wishing to create, to belong, to be central somewhere, somehow. Sick for home, a *safe* home, a home she had never properly had, she had grown up amidst the Biblical 'alien corn', she often thought to herself, reflecting on the sadness of her name. Home for her thus far had been nothing more than the 'alien corn' in which her Biblical namesake had stood in tears.[2]

How she longed to hear the nightingale.[3]

Deciding to linger a while longer she ordered her favourite salad lunch, thinking she may as well give the rain a chance to clear and wanting, she understood, to be a part of other people still, not yet alone.

It was approaching 1o'clock. She had already collected her books from the library, having taken the long route into town, walking briskly through the park on the outskirts of the common, in what had then been bright, but strangely treacherous, sunshine. Ruth clung to the habit of reading actual books learned at her grandmother's house, loving the physical feel of them in her hands and remembering the fleeting sense of security and belonging she had felt in the book-lined sitting room there. Now, a visit to the library also had the benefit of enabling her to check on the educational science books for children, a useful and enjoyable bit of research relevant to her job as editorial assistant for a publisher of science books for children

Remembering that she now had only a quick shop to do for a few essentials and that the supermarket was on her way back to the car anyway, Ruth decided to indulge herself a little more on her day off and have another cup of coffee after her meal. She picked up a relatively recent edition, May, of a glossy magazine entitled *Coasts and Waterways in Britain* and became immediately engrossed by an account of a memorial event that had taken place 2 years previously in Great Yarmouth in Norfolk marking the 170th anniversary of the Great Yarmouth Bridge Tragedy.[4]

---

[2] Book of Ruth. 2:2-3, Old Testament.
[3] John Keats: (1819) *Ode to a Nightingale*
[4] Information from http://www.information-britain.co.uk/famdates.php?id=1473

On 2nd May 1845, she read, *thousands of people flocked to the banks of the River Bure to watch a clown called Nelson journey along the river in a tub pulled by 4 geese. Hundreds of people were on the suspension bridge itself. As the clown came into view they moved en masse to one side of the bridge whereupon their combined weight caused it to give way. Four hundred people toppled into the river, 79 died of which 59 were children.*

During the memorial event, which, by all accounts was very moving, a troupe of clowns paid tribute to the victims, skilfully miming the excitement and anticipation of the event swiftly turning to mayhem and unimaginable tragedy. A ukulele band played haunting melodies of loss and pain in the background. The event was fitting and well received. Two years previously a fund-raising effort led by Mrs Julie Staff had succeeded in raising £5,000 in £1 donations for a black granite memorial plaque on which were engraved all the names of the victims. [5] Ruth had never heard of this tragedy and was struck immediately, like others before her have been, by the pathos of light-hearted celebration turning so immediately to tragedy. The retelling of the tragedy will have this same effect on future generations.

A short while later she reluctantly left the restaurant's sheltered atmosphere, enclosed as it was, not knowing whether the summer shower would be over. She descended the escalator intrigued by her angle of view of the second and first floors. It was only as the ground floor approached with its intrusive, almost threatening, suggestions of outside, that she sensed, rather than saw, bright sunshine again, fickle in its distorting brilliance.

The smells of the perfume counter assailed Ruth nauseatingly as she headed for the wider of the two exits. Anticipating the wholesomeness of fresh air, and the July breeze, harbinger though it might be of more rain to come, she scarcely looked to the right or left as she left the shop. Again, she sensed, rather than saw, his presence.

The young boy was still there, he had hardly moved. The naked mannequin had, however, been dressed as decorously as the late summer offers on 'swimwear' allowed.

Late summer? It's the second week in July, she thought to herself. *They are wishing my life away for me.* She chuckled to herself at the inanity of the suggestion. She was struck though by the boy's rapt pose. A naked child mannequin now lay in bits on the floor of the window display and his attention

---

[5] Eastern Daily Press, 29th September 2013, accessed 18th April, 2017 via www.edp24.co.uk, 'Photo Gallery: Great Yarmouth suspension bridge disaster memorial unveiled

appeared to be focused on the various body parts yet to be assembled. With a kind of relief she quickly realised that he was in fact captivated by the swinging toy monkey forming part of the shoe display in the same window. The monkey, itself wearing shoes as it swung over the bar, paused on the top momentarily before swinging down the other side – spellbinding and strangely very funny indeed.

Ruth put down the bag of books and watched him quietly. There was no obvious sign of any adult in attendance. She found herself as mesmerised by his aura of concentration, his self-possession, his absorption and his little tip-tilted nose, as he himself was by the swinging monkey.

After perhaps five minutes had passed she said, "It's very funny isn't it?" There was no sign that he had heard her. She moved closer to him. Anyone watching would assume she was his mother – she liked that. He did not move away, just continued to watch the monkey, his attention barely caught by the window dresser arriving to assemble the mannequin. "Are you on your own?" she ventured. Again there was no response. Uncertain and suddenly fearful for him she stayed where she was, wondering what to do, but enjoying the monkey's repetitive, soothing antics. She allowed her mind to reflect on another reality – he was her boy and his regular treat when out shopping (she imagined little boys to hate shopping – but she didn't actually know this) was to watch the monkey.

She was not his mother though, and if she had been she would never have left him outside on his own. Instead they would have watched the monkey together and made up stories, perhaps about the monkey escaping from its monotonous pendulum and accompanying them on their trip, coming home with them, uninvited, funny and naughty. They would laugh together... it was as if she knew this 'more suddenly than she at first understood'. Henry James' complicity with his readers and characters sought her out now in this moment of quiet contentment.

As she stood and watched, the weather played its tricks – the sky had blackened without her noticing, the temperature had dropped, the wind had grown in strength and large, fat drops of chilly rain splattered against the glass, noisily. The boy was dressed in a rather grubby T-shirt that was much too small for him, shorts that were much too big, socks that were different lengths and very muddy trainers. Ruth was put in mind of the 'faint appeal of neglectedness'[6]

---

[6] Henry James: (1897) *What Maisie Knew* Heinemann, London, Stone, Chicago, Penguin/Random House

described by Henry James in his preface to *What Maisie Knew,* a book that was still vivid to her, such was its impact, from her recent studying of James as her Special Author in her English Literature degree.

What actually was to be done now though? Practicalities and possibilities ran through her mind. Should she take the boy into the shop and consult a member of staff? Should she ask him where he lived, where his parents were, who he was waiting for? Should she ring the police, and if so should she use 999 or 101? If not, how would she find a local contact number for them without leaving him, and perhaps losing him? She felt the need to stay with him, he was so very young, yet he was still entirely, raptly absorbed watching the monkey. Could she slip away and return with a number to ring, or ring from the payphones way up on the third floor, next to the restaurant and toilets? Did she want her mobile number associated with the call? If not, why not? It struck her too that it was not just that the shorts were too big, but that he looked very thin, undernourished, unkempt, uncared for perhaps.

"How old are you?" she asked him suddenly without preamble. He shook his head in reply without turning to look at her.

Ruth felt a strange sense of excitement as she tried to guess his age. She knew about children though she had none. "Have you ever seen a real monkey?" she asked.

"No."

"Do you think this one has a name?"

"No, it's not real."

"We could give it a name." Ruth's excitement was mounting. She felt a sense of purpose. The boy gave no hint of having heard her but continued watching. A faint rumble of thunder was followed several minutes later by lightning streaks.

"Are you hungry?" she asked. A rhythmic shaking of the head from side to side was the only response. "Thirsty?"

Without warning the boy shot her a glance, turned and ran from the shelter of the doorway into the now teeming rain, heading up the hill towards what they called the 'Village'.

~ *Chapter 2* ~

She knew that the murder had not actually been committed there – 'her park' as she thought of it, but she nevertheless associated the park, which lay to the west of the common, with that horrific crime. Feeling a powerful sensation of loss as the boy fled from her, she felt oddly liberated too. She had been beginning to feel a sense of possession as well as responsibility for this forlorn child. Now, she knew, would have been the time to alert the police to this encounter, but she decided instead to carry on with her precious, planned day. The shopping for one would take no more than twenty minutes, she would then return to the car and if the weather had relented she would let off pent-up energy and, yes, upset, by undertaking her usual fast circuit of the park.

What had the boy seen that had frightened him so, enough to run out into a thunder storm? What did he know? What did he understand? How much did she know about small boys after all?

"Poor little monkey," [7] she reflected, consciously echoing James.

Shopping completed and loaded, she drove up the hill, finding her usual parking space free. The mundane shopping task had given her a sense of release. She had stepped back, as it were, from the abyss. The sun now shone benignly from a clear blue, butter-wouldn't-melt sky. She felt free as a bird: the hackneyed phrase felt apt.

Ruth thought deeply as she walked fast for the sheer enjoyment of it. As usual not a soul was about. Funny expression – would it work if one were to say: *I saw one soul on my walk*? She returned to her reverie. Strange how people with families always assumed all your free time as a singleton was

---

[7] Henry James: (1897) *What Maisie Knew,* Heinemann, London, Stone, Chicago, Penguin/Random House

chore free. You still had to cook, clean, wash clothes, and wash yourself when you were just one. And why were they always so martyred about it all? She would give her right arm…

Her job kept her busy, of course. This was her first proper job and she had actually been asked to apply for it just out of university having worked for the small, but up and coming, publishers throughout her degree having briefly done some holiday work experience with them. Some people perceived her to be starting out as a real career woman not wanting the distraction of children or a husband, or so they believed. But could they ever actually understand the sense of tiptoeing around the edge, teetering on the brink but of never joyously falling in? The warm pit of tangled feelings, the bubbling broth of close family life was forever out of her reach. It eluded her.

Ruth slowed her pace as the path narrowed just before the bridge over the pond. She always lingered here seeing what pond life jumped or stirred as she tossed small pieces of bark or leaves in. But today, as the sky once again darkened, her attention was caught by a movement just ahead of her in the bushes to her right. There he was, sitting, hugging his knees to his chin, looking into the murky water.

"Hallo again," said Ruth, "I remember seeing you watching the monkey in the shop window down the hill this morning. You are out on your own for a long time. That was nearly two hours ago. Do you live nearby? Have you been home?"

"No."

"I expect they'll be getting worried about you. Would you like me to take you home? Is it far?"

"No."

"Shall we race sticks then? That's a good game – called Poohsticks. Have you played it before? Do you know it? Come, I'll show you." Again that strange excitement.

To her surprise, he jumped up and came towards her on the bridge. Ruth heard footsteps on the gravel path and looking up, noticed an elderly couple obviously out for an afternoon walk.

"I don't think we'll get home dry," the man said cheerily as his wife nodded "Good afternoon."

"We'll each have a stick, roughly the same size, then, on my count of three, we drop them in at the same time and see which one gets under the bridge first. Okay?"

At first he was inclined to slither down the slippery bank to retrieve his stick once it had gone under the bridge, so she very quickly had to show him that they needed a new stick each time.

So absorbed were they, laughing when they were neck and neck and one or other got snagged, he thrilled to win more times than lose, that the crack of thunder, followed immediately by a slash of lightning illuminating the rapidly darkening park, made them physically jump. The boy's elfin face quickly turned from absorbed interest in the game to unsuccessfully suppressed fear, as if concealing any natural emotion was already, in his short life, some sort of learned survival skill.

"Don't be frightened," Ruth murmured consolingly, "it's only a bit of thunder. I know a good place to shelter, come on, let's run."

She took his hand, and was struck by its smallness, as they ran together towards the folly and its half constructed pavilion. The folly itself was a stage; there was no other way to describe it. She had often leant on the parapet, ramparts really, and imagined the crowds listening to her, perhaps as Hermione listening to Leontes, sickened by knowledge of wrongdoing, real or imagined: '*I have drunk and seen the spider...*' '*the doctrine of ill doing*', the accused Polixenes yearning for innocence[8], perhaps Ophelia[9] as she descended the abyss: '*There's a willow grows aslant a brook*', witness to Hamlet's own descent into madness.

She kept meaning to discover more about this folly, there were no notices telling its story, but on leaving the park, she always forgot.

As they sheltered from the now driving rain in the barely built pavilion, or gazebo, whatever it was, Ruth found herself simultaneously wondering whether the elderly couple got home warm and dry, and noticing how pale and tired the boy looked. She felt assailed, assaulted almost by responsibility for him, he was so very young. Could she just wait until the rain stopped and tell him she had to return home now, bye bye? Could she say that now and leave him in the shelter of the pavilion, perhaps? He must be hungry, thirsty; she assumed he had eaten nothing. She felt in the pocket of her trousers and discovered the wrapped biscuit so thoughtfully provided by the department store restaurant with her cup of coffee, now nearly three hours ago.

"Would you like this biscuit?" He took it from her hungrily and nibbled it like a hamster, taking tiny bites at a time. "I expect you're thirsty, I've got

---

[8]William Shakespeare: (c1609-1611) *The Winter's Tale* Act 2, Sc 1
[9] William Shakespeare: (c 1603) *Hamlet, Prince of Denmark* Act 4, Sc 7

some fruit juice in my shopping in the car, we'll get it when the rain eases, shall we?" He nodded.

They sat together, almost companionably, she felt, listening to the sheeting rain on the large leaves of the rhododendrons which surrounded them, most of the splendid view from this high place almost obliterated by the torrential downpour. The boy shivered, but she had no extra layer to put round him for warmth. She moved closer to him, hoping to keep him warmer that way, but, almost imperceptibly, he edged away.

Ruth realised he might yet again run, the intimacy of the game of Poohsticks, suddenly lost. She had to keep his attention, his trust; she had to woo him with her playfulness.

So it was of course *Incy Wincy Spider* that came to mind first; she did all the actions, which she urged him to copy, though he would not. Then '*There was an old woman who swallowed a fly*'. At the 'wriggled and wriggled and wriggled' bit the boy smiled, then chuckled, naturally – and she realised this was the first time in their short acquaintance this had happened so she built on it rapidly.

As the rain began to let up she walked to the top of the steps leading to the stage and started declaiming '*The Walrus and The Carpenter*',[10] sweeping her hand in a wide arc to indicate the 'quantities of sand', making the requisite sweeping motion of seven maids with seven mops, and theatrically wiping away the bitter tear shed by the carpenter at the enormity of sweeping the sand clear away. He laughed wonderingly and delightedly and yet made no eye contact.

It was perhaps fortunate that Ruth did not remember the entire poem, but decided they both needed to warm up, and her car was not now far away as the folly was part of the circuit she always did of this park. As they left their rudimentary shelter, she spotted a jogger running up the path towards the folly. They waited until he had passed and nodded his thanks for allowing him a clear passage and then made their way down through the rhododendron bushes, to the gravel path through the lawned area of the park, clearly once the front garden of the big house, now covered in blue security plaques and hidden behind imposingly high brick walls.

The sky remained a leaden grey, reminiscent of an afternoon in late November, rather than barely half past three in mid-July.

---

[10] Lewis Carroll (1872): 'The Walrus and the Carpenter' in *Alice Through the Looking Glass*

~ *Chapter 3* ~

Ruth opened the passenger car door for him and he climbed in but remained standing up, uncertain, his tiny stature barely allowing him to see out of the rain-streaked windscreen.

"Sit down then," said Ruth softly, "and I'll find the fruit juice." He scrambled into the front seat – his feet nowhere near reaching the floor and looked with interest at the gear lever, the steering wheel, dashboard and handbrake. He leaned forward and pressed the button for the CD player, covering the lighted up panel with his hand as Ruth returned from the boot with a carrier bag of shopping. "We can put some music on if you like," she said. "Now, would you prefer orange or apple juice?" He touched the green apple juice packet to indicate his preference. "Right, I'll just find something to pour it into." She remembered she had a couple of plastic cups from the water cooler at work in the driver's side pocket and retrieved them. She poured half a cup for him. Grasping it in both hands he drank it down in one gulp. "You *are* thirsty," remarked Ruth, "have some more," and she filled up the cup this time.

All the car windows were rapidly misting up and the car felt warm, stuffy but secure and intimate, obscured as it was to the outside world. "I expect you're hungry too, let's see what there is in here." She lifted out the bananas and broke off a smallish one, proffering it to him. He took it quickly and held on to it tightly, perhaps unsure of what to do with it. "You remind me of that monkey in the shop window," Ruth chuckled. "Here, I'll peel it for you."

As he slowly munched it she rummaged through the bags for something else. A packet of bread rolls. As a child she had loved bread rolls, preferably freshly baked and with no butter. She remembered that the baker's van used to deliver bread to her grandmother's house and he would give her fresh, warm rolls to eat as she stood near his van to take the bread from him.

Perhaps, she now thought, *I looked thin and neglected. Perhaps he reported his concerns to the authorities*. She hadn't been rescued though so if he had they probably just noted it.

She opened the packet and handed him one. Again, he took it quickly and started biting into it with obvious enjoyment, alternating this with bites from the banana. "Yes, just like a little monkey," murmured Ruth, half to herself. "Once upon a time, long, long ago and far, far away, there lived a woman called Sheba who yearned for a child. Year after year went by and no child was born despite a contented marriage to a man called Frederick, who likewise longed for his wife to bear him a child. The woman craved some young thing to nurture so one day in the days when circuses came to town and had animal acts she slipped out at the dead of night and unlocked a cage behind the circus tent which contained a lonely looking little monkey who was so bored in his cage that he repeatedly swung upside down and howled like a baby for its mother."

She sensed that she had lost the boy's attention and turned to see that he had fallen deeply asleep in the warmth of the car. Ruth stared at his tiny, pinched looking face as he slept, not peacefully but busily and uneasily as if sleeping was just another aspect of physical survival to be done quickly but with care not to lower the guard, not to fall prey to predators, to be ready for immediate avoiding action on awakening.

He looks troubled even if in sleep, Ruth reflected, and remembered the innocent delight she had witnessed in him as he played Poohsticks, and earlier watching the monkey's antics. *But he's not yet five years old,* she thought, *how can he be so careworn?*

She decided to sit out the very heavy rain in the shelter of the car, feeling pleasantly obscured from any prying eyes by the misted windows. She felt as if she was on the brink of something momentous, but she could not define what that was. "I bid adieu to childhood too young," she whispered to herself theatrically, remembering her own sense of drama, aged nearly 8, and using precisely those words having recently encountered the word 'adieu' in a book she was reading. "Well, we all have to face it and move on sometime," she chided herself. Perhaps she came across to others as too needy, too longing, too lost, wanting something indefinable. Certainly, she seemed to scare people away she realised. She could perhaps soothe this little child, ease his fear, whatever it was; she needed and wanted his trust but how to do this? She too had learned at an early age to trust no one, to expect hurt and fear, to fend for herself emotionally, and to be the shaper of her own destiny.

She could hear the single shout as if it were yesterday, the thud as her mother fell to the floor, her stepfather's, Steve, unfocused gaze on her: "See what you made me do?" and the sharp, cold pavement as she ran and ran, only to be found by a policeman as she crouched shivering behind a garage three streets away.

Following her mother's hospitalisation after yet another botched suicide attempt, 'whilst the balance of her mind was disturbed', Ruth was returned to the care of her stepfather, care being a strange word, she'd thought even then. She could tell no-one the truth – ever – as her mother's fragile mental health was known and her stepfather was seen to be the one who coped.

Something was going to happen now. The sound of the engine seemed to lull the boy into a deeper, perhaps more restful sleep as she slipped the car into first gear and, with wipers on full speed, moved gently off.

Home, Ruth thought, *home. We can hole up there and I can make him whole. I will be a strategist; no-one need know he is there.* She was, by chance, living alone in her rented accommodation at that time, being in between sublets whilst the owner of the house was living and working in Canada for a year. London suburban life: she was happy there, but only rarely saw the elderly couple who lived next door, hardly to speak to, merely nod. You mind your business, we'll mind ours; not unfriendly but that was how it was. *Ideal*, she thought. And she could move into her own house, *her own home,* she savoured the words, in about two weeks' time – it was all meant to be.

Her grandmother, her father's mother, Mim, as she called her, had always looked out for her as no other adult had since her father had been killed in a road accident whilst being driven by a colleague when Ruth was only 9 years old. Ruth had, since then, even before her mother, Julie, had hitched up with Steve (as Ruth always put it to herself) used her grandmother's house in Thames Lacey as a safe haven to which she regularly escaped. Her own father was Mim's only and much loved child, Colin. They grieved together.

Ruth had more or less lived at the Thames Lacey house, No 12, as they called it, during high school, only returning sporadically to the now squalid house Steve 'inhabited'. 'Lived in' was not the right term. She always returned to Mim's house during university vacations. In her final year Ruth had lived there full time looking after her increasingly frail grandmother until she died in her own bed at home with Ruth sitting beside her, stroking her hand. The house and her grandmother's entire estate had been left to Ruth as her only living relative and now probate was almost complete. How she loved that house…

She glanced at the clock on the dashboard and saw that it was 4.45pm. She should be just ahead of the really heavy build-up of traffic. Visibility was poor in the still driving rain; it felt more like a February afternoon. She always liked this homecoming time of day, relishing shrugging off the working day, and drawing her own carefully constructed carapace around her, empty though it was of the warmth and welcome she craved.

So how can she tell it? Safety, welcome, security, warmth, unconditional interest in her, instinctive awareness of how she was, *caring* how she was. The soft embrace, home, shelter, food, warmth, the dark night shut out. And in summer too at that time of day, the transition from day to evening with the promise of a longer light, the shadows lengthening heralding a softer dusk, a softer warmth. All of this now only a distant cherished memory. Fast falls the eventide... help of the helpless...

She had indeed been helpless in the face of such tightly controlled fear, such secrets, such holding on... 9 years old and dreading the nights, dreading the distorted cherishing, the demon demands, demon's demands.

~ *Chapter 4* ~

Ruth realised she would probably have to wake him on arrival home... suddenly it really did feel like home, a haven, safe, unconditional... but unconditional on what exactly? Caring perhaps would do it at this stage.

And what stage was this exactly in the abduction and kidnapping of a child? she thought to herself dispassionately.

She was bringing him home to safety, to nurture, away from the dark threats outside, though darkness itself was still at least three or four hours away.

As Ruth parked with practised ease in the one space left outside the house the sky cleared as suddenly as the earlier thunder had arrived lending a piercing clarity to the suburban street. She heaved the supermarket shopping bags out of the boot and dumped them on the front doorstep fearing to leave the boy alone, sleeping in the car, even for the short time it would take to deposit them indoors, even though hardly anyone was about.

Waking the boy very, very gently she said quietly, "Here we are, home safe now."

He looked about fearfully, seemingly irritated at being woken, and clumsily clambered out almost catching his foot in the trailing seat belt. Ruth put a hand out to steady him but, ignoring it, he gazed up at the upstairs windows which the sun was striking, causing almost blinding, bright reflections and walked stiffly along the short path to the front door. Fumbling for her key she unlocked the door, picked up the pile of unimportant post on the mat, ushered him inside and swept up the bags of shopping in quick, economical movements. He stood silent; transfixed it seemed, by the steep staircase which ran up from the hall.

"Come on into the kitchen and we'll unpack this lot and find something to eat, something for tea." Ruth consciously chose the familiar homecoming word. Once in the kitchen, again he stood silent, watching, and watchful, as she quickly put the shopping in the right places. "I'll show you where the bathroom is so you can wash your hands before tea and the toilet is just next door." She added this as an afterthought thinking to put him at ease. "There's just one bathroom and toilet upstairs, come on."

He followed her almost meekly upstairs to the landing and stood small in the doorway as she showed him the light switches, found him a clean towel from the airing cupboard and showed him how to squeeze the soap from the dispenser.

Ruth then quickly made up the bed in the spare room, the smallest of the three bedrooms, which was currently awaiting a tenant. Noting its impersonal décor, the bland, cream walls and brown cushions, she selected a plain cream duvet cover and excitedly started thinking about how to decorate it for him, her 'little monkey' as she was beginning to think of him.

Fortunately she remembered she had fish fingers, chips and peas in the freezer – children's food as she always called it. Just nipping out to the corner shop was not going to be an easy option now, at least not until he was settled perhaps. But he was only 4, she remembered. Instinctively she knew not to leave a 4 year old alone.

They both ate hungrily, without speaking, at the kitchen table, he neatly and competently rather to her surprise, and followed the fish fingers with tinned peaches and cream which she brought to the table, finding him gazing out at the small garden through the French windows, which she opened to let in the soft evening air and to release the cooking smells.

"Do you want to play in the garden for a while?" she asked him gently, noting the dark circles under his eyes.

He stared at her intently as if looking for a catch somewhere in the question and then hesitantly ventured out into the cooler evening air.

Ruth quickly cleared the plates, noting with irritation and some weariness how the strangely bright, low evening sun showed up dust in lost corners and streaks of mud and dead insects on the windows. The relentless light, probing into all recesses, brought her up sharply, revealing the enormity, the reality of what she had done. What had she done? Kidnapped a child. *Kidnapped a child.* She was now beyond the pale, she had crossed a threshold. She was in a fix; she chuckled mirthlessly at the euphemism, but how now to fix it? What should she do? What a to-do. What to do?

Ruth stepped outside into the now chilly evening and saw the boy crouching low, intent on something. Venturing nearer she saw he had neatly destroyed the brick border to the small garden path, with the rectangular bricks all upturned revealing teeming masses of busy insect life, woodlice, pale, skittering, ants scurrying, all with a purpose, a destiny beyond mere survival. The boy was watching quietly. Ruth suggested gently that together they restore the insects' shelter, their protection, and leave them be for the night. There was now just enough muted light to do this.

"Time for bed now," Ruth stated matter of factly. "It's been a long day one way and another. I'll run a bath for you and find you a small T-shirt of mine to sleep in. Tomorrow we'll go shopping for some other clothes for you."

Compliant, complicit really, the boy followed Ruth inside and upstairs where he was immediately absorbed by the ever-increasing pile of scented bubbles. Ruth, kneeling down to feel the temperature, suddenly scooped up the top layer of bubbles in her cupped hands and playfully blew them so that they scattered and danced catching the fluorescent light. The boy caught her eye – the first time he had done so since the game of Poohsticks in the park – and laughed delightedly. He took some in his small, cupped hands and clapped them away.

"Climb in, Captain, give me those," commanded Ruth merrily, turning away to put the T-shirt and shorts into the wash tub. The boy sat still and quiet in the bath, quiescent, almost fearful. "There, you have a good scrub, my lad, Captain Sir," said Ruth trying to invoke the same shouts of laughter with this but the boy listlessly complied. "I expect you're pretty tired," Ruth suggested, making a mental note to introduce hair washing tomorrow, "sometimes baths are good for playing, sometimes just for getting clean. Out you come now." And it was then that she saw them, numerous, finger sized grazes, which were healing, all over his back and legs. Cigarette burns. She gently helped him dry noting how difficult it was to dry another person and realising that this was an absolute first for her and that the only way to tell if the other person was dry was by feeling them; this she did lightly, brush stokes really.

She helped him pull the T-shirt, a souvenir from the Roman baths in Bath, appropriately enough, over his head, and it reached his ankles. Wanting to settle him for the night – she thought this was what a parent would probably do – unpractised as she was, damaged goods really in that line, she decided to read him a story, but what? All she had was Pooh. Fine, that was a start.

As he climbed into bed she went to fetch the copy, returning to find him rigidly staring at the white artex ceiling with its extravagant swirls and loops. She rather liked the ceilings all done in different artex styles though she knew it was not the thing to like and that people spent vast quantities of money painstakingly removing artex mouldings. Nevertheless, she continued to like them perversely and defiantly.

"Here we are. I expect you might know *Winnie the Pooh*." She started the familiar text and completed the first chapter for her own pleasure as much as his but noted that he listened with rapt attention, smiling at *'Isn't it funny how a bear likes honey?'* [11] and actually chuckling at the bears and bees mash up. By the time she got to Winnie the Pooh singing *"How sweet to be a cloud"* she realised he was fast asleep but she completed the chapter for completeness sake, for *'pure loving-kindness'* sake. Hardy's words crept unsought into her thoughts.[12] She found herself starting to ramble meaninglessly in her head, it was tiredness, she knew, but she felt herself to be, with certainty at that moment, full of pure loving-kindness.

"And so to bed, 'to sleep, perchance to dream...'[13] Oh stop it," she admonished herself, "talk sense, think sensibly what is to be done. I am in a fix."

Perhaps she should go away, take a ferry somewhere? No, that would mean passports, border control. Perhaps she could go away in England, go to the seaside with her child, her son. They could have fun, she could show him a good time, show him fun, beach, play, sea, fairground, amusements; somewhere quiet-ish, beauty, tranquillity, larks, song and dance, to quote Eeyore.

She then began to wonder how she could get time off. Easy, the summer holiday period was approaching; she could apply for emergency annual leave to look after an unexpected child, but whose child? A foster child, an adopted child, a relative's child? She had occasionally thought about fostering, just out of idle interest actually, mainly wondering how on earth anyone could do it, that is, return the child.

Ruth picked up the newspaper and put it in the recycling bin; one of her many obsessions was to get rid of old newspapers as soon as possible; being something of a newspaper addict, unusual at her age she knew, but a habit she had picked up from her grandmother, she knew how quickly they could mount up. Most of her contemporaries followed the news online, sometimes reading

---

[11] A. A. Milne: (1926) *Winnie the Pooh*. Methuen and Co Ltd. London

[12] Thomas Hardy: (1898) *A Broken Appointment*, in Selected Poems, ed Davies W (1982) J.M. Dent and Sons Ltd., London

[13] William Shakespeare: (c 1599 – 1601) *Hamlet: Prince of Denmark*, Act 3 Sc 1

digital versions of newspapers or just from the various news sites, but like books, she loved the physical feel of newspapers. Thinking about the day's news she remembered she had not had her usual fix of television news…well, it was late, she didn't want it really, she didn't need it; she had enough to contend with.

Time off would be easy, she reflected. She had an editing task to complete, probably two weeks, pretty full on, home-based work. She also had the usual crop of emails to respond to – and their attachments – a couple of end of academic year reports to compile with deadlines looming. It would all get done, plus, she hardly dared breathe it, a child to look after, to care for, to nurture, the unuttered and the unknown, again James' *What Maisie Knew* [14] sprang to mind. She decided she would buy the boy's clothes online, much easier.

They would hole up here and get as much fresh air and exercise as possible making the most of the long summer days. She would get him gardening and give him his own vegetable patch, all necessary items being purchased online or improvisations made. This would take them to the end of July, still the long summer stretched ahead gloriously, much as it had done for her first eight and a half years. She could recreate a carefree childhood for him, erase anything other.

How much time could she have off work for fostering, she wondered. How did it all work? Money would not be a problem for a while as she was due several weeks leave which she, in any event, tended to save for August and early September as this was the company's down time, all work for the new academic year having been done by June, July at the latest.

Who knows? she thought, with a joyous feeling of just living for the present. Soon she would have no monthly rent and no mortgage… ever. Freelance editing was scarily precarious especially with a little child to look after but that was a realistic option to consider in the very near future; she felt momentarily overwhelmed by the thought, but it was something she could do. But how to conceal it all? The worry was fleeting though and not unduly concerned she made her way to bed looking in on the sleeping child on her way. He had tossed the duvet off and lay curled on his side, deeply asleep

---

[14] Henry James: (1897) *What Maisie Knew* Heinemann, London, Stone, Chicago, Penguin/Random House

Ruth awoke very early the next morning as the sunlight relentlessly pierced the cracks between the rather too short and too narrow curtains. She tiptoed across the landing and saw the boy had scarcely moved in his sleep; still curled on his side, the duvet tossed to one side, small, vulnerable, helpless in sleep.

Showering quickly she headed downstairs, opening the French doors and stepping onto the short, damp grass, wet with dew. She loved this feeling of the long summer day, days really, stretching ahead with purpose and commitment. She needed to make plans but for the moment the priority was to gain the boy's trust by looking after him. She had her own breakfast of cereal and fruit and wondered what the child would like for breakfast. People often had set routines for this meal but for now she would leave him sleeping – children woke when they were ready.

Ruth decided, as a priority, to 'touch base' with work – she hated those clichéd office phrases but they sometimes seemed apt. She emailed her departmental team leader explaining that she would be working at home for the next week or ten days in order to meet the deadline for her current editing tasks. This would save her at least two hours travelling time a day, not to mention the work distractions of chatting to colleagues, telephone interruptions, and difficulty concentrating in her large, shared office. It would also take her up to her already booked annual leave… as was usual at this time of the year she still had a full 20 days of her 25 day entitlement left. She was trusted and well respected by her colleagues and this was an entirely accepted way of working as long as the job was done, deadlines were met and she was contactable.

Part of her strategy now was to keep in contact by responding to emails as quickly and efficiently as she always did, to continue with editing – she loved her job so this was no hardship – and to be available for any video conferencing if necessary – this did not, in fact, happen very often. This way she could continue to work from home, complete the tasks and relish the thought of the freedom of the rapidly approaching summer holidays, knowing that she was placing no extra burden on colleagues. This leave had already been booked before…before she crossed the threshold, as she put it to herself, and became a child abductor.

She had of course crossed a threshold before. What was the difference between abduction and kidnap, she mused? She must look it up. It felt important to be clear about what crime she had actually committed.

First things first, she thought to herself. Having attended to all the work emails, all routine, she checked her food stocks. Luckily she had done her weekly supermarket shop – for one, of course – just yesterday. That seemed a long while ago now; so much had happened, she had travelled far. She could do a top up supermarket shop online of course, no problem. She felt fortunate to be so alone in the world actually as an only child, both her parents and her stepfather seemingly out of her life now. She did have some, just a few, friends from school and university but she was mostly in touch with them by email on high days and holidays – as her grandmother used to say. In fact she loved sending postcards from her short holiday destinations, taken alone and rarely, to a selected few friends as an extra way of keeping in touch, over and above Christmas cards and, occasionally, birthdays. She strived to keep the tradition going as even at her age she had noted a moving away from any written communication in this digital age and she wondered at times, where all this stuff would go, where actually was it, what was cyberspace and was it finite?

Work sorted for the time being, Ruth decided she would check on her young charge – he needed a name – of course. She would ask him again, at a good time. Looking in on him she saw him awake and staring fixedly at the artex swirls and whirls.

"Good morning, sweetheart. Time to get up. It's a lovely day again. Are you all right?" The boy nodded slowly, turning almost reluctantly to look at her. "Let's get you dressed." She had washed his T-shirt and shorts and though they still spoke of neglect, at least they were clean. She lifted the T-shirt he had slept in over his head, quickly slipping on his old one, then the shorts, socks and trainers. She opened the door of the toilet for him, waited outside and then made sure he washed his hands.

Downstairs she poured out some cereal and milk and watched him tuck in hungrily, picking up the bowl to drain the last of the milk. She made some toast, spread marmalade on it, poured out orange juice for him, and then sat next to him as he ate and drank hungrily. All this time he neither spoke nor looked at her.

If they were to hole up here she felt fresh air was important and as much activity as possible. "Let's do a bit of gardening," said Ruth, taking him by the hand. "You could have your own patch." They spent the morning happily engrossed, she weeding, he digging his patch of flowerbed, shaking in the seeds she gave him (free with a packet of cereal) – cornflowers. He loved to turn over stones and bricks and watch the insects scuttling around in the glare of bright sunlight. She gave him a large, empty biscuit tin and showed him how to make a pretend garden with paths of tiny stones, flowerbeds, and grass. Ruth longed to know more about him, his name, who would be missing him, where he had come from, but decided she would just quietly gain his confidence, and not rush it.

At about midday a rather imperious sounding ring on the front door bell shattered the companionable silence. Ruth started, suddenly fearful that the game was up – 'game was up' – what was she thinking? This was no game. Hot and thirsty, she pushed her hair out of her eyes leaving a streak of mud across her forehead and, turning to check, was amused to see the boy rush to the shed; finding it locked, he quickly slipped behind it and was out of sight in no time.

Unlocking the door she was relieved to find that it was only someone collecting for the local children's hospice and willingly donated some money to that good cause.

She found him still hiding, almost holding his breath, and held out her hand to show him all was safe and well. Feeling his small hand in hers she could sense both his trust and his fear – he was so small.

"Time to cool off a bit, I think," she said as they walked up the garden to the welcome cool of the dining room into which the French doors led. She handed him a glass of orange squash which he drank very quickly, wiping his grubby hand across his mouth.

Although Ruth was aware that she was rather deprived of news, taken up as she had been with events of the last 24 hours, she decided she would wait until he was in bed to catch up on the radio or television news, but she was able to quickly check the news on her phone. There was nothing high profile about a missing child she was relieved to see, just the usual doom and gloom about the economy, a bit of repetitive and pointless speculation on forthcoming football signings, something about the German Chancellor's visit to London, an accident on the M25 with a lorry shedding its load of plastic dustbins but nobody hurt, and something about a couple of bodies found in a garden in Enfield, which had not yet been identified.

Lunch was ham sandwiches but, on a sudden whim, Ruth cut the little boy's sandwich into fingers and constructed a smiling face with them, using cut up tomatoes for ears, raisins for eyes and nose, some carrot sticks to make the arms, legs and body of a stick man, and some crisps for curly hair. Putting it in front of him, having helped him wash his hands, she watched a slow, delighted smile spread across his tiny, pinched, careworn face as he looked up at her with cautious delight.

"What shall we call him?" Ruth asked. "Mr. Sandwich would be a good name wouldn't it?" and they ate in companionable silence, the little boy eating more delicately than earlier and selecting the different pieces carefully.

~ Chapter 6 ~

And so the first few days passed companionably enough, each following a languid, tranquil pattern. Ruth made sure the little boy knew his way about the house taking him by the hand and showing him every aspect.

During the hot afternoons they would watch children's television or she would read to him from some of the childhood favourites she had remembered she still had in her bookshelves. She also had on her shelves a few science books for very young children which she had helped to edit – she usually helped with those for older children – but he particularly loved the one about water on earth and would laugh delightedly at the page with just '**PITTER PATTER!**' on it in very large letters. He also loved a little book about garden insects and was able to read it fluently in no time at all following the words with his finger and looking at each picture carefully.

The clothes she had ordered for him arrived in exciting parcels and they enjoyed unpacking them together, the boy stroking the fabrics and smelling their newness with delight and some awe, the postman being the only adult contact she had during the day. She made it clear that the clothes were just for the boy and they enjoyed putting them in the empty chest of drawers. He slept well at night and was starting to look less pinched and less – well – starved-looking really.

Ruth decided she *must* have a name for him. "What do they call you?" she asked. "What's your name? Mine is Ruth." At his silence and sudden withdrawal she decided to move things on and suggested she give him his very own name, like Mr. Sandwich. "I think you look like a Matthew," she said confidently, "that reminds me of a boy I nearly knew. I shall call you 'Matthew'."

He smiled shyly and lost his worried look. "Mimi," he said quietly.

Ruth paused, quickly suppressing any surprise or shock. "Okay, I am Mimi," and she lifted his chin slowly and gently, looking at his little face, making real eye contact, it seemed, almost for the first time.

She was able to work hard and with focus in the evenings, meeting all deadlines and she found herself suddenly starting to plan a 'proper' summer holiday with Matthew's needs always at the forefront of her mind. The school summer holidays were about to start and she relished the thought of Matthew playing on a beach perhaps with other children, herself chatting to other mothers… mothers – she stopped herself.

It was easy to arrange. Angmering-on-Sea, she decided quickly, easy and accessible. Ruth booked ten days holiday in a terraced cottage via a holiday lets website. They could have an evening meal at the nearby hotel if they wished and she liked the idea of the security of being near other holidaymakers without the constraints, carpeted corridors and general 'indoorsiness' of an actual hotel. The most important thing was to be as near the beach as possible with the sea a quick run down a path and in sight of the cottage.

During the last few days in London, contentedly holed up, as Ruth put it to herself, Matthew slowly grew in confidence. He loved the garden, loved his own little patch and she felt torn between maintaining this secretive existence and her own desire to flee, to escape to wide open places, to have fun, to be free. So, knowing she only needed to return to pack her relatively few things, she let the solicitor dealing with probate know that she would be contactable only by email or mobile for the next two weeks as she was away on holiday. She had given her landlord the required month's notice and intended to move into her own house, *her own house;* she was awed by the thought, in mid-to late August.

First though, she needed to find a school for Matthew as soon as possible. A quick internet search revealed that the local infant school had an excellent Ofsted rating so she decided to apply. In theory this was easily done online because she felt no need to go on an actual tour since the internet information was so comprehensive and she could upload the relevant documentary evidence, i.e. solicitors' letters for proof of address and the birth certificate which she had so carefully secreted away. Additionally, as this was the only school she wished to send Matthew to because she felt a deep need to be part of a community, she did not want to put second and third choices on a relatively 'anonymous' application.

In fact so strongly did she feel this that she believed that, whatever the local school was rated by the powers-that-be, sending her own child, Matthew, there, *her own child*, would enhance the school for all. She had read somewhere that a critical mass of 'bright' or 'able' children, to use the school teacher-ish term, was all that was needed to raise a school's standards. And she sensed a certain innate 'brightness' in Matthew. He was quick to pick things up, follow instructions and, lately, to ask penetrating questions beyond the usual childish – 'why?'

They so enjoyed their bedtime story reading that Matthew would now grasp the book himself, follow carefully and point to the pictures. Ruth thought she would let reading happen by osmosis, as it were, so, sitting him on her lap during day time reads, she would run her fingers along the familiar words as she read with no demand that he read to her. But in no time at all, he was pointing to words such as 'no' and 'in' and sounding them out, just occasionally needing some minor correction.

And so it was that Matthew learned to read gently, with no effort, just as he assimilated many other experiences in this way. Ruth therefore decided to make an appointment to see the head teacher to explain why she was applying so late for a September school place for her child who was young in the school year being born in June.

This was easy to explain – they had only just moved to the area – and had the merit of being partly true. She had no idea that her grandmother would have died when she did and that she would have left the house in Thames Lacey to her in her will. She was reassured, and wryly amused to note that the school's website listed 'looked after' children as having first priority for a place. She liked the ethos this demonstrated but reflected that realistically this was probably a local authority rule, enforced nationwide. She knew that such children were now referred to as 'Children Looked After' – 'CLA'S' as opposed to 'LAC's' and wondered idly what had precipitated this change, what non-politically correct term did 'LAC' suggest? 'CLA's' was certainly less user-friendly as an acronym, she mused.

Some of the stories surrounding benign and malign neglect of so-called 'looked after' children shocked her to the core, the headline-hitting Rochdale and Rotherham scandals of course, but also the cruel abandonment of children on the cusp of adulthood when choices and adult support and facilitation of those choices was just so vital. If it had not been for her beloved grandmother...

~ *Chapter 7* ~

Thoughts of 'looked after children', her grandmother and the accompanying sadness, never-to-be-assuaged, she felt, that she had not been able to do enough for her beloved Mim as she entered the last few gruelling months of her life, catapulted her back, it felt almost literal, to a terrifying memory. That cold, hard pavement, running, running in the dark, was brought vividly to Ruth's mind just by that clumsy nomenclature, 'CLA's', with all its irony, heavy with irony, she liked the tautology in that phrase.

Aged 9 and running as if her heart would burst, the rain beating down, forcing her into the shelter of the disused garage's overhanging roof. The policeman on the beat, his steps slowing almost theatrically as he peered into the darkness and made out her sobbing figure, his torch casting even more threatening darts of bouncing light as he leaned towards her.

"Whatever's the matter? What are you frightened of, love? What's your name?" As she whispered her name, he said, "Well, that's a start. Your parents will be worried sick, looking for you... Where do you live? How old are you? You look too young to be out on your own at this time of night." She told him quickly and exactly her grandmother's address in Thames Lacey, parrot-like, learnt, almost as if she was addressing a letter. "Well, I'll call for somebody to get you there safely and get to the bottom of this. You're quite a way from home on a horrible night like this."

Then the warmth and smell of the police car, the efficient, kind woman police officer who had seen so much, helping her into it, sitting with her in the back, not asking too much. Arriving at her grandmother's, being given hot chocolate and custard creams, and being put to bed. Soft, warm, clean, crisp white sheets in the spare bedroom, *her* bedroom, the one she always slept in, where she had been allowed to keep some clothes and books, safety, refuge.

And later, the discovery of her mother's inert body by the police; scared into stillness on that freezing night, and scarred for life as her stepfather's knife blade had done its work, skilfully disguised by him as one of her many botched suicide attempts whilst he was out, and not there to prevent it. Questions, gentle, probing but never, ever would she tell the truth because she would not be believed, her drunken stepfather spinning so many lies, the truth never emerging. It must lie hidden always, the threats, the fear, the shame.

Her grandmother, then aged 73, and just diagnosed with lung cancer, frail and loving, but unable to look after her as she faced months of gruelling hospital treatment. Her mother hospitalised, sectioned under the Mental Health Act, returned to her stepfather's care, so solicitous-seeming, so two-faced – she used the childish phrase even now. She did, as it turned out, spend more time at her grandmother's during those turbulent years, visiting her fragile mother in hospital as often as she could.

It was ironic really, she again reflected, that there she was without a biological mother and father to care for her, she who had known violence of some sort in the household, aged only 9, choosing to return to her sick grandmother, and travelling an hour and a half each day by train and two buses to care for her when she was too sick to get out of bed. It was only there that she found the love, succour – she savoured the old-fashioned sounding word – which she needed to survive and, in fact, against all the odds, prosper.

Her grandmother, Mim, as she called her (a hangover from first baby words which had stuck and was accepted with delight by her grandmother and her father as her special name for her only grandmother) took a keen interest in Ruth's school activities, her successes, and frustrations. She it was who did all the answering of letters to parents when needed, and gave all permissions and payments for out of school activities with no-one ever questioning any of this. She did not regret that she had slipped below the radar of the local authority; she had her beloved grandmother.

How Ruth loved the calm quietude of Mim's house, again an old-fashioned but strangely apt word. It stood tucked away down a drive, the lodge to the big house next door in earlier times, but retaining the character of a large country house though it was not actually very large. Set back slightly from the unmade road with a smooth, 'striped' lawn in front, beautifully tended by the gardener once a week, it was surrounded by well-established flowering shrubs, and an almost completely hidden side garden, secretive and pretty. Most of the rooms had one or more floor to ceiling bookcases and Mim instilled in Ruth a deep love of reading. Time out of mind, she called it when she was there, even then.

She would return to Steve's squalid house, her home technically, only sporadically, usually when she was sure he would be out. But it was Mim who saw her through; her very dearly loved Mim it was who, shortly after her 12th birthday, found her crouched in the bathroom on her way to bed, clutching her stomach, frightened by the blood, her first blood.

"Oh that's just the curse, my love," Mim chuckled, "it comes to us all of the fairer sex, my sweetie pie, shows that everything's working normally. Come, I'll explain properly. You've probably only heard half-truths, half-lies from the girls at school." And, she had sorted out temporary protection for Ruth that night, using cotton wool, gauze, and a crepe bandage from the bathroom cabinet. She had made her a hot water bottle for the stomach cramps, given her some paracetamol and hot milk and tucked her into bed, explaining that they would nip to the local shop, which sold everything and was open all hours it seemed, and get what she needed before school tomorrow. The safety, comfort and security, so, so safe, she had thought as she drifted off to sleep strangely proud that she had reached this milestone and that all would be well.

It was Mim who paid for her driving lessons when she turned 17, as a birthday present, insured her own car for Ruth to drive, first on a provisional licence, then on a full licence when Ruth passed her driving test. Ruth loved her grandmother with a deep, unconditional love; she loved her calm, practical approach, her quick wit, her sharp intelligence. Mim took an interest in everything that Ruth did, her only grandchild from her only, cherished son.

Ruth had vague memories of coming to her grandmother's house with her father. She recalled her father relaxing, the affection between mother and son, Mim wanting to feed her grown up son, wanting to smooth his way, never saying a word against her mother. She remembered her father thawing out, as it were, in the warm embrace of the house, the house that was now hers, unbelievable, fairy-tale-like, though that seemed.

She understood now how damaged her mother had been, her mental instability, the anxiety and depression which had pervaded everything. It had always been her father she had turned to, knowing, from babyhood it seemed, that he would be the only one who could help her. But he had died.

And then Steve; the hurt and abuse; she spoke the words slowly and deliberately: 'only physical', and humiliating, living in fear, learning to placate, until she reached 18 and the explosion of violence on that very day, 31st August, and her brutal rape. It had been Steve's idea of a warped celebration of her reaching adulthood, her mother, recently discharged home from another hospital stay, oblivious or turning a blind eye.

~ *Chapter 8* ~

Driving up to the welcoming school with Matthew sitting beside her dressed in smart T-shirt and shorts, excited and wondering, Ruth felt as if she was joining the world of normality so long denied to her. She had prepared Matthew for this visit gently; they had read some starting school books and she had explained how exciting and fun school was.

Matthew skipped along beside her, holding her hand and looking all around.

The head teacher, Mrs. Pinkerton, Maureen Pinkerton, brisk, kindly and efficient, "on top of her game," as Ruth put it to herself, gently explained that the reception class was already fully – and in fact, over-subscribed for September. However, she made a point of never turning away prospective pupils and parents because no matter how long the waiting list, and it always was long, she explained, slightly smugly, Ruth thought, things happened, prospective children could melt away, literally melt away. She spread her hands wide to illustrate the point and smiled in a controlled way though the smile was not without warmth.

"My suggestion is that you look at the other two schools and put Matthew on their waiting lists too," she said before turning to smile at him, "but I would strongly recommend that you don't buy any uniform items until right at the very end of the holidays, because sometimes there are really last minute changes."

Was this professional, efficient woman trying to tell her something? Was she planning to admit this special child, *her* child, to the school? Was she going to queue-jump him? Had she detected something special, some amazing potential in her child? Did this count for anything in school admissions bureaucracy even if she had? How much power did she have?

All these questions were unknowable, certainly unanswerable at least, so

Ruth shook hands politely, inviting Matthew to follow suit and they left, Ruth trying hard to swallow her sharp disappointment and planning to complete the other applications without necessarily visiting the schools. Her own school had been in 'special measures' for her entire high school career after all, she mused, and it hadn't done her any harm, any *more* harm, she corrected herself.

A longing for the planned escape, for the shaking off of this new responsibility of having a child, for a time of taking stock, for 'growing' the relationship, for continuing the healing, obliterated all other considerations quite suddenly.

"Come on, Matthew," she urged, laughing gently, "it's the open road for us, my boy, sunshine, fun, laughter, song and dance, poop, poop!" she cried.

Matthew laughed delightedly and kicked his legs backwards and forwards in excitement. "Poop, poop, poop!" he cried, almost shouting the last rendition.

They often read *The Wind in the Willows* together, and had in fact planned to 'let the train take the strain', leaving the car in the garage at the house at Thames Lacey, the train itself further representing freedom from responsibility, from the daily grind. Ruth at once realised that the train was a completely new experience for Matthew so she was quick to explain and reassure him quietly about the noise and rush of railway stations.

And how it exceeded expectations! They arrived at about 4pm, with hours of bright sunshine and cloudless skies still ahead of them, first making the acquaintance of Caroline, the owner of the cottage they had booked, one of a terrace known as 'Sea View Cottages' – with startling originality, smiled Ruth to herself, though not critically. The holiday deal included a 'Welcome Pack' of goodies and treats and practicalities for the first night and morning at least: milk, half a dozen eggs from Caroline's own hens, she had explained proudly, bread made fresh at the local shop every day, butter, bacon, a pot of her own marmalade, some apples, homemade fruit cake, homemade shortbread, and some muesli. Tea, coffee, drinking chocolate and all necessary cleaning materials were in the kitchen cupboards.

Between the terraced cottages and the beach, lay a small, unfenced garden, just some grass really, with a stepping-stone path leading to a slightly raised, sandy bank of bizarrely shaped casuarina trees. This meant that the sea was literally a two minute walk away down their garden path, "As well-trod as a path to the beach," Ruth murmured to herself as she gazed around with barely concealed, childlike delight.

"This is lovely, isn't it, darling?" she said to Matthew as they followed

Caroline on a brief tour of the little cottage. He nodded excitedly and clutched her hand more tightly. "Is there anyone staying in the other two cottages?" Ruth asked Caroline.

"Oh yes," replied Caroline, "from about May half term onwards until mid-September really, we are always fully booked. You were lucky to get this; I had literally just had a cancellation – due to serious illness; poor things." Her voice sounded soft and concerned. "People just love the closeness to the sea, I think. And there is a definite move towards these staycations, as they call them," she chuckled, "great for us, of course. Who would ever want airport queues, frustration, hours of extra travelling time and being herded like cattle, when you could have this?" Her gaze moved to the sparkling sea whose comforting roar could be heard as a soothing backdrop everywhere in the cottage. "Well, I'll leave you to settle in then, here's my number. I live not far away if you want anything." She looked down at Matthew who was still clutching Ruth's hand tightly as he looked about, seemingly awestruck by his novel surroundings. "How old are you, sweetheart?"

Matthew held up four fingers looking from Caroline to Ruth.

"He was four in June," explained Ruth proudly, "so he'll be starting school soon." She bit her lip, suddenly not wanting to give too much away.

"Oh that will be exciting, won't it my lovely? Where do you live?" she asked Ruth. "We never know with online bookings."

"South London," replied Ruth quickly and with conscious vagueness, blessing the anonymity of the metropolis.

"Oh well, you'll love this peaceful place, fresh air and space then," Caroline said brightly. "I'll leave you to start your holiday."

She's probably in her 50's, Ruth thought to herself, *well-heeled, well-preserved.* She chuckled inwardly at the judgements she was making. *She's probably running this successful holiday business on her own, with a businessman husband safely stashed away; a commuter – perhaps to London, perhaps to Brighton, children grown and fled the nest possibly, or perhaps no children at all.* She wondered what instant judgements Caroline was making about her…single mum, widowed, separated, divorced, child abductor…

They unpacked their one small suitcase quickly and efficiently into the only bedroom and decided to get to the beach as soon as possible, not wanting to miss one minute of this glorious, liberating holiday. When they reached the beach which was rapidly emptying of the day's visitors, "heading home for their tea," Ruth explained to Matthew, they found soft sand interspersed with large, easily avoided pebbles and shells. Ruth kicked off her sandals before kneeling down to help Matthew undo his own velcroed summer sandals, one of her very first purchases for him, as he sat with his legs stretched out in front of him. His little toes wriggled excitedly as he proudly closed his hand over his first shell, just an empty crab shell, and clutched it as a trophy.

As the tide was only just on the turn they did not have to walk far, soon leaving the pebbly part of the beach behind them as it turned into first soft, dry, then firm, wet, sand, ridged and salted by the suck and pull of the sea as it quickly receded. Matthew squealed with delight and shock as the cold water buffeted his warm feet, splashing as far as his knees as they reached the edge, jumping over the lacy bits of waves as they advanced and retreated. Ruth showed him how the seventh wave always seemed bigger, stronger, fiercer, advancing further than the others, so they counted them in and out.

"Feel the suck and pull, Matthew, isn't it strong? It's noisy too isn't it?" she said. Matthew nodded, jumping the waves. Ruth said quietly, "If you stand as still as a stone in one place for just a couple of minutes it'll feel as if the world is turning round you… it's a really weird feeling, let's do it."

They held hands and let the sea work its timeless tricks on them.

"Splash, splish, splosh, splish, splash," shrieked Matthew, fearless as he paddled further in.

"I expect there'll be rock pools when the tide's out," Ruth responded excitedly, "we can explore them, and oh, Matthew, the very best of it is that we have our own little house to go back to, we can stay on the beach and watch the sunset. We don't have to get back to a stuffy hotel with meal times and carpets and rules and when we wake up in the morning it'll all still be here, and the next morning, and the next, next, next, next," she laughed with him, at one with his childish delight. She needed a holiday, so did Matthew, poor little mite.

~ *Chapter 9* ~

And that very next morning Ruth woke to feel her face being stroked by Matthew, just as she stroked his whenever she needed to wake him.

"Mimi, Mimi, door knock, door knock," he was saying urgently.

"Oh my goodness me, I *have* overslept." Ruth smiled sleepily at the worried looking little boy as she glanced at her bedside alarm clock. "9.30…well, that's a holiday-ish start," she said, pulling on her silky wrap, slipping into her flip-flops and making her way down the narrow spiral staircase. "Just coming," she called as she reached the small hallway.

Opening the door she saw Caroline just turning out of the gate at the end of the front path but, hearing the door, she turned and looking relieved, smiled broadly. "Oh, I'm so pleased you're there. I saw Matthew through the sitting room window when I knocked and when nobody came I saw him scamper off and I had a worry that he might be on his own, that you'd nipped out for some shopping or something. Anyway, I've brought you some eggs. The hens are laying like mad things and I can't use them all."

"Oh, thank you, we'll easily get through some more eggs and I might make a cake or two," said Ruth, brushing her hair out of her eyes. "We had boiled eggs and toast for tea yesterday – it was quite late by the time we got back from the beach. They were delicious, not like the ones I get in Tesco. We were really tired, must be the sea air," she laughed lightly, "I can't remember sleeping this late since I was a teenager. But, Caroline, you must know I would never, ever leave Matthew on his own – he's only four…" She stopped herself as she felt she was about to start protesting that she may look young but she knew how to look after a child. *That would sound weird*, she thought to herself. "I would ask you in for a cuppa but I need to get a move on now – another day when I haven't been so lazy perhaps?" She laughed sheepishly.

"That would be lovely, Ruth and I must get on now myself."

Ruth was looking forward to a quick shower, slipping into shorts, *wearing bare feet* – she used to say that as a child making her grandmother chuckle affectionately – when she remembered she had Matthew to see to first. She was still getting used to having somebody else to put first, somebody who was pretty much entirely dependent on her for his well-being and safety.

"Matthew," she called out, "Caroline has gone now; she was just bringing us some eggs. Would you like bacon and egg for our first holiday breakfast?" Silence. "Matthew? Matthew, you can come out now, it's all safe." Ruth found she was used to Matthew making himself scarce with great speed and skill whenever anyone appeared in London, and she, feeling the weight of her crime, or crimes, she reminded herself, had not stopped him.

It seemed helpful that he was complicit in the deception but here, away, free, in Angmering, she did not think he had to keep doing that. There was no hue and cry it seemed. Nobody appeared to be missing Matthew.

"Matthew, it's okay now, darling, everything's safe, come out now. Breakfast time then we can explore." As soon as the word 'explore' was out she felt suddenly so, so afraid for Matthew and she felt instantly the real meaning of the expression: 'her heart was in her mouth'.

"Matthew," she called out in a higher note now, anxiety causing her almost to scream his name, "Matthew, where are you? Don't frighten me, darling, come out now!" She emphasised the last word hoping to convey the urgency. She ran from room to room, looking behind furniture, curtains, and under both beds. Then she moved all the sofa cushions, calling all the time. She knew Matthew was excited to be there, he would surely not have run down the short path to the beach on his own would he? Well, he had run away before, and he had run away from *her* before too – off to a park adjoining the scene of a notorious murder, no less.

"Stop, stop," she whispered to herself, "he'll be somewhere safe, just hiding, distracted by some new experience." Here she was, alone with a stolen child and that child had gone missing. She would need to phone the police to find her child...

Then she saw him, standing rigid, still as stone, looking fixedly out of the very dusty, slightly broken garage window, the garage empty apart from some old packing cases and a bicycle with no chain.

"Matthew, sweetheart, there you are. Everything's fine, come and have breakfast." She pushed open the rickety door as she spoke and then saw that he had actually managed to climb inside a cardboard packing case as if ready to pull the top closed over him should he need to. She held out her hands ready to lift him out when, after just a moment's hesitation, he lifted up his own arms, just as a much younger child would, ready and wanting to be carried. Again a clichéd expression came to mind as, *weak with relief*, she carried him towards the back door leading straight into the kitchen.

After that inauspicious start to the day – that first day of their holiday – their bid for freedom, as Ruth put it to herself – could not have been more perfect. The bliss was in having the beach – 'nature's playground' as she had seen it dubbed – on their doorstep. So, washed, breakfasted, and generally restored, they set off down the path to find the tide on the way in – a tide table in the local weekly paper, helpfully left by Caroline in the house, told Ruth that high tide today was at 10.45am. She thought it would be fun to get down onto the small amount of beach left and watch the incoming tide, showing Matthew the sevens game again with splashier and splashier waves.

As the rising water took him by surprise again and again with its sudden surges, wetting his shorts and even reaching his chest, he shrieked with fearful delight. They decided to walk along until the beach disappeared and explore the front; after their restorative bacon and eggs breakfast they would have a cafe or kiosk snack for lunch she decided.

After all, we are on holiday. She hugged the thought to herself. *We need the odd treat.* How many treats had Matthew ever had in his short life she wondered?

Ruth worked out that by about 4pm it would be low tide and they could explore the rock pools whilst the beach slowly emptied of the day trippers and people returning to further afield holiday accommodation. The beach would be theirs with their little, comfortable haven just a stone's throw away. Matthew's small hand in hers, they made their way along the pebbles which had been thrust against the sea wall time and time again making quite a shelf of stones which crunched and rattled as they stomped along. It was tiring and soon they decided to climb the steps to the concrete promenade and return to 'their' part of the beach more easily that way.

"Mimi, where does the sea go at night time?"

"It stays right here, sweetheart," replied Ruth, "in and out, in and out. Actually the tides are governed by the moon, isn't that amazing? We've got a lovely book about it at home," she said, "I'll show you."

"Will the big pebbles turn into sand soon? Does the sea get deeper when it rains? Where does the wind come from when it blows?" And so the questions went on from the excited little boy.

They bought their lunch from a tiny kiosk just at the end of the concreted promenade jam-packed with anything and everything you would need for a day at the beach. Their lunch: ham rolls, crisps, and a chocolate mini roll for Matthew, a slab of fruit cake for Ruth, was put into sturdy, wooden green baskets and they left with a couple of beach mats and a bucket and spade which the owner of the kiosk had let Matthew spend some time choosing from the display in front. Ruth had brought bottles of water and apples, and she noted that the kiosk managed to produce tea, coffee, hot chocolate and even soup from its diminutive kitchen area.

They made their way carefully towards a not too crowded area of the beach, next to a breakwater which would provide some protection from the glaring sun as the afternoon wore on. Ruth laid out the mats so that she could lean against the warm, bleached wood of the breakwater with Matthew next to her as they tucked into their picnic.

"This is the life, isn't it, sweetheart?" said Ruth, passing Matthew a roll and a bottle of water and using the paper napkins as plates on the mats. "We'll stay here and perhaps build a sandcastle after we've had our lunch, shall we?"

Matthew was watching a family who had set up camp nearby with wind breaks, lilos, bags and towels. There was a boy about his own age, two slightly older girls, and a baby wearing only a sun hat and a nappy, staggering to its feet and seemingly taking its first few steps, landing on its bottom unexpectedly every three or four steps or so. The parents were fully occupied keeping an eye on all four children as they dug, collected shells, filled buckets, and ran backwards and forwards to the sea with water to fill the channels they had dug. Ruth was struck by Matthew's solitary state as he gazed at the children and determined that whatever it took she would give him the best possible time there at the beach on holiday and onward.

Having returned the wooden basket to the kiosk, leaving the mats and bucket and spade to mark their 'campsite', Ruth showed Matthew how to collect the slightly damper sand nearer the sea, fill the bucket to the brim, pack it tightly in, pat it down and up end it to make a series of turrets for their castle. She quickly realised that they really needed a bucket and spade each so that was another trip together to the kiosk.

She was starting to feel tired, still recovering from the events of the last ten days or so: packing up, planning, caring for a child. *Caring for a child*, she reflected. She would be making decisions, even those as simple as keeping him away from fizzy, sugar-filled drinks, and teeth-rotting calories, she thought to herself. Though she had never been an obsessional or fussy eater – this was just plain common sense to her. Why sully something as perfect as a small child? She thought now fleetingly, in her tired state, of the pleasure of simply lying in the sun reading a book, swimming when she wanted to, and people-watching, but this was not to be. She had an overwhelming and all-consuming responsibility for this small child which she would never shirk, and she would never give up on him. If others could do it, she looked around the beach, then so could she.

And so they spent that hot afternoon, and many similar, building an impressive sandcastle, with turrets, a moat, a drawbridge made of seaweed, shells for windows with another trip to the kiosk for a packet of colourful flags which seemed to reflect their own triumphant achievement as they fluttered gently in the occasional warm breeze. Matthew was totally absorbed in the task, enjoying filling the moat and Ruth was able to relax enough just to watch as he trotted backwards and forwards to fill the two buckets rather than going with him each time. He would turn back to look at her on his way down to the sea's edge several times, and then, reassured that she was watching, would carry on with renewed confidence it seemed.

As the first full day of their holiday drew on, Ruth felt herself to be gradually unwinding from a tension of which she had been largely unaware. The bright, warm sun felt both beneficent and somehow cleansing. At the same time she was aware that Matthew too was relaxing, giving way to normal childish delights, instead of holding himself in a kind of tense readiness for... well, flight or fight really, she thought to herself musingly and she had certainly seen the former. She felt a visceral, fierce protectiveness towards him, her little child, her responsibility, her duty. She noted with tenderness some of his characteristics. He would place his small hand on any part of her when he was tired, and, as he grew in confidence and trust, he would gently knead her skin, subconsciously, whilst sitting close to her. She wondered how much he thought about his former life, whatever that had been, and how quickly that was fading for him to be replaced with new, lasting childhood memories generated by her.

"Oh, look, Matthew, the sea has gone out miles now and you can see the rocks and rock pools appearing. Let's have a cup of tea, water or hot chocolate for you, I should think, and some biscuits and go and explore a bit."

So they set off, hand in hand, back to the by now friendly kiosk.

"Oh it's you again, young man. What can I do for you this time?"

Ruth felt Matthew squeeze in closer to her as she was eyeing useful backpacks strung from every possible point on the kiosk. "We'll have one of those, please," she said, "as we are busy buying up your stock we need something to carry it all in. And a banana milkshake for my son please, cup of tea for me and a couple of *Kit Kats* to share. Thank you."

Newly kitted out, they loaded the buckets, spades, some shells that Matthew wanted to keep, the *Kit Kats* and water bottles into the pack, secured the mats to its straps and sat down on a bench nearby to drink, and eat their chocolate bars. By this time the numerous rock pools gleamed temptingly in the bright, late afternoon sun.

"Who lives in rock pools, Mimi, will we find sea creatures?"

"Well, they'll probably hear us coming and scuttle off for shelter," explained Ruth, but I'm sure we'll catch sight of some, even if it's just a lazy old crab, basking in the sun, waiting for his dinner." Matthew laughed delightedly and kicked his short legs backwards and forwards in excitement. "Just put your cup in the bin over there, sweetheart," said Ruth, "and I'll take my cup back before they close for the day."

And so it was that they happily spent the whole of the late afternoon, early evening, exploring rock pools, clambering carefully amongst tiny, hidden, deep pools made dark and mysterious-looking by overhanging rocks, and shallower, luminescent pools full of darting creatures skimming the surface and diving to catch the sea life fleeing for its life. They were only wearing flip-flops so Ruth showed Matthew how to tread very carefully to avoid the sharp rocks, and how taking off the flip-flops altogether made it easier to walk quietly in the deeper pools. The beach by now was virtually deserted, and in fact they only saw one elderly couple walking their dog that first evening, dogs being allowed onto the beach from 6.30pm onwards.

"Ooh, Matthew we must remember we have to walk all the way back again and not get carried away by going too far. You must be getting tired and you're a bit too big to be carried. We'll head back now," she added, whereupon, quite out of the blue, Matthew sat down, covered his face with his hands and sobbed as if his heart would break. "Matthew," cried Ruth, aghast, stumped by this uncharacteristic behaviour, "whatever is it? We have to go back to our holiday home now, we can come back tomorrow." The sobs turned into wails of distress. His face was streaked with sand and tears. Ruth knelt down beside him, suddenly realising that stupidly she had treated Matthew almost as an equal. He was only 4, and must be exhausted, she realised. *She was an idiot, a novice mother who did not understand first principles,* she berated herself unmercifully. "Poor little monkey," she said under her breath, again consciously echoing James. "But what to do?" Any self-respecting, proper mother would know. On a sudden inspiration she remembered she still had one finger of her *Kit Kat*. "You have this, Matthew," she said, "then we'll set off back the way we came and have fish and chips for tea, then home, bed, and cosy down."

The restorative power of a *Kit Kat* finger worked its magic immediately. Matthew savoured the chocolate, got to his feet and set off holding her hand tightly. She pretended they were explorers nearing land from a shipwrecked boat and this caught his interest enough for them to spot the café at the other end of the promenade and play a kind of *I Spy*, as they got nearer to it, spying features such as its colourful awning, its flashing red 'ICES' sign and tables with umbrellas still outside.

Ruth congratulated herself on a crisis averted as they tucked into fish, chips and peas sitting at an outside table, as she felt it would be easier and more settling like that for an over-tired, small child. Back home, as they called it now, she ran a bubbly bath for Matthew, noting his smeared face, grubby knees and filthy feet and cuddled him closely on her lap as she towelled him dry.

"Sea air always makes you sleepy, my granny used to say," she said to Matthew. "Come on; see if you can get into bed *before* you fall asleep, sweetheart."

The first week of the holiday passed in a blissful haze of bright sunny days, warm, bright, moonlit nights, sea, sand, easy meals and general ease of living. "*La dolce vita*," Ruth would murmur to herself several times a day. Caroline dropped in from time to time, usually timing it just after breakfast and interested to hear their plans for the day. She was friendly and open, clearly wanting to chat, but Ruth found herself, as usual, she noted wryly, inexplicably keeping her at arm's length.

Was it so inexplicable though, she mused? She had always done this with her friends, and potential friends, because she just had so much in her life that did not fit in, was not normal, needed hiding – and, she supposed, this was still, and would for evermore be, the case.

She listened to Caroline talking about her only just grown up daughters, how bereft she had felt when one after the other they had left home to make their own way, how she had strived to keep busy and happy and not to seem needy to them. They had their own futures to carve out. Ruth was a good listener, empathetic, not aloof, but always retaining her own secret inner self, like a protective shell. She gave minimal information away, responding with bland answers. Yes, Matthew was her only one, he would be starting school in September, and she thought he was looking forward to it but had probably forgotten about it during this wonderful holiday. She worked freelance in publishing as an editorial assistant (she had written and sent her letter of resignation the day after bringing Matthew home, as she thought of it, realising this could be the only way so felt pleased that this was not actually a lie) and could extend her hours once Matthew was in full time school, which would be useful as she loved her job and they needed the money. No, his father was not in the picture – we're both better off without him.

She said this with a vehemence borne of her own childhood experiences of her stepfather and of her own dear, much loved father leaving her so suddenly but, when alive, being unable to cope with her mother, leaving Ruth fearful, alone and needing to fight her own corner from an early age. Caroline's company was enough adult contact for Ruth. Her unconditional love for Matthew, her need to protect him, provide for him, guard him, shelter him, fulfilled all her needs. Occasionally though, particularly after dark and when she herself was tired out by the days spent in the open, in the hot sun, tending to Matthew, anticipating his needs, she was overwhelmed by the thought of the ongoing responsibility for this little person, a responsibility she could share with no-one.

~ Chapter 10 ~

As the year continued deep into August, as Ruth always thought of it, the ever darkening green leaves beginning to look tired, literally ready to drop in the heavy heat, each day dawned relentlessly bright and clear and followed a reassuring pattern of beach, walks, rock pools and splashing in the shallows. Their holiday home was a haven, a refuge for them both.

Ruth still found herself instinctively keeping Caroline at arm's length, less because she felt like a fugitive; more, she reflected, because this was what she always did, always had done.

Her life had never fitted into any routine order, had always been so different, she had always had so much to hide, and, she kept returning uneasily to this thought, she had transgressed. That sense of being on the periphery, on the outside looking in was entrenched. She was friendly and welcoming when Caroline dropped round, usually with eggs, sometimes freshly cut runner beans or delicious tomatoes, and listened to her talking about her daughters, her marriage, her mother's illness but she, Ruth, never shared confidences, nor would she, she vowed.

She continued to make it plain that Matthew's father was not in the picture and that that was not a problem. She talked about how much she enjoyed her work, how easy it had been to work around Matthew's needs, but nothing more, though she sensed Caroline's interest in her, curiosity even, and an unspoken reaching out to her almost as a mother to a child. But as Ruth had never had such a relationship with her mother she did not quite know how they worked.

It reminded her of the time that a friend from university, Laura, who had been very close to her slightly older brother, had struggled to make her tutors understand how his death in a drowning accident, aged 21, affected her. It transpired that the two members of staff required to sanction her request for some extended time away from the course were both only children. If you have never had something, you cannot miss it, Ruth had always thought, but perhaps there was something just so immeasurably different about a mother/child relationship. Never having had this, felt to Ruth like an unfillable void, damaging, alienating, and ultimate aloneness was therefore hers.

Her mother had been so mentally fragile, unable to sustain any relationship and Ruth had found something akin to a mother's love in her grandmother, enhanced by a wistful longing for her lost father. She sought that closeness in her relationship with his mother, searching, vicariously perhaps, for a mother's love for herself, and feeling almost jealous of her father's relationship with Mim.

This closeness to her grandmother had too quickly turned though to a mutual dependence due to Mim's physical frailty so that Ruth's sense of being abandoned, being responsible for her own destiny from an early age, for her own survival really, resulted in a default aloneness that felt different from the more common transient loneliness. Perhaps Caroline sensed a need of which Ruth was unaware; perhaps she wore her heart on her sleeve. Whatever her motivations, Ruth was giving nothing of herself to this woman because that was how it had always been.

On the sixth day Ruth and Matthew woke to a changed world. The lashing rain had penetrated her early morning dreams and the grey, sodden view from her bedroom window was relieved only by a torn piece of colourful awning being tossed along by the ferocious wind. The casuarina trees looked as if they would imminently be torn from their sandy soil by their roots.

Well, there's a turn up for the book, thought Ruth to herself sleepily; she had watched no television, read no newspapers, and heard no weather forecasts. This weather suddenly vividly recalled double geography on a Monday morning. The weather was nothing less than a metaphor in fact for double-geography-on-a-Monday-morning. *Actually it could be quite nice to have a homely, indoor day*, she thought, *rest up, cosy up.*

As she showered, noting the new chill amidst the bathroom steam, she murmured the first few lines of a prose poem written by her closest friend from sixth form college, Louise: *"Bored, Summer, with your prattle and chatter of inconsequential things, full to the brim with your grass cuttings, your constant hum and buzz and heavy heat, and everlasting jollity, gratefully I watch at the window for your passing and with relief feel the touch of the curled and crinkled leaves on my face, tramping homeward listen with joy to autumn's doleful whine in the chimney pots...* "[15]

Well, it certainly wasn't autumn yet, she stopped herself, just a rainy August day... autumn with its changes and new beginnings would be here all too soon, she thought. Live for the moment, *carpe diem,* and all that.

"Matthew, are you awake, sweetheart? It's an indoor day today. It's raining cats and dogs." He turned and smiled at her sleepily.

"Cats and dogs....where?"

"No, no it's just a silly expression, darling."

So they spent that first rainy day contentedly together. Ruth taught him noughts and crosses, found the colouring books she had brought for just such a rainy day, and gave him sheaves of the scrap paper she had brought for painting. In the afternoon she devised a secret den by turning a dining chair upside down and covering it with a towel. Matthew had just scuttled inside it delightedly when a knock on the door announced Caroline's arrival.

"Oh, hallo, Caroline," said Ruth, "come on in, you're soaking," feeling a sharp stab of disappointment and resentment at the intrusion. She would have to be sociable now; it would be difficult to pretend they were just venturing out. Well, perhaps some adult company for a while would be all right.

"Would you like tea or coffee?"

"Tea please," replied Caroline, shaking the water off her hair, and sitting down next to the 'den'. "Oh, that looks fun," she said brightly. "I remember wet days with small children," she smiled ruefully and sympathetically, "but you look as if you're enjoying yourselves."

Matthew was sitting quietly colouring now as if needing to draw any attention away from himself. "Oh you are a good, quiet boy," said Caroline, approvingly. "Not like most little boys," she laughed. Ruth, surprising herself, felt an immediate and fierce need to spring to his defence, and to the defence of all small boys, but she bit back such a retort, only commenting that, yes, Matthew was a good boy and could concentrate for a long time.

"I think it's going to be like this again tomorrow," said Caroline, "you'll be going stir crazy. The fair at Littlehampton is going strong though and most rides are under cover, that might be fun. It's only about 20 minutes on the train, a bit longer on the bus. I could run you into the station tomorrow morning if you like."

---

[15] Unpublished prose poem; see author's citation

Ruth sensed Matthew listening intently, it sounded fun, a treat and it was good for children to get out and about, she knew that.

"Oh, that would be kind, what a good idea," responded Ruth warmly. "That will be fun won't it, Mat?" He nodded solemnly as she realised it was the first time that she had used this name for him.

They chatted on and it *was* actually good to have some adult company, Ruth reflected. Again, Ruth diverted attention from her own personal circumstances and asked Caroline with real interest about the business of running holiday lets, the details, how much she got to know the holidaymakers, that sort of thing. Ruth found herself considering her own situation: a house of her own, mortgage free, a job she loved, health and of course, best of all, a child. The obvious blank to some, the lack of a partner, any partner, did not in fact, at that time, enter her consciousness at all.

The day at Littlehampton passed in a childlike whirl of excitement for both Ruth and Matthew. Familiar now with the noise and rush of train travel, he sat with his little face glued to the window for the twenty minute ride, asking perceptive questions, from time to time, about the new sights assailing his senses, such as why are all the cows left to get soaking wet? How does the driver know all the carriages are following his engine cab? Sensible questions.

And the fair itself: the noise, colour, shouts, smells of fast food and sickly toffee apples and candy floss, was just plain, simple fun. Ruth selected some gentler roundabout rides to begin with, which Matthew loved, but she soon saw that he was pretty fearless on some of the faster ones; she drew the line at the dodgems though.

She had told Caroline that they would make their own way back from the station at Angmering having realised that it was not that far from their holiday haven and she was pleased to see that the rain was certainly relenting as the day progressed, exactly as forecast, with even the likelihood of a return to sunshine forecast for the next day. This was three days before they had to leave.

It felt like being reborn as summer returned, unsullied, the next morning. Ruth and Matthew made a joyous return to the beach, fully equipped with buckets, spades, towels, and snacks, to find a sparkling sea, seemingly re-energised by the two days of rain, the beach itself washed clean by the wind and rain and the whole lively scene resembling a newly cleaned water colour painting. They planned to build a sea boat which Ruth had a very vague memory of doing with her father, the summer before he died.

This time their closest neighbours where they set up camp were a father and his tiny daughter, probably only about 18 months old. He was showing her how to fill a bucket and helping her carry buckets of water backwards and forwards from a nearby, quite deep, pool next to the breakwater. She was toddling with the staggering, over-confident air that comes with having only recently mastered that skill, and frequently landed very suddenly on her bottom. This did not faze her at all. Her father was totally focused on her, absorbed in her gentle play, seemingly enjoying the beach trip as much as she was.

Ruth showed Matthew how to draw the shape of the boat first, big enough for both of them, and then start digging out the sand, no small task, and building up substantial benches of sand to make front and rear seats. They stuck a union jack flag proudly on the prow and even found a piece of driftwood to make a tiller; the rudder was left to the imagination. It was hot, tiring work and they stopped frequently to look around, taking a break from digging to drink the delicious fresh lemonade Ruth had made and put in a thermos flask.

"Okay, Matty, we're ready to set sail now. We can head for Smugglers' Island in our trusty craft."

"What's 'smugglers'?" asked Matthew, wiping a sandy hand across his sweaty forehead leaving a wide, dirty streak.

Ruth explained what they were as they pretended to row across to the 'island'. "After lunch we'll be able to explore the rock pools, Matthew, the tide's going out fast – look."

Ruth stole a look at the father and daughter as they made their way haltingly to the rapidly receding water's edge for a gentle paddle. He was lifting her high, and gently splashing her feet which were wriggling with excitement as he whooshed her through the shallow waves. She was squealing with delight and they sat together in the shallow water watching it tease as it trickled over their outstretched legs. She could imagine the suck and pull beneath them and vowed to do the same with Matthew after lunch before the sea had gone too far out. It would be fun and they could count sevens again.

"One, two, three, four, five, six, seven," shrieked Matthew reaching a crescendo of excitement as each seventh wave fulfilled the folklore promise of being bigger and splashier time and time again. They were both laughing delightedly, fully focused on the task in hand when Ruth became aware of their father and daughter neighbours walking, and toddling in the baby's case, hand in hand just in front of them.

"It's amazing how it works every time, isn't it?" he said.

"It is," said Ruth, aware of Matthew leaning in close to her, suddenly completely quiet and still.

The two walked on hand in hand, the toddler finding it difficult to stay upright for any length of time.

She's probably tired, thought Ruth, *sea air*, as Mim would say.

Her father reached down and competently swung her up on to his shoulders striding on before turning back to their encampment near the breakwater.

"Look at that sand boat, Emmie," she heard him say. "We'll build one tomorrow; time for a nap now, sweetie pie."

Ruth and Matthew set off hand in hand towards the rock pools for a quick explore before the tide turned again. They clambered around their usual route, Matthew stopping to peer intently into the limpid pools which appeared to hold close all the secrets of the sea bed. He was collecting shells in his bucket and Ruth explained about not disturbing the sea life whose homes and families were in the rock pools, that they needed their security and safety, "Just like we do, Matty."

Momentarily distracted by the sight of a hang-glider over the cliffs, Ruth had turned to watch its graceful sweep and turn against the cloudless blue sky, when she heard a piercing scream from Matthew. She turned rapidly to see him covering his eyes with his little hands as blood poured from a cut on his foot into the previously tranquil rock pool in which he was standing.

"Mimi, Mimi," he wailed piteously, and she noticed his healthy tan had faded to a ghostly pallor which frightened her almost more than the swirling pool of blood.

"What's happened?" It was the father of the toddler, Emmie, calling over to her from the breakwater. Matthew was by now crying uncontrollably and would only sit terrified as Ruth tried to cajole him to hop along with her out of the pool.

"No, no, no," he sobbed, "no, Mimi, no Mimi."

"If you come and watch Emmie – she's asleep – for a minute, I'll get him, don't worry, I'll be gentle. He'll probably be better with someone who's not his mum, and he'll need carrying anyway across the rocks with that cut," he said with conviction. "What's his name?"

"Matthew, Matty," replied Ruth as she quickly made her way towards the sleeping Emmie, desperate to have Matthew back on dry land and heading for help with that cut. Anxious as she was though she could not help but think what a bizarre situation this was in some ways – two total strangers trusting each other with their small children, one a terrified, screaming, bloodied small boy, the other a toddler asleep in a buggy completely vulnerable. But this was what people did in emergencies wasn't it? They helped each other and she was hardly likely to make off with the buggy across the pebbles with Emmie's father just a stone's throw away. Likewise he could not easily make off with her screaming, injured child – and she certainly needed his help. The irony of these thoughts eluded her. She had rescued, not stolen, a deeply damaged child, she would make him whole again… or so she thought. Perhaps all child stealers thought this way - that they could do it better?

*August **is** a wicked month,*[16] she thought to herself almost hysterically, plucking children to their deaths on holiday, on beaches, in the full glare of the summer sun, so bright, so alluring, the merciless, empty blue sky revealing and concealing nothing just like the laughter of clowns, frightening, false, empty and strangely unnatural.

All at once Matthew's sobs and yelps of pain and fear brought her back sharply to the present. She looked across the rocks to see Matthew being carried by Emmie's father, his little face turned rigidly away, sobbing quietly, *too* quietly, she realised. He seemed terrified and… somehow resigned. As they drew nearer he held out his arms to her as a much younger child would and started crying more naturally, his sobs rising to a crescendo and succeeding in waking Emmie who immediately came out in solidarity with him. The noise was deafening, though Matthew did at least pause, turning to look at Emmie with something approaching awe. The two adults looked at each other ruefully, people would think they were doing something dreadful to their children, Ruth was fearful, Emmie's dad, wryly amused.

"Come on," he said, "I've got my car parked on the prom because of all Emmie's luggage – things needed for a beach trip. I'll take you both to A&E, that cut will need stitching –Dawthing will be the nearest. It's only about 15 minutes away. Traffic shouldn't be too bad, though it's probably rush hour now. Come on," the man sensed her hesitation, "two distraught children need at least two of us…What's your name, by the way, I can't keep thinking of you as Matthew's mum?"

"Ruth, Ruth Forster," she said. "You?"

"Mark, Mark Williams," he said mimicking her serious tone, though not unkindly or rudely.

---

[16] Edna O'Brien: *August is a Wicked Month,* 1965 Penguin, UK

~ *Chapter 11* ~

Ruth sat between the two distressed children in the back of the car. Luckily Mark had a booster seat in the boot which they used for Matthew and, once Emily was safely strapped into her car seat, she was only interested in the fact that Matthew was now sobbing quietly and intermittently leaning against Ruth for comfort. She gazed at him with frank and unselfconscious curiosity as only toddlers can. Ruth talked reassuringly to the children about the things they could see from the window explaining to Matthew what would happen on arrival at A&E and she was thus able to forget the tightly coiled knot of tension inside her. Almost simultaneously though, seemingly soothed by the engine noise and lulled into sleepiness by the motion of the car and the sea air, both children fell fast asleep.

Ruth's mind started to turn somersaults. Would she be unmasked – the dramatic word seemed apt – in the sterile atmosphere of a busy A&E department, in front of this kind stranger, by knowledgeable professionals able to see into her very soul? They'd be on to her in no time. There'd be a hue and cry, as she thought of it. She always found herself reverting to rather old-fashioned, literary phrases when thinking deeply, she realised. The police would be called – oh so discreetly – social workers, an interview room would be found, she would be quietly taken from the patients deserving help, away from Matthew, the person who needed her more than anything or anybody else in his short, troubled life, as she believed it to have been. They would need to access Matthew's health record and she would be giving them a fabricated name, a fabricated date of birth. Would he need something like – what was it – a tetanus jab, perhaps? Had he had this as a baby? How would she respond to routine questions about his past medical history? She quickly *Googled* information about tetanus on her phone, thinking to herself that knowledge is power.

Mark's voice cut in, "If there's someone you need to ring… Matthew's dad? Don't worry about me, just go ahead."

"No, it's fine," said Ruth quickly, thinking hard about what was best to do.

Mark could feel her tension. "Don't be too worried," he said, "it's a nice, clean wound, already bathed by the salt sea, he'll probably need a few stitches, which he'll think is really cool – I think they use stitches rather than glue on feet because feet get quite sweaty so glue doesn't stick too well. Kids mend easily," he declared confidently.

Ruth had previously objected in her mind to people calling children kids, but somehow from Mark it sounded fine and caring. "Is Emily your only one?" said Ruth. "You sound experienced."

"Yes, she's my only one but I know about kids because I'm a teacher – primary – they're always breaking bits, cutting themselves open, it goes with kid territory."

"Oh, oh yes, I see it would," said Ruth, conscious of sounding rather formal. "Where do you teach?"

"Well I'll be a starting at a new school next term – scary thought – and they think it's only the pupils who get anxious starting a new school!" he chuckled. "It's in Natton-on-Thames, a sort of large village – south of London, you probably haven't heard of it. I used to teach at a smaller 'sort of village', Thames Lacey, it's not far from there."

Ruth was silent; she needed to collect her thoughts.

"What do *you* do apart from the most important job in the world of course, being a mum?" Mark asked her after a few minutes in response to her silence.

"I help edit children's text books, mostly science books, primary age and younger," she laughed lightly. "So we're both about educating children, investing in the future. Coincidence, especially as we live in Thames Lacey."

Now it was Mark who seemed to go silent before saying, "Oh, hang on, we need to look out for the hospital signs now…"

Whilst Mark was navigating first a roundabout then two mini roundabouts to take them to the entrance to A&E, Ruth quickly devised her strategy. Matthew needed her care, her protection, she was his rescuer; this, of course, included health care. She had, in fact thought about this whilst thinking about the future before they'd even left for this time-out-of-mind holiday. She decided that she would tell the staff that Matthew had not had any immunisations as a baby because she, an obsessional, right-on, free-thinking, middle class, *Guardian*-reading mum, had refused them, but that she had now seen sense. She would put it that way, grown up, as she put it to herself, and they would probably give Matthew some 'imms' there and then or tell her to go to her GP. Well, she would need a new GP anyway as she was in the process of moving so she would ask if they could give some now – especially as he would soon be starting school. She knew from her internet searches that children of 4 and a half plus would be given pre-school boosters – they could do it that way – and that A&E staff would sometimes do this after an injury. It may depend on how busy they were but Dawthing A&E was not near a major motorway, she mused – well, they wouldn't know until they got there.

In the event, the A&E experience made Ruth almost tearfully proud of the National Health Service.

The unit was cheerfully busy, not manic or out of control, and the bustling, efficient staff were professional, friendly, caring, down to earth and full of practical common sense and good humour.

Well, you'd have to be really, Ruth thought to herself, *working in this sort of environment, but it may not always be the case.*

Ruth and Matthew were efficiently triaged through to a children's waiting area and Mark took Emily with him while he went to park. He returned with her in the rather beach worn buggy cheerfully hugging a battered, cuddly zebra, who, she was told, was called Stripey. Matthew, meanwhile, was fully absorbed at a Lego table building an idyllic-looking, Toy Town type, colourful, very homely and welcoming house, his injury seemingly forgotten. The only other waiting patient was a pale, listless, clearly very unwell baby held in a troubled-looking dad's arms. Ruth assumed he was the baby's father, yet strangely and so unnaturally the baby made no eye contact with him at all. The dad looked very young, maybe 18, 19, thought Ruth, and spent the time flicking through his phone messages and likewise making no eye contact whatsoever with Ruth, Mark, his baby and the two children.

Matthew was called through after about forty minutes into a minor injury area – Ruth was somehow mightily relieved that this is where they were put… minor injury, pfff, nothing then really. She had heard A&E dubbed 'anything and everything'. An efficient, but kindly and reassuring nurse took the history of the injury and ticked various boxes. When it came to it, it was Ruth herself who brought up the subject of immunisations.

"Will he need a tetanus jab?" she enquired once the kindly doctor, a mother herself with a son just a little older than Matthew, she told him, had finished stitching the wound.

"No, he won't because rock pools are not a tetanus risk area," she informed them comfortingly.

But Ruth was now in protective mother mode so, throwing caution to the winds, as she put it to herself later, she said hesitantly, "Well, I do feel really worried because I was stupid when he was a baby..." and went on to her prepared script about being an over-zealous, *Guardian*-reading... This was whispered by Ruth, away from the couch where Matthew was still being charmed by the young, very young-looking medical student who had observed the suturing and succeeded in winning Matthew's trust by calling him 'mate' and high-fiving him as he left.

The doctor thought for a moment and then said, "Actually, as he'll be starting school next month we could give him his pre-school boosters, start from scratch really – better to be safe than sorry. We're nice and quiet at the moment and we even have a Nurse Practitioner on duty this evening. I'll sort it. Can you explain to Matthew? That's the benefit of jabbing when they're tiny," she said to Ruth, mother to mother with a conspiratorial smile, "they just yell, get a cuddle, a sticker perhaps, and all is forgotten and forgiven! Good luck!"

So Ruth carefully explained to Matthew about the protection from illnesses needed and how all children got these jabs, and yes it might hurt just when the jab went in, short, sharp, but it would be nothing like as bad as the rocks and he had already been so brave, she was so proud of him. Matthew nodded solemnly and so it was that he received the vital protection – no questions asked. A new record was started for him, better late than never, as the efficient nurse had pointed out.

Gosh, thought Ruth, *no wonder children can just disappear, slip through the net, and child protection can go so wrong, so often. These people were sort of too kind, too naïve – or something. Forgive us our trespasses.*

She still had the hurdle of registering with a new GP when they got home, but she would cross that bridge when it came to it. Some story about a failed IT system at her previous GP practice, lost records, something vague. They would need to start a new primary care record. There must be some sort of right to health care and at least she had his birth certificate. Well, no stark interview room after all and Matthew was still safe in the care of the person who loved him most and, she suddenly realised, who loved her most.

So they left with an impressive dressing around Matthew's foot, which Emily gazed at in awe, instructions to go to their GP for removal of the stitches in 10 days, and drove companionably back to Angmering, Mark asking for directions as they got closer.

"Well, I know it's late and the kids need to get to bed but I'm starving, I expect they are too, shall we just pick up some fish and chips while we're passing Jim's?" asked Mark.

"Good idea, we'll take it into our place as we get there first," Ruth didn't hesitate, it was the obvious thing to do and she had already entrusted Mark with her bleeding, frightened child. She realised too, quite suddenly, it seemed that she would enjoy adult company for a while longer and found herself correcting that thought, enjoy this kind, reassuring man's company.

Matthew was very tired, very clingy, Ruth noted and simply would not look at Mark – his rescuer. It seemed almost rude, Ruth worried, and she apologised on his behalf.

"Oh, it's nothing," said Mark, shrugging it off dismissively, "he's had an awful time; he's hungry, hurt and tired. I am a stranger and a man, who he's not used to."

Strangely, Emmie, too, would scarcely look at her – she knew you had to wait for young children to come to you, rather than rush them, and it had certainly been a strange day for her as well. At least she was making a good job of the little plate of fish, extracted from its batter, some chips, ketchup and a few peas which Ruth had put on a plastic plate for her and given to Mark to give to her with a brightly coloured tea towel for a bib.

As they left Mark asked tentatively,

"Can I ring and find out how Matthew is tomorrow? It's your last day isn't it?"

"Yes, yes, it is. Give me your number and I'll text you – so you have mine, I mean." At first Mark felt rather dismissed – she might or she might not – but then, as he saw her reaching for her phone, he realised, with a shock of relief and, well, excitement really, that she meant now.

"Oh right, it's 0737 451 3265." It was done in seconds.

~ *Chapter 12* ~

Her phone buzzed in a text at 9am the next morning.

How is he?

Still asleep!

Who, him or you?!

Ha ha.

Wondered if you'd fancy a trip to a "local attraction" today as the beach is off limits with his foot? Was thinking of Hotham Park, it's not far – little animal houses and a few gentle rides, I think. You don't want to waste your last day. Kids 'ud love it.

Good idea. Sounds great. 10.30 pick up here?

Fine. See you then.

Ruth felt relieved to see he wrote texts in plain English. Text speak was so yesterday and only for oldies who thought they were being youngies, she smiled to herself. She felt light-hearted and realised she was really looking forward to the day.

But there was more to it than that she understood, in her reflective way, as she quickly got up, showered and dressed. Matthew's accident on the rocks had really shaken her; the responsibility for one small, dependant person, threatened to overwhelm her at times and at these times she believed that she would not be able to hide forever, that she simply could not do this alone. She knew some people were capable of this, and in fact, chose this way, but she knew too that she was not such a person. She craved safety, security, *normality*, as she put it to herself, whilst acutely conscious of how non-PC this word may sound, normality not only for herself she knew, but also and more so, for the little damaged person she had removed from the streets and now wanted to *repair*, again the strangeness of the word did not elude her.

She who had so early learnt to fear, not trust, had somehow developed a heightened awareness of any hint of trustworthiness in people, honourableness even. She had noted this in some of her teachers at school, and tutors at university and she sensed this quality now, sensed it strongly and intuitively in Mark. She knew with absolute certainty that he would have no reason to believe she was not Matthew's mother and so trust was born and she willingly, excitedly embraced the thought of spending time with him.

Hotham Park did not disappoint. It was gentle, undemanding. Mark had brought a very sophisticated, E-type, as he called it, buggy for Emmie so that they could use yesterday's beach battered, lighter and much simpler buggy for Matthew should he want to rest his foot.

"Wow, that's a buggy and a half," said Ruth, "it looks as if you'd need a PhD in engineering to unfold it. Lucky you had two."

"Yes, it's a nightmare, very heavy too. This is the one her mother uses, that one is our little secret," he chuckled. "Her mother doesn't do beaches," he explained quietly.

Matthew took to the buggy quite early in the day, it was obvious his foot was hurting; he was much quieter than usual but did not complain. Emmie gazed at him with something akin to hero-worship, obviously delighted to have a 'buggy partner'.

After a snack at a café with outside tables Mark suggested they take a look at the pier which had recently been damaged by a storm but was an impressive sight and would get them in touch with the sea and the beach on their last day without getting Matthew's foot wet.

Again Matthew and Emily were awed into silence by the walk along the pier surrounded by swirling breakers which they could see too between the gaps in the wood. The children were both safely strapped in their buggies and Ruth felt a quite overwhelming and totally unexpected sense of peace and contentment. There was a sense of lifting of a burden, a burden which she did not even realise she was carrying, just by being with another adult, both of them with the children's interests at heart.

They were intrigued to discover that a group called the *Friends of Bognor Pier* had formed. They read with interest the leaflets and posters displayed and commented on the enthusiasm shown by the local community for what seemed to be quite a daunting project of restoration.

"I can't believe it's our last day," she sighed. "How much longer are you staying?"

"Just another couple of days – we leave on Saturday – can't believe that's the last day of August," he said. "I'll need to be sharpening my pencils, cleaning my shoes, all that new term, new school year stuff, you know. And Emmie, well, she has all that to come," he tailed off.

"Where are you staying?" asked Ruth, realising that, in her anxiety, she had hardly talked to him at all yesterday and this morning they had been fully occupied explaining different things in the park to the children.

"Just a little way along from you actually. My sister and her husband have a holiday flat which they let out all year round. Sea view, well-appointed," he framed quote marks with his fingers, "they're so generous and kind to me and Emmie and just let us use it when we want to, more or less."

Ruth was, with difficulty, stifling her curiosity about Emily's mother when Mark cut in.

"I looked after Emily after we split up, awarded care and custody by the courts," again he framed quote marks, "from when she was 3 months old to nearly 9 months, as her mother was deemed unfit to look after her. Then she was returned to her so-called care." He sounded bitter, angry, and anxious. "I feel I want to tell you the back story," he said, "but not walking along the pier. It's 4 o'clock. Shall we head for home? You need to pack up a bit, get Matthew to bed on time I should think. Suggestion: we give the kids pizza for tea, get them settled, Emily will sleep anywhere, I then go and get us a takeaway – Indian? Chinese? Something like that and we have an adult conversation," he smiled. "Adult themes," he then said sombrely.

Ruth was silent. *Well, that was enough to make anyone run for cover,* thought Mark.

"Yes, let's do that. I was thinking my place – or yours – but really it would be better if you came to us because then Matthew will be in his own bed. I can pack – kitchen stuff and all that, and, as you say, Emmie is a bit more transportable at her age really. Indian," she said.

The children were sleepy and quiet and uncomplaining as they were programmed gently through their bedtime routine. Emily was tucked up on the sofa underneath a spare duvet which Ruth found in the airing cupboard, whilst Matthew's eyes were closing almost before his head touched the pillow. Once his daughter was properly asleep Mark slipped out to the Indian restaurant to pick up the takeaway, already ordered by phone – Caroline had a whole raft of useful numbers on the table in the hall. So it was that twice in as many days, Ruth was left in sole charge of a stranger's child.

When is a stranger not a stranger, though, she mused to herself. *When he rescues your child, drives you, feeds you, confides in you, takes burdens from you... What on earth do you mean?* she interrupted herself almost crossly, certainly with bewilderment.

The Indian meal was delicious and they washed it down with fresh lemonade – it needed finishing – and followed it with green tea.

"So the back story," she said, after some general and easy-going chitchat. "Why has Emmie been returned to an unfit mother? Why is she unfit?"

Mark rubbed his hands across his eyes. He looked tired, careworn, she thought. They were sitting up at the dining table; Emmie had sprawled across the sofa and was breathing deeply in sleep, *in the land of baby nod*, thought Ruth to herself out of the blue.

"She was taken away from me following my suspension from my job on suspicion of inappropriate touching of a young child."

The abruptness of the stark statement caused Ruth to recoil involuntarily though she wanted and needed just to listen.

"Go on," she said quietly.

"I'm a primary school teacher for God's sake, I have young children in my care; they get hurt... I was completely exonerated during the enquiry but it took 9 months, 9 bloody months, only got the verdict in June, half of Emmie's life. Some people think male primary school teachers are weird anyway – there aren't many of us, you know. But I love my job, I love children. I loved Emmie's mother once, Meg, I would have stayed out of loyalty, commitment, making your bed and lying on it sort of thing but believe it or not she beat me up – regularly, physically attacked me... she nearly killed me several times."

Ruth listened attentively, only moving to replenish their tea cups.

"It was an ordinary Wednesday lunchtime. Just after playtime one of the littlest boys, young in the school year, late August baby, 7 years old, came running to me crying, really hurt, clutching his privates, howling, really howling in pain. I comforted him: he was in so much pain and he thought he was bleeding. He was frightened out of his mind and he pulled his trousers down to have a look, show me – whatever. He wasn't bleeding but he was really hurt, he had a bloody great bruise, excuse the pun, expanding before my eyes, a haematoma on his little scrotum, and needed to go to A&E – I'm good at that it seems." He looked at Ruth sideways.

"What had happened was that one of the Year 5 girls, big for her age, autumn born, September 1st actually, so the oldest child in the year – 10, had kicked him hard in the balls when he went to retrieve a tennis ball which had rolled a couple of feet from her. She was known to be a nightmare – you have to look at the parents, sorry but you do. No child is born evil. Her parents were not the stereotypical, benefits-seeking, work-shy, overweight, fag-smoking, booze-drinking idiots – there were plenty of those in nice, middle class Thames Lacey, I can tell you. No, this woman was as skinny as a rake, always on her mobile, worked as an HR manager, never at home, and was on her third partner, I think. We never saw the child's father. The little boy had the other sort and it was *they* who complained about *me*. I still can't believe it. His mum and her partner, not sure if he was Jordan's dad, whoops, probably shouldn't have said his name, sorry. And, I'll never forget his fat mum arriving at A&E, not even looking at Jordy, striding in looking for blood; she made straight for me and swiped me across the face, her rings, great huge things, drew blood and left weal marks for days. Common assault, actually, if we're talking crimes. And Jordy's little face, it was like a second assault for him; well she certainly got her blood and I don't mean my face." His torment sounded in every tortured word as he told it, every gesture of despair. "They poisoned his mind actually. He was bewildered by having to talk to social workers, and draw pictures of willies..." He broke off laughing hopelessly. "These people are so weirdly terrified of that sort of thing," his fingers indicated quote marks again, "paedophilia, and yet they virtually kill their own kids by neglect, horrible, unhealthy food, passive smoking and worse. I mean, what is it with them? With society generally? Paedophiles have a worse reputation than nice wholesome murderers, rapists, robbery with violence – you name it. During the time I was off, suspended on full pay, I looked into the whole paedophilia thing – if I was being accused I needed to know, had to know more about it."

Ruth was sitting as still as a statue, listening intently, attentively, and was watching Mark's troubled face the entire time. It was set, rigid, tense with emotion.

"So I started 'researching' it. It's interesting actually. I mean of course there are sadistic, sad, sick weirdos out there who probably need castration, chemical or otherwise, but also serious mental health treatment followed by possible hanging, drawing and quartering. But there are others – these people love children, wrongly of course, but they often don't wish to hurt them physically or mentally – of course they *do* hurt them, do irreparable damage in many cases I should imagine, but sometimes it's more gentle, to do with love and protection and almost *preserving* their innocence, ironic though that may seem.

And of course they need help, long-term, skilled help, not locking up with the aforementioned murderers, rapists, and violent robbers who take delight in using their so-called 'moral high ground' to hurt and maim these people. How can that ever help?"

"Go on," said Ruth quietly, still not moving a muscle it seemed.

"Oh goodness, Ruth," said Mark just as quietly, "all my skeletons are emerging. I should just shut the cupboard now, firmly. You must have some skeletons of your own, I imagine. It's struck me that Matthew looks like a boy who's frightened of men. I can't help noticing he pulls closer to you whenever any man moves into sight almost, and he makes no eye contact with me at all. Do you want to tell me about his dad?"

"I really, really don't want to or need to, trust me. Reason? Because he has just never, ever been a part of Matthew's life and never will be. I think Matthew is just not used to men. My dad died when he was young – he has no grandads or uncles even." She abruptly and urgently turned the conversation back to him. "So, what happened after all this research of yours? Did that help?"

"Well, of course the worst thing, the very, very worst thing, in amongst being considered not fit to teach children; everyone knowing the reason why; my own family knowing... was losing Emmie, my little precious Emmie." He turned to look at her sprawled in blissful, deep toddler-sleep on the sofa, her cheeks lightly flushed, hair tousled, tiny lips set in a small, perhaps dream-induced, smile.

"People just go crazy mad at a sniff of something weird, paedophilia, whisper it if you dare. I mean do you remember that terrible story that hit the newspapers about the vigilante groups somewhere or other hounding a paediatrician out of his – or was it her – home? Well, that shows a certain level of unbelievable ignorance doesn't it, to start with?" He shook his head in weary despair. "And the bullies seeking out vulnerable people, pursuing them unmercifully."

"They returned Emmie to her mother's care," he virtually spat the last word, "for fear, I suppose, that I might abuse her. God, the idiots! Following procedure, protocol, tick box, cover your back, best interests of the child. But the woman could not look after a fly." The despair, anguish and anxiety he felt were evident in every gesture. "She's sick, she's mentally..." he searched for the word, "mentally fragile. Unhinged. Always was. I thought I could help her. I loved her fragility at one time but now it's terrifying actually. Emmie was an 'accident' as they say, well, Meg assured me she was on the Pill... that old chestnut, she simply was not – never had been. So, of course, I stuck by her, I mean I loved her but she was impossible to be with and became more so. She rejected Emmie from day one, wouldn't hold her, look at her, or feed her. She was admitted with what they thought was postnatal psychosis, the serious one, you know, not the bog standard baby blues. And she still rejects Emmie, neglects her physically and emotionally... how could she, how could anyone?" again, he looked across at his sleeping daughter. "And those pen-pushers with heavy workloads and stupid bosses just cannot see it. And I have been completely exonerated," he actually thumped his closed fist on the table. "And when I have to return her each time, to comply with that bloody court ruling do you know, Ruth, she clings to me, and whimpers. Emmie will not look at her mother; her mother grabs her and locks her in her bedroom – can you believe it? And do you know almost the worst thing is that Emmie goes immediately quiet – that is so scary. What does she think to herself in her baby mind? She's a tiny child – for God's sake. They are..." he paused for a moment, "...mutilating, yes, mutilating, her childhood. And as for me, well the pain is physical, searing and I sob and sob and sob and sob, not cry or weep, but great gulping sobs for hours and hours afterwards. I read somewhere that sobbing, as opposed to other types of crying, is associated with loss. Oh, Ruth, I'm so sorry to be pulling out skeleton after skeleton after skeleton when we hardly know each other but you live too close for comfort and I wanted you to hear it from me, not those playground gossips, tittle-tattling in their self-righteous, know-it-all-at-least-our-children-are-safe-from-his-predatory-paws way. No smoke without fire, you know. I mean, Matthew is your first; you wait till you encounter the world of primary school gauntlet running." He laughed, not with mirth but with deep, resigned sadness.

Ruth remained silent, still, attentive, noting the despair, bitterness and anxiety in every fleeting expression, and struck by the word 'mutilating' recognising, with a kind of jolt, Mark's unintended allusion to *What Maisie Knew*,[17] and its depiction of a childhood wrecked by knowledge. He pushed his hands wearily through his dark hair, just beginning to show tiny flecks of grey here and there.

"Why not move away, you might ask? Mud sticks, no smoke without fire,"

---

[17] Henry James: (1897) *What Maisie Knew*, Heinemann, London, Stone, Chicago, Penguin/Random House

he repeated. "I cannot, Ruth, *cannot*," he said firmly, as if she really had asked this. "I cannot leave Emmie, how could I?" He turned to look at her almost accusingly.

"Gosh, Ruth, you told me you were only 22, nearly 23; at the end of August did you say? I can hardly believe you're the same age as my kid sister, who's a free as air student still! I mean I love her to bits, I love all my sisters – all 3 of them and a brother – how about you?"

"I'm an only one," said Ruth quickly and dismissively, reluctant as ever to share confidences. The difference now though, she suddenly realised, was that she felt a quite overwhelming sense of compassion – strange word – for Mark in his situation. And, poor, poor, poor little Emmie. How could adults do this to children? And this was all sanctioned by... by officialdom. It was unbelievable, just unbelievable. Yes, she *was* only 22 still, just, her birthday fast approaching, but she had lived, oh how she had lived, you could say, compared to, for example, a feckless, 'free as air' student surrounded and supported by a large and loving family.

"Mark," she said urgently, leaning towards him, covering his tensed, closed fists with both her hands, "we – you," she quickly corrected herself, "*have* to do something. You *have* to help Emmie, rescue her." She stopped herself abruptly. "You can do it. Are you ever allowed into the house with her? I read some newspaper report the other day about a father who installed hidden cameras and saw the mother of his 5 year old daughter smacking her really, really hard, grabbing her by the leg when she tried to get off the bed, and then asking for cuddle under the duvet and the child saying, "No, Mummy, you hurt me.""

Mark looked straight at her. "Allowed in with her? I often have to put her to bed when she doesn't just grab her from me; as I said, Meg is just out of it most of the time. Emmie's hungry and dirty and so, so quiet when I collect her. Just so dead quiet, Ruth, it's unnatural, just so unnatural the whole bloody thing."

He turned away and said, "I must get her to bed." He lifted Emmie quickly, quietly and competently into the car with practised ease and dear familiarity with her small body.

~ *Chapter 13* ~

So it was that the next morning, desultorily finishing packing up for their departure whilst Matthew followed her around, uncertain of what was to happen next, clutching a colouring book tightly to him, Ruth found herself almost struggling to recall the early, bright, sun-filled, fun-filled days of their holiday. Their haven was taking on the character of any old holiday home now as she packed their things and put the bags in the outside porch ready for the taxi to the station. She was thinking about poor little troubled, sad Emmie and a childhood to be rescued but she found herself also thinking of Emmie's distraught, tormented father, the searing grief he spoke of, and the destruction of lives.

The last few days of the idyll had been pretty heavy really: the bleeding child on the rocks, covering her tracks in A&E, relief, Mark's skeletons, as he called them, emerging in fits and starts, but relentlessly, through his tortured retelling. It was hard even to recall the light-hearted, companionable morning at Hotham Park, the stroll along the pier, discovering all the work that the *Friends of Bognor Pier* were putting in to restore the storm-battered but still proud edifice, enjoying the human endeavour, the pleasure in sharing goals, almost restoring her own faith in... *in what exactly*, she wondered, *well, just people really*, she thought to herself.

But the holiday was now well and truly over; it would be September the day after the day after the day after tomorrow, she thought to herself, relishing the childish phrase. She still had no idea which school would have a place for Matthew in just a few days' time, she realised.

Well, let's make the train trip home, home, she said to herself slowly savouring the word, *let's make it really fun for Matthew and a birthday treat for me.* Her last four birthdays had passed without fanfare, an anniversary to be forgotten.

And it *was* really fun, a real birthday treat. Again, Ruth and Matthew loved the whole experience, the clackety-clack of the train, the buffet snacks on their tables whilst rattling through the countryside, the feeling of being cocooned safely together, getting nearer and nearer to a different haven, full of hope and expectation.

Looking out at the myriad patterns of others' hopes and expectations, their fleeting joys, disappointments, even longer lasting tragedies perhaps, the tidy gardens, the untidy gardens, the trampolines, empty paddling pools, discarded plastic toys, the odd sandal, washing on the line, the end of summer, outdoor fun, Ruth sensed sharply the anticipation of subtler, softer experiences. She found herself to be looking forward to this annual renewal ironically foreshadowed in the ever darkening greens of the still plentiful leaves on the trees. She was ready to bid farewell to that 'everlasting jollity' of Louise's prose poem with this opening up to new learning, new growth as the nights drew in, garnering strength in the longer darkness, the later dawns.

Lying on the mat amongst the circulars and flyers and charity bags for discarded clothes was an official looking letter from the local council informing them that Matthew had after all been given a place at Thames Lacey Primary. There was, too, a message on the answerphone asking Ruth to ring Mrs. Pinkerton as soon as possible. The message had been left two days previously and it was already 3.45pm on the last Friday of the summer holidays. Well, she supposed, Mrs. Pinkerton might be there, setting up her school for the new term, the new school year, talking to the caretaker – whatever head teachers did. Or she may be relishing the end of her holiday. Ruth quickly set Matthew the task of putting the books he had taken on holiday neatly back on the shelf whilst she turned on her laptop to check her emails. Yes, one from Mrs. Pinkerton explaining that a child due to start in Reception had been taken very seriously ill so would not be taking up his place therefore the place was Matthew's if he still wanted it. Ruth zapped off her delighted response, and then left an answerphone message as well. The new term started on Tuesday.

The weather stayed very warm and dry for that last weekend. Matthew loved exploring his new garden which was much bigger than the garden belonging to the rented house had been. Bobby, her grandmother's gardener and general handyman for many years, now in his late 60's, had been keeping an eye on the house and garden whilst they had been away so, despite the brown patches on the grass, it looked well cared for and inviting with a lawn that turned a right angle at the far end from the house providing a kind of secret space.

Here there were large, well-established flowering shrubs: rhododendrons, azaleas, lilac bushes which her grandmother had so loved and which had afforded hideaways for Easter egg hunts and hide and seek itself though Ruth had always felt deeply the lack of other children during such games. The front lawn, as it were, was mostly surrounded by flowerbeds with roses, bulbs in the spring and plenty of purplish blue ground cover, interspersed with yellow. Her grandmother had always commented on the garden's different colour phases at different times of year. The whole gave the impression of a sweeping lawn and drive of a much bigger house lending space and an expansive, open view.

The house itself was very late Georgian, with four bedrooms, three fairly spacious, one rather smaller. Downstairs a large airy sitting room overlooked the lawn with French windows opening directly onto it via a brick lined gravel path – plenty of spaces for Matthew to look for insect life, Ruth realised.

What was amazing was just how quickly the house became very small-child-friendly indeed. Ruth found some blu tack in her grandmother's 'bureau' and together they put up Matthew's holiday pictures in the kitchen and dining room. Matthew had put the still sandy buckets and spades under the dining room table until Ruth told him that the best place for those was the back door porch. Matthew's little flip-flops lay discarded by the kitchen door and his toy wheelbarrow, the first toy Ruth had ever bought him, stood ready for action by the garage door.

They spent the weekend unpacking, including the boxes and suitcases from the rented house which Ruth had hurriedly stacked in the fourth bedroom just before leaving for Angmering, and generally settling in. They enjoyed having a breather by walking to the local parade of very useful shops including a newsagents and small stationers where Ruth was able to buy Matthew his first pencil case, and stock it with the necessaries. Matthew looked pleased, proud and apprehensive all at once.

Ruth bought the first newspaper she had read in just over two weeks and was horrified by a story of gangs of clowns roaming around threatening and frightening people in Nottingham. The clown community was outraged as they said these fake clowns gave real clowns a bad reputation. *Clowns' reputation,* mused Ruth to herself, *what is* their reputation exactly? *Fake, a covering up, the sadness of clowns, false jollity, lovely fun, funny people, skilled entertainers, love children, can reach children through disguise, disturbing, pretence*. It was like a word association running through her head. She had only seen a clown at close quarters once as a child. On that last holiday with her father there had been a clown strolling along the promenade approaching children to advertise a circus coming to town. She had been terrified of it and briefly inconsolable as the clown was inappropriately persistent commenting he had never known anyone to be frightened of clowns. This was patently untrue of course, as her father had commented at the time, as fear of clowns is such a well-known phenomenon. She could almost hear his calm measured tones as he said this.

On Monday 2nd September, still heart-breakingly full of bright sunshine, Ruth expected and dreaded the phone call from Mrs. Pinkerton or the ping of an email into her inbox saying, "I am so sorry, we hadn't heard from you so had to give the place to the next child on the waiting list." Knowing she had to buy Matthew's uniform though and realising if this was to happen she would have to spend the day trawling around for a school place, she picked up the phone herself after breakfast and felt relieved to hear Mrs. Pinkerton's steady, motherly, professional tones. "Thames Lacey Primary School, Maureen Pinkerton speaking."

"Oh, Mrs. Pinkerton," Ruth almost stuttered much to her own surprise, "it's Ruth Forster, Matthew Forster's mother, I got your messages but we're only just back from holiday."

"Yes, I knew you were going away as you told me you were, Mrs. Forster. I'm so pleased that Matthew can take up the place. I'll send you a uniform list by email now if you like. They're just everyday items, *Asda*, or any of the bigger *Sainsbury's* or *Tesco's* will have them. *John Lewis* of course if you really fancy a trip to Oxford St. on a beautiful day like today," she chuckled doubtfully. "The boys can obviously wear school shorts rather than longs in weather like this, I leave it to the parents and children to decide, I don't believe in any rigid date rules about summer or winter uniform – you know what our English weather is like. I am quite strict about uniform looking smart though, I'm afraid, and no trainers please."

Ruth felt herself suddenly to be subservient to authority, and again it took her by surprise; she was Matthew's mum, his rescuer… but she stopped herself short, she would, of course, comply. Anyway, children liked to be the same as their peers; oh she knew that, how well she knew that.

Ruth often thought back to that last trip *before the school gates clanged shut*, as she put it to herself dramatically, reminiscing on Matthew's early days with her. They bought some very special items, a dolphin themed duvet cover and pillow case set, with two of each in slightly different dolphin material, some colourful and practical, plastic covered place mats with different sea creatures on them, some wellies, a paddling pool with a very good end of summer reduction in price and, of course, the necessary school items. She also bought him a colourful towel for swimming thinking that this was a vital skill she could help him achieve; she would find some local swimming lessons, she did not know yet whether children were taught swimming at school.

They then decided to cool off with an ice cream sitting by the fountain in the main square. This was when Ruth remembered the park with the boating lake and ride-on vehicles for small children which she had been taken to by her father and grandmother up until she was about 7 or 8, she supposed, after which everything had changed for her.

"Let's see if we can find it," she said to Matthew excitedly and of course, like a children's book, there it was, just as she remembered it, if anything even more magical as she saw it through Matthew's delighted eyes. The tarmac area with vehicles had, it seemed, more and better to choose from, and Matthew tried out all of them as they became free whilst she sat on a bench with other parents or child minders perhaps, she realised, whilst the children careered around. She also realised that many children had been brought there for a last taste of summer holiday freedom before school started, and there was a smattering of lone dads, most reading newspapers, more or less oblivious to the usual crushed fingers, scraped knees, and queue jumping for the favoured vehicle, and the odd shove out of the way of the smaller children. This was all policed or observed, good naturedly enough, by the mums who generally saw fair play.

After this they found the same café for lunch, overlooking the boating lake, the granddaughter of the old man who used to run it, now in charge, she explained when Ruth told her she was last there about 15 years or so ago. They both chose ham salads; Matthew always loved salad, and Ruth still remembered that the cucumber had always tasted extra delicious there and had once been taken out to see the rows of them growing in the café garden. Sure enough it still did taste delicious.

"We'll grow cucumbers, Mat, and we'll never have to eat stale shop ones again, you'll be spoilt for life," she told him gleefully.

As they paid their bill Ruth spotted some little wooden sailing boats, obviously sold for use on the boating lake just in front of the café. "Would you like one, sweetheart? End of summer treat?" Matthew nodded and in his tactile, affectionate way leaned against Ruth as they made the selection.

"Thank you, Mummy," he said softly as he clutched it tightly to him and chose a clear launching spot.

And the afternoon drew on enjoyably but inexorably towards 'fin de vacances' with its sweet melancholy and hopeful anticipation whilst Ruth savoured the fact of having been called Mummy by this little, healing child, *treasured the word in her heart,* [18] the Biblical allusion seemed to her apt.

---

[18] *St James Bible*: Verse 2 Chapter 19

~ *Chapter 14* ~

And then it was that she tumbled in, finally and completely, or so it felt. Sudden, unexpected, unbidden, never even hoped for she realised. She loved it; that joining in, the teeming mass of humanity doing its shared business, with fervour, with energy, with commitment and this business for her now was the school run, or walk, actually. The third of September, first day of the new school/academic year.

Having resigned from her publishing job with some momentary reluctance, realising that she had no real choice, she planned to set up as a freelance editorial assistant in her field using the many contacts she already had as soon as possible. Needs must. She had to kick over the traces of her old life... let time pass and Matthew could and would be her own child, nobody need know. Five or six months would be enough. She had always kept herself to herself anyway, respected and liked though she was for her quiet ways and high standard of work.

Ruth had always felt that September was a time of renewal, of beginnings, much more so than dark, gloomy January, ever felt. She had always 'thought' and 'lived' according to the academic year, obvious through school and university but even her academic publishing job followed that pattern of course. Books had to be ready for new intakes of students, new intakes of school children, it just worked that way. Her annual leave entitlement had for the duration of her working life to date been calculated from October to October; only her P60's reminded her of other sorts of years.

And how she loved it now! How unexpected that was too – she thought back suddenly to Mark's embittered, "You wait... gauntlet-running playground" comment. She shook herself free mentally and almost physically as she walked briskly on, Matthew's small hand in hers, but not before she remembered that Mark too would have sharpened his pencils and cleaned his shoes... She stopped herself, returning deliberately to the 'present joy'.

Walking along with Matthew beside her, sometimes skipping, morning and afternoon, mid-afternoon really and even late morning until Christmas as summer born children only went in for a half a day that first term, she reminded herself with positive pleasure that the day still stretched ahead and that Matthew was safely back in her care. She had managed to get him registered at the GP practice when she registered herself. She gave them the letter from A&E, explained that some mix up at his previous surgery had caused his record to be lost, "some new IT pilot scheme, I think it was," she had explained with deliberate vagueness, and they had just registered him as a new patient.

The smiling practice nurse had taken his stitches out, given him a sticker, and commented on the impressive scar. "That'll fade though," she explained, "surprisingly quickly at his age."

But he loved school, she was delighted and relieved to realise. And it was lively and fun being such a part of it all, a key part. Letters home to parents, waiting to hear Matthew's excited burbling out all he had done. So much going on all the time, every day.

So what exactly was this tumbling in? It was the shared experience, the playground experience for mums and some dads, the unspoken understanding, the rueful smile, conspiratorial almost, between parents, the catching of an eye, no words needed, the mutual trust. She felt part of it all for the first time, the very first time, she felt the same as others and how she relished it.

Ruth had read about the competitiveness of school gate parents, especially mums, in weekend newspaper supplements mostly, but she saw none of it. If it was there she consciously or unconsciously tuned it out. Certainly, she found no need herself to put on any sort of show; by contrast she felt entirely grounded, grounded by and in her child, as she put it to herself, as others were, she noted. She quickly joined the fund-raising group – all Reception parents were targeted from day one – and she readily volunteered, feeling a need already to give something back, to contribute, to share ideas, to be part of it all.

And it worked so well, the whole pattern of the school day. As Matthew was a summer baby he attended only in the mornings until Christmas – the head teacher, Maureen Pinkerton, had told the new parents with a knowing twinkle in her eye that the children soon wanted to stay on for all the afternoon fun. Ruth collected Matthew with the other 'littleys' at lunch time and enjoyed the gradual weaning from her full time care of him – he had, after all, been hers for such a very short time. There was no shortage of freelance work, she discovered, and she relished the freedom of being absolutely her own time-manager, working diligently and quickly on the task in hand, easily able to prioritise and developing good working relationships with her growing clientele.

During the morning drop-off and lunch time pick-up she got to know Melanie whose son, Sam, was her youngest of three. Melanie was fun with a quick sense of humour, a no nonsense approach and a wisdom borne of mothering experience, as Ruth thought of it. She had just turned 30, she told Ruth, and it felt like a big birthday – the big 3 0. Her daughter, Jess, had just started high school in year 7, and her middle one, another boy, Liam, was in Year 4. When Sam started attending school full time after Christmas she would be returning to her job as a hospital pharmacist from which she had taken extended maternity leave, planning that Sam would be her last one. She was looking forward to returning with some apprehension – she had taken longer off work with Sam than she had with the older two and felt worryingly rusty, she explained.

Melanie was good to talk to, a good listener, always interested in what Ruth and others had to say, always something interesting to contribute without taking over conversations. She was tall, slim, her dark curly hair attractively unruly. As well as turning 30, her daughter starting high school – now that *is* a leap – delivering her last to the maws of school life was giving her some unexpected feelings of loss, she told Ruth during a shared coffee after the morning drop-off one day.

For the first time, Ruth found herself giving something back, sharing her trepidation about Matthew starting this big new phase. They discussed the fact that this was entirely natural and chatted easily with each other, Melanie mentioning a couple of people who had "fallen for their third", she deliberately put it in quote marks, just when their children were leaving primary school. Melanie looked thoughtfully at Ruth, "Actually," she said, "I'm suffering the pangs of the children growing up too fast and we've decided to go for it again but it isn't happening and I feel ridiculously desperate, so much so I am going for an exploratory D and C next week to see what's causing this secondary infertility, as they call it. Horrible, but I can't just let it go and Richard's supporting me completely."

"Oh, Melanie, I had no idea. I hope it works out. Actually I've heard that D and C's can work as some sort of crud clearance and clear the way for the sperm to whizz along to its target… sorry too graphic perhaps." But she saw that Melanie was laughing helplessly.

Happily Sam and Matthew seemed to be becoming firm friends, gravitating towards each other at the beginning of the day and choosing each other as partners when any activity called for that.

There were of course, the other sorts of mums. Those were the ones on their mobiles, in smart business suits, who gave their children a quick peck on the cheek, and had no real contact with any other playground parent, 'just no time for anything', metaphorically tapping a pocket watch, White Rabbit like, [19] with just as much pretension. And the Jordan-type mums too, Ruth realised. The "Kyle... get your arse over 'ere now," types. These disturbed Ruth more than she liked to admit but she was, nevertheless, able to tune out from them in some kind of self-preserving way, as she herself thought of it.

Another aspect of primary school life which struck Ruth forcibly, unexpectedly and disturbingly, was how startlingly loaded in favour of little girls the whole experience was. She found it hard to believe and wondered whether it was because all the teachers at this particular school – if they had children at all – had much older girls, mostly grown up. They were perfect sounding girls, she discovered from the teachers she chatted to at fund-raising events or when offering her services to help with reading as a freelance working mum.

There were just so many examples of this. Melanie was explaining that her own brother, Sam's "cool, bachelor uncle", worked offshore as a geophysicist and had recently been in close proximity to pirate gangs off the coast of South America. He had of course regaled Sam and the others with this story and of how they had managed to avoid the pirates so Sam decided, of course, to share this exciting, true story with his class in 'show and tell'. The comfortable, motherly teacher of the Reception class, Mrs. Wilson, a mother of two twenty-something girls, had dismissed this as a tall tale and moved quickly onto a model pupil called Laura who had told the class she was to go swimming after school. This was greeted approvingly by the teacher and much was made of it. Melanie had, by chance, chatted to Laura's mum in the playground after this episode – to which she had been witness as she had been hearing reading in Reception that morning – and asked her where they were going swimming that evening as she had planned to get Sam started on swimming nice and early for his own protection.

Laura's mum, Sarah, had looked bemused, "We're not going swimming," she had replied, "I wonder where Laura got that idea from."

---

[19] Lewis Carroll: (1865) *Alice's Adventures in Wonderland* – Macmillan UK

On another occasion Ruth had been walking home along the footpath beside the school playing field when she noticed about 50 yards ahead of her a mum with a little girl toddler – perhaps about 2 years old. The mum had stopped while the child did a wee in the hedge with her mum holding her in position. When the mum caught sight of Ruth she was very apologetic.

"Oh sorry, she just couldn't wait," she explained, flustered.

"Oh, don't worry," said Ruth easily, "it is the obvious thing to do, no matter."

The mum looked relieved, "Yes, and at least she's a little girl," she unaccountably responded with a chuckle.

Ruth walked on, inwardly infuriated, thinking, *Well, at least any little boy would have a better aim into the hedge.* She felt a need to be protective and to champion the cause of all little boys against this ridiculous early prejudice.

Another friend at the school gate, Jan, recounted how her eldest, Danny, had been really upset one day when he was in Year 5 by a group of his girl classmates ogling the Year 5 boys who had been sent to their mobile classroom to change for an after lunch PE session, there being no proper changing room for boys. One of the girls who had severe asthma, had been allowed, rightly, as Danny said, to return to the classroom to collect her inhaler – "but she didn't have to bring all her giggling friends with her to laugh at us."

Jan just ruefully commented that, "If that had been boys ogling girls, there would have been letters home to parents, and they would all virtually have been put on the Sex Offenders' register for life." There were many similar examples but actually it was comforting to regale each other with such experiences, mothers of boys, it was all part of having, at last, tumbled in, as she put it to herself.

And what of Mark? Ruth thought often of Mark and Emmie, wondering how they were, how Mark's new job was but, used as she was to holding back, keeping herself apart, it never occurred to her for a minute to contact him – she had his number after all – and find out. This was not a deliberate, coy, I'll-let-him-call-me-first strategy, it quite simply was not her way.

Mark, meanwhile, was fully occupied getting to grips with his new job at Natton-on-Thames, meeting new, all female, apart from one much older, fellow teachers, a dragon of a school receptionist and a head teacher who seemed to be struggling but who was ably supported by her competent and loyal senior management team. Mark had the insight to understand that he himself was suffering stress. He was busy at school; days were full on as always in primary teaching and being the only younger male he took it upon himself to start some new lunch time and after school clubs.

So he ran a running club after school on Wednesdays, a chess club during Tuesday lunch times, a debating society for Year 6's at Monday lunch times and planned some more sports-based activities for the spring and summer terms. His anxiety about Emmie meanwhile was almost all-consuming since Meg's health seemed to be deteriorating rapidly. Sleeping was difficult for him, eating was merely a necessity, always rushed, even in the evening. He had so much to do. If Meg were to be hospitalised Emmie would be removed into Local Authority care. Of course many would think this was the answer to his prayers, as she would be returned to her father, but no, oh no – he had been accused, accused of dare-not-speak-its-name. And the no-smoke-without-fire brigade pushed paper around whilst his little Emmie, his precious daughter, suffered in her innocence.

He had taken Ruth's advice and installed a couple of hidden cameras, only to find that one of them had a faulty battery and the other one was badly positioned. That was quickly rectified once discovered but it all took time and time he just did not have, neither did Emmie of course. Additionally the concrete evidence was elusive. Not because Emmie was not suffering but because Meg, to put it bluntly, was so out of it that her taciturn, current partner, Jeff, took Emmie wordlessly from Mark, shutting the door in Mark's face – thank goodness he had managed at least to install the cameras before this behaviour had taken over – and, it seemed, just put Emmie in her cot, shutting the door on her unnatural and haunting silence. As Mark always fed her, bathed her, and put her in her little pyjamas before bringing her back – he could not use the word 'home' – nothing was obvious on camera. He would just have to bide his time.

He too thought about Ruth and Matthew but was actually too overwrought, too busy to ring. Subconsciously he had a strong feeling that Ruth would be scornful of his inability thus far to rescue his own child.

Finally though, he managed to retrieve some very distressing footage of Meg shouting at Emmie, slapping her face, carrying her upstairs, not screaming but quiet, and throwing her into her cot, before slamming the door, without leaving a light on. Emmie lies, eyes open, rocking from side to side until she falls asleep, and the slightly distorted camera image only enhances the sense of dark abandonment of this little child.

But the paperwork, the time, the expense. His solicitor was sympathetic but seemed somehow out of his depth against the full force of so-called Child Protection. The charity, *Fathers for Justice,* had no more advice to offer, other than suggesting he join a support group for fathers who wanted more access. But his child, his little child, was in real, urgent danger. It had been agreed that a meeting would be held with the aim of applying for revised custody arrangements in view of Meg's health – Mark was sent a date four weeks away.

This was impossible. He felt it had moved beyond mere docile compliance, he had done nothing wrong, and more importantly, Emmie had done nothing wrong and he felt that this meeting might at best result in Emmie being moved to emergency foster care. Well, of course that was better than what she was going through now but the wheels would grind slowly, she could be put up for adoption and neither of her parents would see her again.

He knew that he was so tired, so stressed that he could hardly think straight. He did not want to burden his own siblings and parents with all the sordid details, as he put it to himself, and of course he could not talk easily to his new work colleagues – they all seemed to be under mostly work-related stress it appeared. He thought suddenly of Ruth, her calmness, her listening, her integrity, that quality which he sensed in her came to him out of the blue and he thought about the root of the word and the way in which estate agents used it. 'Tegare' – Latin – to touch, integral garage, unable to be touched, moved from a position once taken, he felt his mind wandering at a tangent. He wondered how little Matthew was doing too and scarcely hesitating reached for his phone:

Hi Ruth, it's Mark – Angmering, how's Matthew's foot? How's he liking school?

Hi, both fine, thanks and thanks for all your help that day. How're things? Job? Emmie? Been thinking about you both.

It's complicated. Wondering if we could meet up, could use some of your wise-beyond-your-years advice actually.

Fine. When were you thinking?

ASAP. Wondering if you're free on Friday, well, maybe not free exactly but we could do what we did before. I'll have Emmie, collecting her that evening after work. We could come to you and talk after they've had tea, Emmie is still very transportable.

Sure. What 6, 6.30? Whatever suits.

And she added her address and post code so that he could use either satnav or *Google* directions or whatever.

~ Chapter 15 ~

It was a foul night, early dark, splattering autumnal rain, with a real chill in the air when Mark rang the doorbell, holding Emmie tightly to him.

"Oh, you're both soaked, come on in. I've even lit the wood burner for the first time."

Mark put Emmie down gently on the sofa where her attention was caught immediately by the leaping, welcoming flames, then by Matthew, engrossed in a *Lego* construction. Mark slipped off her little coat which Ruth took from him, whilst he took off his own.

"I'll hang these in the hall, they'll soon dry, heating's on – for the first time too," she said.

"Shall I get a towel for Emmie's hair – and yours maybe?" She grinned at him easily, surprised at how immediately relaxed she felt in his company and how familiar to her both he and Emmie seemed. Well, they had spent two pretty eventful days together, she mused to herself. She was pleased to note that Stripey had landed on a chair and was sitting on it with a proprietorial air.

"We'll just let Emmie's hair dry naturally," he said. "She hates having her hair washed and dried anyway, let's just let her settle and recover a bit." He rubbed his own hair and shook it like a dog, "Soon dry," he said.

Emmie continued to follow Matthew's every movement it seemed with adoring eyes, but it was clear that she was very tired. She looked to Ruth to be pale and underweight and still she made no eye contact whatsoever with her, just snuggled closely to Mark, and actually turned her head away whenever Ruth approached. This was a damaged child, reflected Ruth, but rescuable, oh so rescuable if they acted quickly. She was so very young after all.

They had a simple meal of pasta with a bacon, onion and tomato sauce, which Ruth had made as a two-day meal yesterday, so it just needed reheating and some mushrooms and more tomatoes adding to bulk it up whilst the pasta cooked. Always tastier on the second day, as her grandmother used to say; it certainly seemed to be true.

Once the children were safely asleep, Matthew upstairs, Emmie on the sofa having enjoyed Matthew's bedtime story, held snugly in Mark's arms whilst Ruth read *Mr. Gumpy* with its lovely rhythms and pictures, Ruth and Mark sat opposite each other at the dining table where they could still see Emmie. Mark looked intense, sad, and distraught.

"Ruth, it's desperate now. Meg just cannot look after Emmie any longer even as far as the basics go, let alone the emotional and physical neglect. I mean look at her – she's being destroyed, such a sweet natured child. Meg is not well actually…" he faltered.

"But, Mark, she is rescuable, she will heal, she's so young. But we…" she did not correct herself this time, "have to act quickly. What's been happening? Did you get anything on camera as I suggested?"

"I did, yes," Mark sounded guarded and weary, "it's horrible. Thing is, Ruth, I actually *cannot* take her back there. I just cannot. No father could. No human being could." He rubbed his hands across his eyes as the rain and wind continued to lash outside lending an extra sense of refuge there in that warm, calm environment.

"No, I can see that, definitely," said Ruth thoughtfully as the silence grew. "But what's to be done?"

"Well, I've been thinking… I'm supposed to return her on Sunday evening as usual but no-one dictates how we spend the weekend… yet." He looked at her quietly. "She needs some fun. Have you noticed how she worships Matthew? I think she senses a fellow childhood spirit there, despite the age gap. I mean, what adult could she ever really trust? Not me, because I keep returning her to that hell hole to comply with the bloody law, child so-called protection bloody diktats. Sorry." He laughed angrily and emptily. "If we were to stay with you and Matthew this weekend, just have fun, like we did at Hotham Park, remember, she could get used to you. Young children *do* heal. Then perhaps she could be with you on Monday while I go to work, you could take her along when you take Matthew to school, just normal life, children, routine, and all that…" He tailed off. "I could sleep down here with her so she's not frightened and is safe."

Ruth was silent, watching Mark not meeting her eye.

He continued, "On Sunday evening I would ring Meg – she'll be out of it, will probably get Jeff, and explain that Emmie has a tummy upset or something and she'd be better off with me until she's over it. If he asks I'll say I've had to take some leave from work to look after her and anyway it's probably infectious so I cannot be with other children for 48 hours. I'll tell him the nappies are pretty awful and the puking is not much fun either. Then, Ruth, the court hearing is on Wednesday. I *must* get her back, it stands to reason. Social workers cannot take her, nor can her mother have her."

"It's the obvious thing to do, you're right," said Ruth with the sudden calm decisiveness Mark had seen before.

The weekend felt like a kind of oasis to Mark in the dry, burning desert of sadness he found himself struggling through, sometimes almost literally gasping for succour, some kind of reaching out, much as his own little daughter reached out to his care. The rain and wind continued all day on Saturday only allowing for a brief foray to the local shops, feeling like brave explorers, all in cagoules with hoods tightly drawn under their chins, Matthew showing Emmie how to jump puddles and both children, despite their wellies, ending up muddy and soaked to the skin. It was gentle, undemanding, two adults, two children, holed up *contra mundum* – Ruth remembered that phrase, appropriately enough, being used by Sebastian Flyte in *Brideshead Revisited*[20], both he and Charles Ryder outcasts, criminals actually, just as she was.

Sunday, though, was a glorious late summer's day. The capriciousness of the weather teased them, actually Ruth generally thought of September as being softer, more benign, than its wicked predecessor, August. But what was it about these bright, shiny, perfect days that caused hearts to hurt, somehow? Was it their ephemerality, their beauty, their masking of something untold, their half glimpsed memories of some forgotten childhood idyll, their demands for that 'everlasting jollity' of Louise's prose poem? She did not know.

Mark was distracted by anxiety, Ruth could see that but, at the same time, he seemed to relax a little as he watched Emmie and Matthew playing and they were both struck by Matthew's solicitude for Emmie. He helped her down the garden steps, saying to her quietly, "One at a time, steady on, steady on." Ruth and Mark caught each other's eye when they heard this and smiled in shared delight.

Mark frequently looked at his phone, waiting for who knew what? He showed Ruth a text from one of his sisters, Jane:

---

[20] Evelyn Waugh (1945) *Brideshead Revisited,* Chapman and Hall, UK

Keep thinking of you and Emmie – and Meg, I guess. Are you OK? Anything I can do to help?

He replied:

We're OK, don't worry. Everything is under control. I might have some news soon.

OK, sounds as if it could be good? Don't shut your family out Mark, we all love you. M&D really worried.

I know you do. Tell them what I told you. Give them my love. Be in touch very soon. Love you all too.

Ruth consulted Mark, "They seem to be having such fun, shall we just have a garden day – they may be coming to an end soon I suppose?"

"Oh, definitely, it's so relaxing and lovely out here."

"I'll get our brand new paddling pool. Matthew and I fell for it on our school uniform buying trip on that last Monday of the holidays once we knew he was in at Thames Lacey. I think we were trying to hold onto the summer holiday idyll – it didn't end so well though on the rocks, did it?"

"He seems fine now, does he have a scar?" Mark asked.

"Quite an impressive one actually but the nurse who took his stitches out thought it would fade quite quickly at his age."

"Let's hope Emmie's mental scars do too." Mark immediately regretted turning the conversation heavy but it just slipped out.

Filling the paddling pool with the hose was almost as much fun as jumping over the side and skidding across the bottom. Again, Matthew's solicitude towards the much younger Emmie was literally heart-warming. He did not need to be told to be gentle, that she could not go as fast as he could; he saw it and helped her.

As for Emmie, Ruth and Mark could see almost visible healing of mind and body. She had developed a rosy flush in the sun, lost her closed in, wary look and had even allowed Ruth to take her on her lap and dry between her toes making a tickly, nursery rhyme, joke of it as they sat down on rugs for a simple picnic lunch, "this little piggy went to market..." Emmie looked up at Ruth, made brief eye contact and laughed. Ruth was taken by surprise by her feelings of tenderness towards this little damaged child. It was not yet the deep, unconditional love she felt for Matthew but the tenderness was there, the need to protect, to rescue. Mark watched all this, watched Ruth, watched Matthew, watched his little Emmie and seemed himself to thaw a little, as Ruth put it to herself.

And what of Matthew? Well, he certainly seemed to be less terrified of Mark. He looked on in awe as Mark dealt with a minor two year old outburst of frustration when Emmie found she just could not catch the ball that Matthew threw to her. It was too big for her little hands actually, and he watched carefully as Mark showed him how to roll the ball along the surface of the water towards Emmie, creating an exciting whooshing wake which she loved.

A little later Ruth quietly alerted Mark to Matthew trying to do up Emmie's tiny topknot in her still scant toddler hair as he had seen Mark doing earlier with her little Minnie Mouse scrunchie. Again, Ruth sensed not only a thawing but a positive, if tentative, reaching out by Matthew towards Mark who sensibly did not try to rush this. She was aware at times of Matthew watching her watching Emmie but she could not quite fathom out his feelings.

It was Ruth who had the idea of making a wigwam for the children out of an old candlewick bedspread of her grandmother's which she remembered fondly, and happily located it at the back of the airing cupboard. Matthew took Emmie by the hand to find some of his favourite toys and books, including some Mr. Gumpys, to take out to their den. There was a distinct element of hero-worship as she trotted along beside him.

So contented were the two children that, as they made a cup of tea having cleared away the picnic things, Mark and Ruth managed to have a one to one 'adult' conversation.

"So what about you, Ruth?" he asked. "All my skeletons are out, free, and dancing around us," he chuckled sadly. "You don't need to release any skeletons if you don't want to; perhaps you haven't got any, but what about you, something, anything? I know you're very alone in the world family wise. You're a touch mysterious and not mysterious at the same time. I still cannot believe you're only just 23. There, I'm doing all the talking again, still." He laughed quietly. Looking at her serene profile, her clear skin, he suddenly realised with a shock that it was as gorgeously sun-flushed as Emmie's.

That same youthful glow. I bet it's just as soft as Emmie's, he thought to himself, 'shamelessly', as he reflected later.

Ruth was thinking hard. And this is what she thought:

What was it with all this telling it all, letting it out? Some things were surely better left, left unsaid, left inside, weren't they? Why the need to lay it all bare? What was that all about? Probably not the damaged victim, the rescued victim. Why would Mark ever need to know her story? It would make him complicit in her crime, crimes. An accessory after the fact was the cold phrase. No, best kept in, her secret inner self concealed, her secrets intact, untold. As for Matthew, he certainly would never need to know. What on earth would be the point? There must be hundreds of children, thousands, tens of thousands probably, millions even, not being brought up by their 'biological parents', especially their biological dad.

It was not that she believed she had given birth to Matthew – she knew what she had done, but she knew too that she could rescue him completely, make good out of evil, give him a background, family of a sort, education... just as she had been unable to do for the pile of tiny bones in the back garden of her stepfather's filthy hovel...

"Penny for them," said Mark softly, watching Matthew helping Emmie carry a little bucket full of paddling pool water over to his part of the garden where he had sown some lettuces and radishes with Ruth's help.

"Well, there's really nothing to tell. I suppose I did grow up quickly because of losing my dad so young and my mother being... unwell... possibly a bit like Meg, I don't know. She was never deliberately cruel, just..." she hesitated, "...not capable really of any normal things, bringing up a child, choosing a replacement for my lovely dad, hopeless really and never any, any..." again she hesitated, "tenderness, really. I guess she just needed so much looking after herself. There, that's it. Enough."

Again her literary background found its way to the fore. She was aware that she had voiced some thoughts for the first time and it did feel painful so why keep prodding the wound?

Where words are scarce they are seldom spent in vain
For they breathe truth that breathe their words in pain.[21]

Yes, all that was the truth, but it was over. Let us return to the present joy, she thought again.

Mark was certainly a good listener. He just nodded, looked at her and asked for no more then said, "Do you think it would be really irresponsible if we showed them how to light a little fire and cook on it?" He grinned boyishly, sheepishly almost. "There's the Boy Scout in me revealed, unmasked."

"*Were* you a Boy Scout?" Ruth asked, intrigued and relieved to be leaving her own past behind.

---

[21] William Shakespeare (c 1592) *Richard II Act 2 Sc 1*

"Oh yes," replied Mark, "loved it. All of it – the big outdoors, the gaining of badges, the singing round the campfire."

"Just thinking what I've got that we could cook without killing everyone," she said. "I could defrost the sausages from the freezer in the microwave perhaps, and then we could cook them for as long and as hot as poss. Does Emmie like sausages?"

"Yes, definitely. One thing about Emmie is that she'll eat anything, absolutely anything... for obvious reasons really," he broke off as the weight of returning sadness immediately threatened to pull him under.

Ruth remembered the recent story of the little boy who had 'slipped through the net' of child protection. He had been seen scavenging from his school's litter bins, and had died of starvation aged about 4, Matty's age, she realised. His mother had told the school not to allow him extra food and he had been told off in the weeks before he died for such scavenging. You couldn't make it up.

"Let's get Matty and Emmie to collect a few windfalls, we'll show them how to avoid the wasps and we can bake some apples in the embers, with butter, brown sugar and raisins. And we'll have sausages, baked beans, and baked potatoes cooked over the fire but mostly in the microwave otherwise we'll be waiting until midnight – mmm, yummy, very Enid Blyton really."

"Yes," responded Mark relaxed again, "and I suppose it would be Anne defrosting the sausages in the microwave while the boys, George included of course, would be doing the fun hunter-gatherer thing, fetching wood, finding apples, building the fire, whilst Timmy the dog rushed ahead barking madly and looking forward to his share of the feast!"

"Yes, but no lashings of revolting ginger beer for these children's pearly teeth of course. Water it is, and not from a running stream," she laughed.

Mark took the children off on the apple quest carrying Emmie at times; she was tired having been out in the fresh air all day, with no nap, he suddenly remembered, whilst Ruth prepared the sausages, and potatoes for cooking over the fire, and found an old-ish saucepan to heat the beans up in.

They loved it, all of them. Mark was a skilled and safe fire builder but they left the water in the paddling pool nearby for added safety. It all tasted ridiculously delicious and Ruth went off to do the Anne thing whilst Mark showed the children how to empty the pool by standing on the sides. Emmie was not heavy enough to do this very efficiently but she got the idea and added a bit of weight by going down on all fours, screaming with delight as the water tumbled out at speed. They made sure the fire was completely out and went in 'tired but happy' as the well-worn phrase puts it.

Despite the pool the children were actually filthy from their day in the open so Mark and Ruth decided that bath time could be a joint enterprise. There was no doubt that this would need to include hair washes. Mark made a grimace but in the event Ruth entertained Emmie royally by showing how she could lather up Matthew's hair into pointed spikes so that he looked like a pixie. Matthew entered into the spirit manfully, as Ruth noted, and made naughty pixie faces as he pretended to hide behind his sponge and play peek-a-boo with Emmie.

"Let's make Emmie into a pixie shall we?" said Ruth bravely. Feeling rather perturbed by the tangle count in Emmie's hair (boys were easier, she reflected) Ruth nonetheless set out to make the hair washing game fun... with great success as it happened. But again, that tenderness, talking gently to Emmie all the time pretending to whisper so that she could hide from that naughty pixie, Matthew, Ruth trickled the warm water over Emmie's head, with Mark looking on in ever-reducing trepidation.

"Wow, Ruth," he whispered over Emmie's head, "this is amazing. She's putty in your hands. You must be some kind of toddler whisperer or something," he said admiringly, "you should run classes perhaps."

Not so much a toddler whisperer, thought Ruth to herself, more some kind of child rescuer really.

~ *Chapter 16* ~

Next morning they were all up early as Mark had a longer drive than usual, through the rush hour and school run, and he usually liked to be in school by 8am at the latest.

"Children often arrive then, dropped off by working parents, or they sometimes get themselves there just because it's a better place to be than home," he explained. He was planning to try to start a breakfast club too, but the head teacher was not that well and any new ideas easily fazed her. "Actually, I feel I can't quite get to that right now, I've just got too much going on, but it's an idea to be followed up as soon as I've got the head space to do it."

He tapped his scalp, rather hard, Ruth thought.

Teasingly, the late September morning was just as beautiful as yesterday had been, but the Sunday summer idyll seemed remote as the scramble to get everyone ready took over. Matthew seemed delighted to have Emmie for company on his trip to school. He held onto the buggy and told her about some of the landmarks on the way, the post box, the lollipop man who always gave him a high five, and the wall he could walk along beside the churchyard path which led to the school. As soon as he saw Melanie and Sam walking along though he ran off to catch up with Sam without a backward glance, leaving Ruth to walk along with Melanie and introduce Emmie. She explained straightforwardly that she was the daughter of a friend and that she would be looking after her for a few days.

Melanie made a suitable fuss of Emmie without going over the top, and just quietly said, "Emily, Emmie, what a pretty name."

The two women chatted about their weekends, how quickly that precious time had passed, and Melanie remarked that Sam talked a lot about Matthew –

Mat, as he called him, and would like him to come to play after school one day soon.

"Oh, I'm sure Matthew would love that, and Sam must come to us too," replied Ruth without hesitation. This was a whole new part of her life, all part of joining her fellow journeymen, human race, that tumbling in, as she again put it to herself.

"Gosh, Ruth, you've got a 2 year old for a whole day. Do you want to start with a coffee?" laughed Melanie.

"Love to," said Ruth, "but don't forget we're still picking Matthew up at lunchtime. It's really good because they get on really well. He's so sweet to Emmie, really considers her needs, you know? Shall we just go to mine so that we can release her from her buggy and not have to worry about her in the café?"

"Good idea," said Melanie, and the two of them chatted about this and that with Ruth explaining easily how she had inherited the house from her grandmother, how she had loved her, looked after in her last illness, and, with Melanie now a trusted friend, was even able to explain a little about her mother's problems.

Melanie was a good listener, interested, never making assumptions. She commented, "You must have learned your 'parenting skills'"- she formed joke quote marks with her fingers – "from your grandmother then as your dad died when you were so young. I wonder how different it would have been for you if he had lived."

"Umm yes. How about you, Mel? Who have you got apart from the lovely Richard?" she raised her eyebrows quizzically.

"I'm close to my sister, she's only eighteen months older than me, but she lives so far away – Edinburgh, of all places. They moved there with her husband's job. Alistair. He's okay, a bit dour, thinks I'm bit giggly and girly when I'm with Susie I think. Taciturn but solid. Lives on porridge… not really," she added quickly. "They're happy. And they have two kids, boy and girl, pigeon pair, 10 and 12. Iain and Alex."

Ruth bent down to accept a plate of nameless plastic food from Emmie who was playing with the toy kitchen which her grandmother had played with as a child, as had her father, as had she. Visiting children, it seemed, loved it too.

A text buzzed through:

All OK with everyone?

Fine. Emmie's making me a plastic meal, Mel's here for a coffee.
Sounds good.
You OK?
Difficult to concentrate.
Not surprised.
Emmie might like a nap about 11, after her busy time yesterday!
Fine, I'll try her before we go to get Matthew.
See you later.
Keep calm. (:

The day sped on: Ruth had Mark constantly on her mind. As for Mark, distracted as he was, the school day took him over and he felt a sense of relief, serenity even, knowing that Emmie was safe. He found himself actively looking forward to 'home time' when he would see her and Matthew and Ruth. Running club took his mind off any sort of clock-watching which, in any case, was just not in his nature but he was pleased to see the last child safely collected when he could quickly shower and head for Ruth's, stopping only to pick up a bottle of chilled white, South African chardonnay.

Shall I pick up something up for supper?
Kids are sorted. Fish fingers. You could get a takeaway for us. Or a ready-made something or other? I was going to do something original like mac cheese as they don't like it, but a takeaway sounds better.
Will do. Any hates?
None.
OK.

Once again bath time was fun. Ruth had been gratified to see that Emmie did not actually leap into Mark's arms as if needing to be rescued. She toddled over and clutched his legs to her and then returned to offer him a plateful of plastic food. Matthew was solemnly taking the orders using a notebook and pencil and a tea towel for a waiter's apron. Ruth was pleased to note that he could easily write eggs and bacon with no prompting. She found herself oddly regretting not having been able to get ready for Mark's arrival. She felt horribly end-of-the-day-ish, fish fingery, and had ketchup on her T-shirt sleeve, she realised. In her reflective way she stopped to consider why she should even think about this 'getting ready'.

She knew that she was tired, it was tiring of course looking after two small children all day including two school pick-ups; a shower would revitalise her for the evening. She was suddenly aware of Mark looking at her.

"I really appreciate being able to leave Emmie with you, Ruth, it's such a relief. It's a lot for you though, I know. What about your work?"

"Well, with Matthew still being picked up at lunchtime I never have that much time during the day anyway at the moment so I burn the midnight oil a bit – I have to meet deadlines otherwise we wouldn't eat," she laughed. "I wouldn't have it any other way though. I love seeing Matthew at lunchtime." She glanced at him, still absorbed in 'cooking' and 'waiting'; he and Emmie had lined up some soft toys and some *Playmobil* figures as more restaurant customers and had seated them rather randomly to eat their even more random meals. "And it's only until Christmas that he's part-time at school; then I'll miss him in the afternoons but will get more done."

"How's school going?"

"All fine, he seems really happy. I've joined the fund-raising parents, I love it. I haven't encountered any of those playground horrors you warned me about yet, only a matter of time perhaps, or maybe they are there and I just tune them out in a haze of new-found belonging."

"That's good to hear." Mark sounded genuinely pleased for her.

"What takeaway did you get?" asked Ruth, suddenly realising she was hungry *and* tired.

Mark pulled out the chilled white wine with a mischievous grin.

"Oh… oh, great," said Ruth.

"And this." He pulled out a 'pretend', guilt-assuaging takeaway, a new range of upmarket dishes that Sainsbury's was doing – this was a delicious-looking Thai curry which just needed 'putting together', hence the pretence.

"Mmm, looks tasty. Oven will take about 15 minutes to heat up. But these two need to be steered towards B – E – D. They're very contented at the moment I know but early starts again tomorrow. Do you fancy reading to them while I run their bath? And I could 'sneak' a shower at the same time, I could do with one."

"Sure thing. Shall I choose or is there one on the go?" He looked towards the well-stocked bookshelf.

"Mr. Gumpy's always popular but they might like a change. You choose. Matthew, Emmie, I'm just going to run your bath while you have a story with Mark/Daddy," she said to them both, "so you need to put the closed sign on the restaurant door and tell the customers it's last orders now."

Matthew proudly found his closed sign and called out, "Last orders now," very fiercely and bossily.

Ruth looked at him thoughtfully. "Mat, you need to be friendly to your customers so they come back again and always be very polite so you could say something like, 'Ladies and gentlemen, the night is moving on so I am afraid it is now time for your last orders. I hope you have all enjoyed your evening. We have enjoyed being of service to you. Thank you and good night."

Matthew looked at her with delight as he mimicked her exactly; Emmie was watching them both, smiling quietly.

The shower was 'just what the doctor ordered' as her grandmother used to say, she remembered fondly and happily. As the bathroom filled with restorative, scented steam she simultaneously ran a bath for the children filling it with bubbles for some last fun, not too raucous though, she thought to herself tiredly, though by now much revived.

She returned to find them contentedly enjoying *Mog the Forgetful Cat* [22], both gazing at the wonderful illustrations with that complete small child absorption, Emmie mouth-breathing a little as she had a slight cold. It was good to see and further restored Ruth. The closed sign was firmly in place on the little wooden kitchen, and the 'customers' bundled rather unceremoniously into the toy wheelbarrow. Bath time was a joint venture again, Emmie now positively enjoying a bubbly hair wash, and Matthew proudly showing her his plastic steamer as it chugged through the froth with its detachable little plastic crew members, four lifeboats, six life belts. Both children snugged down quickly, naturally tired out and were asleep in minutes.

Ruth turned the oven on whilst Mark splashed wine into large glasses. They returned to the sitting room and let the wine do its work.

"How are you feeling about Wednesday now?" asked Ruth.

"Still fraught, but I must say it's great being here like this. It feels safe somehow. Tell me about your grandmother, I can sort of feel her presence here – in a good way," he added quickly.

"Yes, I can too," agreed Ruth, "it makes me feel grounded, less rootless, I guess." She enjoyed explaining how it had been for her as a child, leaving out most of the really awful bits – for the moment – she thought to herself. She described to Mark how she had seen this house as a refuge, a grounding, how her grandmother had been her mainstay, but how difficult it had been to have friends round in the normal way of children growing up. She told him how they used to talk about her father together, how her grandmother had never said a

---

[22] Kerr, J (1970) *Mog the Forgetful Cat*, Harper-Collins UK.

single word against her mother, and how her grandmother had gradually started to depend on Ruth physically as the illness took hold but how that had never detracted from the emotional support she was able to give Ruth, even to the very last.

The curry smelt delicious, and Ruth served it at the table for ease because of the varied and sumptuous accompaniments, coconut shreds, yoghurt and stems of finely shredded ginger. The wine perfectly complemented the meal.

Ping. Ping. A text to Mark's phone. He ignored it whilst they were eating, one of his rules he said to Ruth. But later, once they had cleared up, he apologetically looked at his phone.

Meg won't be in court on Weds, you bastard, but I will so watch out, peedo.

Right. I have been warned. Is Meg OK?

What do you care?

Emily's still not well, tell Meg, just a nasty vomiting bug it seems.

Fuck off.

He showed the exchange to Ruth. "Oh… lovely," she said uncertainly.

The relaxed mood was destroyed of course and Ruth did have a deadline to meet so she, in her turn, apologetically got out her laptop and set to work in the sitting room alcove. She explained she could completely tune out any television noise whilst she was working so if he wanted to watch and wind down he must feel he could.

Mark leant back against the sofa cushions with a sigh. "I'll just have my news fix," he said, "then go and join Em I think. Running club takes it out of me," he sighed.

Ruth had allocated the third, not too small bedroom for Mark and Emmie. Mark had brought her travel cot and he would have the very comfortable single futon in with his little daughter.

He found himself studying Ruth's profile whilst she worked, noting the neat jaw line, the unlined skin, her long yet somehow 'dainty' neck. His interest was captured briefly by a travel documentary about India whilst Ruth worked with complete focus on a book about the universe for 8 to 10 year olds.

Despite her ability to 'tune out' as she had said, her attention was caught by news of a discovery of tiny human bones in a garden in Northampton – the travel documentary having turned into the 10 o'clock news. She saw the white gowned, 'forensic' figures moving eerily in the darkness, the police cordons, the vans, the lights. The bones had been discovered during a garden landscaping job which was being undertaken by the new owners of the ordinary looking suburban house.

"Sad," muttered Mark, almost inaudibly, "there just has to be a sad story there, not just a crime, and sad that the baby could not be left in peace really. On that profound note I will say good night and thanks, thanks again for everything. How long will you be working?"

"Probably about an hour or so, mustn't be too late. Hate getting irritable which is what happens when I get tired, not good. Good night. Get some good sleep. See you in the morning." She knew she tended to lose track of time when she was working but she did need to get on.

Having concentrated with focus, absorbed commitment to completion of the task, she loved her work, Ruth discovered that, after final checks, 3 hours had passed, but she knew it was time well spent and sent the work off in her usual competent way then and there, enjoying the thought that it would be there at the start of the working day.

Deciding not to be tempted by a final wind down, it was now 1.45am, she made her way quickly to bed, tired out, in a good way – or so she thought. It felt like a physical assault therefore when out of the blue, the memories hit her, thwack, full on.

That early July, hot night, 9th July to be precise, exhausted by the relentless feeding demands of 33 day old baby Matthew, who still slept only fitfully and unhappily, it seemed, as if able to sense her own distress, her own helplessness perhaps, she had that night not even attempted to return him to his Moses basket after his 2am feed which took about an hour. Instead she cuddled him close, cradling him, rocking him, making real eye contact, knowing him, learning to give of herself, loving every perfect aspect of his tiny body, trying to read his thoughts but knowing, deeply and instinctively that she would do all in her power to keep him safe, to nurture him, to protect him, with every fibre of her being; the metaphor seemed apt so physical, so elemental were his needs at that time.

In such ways she would enable him to grow, made strong by the force of her love; she knew now that she could do it. Feeling new strength and a sense of capability literally flowing through her, she remembered that so clearly now, she had placed baby Matthew carefully on his back, as instructed, and had fallen deeply into the first really refreshing sleep she had had since he was born.

She had slept thus until 9.30am when, turning to look at her baby, had seen that his perfect features were a mottled grey, his tiny lips completely white, his body cold and already stiff. Baby Matthew had died lying next to his mother, his protector, his nurturer. This same person, Ruth, now changed forever, then went on to collude in her inadequate mother's crazy idea of concealing her grandson's death and unlawfully burying him in the garden. Steve, too, her baby's father, her rapist, was, with obvious relief, which he made no attempt to disguise, complicit in this whilst leaving the two women, Ruth, aged 18, and a new, now recently bereaved, mother, the other, her mother Julie, mentally ill, to complete the task, unaided, unsupported, unshriven.

Now, 4 years later, these memories returned like malevolent clowns, endlessly circling through her tired brain, gyrating, taunting, mocking *...thought you'd got off scot free did you? Oh no, you won't, oh no won't, oh no you won't, free you'll never be. You're damaged goods, you have 2 damaged children, a damaged man beside you... who knows what he gets away with? Haha, haha, haha, others will laugh, you will weep forever. You killed your baby.*

The weight of sadness threatening to overwhelm, to crush Ruth's spirit beyond repair, enabled her at last to close her eyes, if only to shut out the clown images, the dead, cold baby images, the digging of the grave and she slept for about an hour and a half when the shrill blast of her alarm clock woke her at 7, followed by her failsafe phone alarm, set for 7.10am, just in case.

~ Chapter 17 ~

To her surprise Maureen Pinkerton made quite a beeline for her the next morning in the playground.

"Would you have a minute for a quick word when the children have gone in, Mrs. Forster, or can I call you Ruth? Don't worry, everything is fine with Matthew, he's doing well I hear from Mrs. Tachet and see from all the records, I just want a quick word with you if you've time?" She glanced down at Emily uncertainly. "That's if this little person doesn't mind?" She looked at Emmie fondly.

"Oh, fine, no problem, shall I just come in and find you when the bell goes?"

"Yes, I'll be in my office. Would you like some coffee?"

"That would be nice," said Ruth surprised. This didn't sound too bad, she thought.

"I'll put it on now," said the head teacher as she turned to greet some other parents, picked up a stray ball, holding it aloft until it was claimed by a small boy in Matthew's class.

"Wonder what all that's about," said Mel, intrigued. "Summoned to see the head... ooh."

Ruth looked innocently bemused and stopped to check Matthew's book bag to see if he had remembered his reading book; he had been showing it to Mark last night, who had kindly heard him read.

"Busman's holiday," Ruth had said apologetically.

"Not really, feels different somehow." He had ruffled Matthew's hair. "Lovely reading, Mat, well done. Bit of a silly story though, heh? Never mind, getting through these 'readers' will just give you the reading wings you need... *A Trip to the Shops* today, *Harry Potter* tomorrow, kiddo!"

The bell rang out, Mel waved goodbye and mouthed a joking good luck, see you later, and Ruth found her way to Mrs. Pinkerton's pleasant office which she remembered well from her visit in August with more pleasure than trepidation so much did she feel, even then, that they, she and Matthew, belonged there.

"Ah, there you are dear. Sorry to appear to accost you in the playground, would... Emily, isn't it? Would Emily like to play with bricks over here perhaps?"

"Yes, good idea," said Ruth unbuckling her, setting her to her feet and showing her the box of colourful bricks obviously put there to entertain or more likely keep small children quiet whilst their parents talked to the head teacher about serious matters... there would be no disturbances in this office, the box seemed to say. Emmie got the message too, Ruth realised thankfully as she settled to playing quietly, occasionally looking at Mrs. Pinkerton rather doubtfully but wisely thinking better of interrupting.

"Milk, dear, sugar?" asked Mrs. Pinkerton.

"Just milk please." Ruth took the steaming mug gratefully, she had worked far too late last night but had satisfyingly met her deadline – which was 12 midday today.

"I need to tell you that I'm not going to be in school tomorrow..." She paused. Ruth was lost for words momentarily, feeling "So?" not to be an appropriate response. "Because I'll be in court. I feel I must tell you, Ruth, can I call you Ruth?... that Mr. Williams, Mark, Emily's father, was not only the best teacher I have ever worked with during a very long career but also the best man I have ever known... and I have known a lot. Unimpeachable is a word that springs to mind when I think of Mark Williams. I would trust him with my own child if I had one, which I don't, not for want of trying." She paused reflectively, obviously in the mood to confide in this relative stranger. "My partner and I – Sheila," she looked straight at Ruth so there was to be no misunderstanding, "we have now been together 30 years and applied to adopt about 25 years ago now when we were both 30. Sheila, bless her, had already undergone IVF three times, nearly bankrupted us – it was just not to be, I suppose," and she turned to look at Emily playing happily. "But of course I have always been surrounded by small children..." She broke off. "Anyway, I will be there to support Mark *and* to speak up for him both as his former employer and as a character witness. I will not mince my words. That investigation... they crucified him, he was hanged, drawn and quartered really as soon as that oaf of a woman – sorry, opened her foul mouth, sorry again. How do you know Mark, if you don't mind my asking… you don't have to say if you'd rather not of course?"

Ruth was rewinding a bit, realising that Maureen, as she insisted Ruth call her, had called Emily by her name in the playground. Ruth had not registered it at the time, somehow it was a given that Mrs. Pinkerton would know the names of all the children in her playground and had to rouse herself to reply. She had noticed, irrelevantly she thought to herself, how Maureen had used the right past tense of 'to hang'; a rarity. *Well, she is a teacher of course, but she cannot be teaching children that word very often can she?* She suddenly remembered the rather pointless games of hangman at the end of terms at school.

"Oh no, that's fine. We met on holiday in August down on the south coast. Matthew and I were staying nearby. Matthew and Emily get on really well. Mark sort of rescued Mat when he cut his foot badly on the rocks on nearly our last day. Quite dramatic really. The screams."

"Oh yes, his lovely sister – Jane isn't it – has a holiday house down there doesn't she? Angmering? I've met all three sisters actually at their parents' silver wedding – it was a lovely occasion."

"Yes, that's right, Jane. I haven't met her yet."

"Typical of Mark to come to the rescue of a child in distress, anyone in distress really. How is Meg, talking of that?"

"Not too good, I understand. Not well. Mark explained it all to me. Tragic."

"Yes." She paused. "Integrity – that's a word I think of to sum Mark up. Such a brilliant teacher too. Natton's gain is our loss. We can never replace him. Bloodhounds," she muttered almost under her breath. She shook her head as if to free herself of the image of Mark being hounded almost to death.

"I presume you'll be looking after Emily then and won't be there?"

"Yes, that's right; and Matthew of course."

"Oh yes, lunch time pick-up still," she smiled. "How has he settled do you think?"

"Oh he just loves it, full of it all, can't wait to do afternoons and school lunch – imagine!" Ruth laughed lightly.

"You know we're about to be holding parent governor elections? Have you thought of putting yourself up for it?"

"Well, I hadn't actually… I feel such a new girl, really."

"Well, don't forget it's a 4 year term so it could be good to have a Reception mum, fresh eyes. They're a nice bunch, competent too. It's such an important role. Think about it." She handed her the flyer and got to her feet. "I'll do my very best in court tomorrow, trust me," she said warmly, clasping Ruth's hand in both of hers, and ruffling Emmie's hair affectionately.

"I'm sure you will, thanks," she said hesitantly. "The alternative is too grim to contemplate."

A text from Melanie buzzed through as she crossed the deserted playground wheeling Emily briskly along rather wanting to make up for lost time, though not actually lost at all, she realised.

Is everything OK? Has she released you?

All fine, nothing drastic. Might go for parent governor actually (:

Good idea. Hard work, quite a commitment. Been there. Did it when Lauren was in year 1, eye-opener.

Sounds intriguing. See you later xx

See you (:

Melanie was becoming a good friend Ruth reflected as she walked on fighting the tiredness from the previous late night working, the worry about tomorrow and simply from the relentlessness of looking after small children. Unable to stop herself she suddenly remembered, felt it viscerally really, her 18 year old self as a new mother, cast adrift in a sea of sleeplessness, her body and mind rent asunder, as she thought of it, first by that perverted act of violent procreation, then by the equally violent, it felt, birth itself.

Her mother had been there, wringing her hands, crying, ineffectual, no help at all actually. Ruth had felt more terribly and terrifyingly alone than ever. The baby was thrust into her arms, and then another assault, a bolt from the blue, the sudden intensity of tenderness, all suffusing, unbidden, and the overwhelming sense of responsibility. These assaults, as she thought of them, were almost as overpowering as everything else at that time.

Getting home, the horrifying squalor, trying to create a small space of cleanliness and calm for the innocent victim in this, the escalation of violence between her stepfather – hated, unnatural word – and her pathetic mother, pathetic in the true sense of the word – arousing pathos. She had nursed her child alone and, left to it, she had suffered the nights of endless feeding, the waking, fretful, insistent, unsatisfied baby, and his accusatory blue eyes. What was she doing wrong? How she had thought of hurling the tiny thing out of the window at times just to stop the noise, just for a moment to stop the noise. Sometimes she did indeed want to tell it all, to let it out, but more often she felt it safer to keep it all in, locked inside forever.

Emmie was watching, fascinated, the dancing, russet red, biscuit dry, autumn leaves bouncing and bowling along in the brisk, slightly chilly wind, harbinger of more to come. She made swirling movements with her hands as if to mimic their motion. *How topsy-turvy it all is*, thought Ruth to herself, suddenly so sharply aware of that childish story book phrase and its myriad meanings. *Here I am, an accessory after the fact of child killing and concealed burial, a child stealer to boot, left to care for this little damaged person, and my own little damaged Matthew and able to do that so whole-heartedly, so relishing it all, so accomplished at it, so successful*, she chuckled softly out loud, *so sought after to do this*.

Then it came to her, like a bolt from the blue, as she was to realise later. What was to stop her revolting, sick, violent stepfather from destroying all this by spilling the beans, grassing her up? The clichéd phrases came rushing in. He would do that from spite, the need to destroy anything good, anything he perceived to be weak, controllable. She thrust the thought from her; no, she almost shouted it out loud. And it was only much later that she understood that he would just never do that, could never do that because it would, of course, incriminate him.

She sat down on the low wall just outside the school gate, unpeeled a banana for Emmie to keep her going, stifling her sudden irritation at Emmie's increasingly insistent whining, kicking her legs out, preparing for a full blown wail. This was irritation borne of fatigue, she said to herself. *Control it now*, she commanded herself as she quickly completed the school governor election form by hand, dropping it in before she could change her mind. She could always bring Matthew to the meetings she thought. They were relatively early in the evenings; he could read quietly somewhere safe; Maureen would sort it, her new ally. She smiled as she, tongue in cheek, thought of herself as the teacher's pet. Still, it could be helpful and actually she realised she liked Maureen; she was a strong woman, as she had understood during that first meeting in August. It was a good feeling, a trusting feeling.

~ *Chapter 18* ~

That evening she made macaroni cheese as planned, Mark having said it was one of his favourites, and served it with a tomatoey basily sauce. This was followed by tinned peaches and plain yoghurt, which was a new combination for Mark but they both agreed it was not only food of the gods, but went very well after mac cheese, and that tinned fruit was a much underrated commodity.

"Like sardines," commented Ruth, "I think if they were not so cheap they'd be really expensive. I only learnt to like them when I was in my final year at uni though, cheap, needs must, used to hate them. Matthew still does."

"Yes," agreed Mark, enjoying the light-hearted, footling conversation, "I always think mushrooms are a bit like that, a real delicacy, you know even just the ordinary supermarket ones, I wouldn't trust myself to know a safe wild mushroom to be honest." And he quite suddenly burst into song, in a perfect pretend Italian accent:

"Just one mushroom-o, give it to me, delicious fungus from *Sainsburee*."

Ruth found herself laughing helplessly, seeing this new Mark and the children loving the laughter, a rarity for them, she realised sadly. Matthew and Emmie were now turning back to look at them, joining in; *laughter really is infectious*, thought Ruth.

"You'll be accused of 'cultural misappropriation' next," she said, "luckily the thought police aren't about." Mark was still thinking about food delicacies though. "Radishes too, Matthew's growing them isn't he? Just one radish-o," he started, and then stopped almost as suddenly as he caught sight of Matthew and Emmie holding hands as they jumped pretend, tiny waves, in the rivulets of water still flowing freely from the rapidly emptying paddling pool. They had filled the pool after school as it had been one of those glorious, golden sun-filled days often seen in early October and the children had run out in the setting sun after tea to help Mark and Ruth empty it as twilight approached.

Mark went indoors to replenish theirs and the children's drinks whilst Ruth took out her phone to take a quick picture of the children jumping, sending it to him too. They drank cold water only, conscious of the need for complete concentration on what was to come.

And the reality of the next day was never far from either's thoughts.

"I feel like Jesus must have felt in Gethsemane," said Mark suddenly when they were clearing up companionably enough having put the children to bed.

Ruth got up from her haunches where she had been returning the day's saucepans to the cupboard under the cutlery drawer, turned to look at his driven, careworn features, and moved towards him. She put both her hands on his strong wrists noting the fine dark hairs just tickling the bottom of his hands. "Mark, I am with you all the way. They *have* to see sense. They do not want more parentless children on their hands surely? Also…" she hesitated, unsure of how much to tell him, "…Maureen… Maureen Pinkerton summoned me to her office today – it was a bit scary at first, Emmie was a credit to you, sat and played happily with the famous bricks, while Maureen told me she was going to be there tomorrow, to speak up for you, what a brilliant teacher you were, Natton's gain Thames Lacey's loss etc. etc. She remembered your parents' silver wedding celebration, knew your sisters and brother, she was lovely, Mark, I really like her. I thought I did when I first met her in August. Matthew does too."

Mark was silent, looking down at her hands on his wrists. "Ruth, that really means a lot to me." He drew her towards him, "Can I do this?" he asked gently, as he released her grip, took her face in his hands and kissed her so, so gently on the lips, pausing to ensure she was acquiescent, willing. She stroked his forehead with both her hands as if to erase the worry and they went together into the sitting room, desire unspoken, unacknowledged between them, but sharply felt by both.

Neither of them slept much that night. Ruth went into the kitchen to get a glass of water at about 2am and found Mark, on the same mission, staring out at the dark garden, the full moonlight throwing up menacing shadows, the screech of a cat fight somewhere shattering the stillness.

"I've been looking at Emmie sleeping, safe and sound, in a house with three people who feel something for her – I'm right aren't I?" he asked Ruth directly not waiting for an answer. "And thinking that tomorrow she could be rocking herself to sleep in a strange cot, sucking her sleeve, in a strange foster carer's home, wonderful people that they are and all that."

Ruth just leant against him, staring out at the darkness with him, unable to provide any comfort at that moment that would not sound dismissive of his realistic fears. He put an arm round her waist and pulled her into him closer, leaning against her, almost literally, for support. They spent about ten minutes just like that, close, needing no words.

At length Ruth asked, "Have you anything to read with you? I find I can read myself back to sleep sometimes."

"I've got a Jeffrey Archer on the go actually. Light, good story, no demands. Good at 'taking me out of myself'." He formed the quote marks with his fingers.

"Let's try it; otherwise we'll be fit for nothing tomorrow."

"You're right of course, you wise little 23 year old," he said with affection as they went their separate ways.

In the event, her fears from the morning in the playground returned to haunt her as did her fears for Emmie and Mark, chasing each other across and through her brain until about 5am when she fell into a fitful slumber – "as they put it in books," she said to herself and Mark in the morning – only to be woken what felt like minutes later by the shrill ringing of her alarm clock.

Strangely it was later that very day, just five weeks into the term, when Ruth became aware of the whispered rumours. They were innocent enough at first. In fact, Melanie's eldest son, William, Will, started talking about Mr. Williams. How cool he was. He, Will, had been there that day and had seen exactly what happened and yet they got rid of the best teacher ever. Idiots! With his 10 year old, going on 11, new-found knowingness, Will was keen to set the record straight. He had taken that snotty little kid, can't remember his name, onto his lap to comfort him after that great oaf, bitch face, whatshername, don't know don't care.

"William, no language like that please," interjected Melanie sharply, both mums thankful that Matthew had not yet come to join them but conscious too of Emmie's little pitcher status.

"They've got filthy minds," he said suddenly in no uncertain terms. "And two of the TA's are not much better," he said resentfully. "They're so rude about Pinky, just because she's a les. They're homophobic and they tell us we're not supposed to be."

William is a bright boy, but how does he know the word 'homophobia' so young? wondered Ruth. Even his mother with older children looked taken aback by this. *Perhaps it's good to be so aware so young, who knows really? Is it good to know things? So young?* There had been a ban on the use of the word 'gay' as a playground insult too, so that had to be good really, she felt.

She felt consumed by anxiety that day and welcomed the distracting chitchat of her playground companions, some of whom were becoming real friends, Melanie of course especially but also Paula. She had two children, one in Reception and one about Emmie's age, both girls, Rebecca and little Alice, who were quite friendly with Sam and Matthew despite the gender divide so marked at that age. Paula was a full time mum and loving it.

Ruth took to a woman called Nicola too, she was good value, lively and quick-witted, and worked for an insurance company as part of the marketing team. It paid the bills, and had some good perks, was her take on it. Her husband was a banker but was looking for an escape as he was troubled by some aspects of that industry, Nicola told them. She had a Year 6 daughter, Emma, nearly 11 going on 18, she told them sadly and a son in Year 4, Finlay, Fin.

The women tended to congregate on arrival for pick-up or drop-off and at the various birthday parties, invitations for which had soon started arriving. All the parties took on similar, tried and trusted and highly successful formats.

It was Melanie and Paula though who Ruth considered to be her real friends. Paula had had a breast cancer scare last year aged only 28 and her mother had died from the disease aged just 37 when Paula was 12 and her sister, Helen, 14. She had a calm, reflective way with her as people tend to when they have seen too much too young, thought Ruth. Paula's father had struggled to cope and had then himself developed a horrible wasting disease aged 42, motor neurone disease; this was three years after their mother had died. So the girls had looked after themselves, aged just 17 and 15 and were, as a result, very close.

On the other side of the playground at about this juncture in the school term, she occasionally detected some curious looks directed at her, and rumours soon spread that she was indeed looking after Mr. Williams', the paedo's, daughter. She had no difficulty in ignoring them and wondered if her new friends realised too but were saying nothing, perhaps waiting for her to confide in them. *Do they talk about this to each other?* she wondered fleetingly. *Maybe*, but somehow she thought probably not.

The text pinged through just after 4pm.

It's over, Ruth. She's safe. She's to live with me.

Pheeeeeew. That is beyond words a relief.

You can say that again. See you shortly. All well?

Fine. See you soon.

Ruth glanced over at Matthew and Emmie companionably watching children's television, leaning against each other in a cosy, after school snug of contentment as they drank milk and munched some animal chocolate biscuits.

"Budge up," she said to them both as she brought over her cup of tea to join them. "Daddy'll be home soon, darling," she said to Emmie.

Mark arrived about an hour and a half later, having called into his flat to collect some clean clothes for himself and Emmie. Ruth had no idea if he would want to take Emmie off straightaway to feed her and put her to bed in her familiar cot in his flat. She felt light with relief so decided just to go with the flow, allowing her tiredness to take her over in a pleasurable, engulfing way, like the deserved rest of a traveller reaching the end of particular road.

She made room for him on the sofa. "Tea, or something stronger?" she asked.

"Just tea, thanks. Great, my favourites." He looked at the children absorbed in their story as he helped himself to some animals.

Ruth brought his tea. "I've made shepherd's pie for tea. We could all eat together earlier if you like, unless you want…" She tailed off, faltering as she suddenly found it hard to think of him taking Emmie off.

"Can we stay tonight again?" asked Mark. "You've been/are fantastic. It sort of feels like home here. Actually I'm starving; I think I've only had undrinkable tea and coffee in polystyrene cups since this morning. We went to the cafeteria at lunch, but I just couldn't eat. Maureen was just brilliant, fearsome, fearless actually." He looked tired out but elated too, Ruth observed.

They all ate together just before 6. It was a beautiful late summer evening, and all thoughts of autumn were put to one side as the warm October sun brought back memories of summer but with the added subtlety of more muted colours, rich and gold. Ruth gazed out of the open French windows and confided to Mark her recurrent equinoctial heightened sensibilities which took her by surprise every spring and autumn. He put both arms round her from behind, stroking the length of her bare arms rhythmically, smiling across at the two children all the while who looked pleased, giggly and embarrassed all at once.

And so it was that later that evening, with both children fast and quickly asleep as usual and both adults needing an early night, and having only had water to drink with their meal, they consummated their growing love and friendship in Ruth's bed, the curtains drawn wide as the sun set burnished gold on this part of their journey and allowed the darkness to encompass them as they lay all night in each other's arms for the first time.

~ *Chapter 19* ~

And thus began for all four of them a new period of slow, gentle growth, of healing, of new beginnings, of rebirth almost, of calm; calm before the storm as Ruth was to reflect later. The autumn term rushed on in the way of school terms. Half term was a new delight for Ruth, it felt excitingly like an *illicit* holiday, a bit like a mid-week lunch out, but it was in fact much needed respite for all of them. They took it gently, enjoying the beautiful late October weather, walking along the towpath, little Emmie delighting in her first proper, more assured, steps, each one of them in their own way feeling the hurt, damage and pain recede as they found new harmony with each other.

Mark did not after all return to his flat. It seemed meant that he and Emmie should move in and that Emmie's bedroom should become her own. She also proudly moved into her own little bed, the cot being folded up and stored in the loft. The deep and light shades of pink on her bedclothes and curtains were in stark contrast to the deep and light shades of blue in Matthew's dolphin sets, chosen on that trip of lasting memories to buy school uniform on their return from Angmering.

Mark felt able to let his siblings and parents become a part of all their lives once more. They lived just outside Godalming, in a beautiful, sun-filled, honey coloured late Victorian house set into the valley of the River Wey. They visited his parents first, on their own, just the four of them, for all the world a conventional, 'nuclear' family unit, thought Ruth to herself. Ruth was welcomed easily into the Williams' fold.

Time spent with them was undemanding, uncomplicated, and full of simple pleasures. Mark's father, Bob, loved to show Matthew his greenhouse, showing him the technicalities involved in growing various plants as soon as he detected his quick intelligence and interest. Emmie and Matthew came to call him

Granbob, a name they devised for him themselves, and of course his mother, Anne, quickly became Grananne.

Gradually Ruth and the children came to meet each of Mark's siblings and their partners, and found themselves liking all of them, again in an uncomplicated, undemanding way. Matthew appeared almost to be stretching, physically and emotionally, in this reaching out to his new extended family, much as a plant puts roots deep into new soil when rescued from a too small, dried up plastic pot like those sold on garage forecourts.

What of Meg meanwhile? She was allowed supervised contact once a fortnight and was at last receiving professional help for her substance misuse and mental illness. Emmie returned from these short visits, confused, eerily quiet and clearly troubled. She would cling to Mark, sometimes to Ruth too, and do little but suck the sleeve of her top, a habit which she had seemed to drop before the visits started. Mark protested to social workers that these visits were damaging Emmie and were pointless.

Meg seemed to be disappearing into darker and darker places despite the help she was receiving. And it was on a grim, dark day in late November that the news arrived for Mark from Meg's social worker. Meg had been found dead in bed that morning having apparently, probably accidentally, overdosed on a mixture of alcohol and drugs prescribed for depression. Her violent partner, Jeff, was nowhere to be found, but no foul play was suspected, and it seemed he had not been seen for some weeks prior to Meg's death.

Mark's relief was tangible; another burden lifted it seemed.

The cremation passed quietly and almost unmarked, only Mark present as close family with Ruth and his sister Jane for support while Matthew was at school on a chilly, grey winter's day when it scarcely got light.

Melanie, having by now been taken into Ruth's confidence about her relationship with Emmie's father, Mr. Williams, the paedo of the playground gossip, the result of the court case and the situation with Meg, looked after Emmie while the tragic, but at the same time liberating, ceremony took place. Melanie, it turned out, had already deduced most of what was going on but had kept her counsel knowing Ruth would tell her if, when and how much she wanted to. They were becoming close friends.

By way of contrast to this gloom Melanie confided to Ruth the day after the cremation, the first of her friends to know she told her, that she was, ecstatically, a little bit pregnant, as she put it six weeks to be precise, the baby being due in late May/early June. It seemed the 'crud clearance' had done the trick. Richard was pleased and excited too and felt that, having already done it twice, the sleepless nights, nappies and so on would be a walk in the park.

All that did not last long it seemed to them both in retrospect and anyway this was what Melanie in particular partly craved, had missed in fact, that warm, engulfing, tumultuous tipping into new baby-dom. Ruth was solicitous of her new friend, frequently offering to have Sam after school so that Melanie could rest a bit and asking interestedly how she was feeling.

To add to this excitement and joy the primary school world, of which Ruth was now such a part, entered wholeheartedly into Christmas.

No wonder the children get over-excited, thought Ruth privately, but actually not so privately she loved every aspect of it. She could scarcely remember any happy childhood Christmases. She had a very vague memory of a brightly lit fire one year and a pink party dress over the back of the sofa after she'd opened it. Probably the same year she remembered unwrapping a little doll dressed all in bright red, fluffy, woollen clothes, including tiny shoes and a bonnet in the same wool. She had called her Rosy and remembered one of the shoes falling off on a snowy walk in the afternoon and finding it on the way back lying brightly red on the untouched white snow.

Other memories were of Steve's alcohol fuelled rages, her mother's total withdrawal, and her own escapes to Mim's using the skeleton public transport service on Boxing Day. Some lower key memories of these times lingered, such as helping to decorate the little tree, putting up lights in the holly bush in the garden – perhaps they could do that again – and arranging the crib figures.

She set out consciously and delightedly to create new, childhood Christmas memories for these two saved children. Mark had his own memories of course and it felt good to be able to share this joyous responsibility. By chance, they agreed on everything, such as advent calendars which told of the approach to the Nativity not chocolate ones; reading *'Twas the Night before Christmas* at bedtime on Christmas Eve, one of Mark's family's traditions, and Ruth introduced Emmie and Mat to Shirley Hughes' *Lucy and Tom's Christmas,* little realising that they would want that story every day from the beginning of December onwards. Stockings – cheap and cheerful – at ends of beds with a satsuma or tangerine – whatever – in the toe, chocolate money scattered throughout, a silly pen of some type or other, magic colouring book; these were opened first thing with the children on their bed once everyone was awake. Church in the morning after breakfast. Stocking presents to keep people going until after lunch. Crackers at lunchtime. Present opening after lunch, and a walk if wanted but not forced.

Mark and Ruth also discussed a Christmas Eve surprise for the children involving a trip out. This year it was to be a surprise trip on a boat on the Thames on which Father Christmas would make an appearance via a sleigh with reindeer landing on the roof bearing presents for the children. There would be mulled wine and mince pies for the adults, juice and decorated biscuits for the children.

And so it was that on Christmas Eve with anticipation and excitement running high they set out on what Mark and Ruth told them was a magical mystery tour, all of them wrapped up warmly for a river trip in December, and prepared to be enchanted, the two children unknowing and wondering.

Waiting in the queue to embark for this trip Ruth was suddenly alarmed to see a clown on stilts making a beeline for their little family group, probably noticing the small children.

Emmie froze with terror, and Matthew leant across and covered her eyes whispering, "Don't worry, Em, they're going now." But, as before, the clown did not take the hint.

"Well, well, well," said the towering figure, caked on bright foundation cracking as he formed what he thought was a smile as he lurched down towards Emmie, "I've never known children not to like clowns, never in all my born days. What about you, little man? You like me don't you? I can make you laugh not cry every time. Smile not weep, eh, no weeping here?"

"Get away from us; get him away from us, please, please, Mummy. Mark, get him away from us," Matthew begged, holding on tightly to both Emmie and Ruth. Ruth held on tightly to Emmie too who was screaming and crying whilst Mark approached the clown and told him politely to move away. The queue was tut-tutting in consternation; Ruth was unsure whether this was because of Emmie's reaction or the clown's reaction to the children's distress. Either way they needed to distance themselves from him and a kindly pixie, dressed all in green and wearing a cap with pointy ears, moved forward to let them on to the sanctuary of the boat, brightly decorated for Christmas, warm and welcoming and showed them to a table with a good porthole view out to the river.

"Oh that naughty clown," she said to the two children, "he's not supposed to be here frightening children. Here are some colouring sheets for you. Let's see if you can colour in these Christmas trees. Would you like a drink and biscuits?"

Quickly restored the two children settled to their colouring with rapt concentration and Ruth smiled gratefully at the cheerful pixie.

"Thanks," she said quietly, "that could have ended very badly."

"They're a real nuisance, we don't want them here, our passengers don't want them here, even Father Christmas doesn't want them here," she chuckled, well in the Christmas spirit. "There are gangs of them roving around actually. I'll get your mulled wine and mince pies now while I'm at it, then you'll be all set." She turned to look at the little group, Mark training his binoculars on the distant bird population, the children happily fully occupied with their task, Matthew suggesting kindly to Emmie that Christmas tree branches were usually green not red.

The highlight of the trip of course was the sudden thump and bang of Santa landing in his sleigh on the roof of the boat, the arrival eagerly talked up by the helpful pixies, as they collected in the colouring for those who wanted to enter the competition and distributed the drinks and snacks to adults and children alike. The present distribution itself felt wonderfully low key, not tacky in any way, and gently magical for the excited children on board. The presents had all been carefully chosen according to the age and gender of the child, and individually wrapped, *presumably by the pixies*, thought Ruth to herself. Father Christmas himself, large, white bearded and benign, made time to talk to each child quietly about their hopes and dreams and being good in a non-threatening, non-patronising, one to one manner.

And so Christmas passed in this magical, time out of mind way, the sense of other worldliness culminating in a traditional, as Ruth discovered, day after Boxing Day trip to Mark's parents, Grananne's and Granbob's as they were now known in this household. The temperature had dropped by about 7 degrees since Christmas Day and on the 27th, the day of this visit there was sparkling white frost lingering until late morning beneath cloudless, piercing blue skies, the low sun blinding at times on the roads made darkly wet in places by the melting frost.

The whole family was there, Mark's three sisters: Jane and her husband, Tim, their 7 and 5 year old girls, Lucy and Georgie, Charlotte with a few days off from her job as a radiographer in Newcastle where she had settled since leaving university, and Sally, just a few months younger than Ruth, the 'feckless student' as described by Mark, in her final year of a history and politics degree. Mark's brother, Simon, his pregnant wife Sue, baby due in early July, with their 3 year old son, Stuart, were staying for a few days as they usually did around Christmas, alternating visits with those to Sue's parents who lived on Guernsey; Simon and Sue lived just outside Bristol.

Everyone chatted easily giving a genuine welcome to Matthew as their new cousin/nephew. This set just the right tone of unforced acceptance which Ruth had come to expect and relish from the earlier, undemanding visits. She had a sense of having suddenly gained three siblings, sisters in particular since Simon was understandably preoccupied with Sue and Stuart.

Jane commented to her that Mark had lost his haunted look and seemed happy and relaxed like he used to be before he met Meg. Ruth found herself able to confide in them their relief and sense of freedom since Meg's tragic death, how close Matthew and Emmie were and how Mark was settling into the Natton job now, and putting everything into it. They talked too about the demands of Jane's job as a high school Maths teacher, and how she was about to apply for head of department, the closing date for which was 13th January.

Ruth found that Charlotte was really interested in her freelance editing work, asking very sensible questions, and Ruth equally took an interest in her radiography job. She asked her about the demands of on-call work, the demands of the radiologists, ridiculous government targets, and the anxiety of patients who knew you had seen their tumour, or perhaps their child's tumour, but with whom you obviously had to maintain a professional 'barrier' as it was not part of a radiographer's role to be breaking bad news.

All the children were enchanted with the Christmas tree in the hall around which were stacked piles of presents, the magic seemingly never ending. They were enchanted too by the outside tree bedecked with lights for the festive season. It handily provided a nicely obvious hiding place for Emmie, who needed to be found quickly in a rather chilly, but riotous, game of hide and seek organised by Mark, Simon and Tim whilst the women put together a wonderful Christmas tea at the large, scrubbed pine table in the dining room where an open fire also blazed in honour of the season and where every picture was adorned with holly branches bright with berries. The leaping flames were reflected in the glass door of the corner cabinet which held various sports trophies from the childhood prowess of the Williams clan, much to their present collective embarrassment and self-deprecation.

~ *Chapter 20* ~

Strangely enough it was Maureen Pinkerton, at the beginning of the new school term, and the new calendar year, with Matthew now proud to be a full time Reception pupil, who first broached to Ruth the idea of applying for a parental responsibility order for Emmie. As ever any mention of form-filling, particularly to do with the children, gave Ruth the heebie-jeebies as she put it to herself, frightened as she was of officialdom, of being found out really, unmasked. It was not so much, she recognised it clearly, to do with saving her own skin, again the clichés leapt in, but it was instead to do with a quite overwhelming need to see the whole rescue through, to bring Matthew, and now Emmie too of course, safely to shore from the turbulent waters of their early childhoods.

If she could do this unfettered, she felt she would subsequently be willing to pay any price, pay her dues to society, face the music – however you wanted to look at it. Meanwhile she sought only to have this time with her son, and with Emmie, as children, to give of her best to them, as she hoped, then launch them into adulthood, salvaged, repaired, *made whole again*, as she put it to herself thoughtfully. People talked about fully rounded adults, quite a pedestrian phrase really, she reflected, for something so life-affirming, so much more. But how deeply she understood now that *"there are no fortunes to be told."*[23]

Maureen, Melanie had teasingly taken to referring to the head teacher to

---

Ruth, as "your friend, Maureen," explained that applying for a parental responsibility order was really very straightforward; she and Sheila had looked into it when they had thought they both might be mothers to the same child at one point. "It was a question of form-filling, permissions. Have a look on tinternet," as she always rather irritatingly called it, she said to Ruth, "see what you think. You might even want to consider adopting Emmie perhaps." Ruth blocked that idea out instantly: the intrusion, the discoveries; no that simply could never be. It seemed these thoughts had just occurred to Maureen when she mentioned to Ruth that if Mark wanted Emmie to come to Thames Lacey he needed to get her name down soon for the nursery class which they entered in the school year in which they turned 4.

This gave Ruth the opening she needed to mention parental responsibility to Mark. It was not that she felt she really needed an opening, though it may have sounded presumptuous: "I need parental responsibility for your daughter," she mouthed the words to try them out, but she was already finding herself, in her freelance freedom, in the position of taking Emmie for the various routine, pre-school health checks. Mark had transferred both of them to the same practice as Ruth and Matthew, since moving out of the Natton flat. She found she needed permission from Mark as her father for immunisations and other checks, though it was invariably and understandably assumed she was Emmie's mother until the record was looked at.

Maureen was right; it was straightforward in every way, not least Mark's reaction, "Oh yes, good idea, it's obvious really. Good old Maureen, I should have thought of it and yes, let's put her down for Thames Lacey Nursery School pronto – can you do it tomorrow when you drop Mat off?" She had already given him the form to complete handed to her by Maureen.

No mention of adoption then, she felt relieved, reprieved almost from having to attempt to explain to Mark that she could never, ever contemplate this because of the terrifying background searches. If it ever came up again she supposed she was could tell him that social services might easily discover by talking to neighbours in Thames Lacey that she had more than once been literally dragged by the hair from the grandmother's house by her stepfather, screaming and crying. They might deduce that this was how she had learnt her parenting skills; she would put nothing past them.

So, paradoxically, that wet, dull January held lots of promise for the new family. Mark had a new tenant in the Natton flat – his 'kid' sister, Sally, embarking on her first job as an apprentice reporter on quite a prestigious local daily paper: *London and South Daily News*. Sally was fun-loving and outgoing, keeping up with her university friends, most in their first jobs, first proper relationships, all tentatively testing the waters of adulthood in so many ways. She loved to babysit too, getting to know her niece and nephew and allowing Ruth and Mark to get to know each other properly, away from the all-consuming demands of looking after small children, much as they both embraced that consuming.

And as that long, dark January drifted into February with the promise of half term in the air she and Paula provided shared support for their friend as the morning sickness reached a peak during February and March, one or other of them calling to pick up Sam in the mornings when she felt she just couldn't leave the house. Paula, from her own experiences of coping with the nausea and vomiting of chemotherapy, her own pregnancies had in fact been free of that scourge, was particularly good at offering practical tips, such as having a tin of water biscuits next to her bed and eating a couple before even getting up.

The parental responsibility order was granted with no hitches and Ruth felt herself again breathing a sigh of relief at another bit of officialdom safely navigated. She felt light with relief she realised, not having fully appreciated the ongoing fear of detection, the cat being out of the bag, a feeling of living under a cloud at times.

Mostly though, nothing could detract from her and Mark's feelings of moving forwards positively into a bright future of fun with their children, as they now thought of them easily. Yes, it was tiring, but life *was* tiring with or without children actually. They were both actively looking forward to the half term break, no early up and outs, no battling through horribly wintry weather, although on the more benign days Ruth had noticed spring bulbs already bravely emerging.

At the few quiet times during the day when Emmie was napping or playing happily and Matthew was at school she would find herself, usually in front of her laptop screen, reflecting vividly backwards in time. It was exactly like putting a video or DVD on slow rewind and watching what had happened unfold. The rewinding went back as far as that violent taking, the rape, through her lonely, terrified pregnancy and birth, the death of her baby, death of her mother, death of her grandmother, the taking of Matthew – her second crime – leaving the rented house, meeting Mark and Emmie and now here they were. She had read or heard somewhere that this rewinding was a sign of recovery from extreme stress and/or distress.

Three days before half term though, out of the blue, there was a peremptory knock on the glass panel of the front door at about 9.30pm on a particularly wild, wet and windy night. Ruth had been working to a deadline as usual, Mark was completing some paperwork for the next day, both concentrating in companionable silence, and the children had both been fast asleep for about 2 hours, when the knock shattered this calm. Mark got there first and opened the door to two police officers, a woman and a man. Behind him, Ruth felt her knees turn to water as the phrase went; it felt literal and she thought she would faint. They were both silent, fearful. The police officers were polite and professional.

"Sorry to disturb you at this time but a young child has been reported missing, a little boy, he's only 4. Not a local though, he was staying with his grandparents for half term, had a two week holiday from an independent school up north. We're searching garages, sheds, outbuildings and gardens locally first, so we were just wanting access. Which is the best way through to yours?"

"I'll just get my coat and show you," said Mark quickly, taking them round by the back gate. Ruth caught sight of her pale, shocked, tense face in the mirror over the fireplace and theatrically slapped her cheeks to restore some colour. She found she could not settle back to work though and as soon as Mark returned she was pleased to snuggle up to his reassuring presence and lose herself in the late news. Both the national and the local news carried the missing child story.

The child was subsequently found safe and well in an aunt's house, some innocent communication breakdown within the family it seemed. It took Ruth some time to recover from this episode; she felt she teetered on the edge at times.

Emmie, meanwhile, was growing into a loving child, tactile and affectionate with all three of them; she loved to snuggle up to anyone sitting still for long enough. She did not knead, as Matthew still liked to, but she would fetch Stripey, clutch his right ear where some silky material was exposed by wear, and lean in close, rhythmically stroking this part of the toy animal. She appeared wise beyond her years in many respects, sometimes to be heard muttering philosophically, "Never mind, it doesn't matter," if anything went slightly against her. Ruth was keenly aware of *"her small expanding consciousness"* just as Henry James was of Maisie's [24] and especially of the

---

[24] Henry James: (1897) *What Maisie Knew,* Heinemann, London, Stone, Chicago, Penguin/Random House

need for his readers to be similarly aware. *Not surprising really*, she thought, as she again quelled her irritation with herself for relating everything back to something else, something she had seen, heard, read, because of course life does imitate art. How could it ever be otherwise? And here she was in the thick of it, loving it and so keen to ensure that neither of her two little charges should be *"coarsened, blurred, sterilised"* by the *"ignorance and pain"* of their early years just as James wished for Maisie. [25]

Matthew, particularly when Sam or any other friend was round, would sometimes show his impatience with Emmie's following them around, wanting to do everything they did though she couldn't of course, and he showed no sympathy with her occasional, sudden collapses into tears of frustration at being left out. When it was just the two of them, brother and sister as it were, he was sweet and gentle with her, asking for her forgiveness for being horrible when his friends were round. She gave it readily.

A strange episode at this time concerned Emmie's collection of leaves. She loved the really big, shiny, crackly ones, the deeper the reds and browns and yellows the better. In her search for leaves to add to this one day, when 'helping' Mark and Matthew with some weeding, she uncovered an almost perfect skeleton leaf, a "skelington" leaf as Matthew explained it. Emmie became inconsolable; she could not understand where the shiny flesh had gone. "Would it come back?" "Why was it like that?" "Where was the leaf?" Matthew looked on fearfully and uncomprehendingly at this outburst. His impatience with his little sister had already been ignited by her use of his wheelbarrow to collect these leaves. This was like lighting the touch paper for Matthew's fury at times.

Luckily, Ruth had recently been editing a beautifully illustrated little book on the cycle of a leaf and this went some way to mollifying her, though Ruth sensed that this wise little girl was accepting the explanation to please Ruth more than anything but perhaps this small child even then knew that: *"There must be reasons why the leaves decay."*[26] Mark then had the bright idea of suggesting Emmie draw the leaf and colour it in brightly but "no," she whispered insistently, "that was not the leaf."

---

[25] Henry James: (1897) *What Maisie Knew*, Heinemann, London, Stone, Chicago, :Penguin Random House
[26] "If I Could Tell You," copyright © 1934 W H Auden: (1934) and renewed 1962 by W H Auden; from W H AUDEN COLLECTED POEMS by W H Auden. Used by permission of Random House, an imprint and division of Penguin Random House, LLC. All rights reserved. Copyright © 1934 by W.H. Auden, renewed Reprinted by permission of Curtis Brown, Ltd.

On Valentine's Day, just before half term, once the children were in bed, Mark and Ruth were idly discussing their limited knowledge of the origins of this day as they sipped wine and exchanged simple gifts – rose-scented bath and shower gel for Ruth, rich dark chocolate bars for Mark. Ruth told Mark that he really was her Valentine as he had made her see the goodness in people, reflected, mirror-like, in him. This was the closest she had come, she realised, to any sort of sharing of her own past; the wine, it seemed, had *loosened her tongue*, she used the phrase to herself, as she changed the subject.

Mark pursued it for a bit, "You've been really hurt, haven't you, Ruthie?" he whispered as he traced the outline of her jaw and neck.

"It's over though," she did not deny it, and, "I have you three now. I love Emmie just as if she was my own," she said wonderingly, "just like Matthew."

Mark smiled and drew her closer. "She's a very lovable child, they both are. We should be proud of ourselves. Do you think we should make some more soon?"

"Mmmm, soon maybe, everything feels right at the moment. I wouldn't want anything to upset the apple cart though."

"You're right, there's no great rush is there? You're just a baby of course," he chuckled. "I think not too big an age gap would be best though."

"Yes, I agree." She was quiet then leaning against him she murmured, "Mark, you know how to make me forget it's dark outside."

He looked down at her head on his shoulder and inhaled the fragrance of her hair, rubbing his face against its silky softness. She had been sharing with him from time to time particularly resonant aspects of her current reading: Hermione Lee's: *Penelope Fitzgerald, a life.*[27] Fitzgerald had been asked whether she had a view on what the novel should be and had commented, with deceptive simplicity, that she thought it had "started as soon as people realised it was dark outside and felt they would like a story to be told to them." She had been asked whether she thought novels should deliver something of importance and had replied, quite sharply, that she did not; that it was just that for the time being you forget it is dark outside.

"For the time being..." made Ruth think; she had, she realised, for some time now, certainly since she reached adulthood with all its violent ripping apart, felt herself watching her own story unfold but never felt she was part of something important, had felt herself to be in a kind of lasting outer darkness.

---

[27] Hermione Lee: (2013) *Penelope Fitzgerald, a life* p278 Vintage, UK, 2014 Knopf, US

And it was later on in bed that Mark, after their tender lovemaking, had brought up the idea of her adopting Emmie, for security, safety perhaps, if anything should happen to him.

But Ruth knew the stakes were simply too high and she outlined her fears about searches into her past revealing too much about her own mother and stepfather as her role models for parenting. "Probably parental responsibility would be enough, they look at the best interests of the child and I just seem to be her mummy now. She called me mummy the other day. Is that okay with you? We can change that if you like. Does it upset you?"

"It is the best thing ever," he murmured sleepily, pulling her to him.

~ *Chapter 21* ~

Ruth very much enjoyed her role as parent governor. She was astonished by the workload for governors and the significance of the role but was heartened to see the due diligence which every governor brought to their respective roles in different ways, using their varied expertise. It was good to see Maureen and the other teacher governor as adults and to be dealing with both of them on an adult, one to one basis, she felt. This sounded odd even to her but what she meant, she said reflectively when explaining this to Mark later, was that so often primary school teachers are necessarily seen only in their role of talking to, and teaching, young children and sometimes, inadvertently it seemed, tended to address parents in the same way. Both teacher governors had sharp wits and dry senses of humour and would spar off each other as only colleagues who know and respect each other well, can. It was good to see. The governing body seemed to be a functional and very effective group. She felt she sounded like an Ofsted inspector when she said this to Mark.

The first snow of winter arrived on the first day of the half term break. The sense of quiet, the stillness, the muffled sounds, the engulfing, and the purity of the untouched snow allowed the family to pull up the metaphorical drawbridge, relishing the fact that none of them needed to struggle out. The fridge was well stocked and they had plenty of firewood gathered during long winter walks, so there was no need to go anywhere.

Ruth was reminded that first snow morning, as if it were yesterday, of a phrase she had used as an 11 year old at the beginning of an English essay in her first year of high school. The class had been required to write about the happiest day of their life. She had started it bravely and compliantly enough thus:

One of the happiest days of my life was when...

and had been struck both by the fierceness of the red pen, pernickety scrawling out of 'when' and the ugliness of the substituted, corrected phrase: 'that on which'. She had in fact received a very good mark for the subsequent, totally fictitious, account of a family boat trip on a lake in Switzerland. But now, as she beckoned Mark to Matthew's bedroom and they silently watched the little pyjama clad figure sleepily pulling back the curtain, and rubbing his eyes as he caught sight of the snow covered lawn and exclaiming with delight, "I'm outta here," it did indeed feel like the happiest day of her life so far as she and Mark chuckled together and urged him to dress warmly and have breakfast before rushing out.

"And you'll need your waterproof gloves, darling," Ruth reminded him. "They're in the porch. No ifs or buts and look after Emmie, it'll be slippery and cold."

The 'drawbridge' remained pulled up for three entire days. There was no sense of cabin fever in the house which was anyway spacious enough for them not to be tripping over each other. This was probably too because they all spent enough time outside to feel refreshed, invigorated and pleased each time to return to its warm welcome. The children built their very first snowman with Mark's help, topping it with an old woolly hat of her grandmother's found by chance at the back of the shed when extracting an entirely serviceable sled which Ruth suddenly remembered was there. They could use this safely enough on the slight slope down which they planned to construct a rockery when the weather improved.

Mark showed Matthew how to make sure snowballs were not too hard for throwing. "It'll be terrible if Emmie just keeps crying," he said man to man, understanding that Matthew simply had not realised how hard the snow had impacted and was obviously frightened by Emmie's screams of hurt and shock as his first snowball hit her full in the chest. "The aim is to keep her happy and wanting to play, old chap."

While Ruth comforted Emmie inside in the warm he set up a snowball aiming game between him and Matthew scoring points for the number of target hits. As soon as Emmie realised she was not to be the target she rushed out to join them. Matthew carefully chose an easy target for her to win some points, which Mark noted with affection and approval in which the little boy basked. Ruth had sometimes noticed a lingering wariness in Matthew's developing relationship with Mark and days like these seemed to push this wariness into the further reaches of his memory, hopefully one day to be buried completely.

Mark decided to construct a bird table using some left over wood he discovered in the shed and Ruth consulted one of her previously edited books to see how best to feed garden birds during snow. Both children entered fully into the spirit of feeding birds who might otherwise starve, Ruth explained, because they could not reach their usual food sources. They even found some garden bird food packets – still in date – at the back of the shed which they distributed diligently and with scrupulous fairness.

On the fourth day they ventured out as far as the small woodland area leading off from the rec. for a brisk walk in the snow. They had Sam with them, whilst Melanie rested. Having sampled all the newly refurbished children's playground equipment: swings, roundabout, and a terrifying looking Ruth thought, swing rope ladder sort of thing, they headed down the steep, narrow, wooded slope, slippery with fallen, dried out bracken spines, and into the woods. Sam and Matthew, out in front, were on the look-out for suitable trees to climb whilst Emmie seemed happy to be in her own more manageable world of looking for fairies underneath the largest leaves with Ruth's help. She collected thistledown for their beds and acorn cups for them to have their tea in, she explained to Ruth, whilst Mark supervised the boys' climbing.

Tired but happy, Ruth went into children's story mode easily these days, she realised, something to do with forgetting the outer darkness perhaps she mused, they headed home as the sun slipped below the horizon, spreading fiery tendrils of ruby red light across the darkening sky, like dragons' claws, said Emmie sleepily, and had crumpets with their tea before Mark dropped Sam back home.

It was noticeable that the days were drawing out now; there was less than a month to go in fact until the first day of spring, yet the snow still lay like a blanket as if defying spring to arrive at all. By Saturday afternoon though, the sun thaw that had gathered momentum from about 10 o'clock onwards really set in and by 5 o'clock with dusk descending, there were only a few pockets of snow left under hedges and in sheltered parts of the garden.

It really was a time of new beginnings as they all settled into family life. Mark was enjoying life at Natton now he had the head space he had so badly needed. The head teacher had gone on long-term sick leave halfway through January and an interim head teacher – Joseph Rayner – was to start after half term. Mark knew of his good reputation and was looking forward to working with him.

And as for Mark at home, he would often find himself watching Ruth with the two children; attentive, tender, they were both truly and equally the centre of her world. He loved her calmness, her can-do approach to life, her liveliness, optimism, joy in small things, and her sense of perspective, astounding in one so young, he thought. But he had grown to understand that this was borne from her having witnessed as a child "more than she at first fully understood", like the fictional Maisie and like his own dear, real, little Emmie probably had.

Ruth had urged him to read *What Maisie Knew,*[28] and he had told her that he found it quite baffling, but at least it was short and it confirmed his resolve to teach his pupils to write in short, clear sentences. Mark felt that with Ruth by his side watching their children grow they would be able to face anything, to experience together all the passion, anguish, love and joy of parenthood.

Melanie's morning sickness subsided as quickly as it had appeared as she entered the second trimester of pregnancy with renewed energy and joyful anticipation. The three women, Ruth, Melanie and Paula's friendship was close, undemanding, nothing of the playground competitiveness and bitchiness she had been warned about by Mark and had, in fact, read about before she had tumbled in wholeheartedly to that world. The three of them had much in common, it seemed. They all had a sense of perspective. They knew life was precious, they knew this time of life was especially precious and fleeting, and they savoured the day to day experiences of being mothers of young children with a sense of fun, realism and humour. The friendship had its own momentum, engendered it seemed, by the hurtling through of this special time.

They talked of their men, as women do, in loving tones, but with exasperated despair at their ability to cause chaos in the management tasks of organising small children; Mark driving off with Matthew's PE kit in the back of his car was one thing, Richard forgetting to pick Sam up from football training another, but they agreed that Jack, dropping off Rebecca, his and Paula's just 4 year old, at her first proper birthday party in a big, multi-functional restaurant with bar at a table full of 13 and 14 year olds at a different party, took the biscuit this time. And it lost nothing in the telling as Paula described vividly how the restaurant staff had rescued little Rebecca and reunited her with the other 4 year olds in the soft play area, one of the other 4 year old party mums having recognised her. Jack, oblivious, had already, blithely, left.

They all spluttered with not quite incredulous laughter but underlying this type of regaling was clear recognition that there were no serious issues, just a

---

[28] Henry James: (1897) *What Maisie Knew* Heinemann, London, Stone, Chicago, Penguin/Random House

gentle tolerance of *'vive la différence'*. Ruth herself was always astounded that Mark, supposedly in charge of the children for any period of time, could be completely engrossed in the newspaper, or a football match, whilst various forms of chaos reigned. The children recognised that he was not to be disturbed and would wait until Ruth reappeared to ask for drinks, paints or to report grievances or triumphs.

Ruth herself was facing a new challenge. Money was tight in the household with just one full time salary and her own intermittent freelance work, enjoyable and childcare friendly though it was, bringing in an uncertain and not vast income. Of course, being mortgage free was wonderful, and she was well aware that very few couples of their age were in this position. They did want, if they could though, to put their mark on the house by upgrading and updating the kitchen in particular and the bathroom, currently second in their to do list. Third on the list was an upgrade of most of the lighting throughout the house. Ruth had always found her grandmother's house rather dark and as she herself grew older and her grandmother frailer, often taking to her bed, Ruth, downstairs alone, would find herself putting on all the lights she could as day turned to night. Even then, she had a strong sense of needing to keep the encroaching darkness, 'th'encircling gloom' as the words of the hymn had it, at bay; the darkness she recognised as being, in part, her grandmother's approaching death. She looked everywhere then for some 'kindly light'.[29]

By great good fortune, a phrase Ruth remembered as one of her grandmother's, she had managed, through her growing acquaintance with Nicola, a fellow governor, to secure a dream job, as she thought of it, at a children's bookshop run by a friend of Nicola's mother, somewhat off the beaten track along a narrow, twisting road leading off from the towpath. You wouldn't know it was there; the rickety pointing arrow sign announcing it looked unlikely in that riverside, countrified setting.

Ruth wondered how on earth it could be a going concern; surely there would be no passing trade in this remote, relatively inaccessible spot, but she quickly realised when researching the business a little that it did most of its trade through supplying schools with text books over a large area of south London. It did, though, carry a fantastic range of children's fiction too. The bookshop, *River Books for Children*, also organised talks and readings in schools and libraries and played an active role in promoting all children's

---

[29] John Henry Newman (1833) *Lead Kindly Light Amid Th'encircling Gloom* Hymn published in 1033 Hymnals

literature whenever and wherever it could, with author signings, exhibitions and themed events to coincide with publication dates not to mention World Book Day when pre-school children and their parents/carers were invited to dress up as their favourite character and enjoy a party at the shop.

The hours were 10 until 2; intentionally designed to be completely ideal for school pick-ups and drop-offs. She was to start after half term and could bring Emmie with her until she started at playgroup or nursery. The owner, Sarah Stangham, now in her late fifties, felt that having Emmie in the shop sampling its wares, as she put it, could only enhance its child friendly ethos. She had herself brought her own three daughters with her to the shop as babies and toddlers more than twenty five years ago when she first started working there for the previous owner. Sarah was passionate about the shop and actually very selective, Nicola told Ruth, about who worked there. Sarah knew that by allowing her to bring Emmie she would enable Ruth to work there.

For their part, Ruth and Mark believed that this was a wonderful setting for Emmie to spend several hours every day; she would be with Ruth whom she had steadily grown to trust and love and would be meeting other adults and children in a safe, relaxed setting, surrounded by books. They would bring a snack lunch each day and eat together at the little low tables, the coffee machine always on the go and there was no need to lock up shop whilst they ate because they were never inundated with passing customers. If people did come in they usually wanted to browse anyway and were always offered coffee and to use the low tables. There was a great deal of unpacking of boxes of orders to be done, checking amounts, sorting onto the shelves and packing up for deliveries to schools and libraries.

Ruth loved every aspect of it: the smell of the new books, the interest in new titles, the appeal of the bright covers, the dealing with different publishers' reps, the distributors and their varied and funny little ways, as Sarah put it, and of course, the pay cheque. Emmie would sit happily 'reading' or colouring or 'helping' as she grew to trust Sarah too and the bookshop itself become a real home from home for them both. Ruth and Sarah became firm friends, a friendship borne of respect and fellow feeling for the cause of books, the age gap meaningless as they became close, sharing the odd confidence – a first for Ruth – and more than the odd joke. It was easy and undemanding and Sarah often turned to Ruth for new ideas and advice on ways forward with the business.

~ *Chapter 22* ~

And this is how Mark planned it as the spring equinox approached – 21st March – when the day splits, rents itself in two, half in darkness, half in light, as he explained to Ruth. He certainly had his own sensibilities, one of the qualities Ruth had grown to love about him, especially the fact that, man-like, he kept these well under wraps most of the time. Mark had purposely chosen that day because of Ruth's talking jokingly about her "equinoctial heightened sensibilities"; he was intrigued by that.

So he did it in the traditional way, as he thought of it to himself, and had told no-one, it had to be Ruth who was the first to know. He asked Sally, who by now was happy in the Natton flat, in her first job and seeing someone regularly whom she had met at work, if she could babysit on that Saturday evening, and to bring her new boyfriend for company if she wished. He trusted her to take her babysitting duties seriously and Emmie and Matthew knew her well by now, usually through visits to his parents, who carried on being there for everyone and each other in their own sweet way, as he and Ruth often thought of it.

The evening out was not itself a secret from Ruth because he wanted her to enjoy looking forward to it. He knew she was tired; it had been a long, if exciting, winter and she was still working hard to meet all freelance deadlines, working in the bookshop, doing the lion's share of household and childcare chores – he was always quick to recognise and appreciate this – it was the way it was. And he certainly pulled his weight in terms of shopping and DIY jobs; the division of labour was not an issue between them but they both felt the relentlessness of daily life at times.

They looked forward to the evening. Mark told Ruth he had booked them a special table at a special restaurant. And there it was, sitting together in the candlelit alcove, in between their first and second courses that Mark asked for Ruth's hand in marriage, in the traditional way. He drew the line at going down on bended knee though as he wanted it to be their private time, and not to draw attention to themselves from their fellow diners. Ruth, genuinely taken by surprise, had, in the traditional way, said yes.

They both entered wholeheartedly into the spirit of discussing and arranging the wedding. Ruth had never understood long engagements, neither had Mark, so they settled on the Whitsun bank holiday Saturday, the beginning of the May half term week, during which, they decided, mentally putting kitchen and bathroom plans on hold, they would go off on a short, inexpensive, family friendly honeymoon/holiday, just the four of them, they planned excitedly, their first holiday away as a family. This was just over two months ahead, at the end of May/beginning of June. They both wanted simplicity and no pointless expense for the wedding; again Ruth had always felt this, even as a small girl dreaming of how this might be one day for her. Mark genuinely just wanted what made Ruth happy, he told her, covering her smaller hand with his as she excitedly outlined her ideas for the wedding, all the while seeking his views too.

Ruth, they decided, would talk to the Thames Lacey vicar who was also a school governor, and she liked his common sense, knowledgeable approach. After careful thought they decided to hold the reception at home and simply hope for reasonably clement weather. They would have a marquee in the garden, which could be heated if necessary should it turn into one of those long, light but freezing cold, they both chuckled, late spring/nearly summer, evenings so familiar in Britain. To reduce hassle and stress they would hire caterers, to which end Ruth would ask around.

One of the many enjoyable aspects of this preparation was the way in which Mark's family embraced the whole idea. They were warm, wholeheartedly welcoming her into the family with renewed affection and, actually, love, Ruth realised. Ruth asked Mark if he thought his mother would be up for a shopping trip to choose her dress.

"She'd love it, Ruthie, ring her and arrange it. Make it a Saturday; I can look after the kids."

They also needed to think about passports of course. Mark had sensibly put Emmie onto his just after he won the custody battle; it felt like a form of added security, so at least that was well in date. Ruth had an overwhelming need and wish to take Mark's name and they discussed the need consequent upon this, to change Matthew's surname. This they did simply enough by deed poll only needing the consent of them both and as they both agreed to it they also changed the name on Matthew's birth certificate to Matthew Williams. They felt this would just simplify everything and for Ruth especially it enhanced that sense of belonging. She had no need or wish to hang onto her old name with all its sad history. As another way of providing a secure base for Matthew, strengthening the launch pad as it were, she applied for a passport in his own name whilst applying to amend the details on her own.

As for the shopping trip Anne was in some ways obviously delighted but sounded rather guarded on the phone, Ruth felt. She was too busy to think too much about it, so the trip was arranged for a fortnight's time, but it was only a phone call from Jane the next evening which confirmed Ruth's perception that Anne had sounded, well, cagey really.

"Did you think Mum sounded a bit odd about going shopping for your dress, Ruth?" Jane sounded slightly giggly.

"Yes, yes, definitely… Why?" Ruth sounded suspicious and worried.

"Well, I was going to ask sooner but time just zooms on doesn't it? I would love it if you would let me make your dress; it can be our present to you… free rein to you. What do you think?" Jane sounded excited but tentative.

Ruth was silent for a moment, she felt quite overwhelmed by the sense of acceptance, belonging, love and warmth surrounding her from Mark's family. Mark had told her earlier that day that Charlotte, Sally, Simon and Sue had all clubbed together to book their week's honeymoon in a child friendly but boutique hotel on Crete having discussed where they would like to go pretending merely to be interested in their plans. This just left Mark and Ruth to book the flights. At the same time the thought of the dress responsibility being lifted from her was a gigantic relief – she could trust Jane absolutely, and would leave it with her. She had the wish for clean, simple lines, she liked the idea of faintly 'virginal' ivory rather than white – she was, after all, only 23, but apart from that she could just enjoy the attention.

"Oh, Jane, you have no idea what that means to me," Ruth breathed softly, "thank you, thank you, thank you. When can we talk about it properly, it needs to be all secret from Mark?" she giggled happily.

They arranged that Ruth and Anne would drop round to Jane's on the way to their shopping trip. Mark would already be safely out of the way looking after the children. It would be fun for Anne to be in on the secret arrangements, and that way they could work out what material was needed, take measurements, and buy everything they needed that day – there was after all not too much spare time before the wedding, given children and work commitments. Jane made her own patterns and always worked competently and quickly as she did at everything she turned her hand to.

The rest of the shopping trip would turn into buying a 'going away outfit' as they would be leaving for an overnight airport hotel stay at Gatwick straight from the reception – in the traditional way. Mark's parents were giving them a very substantial donation to their bathroom and kitchen fund and it was obvious that Anne was relishing this different, close, hands-on, almost intimate, certainly motherly/daughterly participation in the preparations.

Ruth found herself hugging the excitement to her. She felt nurtured, pampered almost, and incredulous that other people should seem to relish the fact of her happiness. She gave herself up willingly to the experience, understanding, with that sense of perspective and knowing of one who has seen too much too young, that happiness such as this could only ever be fleeting, transitory, elusive, to be captured and held tightly for as long as possible, the spectre of its slipping from that grasp ever present.

Emmie and Matthew too seemed somehow to sense this. They were wild with excitement about the whole fairy tale aspect of the wedding. They were seen at times to be playing out their make-believe, with Emmie dressing up as the bride or princess, as she thought of it, in a white gauze skirt with gold ribbon on it found at the bottom of the dressing-up box which Ruth had created for them remembering her own delight in playing with her grandmother's old clothes as a very young child. Squeals of delight could be heard as they paraded around and made pretend wedding food which consisted of delicacies such as ice cream, fairy cakes with silver baubles, candy floss and toffee apples. Later on though Emmie snuggled close to Ruth and Mark on the sofa and carefully presented Ruth with a 'tiara' she had made from some old, definitely used and rather greasy, kitchen foil.

"You are a princess bride, Mimi," she said softly as she placed it gently on Ruth's head.

"She's called Mummy, Emmie, she's *my* mummy," muttered Matthew.

"Thank you, darling," Ruth smiled down at Emmie, "you'll be a princess bridesmaid with your cousins won't you soon and Matthew'll be a prince pageboy, organising you all, won't you, sweetheart?" she said as she pulled him onto her lap. "What about a bit of *Mr. Gumpy*?"

"Mmm," was the sleepy, contented response from Emmie whilst Matthew kneaded her inner elbow gently and Mark went to get the book.

~ *Chapter 23* ~

The Saturday of the planned shopping trip was a beautiful, brightly sunny, early spring day with just that nip in the air to remind everyone that it was still only very early April. Ruth willingly "gave herself up" – this was how she described it to herself – to this once-in-a-lifetime experience. Jane was her usual warm, welcoming yet at the same time, briskly efficient, self.

Coffee, freshly filtered and keeping warm on the hob was poured, and Jane offered delicious homemade *pains au chocolat* which she often rustled up as weekend treats, she said. Thus fortified they set about the task. Jane had drawn some simple, classic designs for Ruth's dress and already had some saved internet pages to show likely materials. Ruth chose quickly the simplest of all, a classic, stylish cut, with no 'meringue features' asking for Anne's and Jane's opinions and thoughts as she flicked through. The material too was easy; ivory coloured silk.

Jane asked what she planned to do with her hair. Ruth had, in truth, not given this a moment's thought so she ventured timidly, "Wash it and brush it?"

Jane and Anne spluttered with affectionate laughter – it was just long enough to make a respectable French plait, Jane felt, and would look lovely with a few fresh flowers from the garden woven simply through it; as she spoke she gently took hold of Ruth's hair and deftly and quickly wound it into a plait before leading Ruth over to a long mirror in the hall and holding up a smaller one behind her just like a professional hairdresser.

"Wow, it looks quite luxuriant; I'd love that – no expense either. What about going really natural and putting daisies in, do you think they'd last the day?"

"Great idea," said Jane, "you could perhaps carry a bunch of freshly picked wild flowers too – you'll have the florists out of business!" she laughed. "That brings me to this thought…would you like me to make the little bridesmaids simple daisy patterned cotton dresses? It's going to be Emmie, Lucy and Georgie isn't it?"

"Oh, that would look lovely and we could perhaps get them to make their own daisy chains that morning for their hair – keep them occupied – Lucy and Georgie will love helping Emmie. It doesn't matter if they're not perfect, even better really, lovely and natural, and they can always redo them at the reception, our grass is covered in daisies, very pretty they are too. They could carry wildflowers too."

Ruth had at first been adamant she did not want a whole trail of bridesmaids but then had quickly come to understand for herself how much Mark's sisters would relish that role. Nobody needed to spell this out to her. So there were to be three big and three little – well, why not Ruth had thought then – it's not all about me, I am being indulged enough even though it'll probably be the first and last time. Mark would love it too, so would Anne and Bob – these people were her family now. It was the least she could do.

"Actually, could you do something similar for you, Charlotte and Sal without it looking silly?" Ruth asked Jane. "It could look stunning."

A quick online search revealed *John Lewis* to be the clear winner of their custom for all the material, which they bought then and there (click and collect) with Jane overseeing the amounts needed, selecting the lining for Ruth's dress and quickly emailing her sisters with the decision adding a link to the material chosen and drawing some word pictures of the possible designs – it may look good if they all had slightly different designs in the same material, she suggested, as they were all different shapes.

By the time Anne and Ruth set off companionably for their shopping day it was still barely 10 o'clock – it was a good feeling. As they descended the quite steep station staircase at Natton, Anne suddenly took Ruth's arm, not so much to steady herself, Ruth realised, but in simple, close companionship.

Oxford Circus was teeming with people and they made a plan not to wear themselves out. Ruth really was not fussy, she just was not that sort of woman or shopper, so they decided to start at *Selfridges*, and possibly call in at any interesting boutiques they passed en route. Ruth did not want to bother with South Kensington shops at all and certainly did not want to toy with posy Knightsbridge shops. This was not Anne's style either so they were in complete agreement there as it seemed that they were about most things so far.

"I wouldn't mind having just a quick look in *Monsoon*," said Ruth, "after all, as Mark can never quite believe and keeps reminding me, "I *am* only 23," making innocent looking large eyes at Anne in conscious self-mockery.

"Oh of course, yes," said Anne, "I have to remind myself of that too. Sally got a beautiful dress there for her graduation ball last summer. I'll enjoy going there."

"Oh gosh," said Ruth suddenly, "what about the boys? I feel we have gone all girl-centric, that's not like me. I'm not keen on page boy outfits or page boy 'roles' come to that," she said as she indicated quote marks round the words. "I'll call Jane when we stop for lunch and see what she thinks, and I must talk to Sue, obviously. I can't see Stuart and Matthew wanting to dress up in a silly way, maybe just proper long-sleeved white shirts, and new school trousers or shorts in a nice dark grey perhaps? If Stuart's anything like Mat he'll always need extras; they go through the knees of trousers as if there were no tomorrow. I sometimes think *Elastoplast* would be a cheaper option, and they cover themselves in glue and paint and food and things all the time. Perhaps some smart, matching ties would make them feel dapper. What do you think?" Ruth turned to Anne.

"I think perhaps nicely cut shorts would be nice for such little boys, it'll be the end of May so they should be warm enough, and white shirts and ties, yes. Perhaps see what the dads say too – Mark and Tim?"

"Good idea," replied Ruth, secretly relishing the joy of hearing Mark referred to as Matthew's dad. Oh how they now belonged, she realised. She was giving Matthew so much already of what she had planned to give him, a loving extended family, roots, love, security, a sister even. During this dream-like day she felt herself tumbling further and further in, just as she had begun to when Matthew started school, but now further, further tumbling down like *Alice* into *Wonderland* but without the terror and incomprehension of dreams. Instead there was the certainty of belonging, acceptance, of legitimately being part of it all, the same as others, of healing, of being whole, of happy endings perhaps.

~ *Chapter 24* ~

Not wearing themselves out turned out to be a pipe dream of course but it was an enjoyable wearing out. *Monsoon* had come up trumps for Ruth's 'going away outfit' which turned into a simple, but beautiful, layered silk summer dress in pale blue which she would change into for the trip to the airport hotel that evening. Practical as ever though, she would of course not fly in it but would preserve it for the odd dinner out on holiday or, more likely, once back home because their trip to Crete was going to be a simple, low key, relaxed, family holiday in a bungalow style hotel.

Selfridges provided a relaxing setting for a delicious, salad lunch during which they treated themselves to a glass of sparkling white wine each in honour of the occasion and to celebrate the rare occurrence of not needing to drive until much later. The decision was taken during lunch that the little boy cousins, Stuart and Matthew, would wear shorts and shirts and ties which were all successfully purchased in *Selfridges*. The middle-aged shop assistant took a great interest in all the wedding plans and came up triumphantly with two little ties with very stylish, surprisingly 'ungirly', daisy designs running through them and, miraculously, some smart socks suitable for wearing with shorts and 'proper' shoes.

Their last port of call was to *John Lewis* to collect the material bought earlier online and they combined this with a very welcome cup of tea and slice of cake – coconut for Ruth, lemon drizzle for Anne. Strangely enough this experience of sitting in an eatery in a slightly old-fashioned feel department store recalled vividly to Ruth's mind the day she had first set eyes on Matthew watching the monkey in the window in *Hardcastle's*.

In *Selfridges* earlier the setting had felt quite different, the clientele, the time of day for stopping for a snack, all somehow more modern but here time stood still momentarily for Ruth and then rewound itself rapidly. Anne noted her distraction, her discomfort and enquired with great solicitude if she was all right but Ruth, remembering the thunder storm, the chase, the rescue, could barely answer at first. Just as she was summoning the resources to return to the present and teeming reality, present and teeming joy really, another bolt from the blue – as she was to think of it later – hit her.

"Ruth, Ruth, it *is* you isn't it?" The voice came from a neatly dressed young woman of about her own age who had been doing something complicated and managerial with the till takings but had come over to their corner table.

"Oh gosh, Louise, is it really you? Anne, this is Louise, a friend." She said the unfamiliar word bravely, strengthened it seemed by her new-found sense of belonging, and thinking under her breath, as it were, *only friend,* "from my sixth form college. Louise, this is Anne Williams, my very soon to be mother-in-law."

"Well, Ruth, of all the people to take that particular plunge I never would have thought…" She stopped herself. "I mustn't interrupt you, anyway I'm at work, give me your number and we can catch up properly. I'm a proper career girl – woman, now. I'm on one of John Lewis' management schemes and I'm already a shareholder in the business. That's the way they do it – great employer… she says from her vast experience." She smiled self-deprecatingly.

"And you, I must ask, are you still editing children's text books? Somebody thought you were doing that when we had our reunion – last year, I think it was."

"Yes still doing that and… some other things too now – we'll catch up soon." Ruth was conscious of how easy it would be to leave Anne out of this old friends' discussion and that they needed to get home. She also did not want any old 'secrets' inadvertently revealed by Louise – it felt slightly, well…dangerous really, suddenly meeting up like this. Ruth passionately did not want any intrusion into her "present joy."

And the present joy continued. The Easter holidays soon arrived with the excitement of an early morning Easter egg hunt for Matthew and Emmie, including finding little eggs underneath their own egg cups on the breakfast table. This was a novelty for both of them as of course Emmie had been too young to remember last year's Easter Day – whatever had happened then – and this was Ruth's and Matthew's first Easter together, truly a rebirth, a renewal.

It was absolutely obvious to both Mark and Ruth that Matthew had only ever seen Easter eggs in the shops before. Mark said lightly and jokingly, "He looks as if he's never had an Easter egg before..."

Fortunately just at that moment his phone rang – his mother asking them if they could stop and get some cream on their way over for lunch.

Matthew clutched the colourful, foil-covered eggs close to him until Ruth quickly found both children, plastic bags to keep their 'finds' in, explaining that the chocolate eggs would soon melt if held close. Emmie needed a lot of help to find her eggs and the look of sheer excitement on her little face each time she uncovered one caused Ruth and Mark to exchange their own grins of delight.

All the cousins and siblings would be at Anne and Bob's for lunch, a real family gathering, so Ruth set the children then to making Easter cards all round. They knew that there was to be another hunt with clues in the afternoon at Grananne's and Granbob's house so the air was hissing with excitement and anticipation of a very special day. It was always touch and go, Ruth heard, whether it would be warm enough for this to be in the garden; how many little eggs would remain undiscovered each year; and how many Toby, the excitable border collie, would find before being put "inside if out, outside if in" as the family saying went.

Ruth found herself, almost subliminally entering into the whole message of Easter, whether pagan or Christian, secular or religious. Re-birth, renewal, resurrection, forgiveness, light after dark, atonement, propitiation, she hated that word and its connotations. She had quietly taken herself off to Stations of the Cross in Natton church on Good Friday evening once the children were in bed – ostensibly to remind herself of her grandmother. That was what she'd told Mark but deeply, more deeply than that, she knew it was something more, something just for her, though she was, as yet, not quite sure what exactly.

Entering the cool, dark church and seeing the baptismal font standing out in sharp relief on its raised plinth as the evening sun struck it at just the angle to turn the light coloured stone to white gold she thought suddenly of her tiny, dead Matthew, the first Matthew. She had found herself tormented some months after the death by the fact that her baby had not been baptised. She had, by chance, read only yesterday of a social worker who had told parents whose baby was being put up for adoption, as the father of the baby had been convicted of rape, that the baby's chances of finding parents were reduced because it *had* been baptised. The judge in the private family court hearing had been so horrified by this that he had ordered an internal inquiry into the conduct of the social worker which was currently ongoing.

She had known that the baptism of her child was something her grandmother would have organised had she but known any of it but at that time her grandmother, then aged 82, had been undergoing arduous treatment for a secondary brain tumour, having it seemed been cured of her primary lung cancer. This first tumour was not quite done though as it had managed without warning or fanfare to spread its seeds to her brain. This secondary brain tumour was ultimately to cause her death two and a half years later though thankfully she retained full mental capacity throughout the toxic and destructive range of treatments intended to alleviate her symptoms and provide the best possible quality of life for the time she had left.

Throughout Ruth's pregnancy, even during the latter stages, she had continued to visit her grandmother easily able to conceal the evidence of the baby growing inside her. A kind, elderly neighbour drove her grandmother to her hospital appointments but it was Ruth who stayed with Mim while he sorted out the practicalities of parking, buying coffees, teas or cold drinks as needed and returning promptly to collect them both when summoned by a text from Ruth.

Ruth helped her grandmother in all the practical ways she could, shopping, preparing meals, filling the freezer with ready cooked, nutritious, small portions of all her favourite foods. But she shared none of her personal turmoil with Mim at this time; it was, she felt, simply too much for her frail grandmother to bear at this stage of her life. She would go it alone.

As she left the church after the intensely moving *Stations of the Cross* service, the baptismal font was now virtually in darkness, the light stone only just visible and she found herself almost physically trying to shake off this particular reflection on her baby's untimely death as she jogged back to her family and sprinted upstairs to check on the sleeping children.

There was no time to fit in any actual Easter Day service but in any event she did not feel quite ready for that. She vowed though at least to introduce Emmie and Matthew to the Christian teaching related to the feast whilst explaining that it had many different origins; in this way they would be able to choose for themselves when older.

Once again she embraced wholeheartedly the family traditions at Mark's parents' gathering, noticing how solicitously the older children helped Emmie and, when necessary, Matthew, find eggs. She found herself making more time to chat to Sue and Simon on this occasion and even managing to 'sneak' upstairs for a secretive, and therefore very giggly, dress-fitting with Jane. Part of the Easter Day tradition was that the smaller children all had tea and baths at Grananne's and Granbob's house and got into 'jammies' for the journey home.

Next morning the bookshop was open only between 2 and 5 as it was Easter Monday and Sarah had asked if Ruth could manage this on her own as her younger daughter had just arrived for a short, precious visit. Ruth was very happy to do this, leaving Mark looking after the children, but it was just as she was locking up at the end of a satisfyingly busy afternoon that quite out of the blue, as she put it to herself later in the way she had of retelling her own story at such momentous times, a life-changing (as she thought of it afterwards, long afterwards) text pinged through from Louise.

Hi Ruth, Lou, Louise here, in case you didn't save my number. Do you want to meet up for a catch up?

Sure. But never seems any free time.... Erm...are you free next Saturday evening and if so could you cope with bath time then catch up? Mark's away for his stag do that night...

Fine, at your Gran's, well yours now I guess!? (:

Yes, say, 6ish? I'll feed you. Adult meal once kids asleep, don't worry.

Cool...see you then. (:(:

~ *Chapter 25* ~

Ambivalent, that's what it was, Ruth decided, she felt ambivalent about the catch up with Louise. It was not hard to analyse why. Louise had been a good friend, through thick and thin really, mostly thin, and perhaps Louise now felt the need of this friendship for *her* sake, perhaps she herself was entering a 'thin' phase. Ruth knew herself to be a fundamentally giving and generous-hearted person; earlier in her life too much had seemed to get in the way of that, but now she had so, so much more she could give.

The evening started well. Louise entered wholeheartedly into the whole bath time routine, offering to read to the children whist Ruth put their own, up-market, ready meal in the oven. As Louise was staying the night – this would be good company for Ruth of course and help with the children – they decided they could indulge themselves in a bottle of chilled rosé.

"So how are things with you, Lou? You can see how things are with me," Ruth chuckled.

"Yes, you seem so happy after... after everything..." Louise paused. "Yeah, *John Lewis* is great, I'm really happy there. Things didn't work out with Tim so I'm single again, pleased we didn't ever get properly hitched, simpler, and enjoying my freedom to be honest. It all just got a bit heavy really; he was always so jealous and became difficult when we were with other friends and boring when it was just us... so *I* finished it actually. He's finally accepted it. Anyway, enough of all that, it's history. I guess Matthew must be what, 4, 5 now? You were so brave to... to keep him, Ruth. But then it was not his fault..." Again she stopped herself mid-flow as she noted Ruth's suddenly closed expression.

"I feel I should tell you though, Ruth, I've thought about it a lot... wondered if you knew, wondered if you were one of those who came forward... Anyway, Steve, horrible Steve, who we vowed to get our own back on one day, was convicted of a violent rape about 6 months after, after, well... you know... And he admitted about 4 or 5 more, all of 18 year old girls, going back about 6, 8 years or so, before he even knew you and your mum. Absolute brute. Anyway, do you remember Rachel, in our year? Well we're in touch regularly and she was on placement at the prison as part of her course, social work, I think, or social work and something – not too sure – and she told me, in confidence, of course, that he's currently very ill, alcoholic liver failure or something and made worse by a series of mini strokes, at least I think that's what Rachel said, and he's now in hospital. But in prison he kind of quite recently 'got religion', she said, and wanted to 'atone' for all his 'transgressions'- he kept using those words apparently and wanted to "fess all'. He asked to see the chaplain as soon as possible but that same evening, about three weeks ago or so I think, he was found collapsed in his cell. The paramedics were called and he's still in hospital – the big one, you know S&G, Surrey and Guildford University Hospital, whatever it calls itself... Ruth, are you okay?"

Ruth's closed look had turned into one, as Louise described it to herself and Rachel later, of desperate, resigned, seemingly immeasurable grief, unfathomable in its intensity. "She suddenly looked terrible, Rach, kinda shutdown, not there, and just so, so, so deeply sad, like she'd lost something, everything...can't explain really, it was weird and scary."

Ruth felt this herself in the form of a physical searing pain... the game's now truly up, she sensed. She thought of the sleeping children upstairs, the taunting clowns of her recent, nearly sleepless, night, Mark out on his stag night, their forthcoming wedding, Mark's family... it was as if her life was passing in front of her, as people say it does when it's nearly over. She got up slowly, as people do when in pain, and brought the bottle of wine to the table, pouring another glass for both of them. Louise put her hand gently over Ruth's.

"Oh, Ruth, I'm so sorry... I didn't mean to upset you. I suppose, I thought, well, I thought you'd be pleased he was safely locked up and that it wasn't just you... I'm an idiot."

Again, she stopped herself, Ruth was still looking closed up and well, stricken really. "I'm so, so sorry, it must just bring it all back. Let's talk about happier things, like your wedding..."

So, once again there it was – Louise looking after Ruth.

"Yes, sure. Sorry, Lou, you're right. It just brings it all back. Anyway, you *can* come can't you? You know the reception's going to be here. My dress is a major secret and we're going away on holiday – honeymoon," she corrected herself quickly, " to Crete straight afterwards...with the children. Nice chance for our first family holiday and actually we can't bear to be apart from them, to be honest."

"I can't wait to meet Mark," said Louise excitedly, "wonder what time he'll be home tomorrow... and how he'll be."

"Actually he's not a big drinker, thank goodness. Likes a drink, but you know, that's it. I suppose they could have done something evil to him of course," mused Ruth. "Well, we'll see..."

"And your job? I always thought that sounded like a dream job – how's that going?"

"Well with both children," Ruth paused, realising she had to think a bit carefully now, "it became quite tricky so I'm now freelance, but I still get lots of work from *Petersons* of course and they'll always have me back as temporary cover for people's leave – mat. leave and things, you know. It can be a bit precarious money-wise but I have this wonderful part-time job in the children's book shop down the road – *River Books for Children* – do you remember it? Off the beaten track – somebody in our year had a holiday job there once I remember – Lauren Smith, I think it was, ginger hair, loads of freckles, got bullied. Remember?"

"Oh, yes, I do. She was a bit strange though – cause or effect, I suppose you might ask. And Mark's a teacher isn't he? Primary, secondary?"

"Primary, quite unusual for a man. He loves it though."

"So, Emmie's mum? Sorry... this sounds like an interrogation, I won't torture you for answers don't worry, but so much has changed for you, it's great, I just care about you as you know."

"She's dead. Suicide. Mental health issues. They were already separated. Long story... but, Lou, let's talk about you. How are your lovely parents? And Annie?" (Annie was Louise's elder sister and only sibling – three years older so in terms of school years this was virtually another planet to the two younger friends.)

"Parents are great... they pretend to be like Darby and Joan, but are pretty on the ball with everything. Both working flat out still, both loving it, Dad was promoted to Inspector about 3 years ago, Mum does some private physio now but mostly NHS still. I'm going over for Sunday lunch tomorrow. Annie and David'll be there... no sign of the patter of tiny feet though. I suspect Mum and

Dad can't wait for one of us to do the honourable thing – give them a grandchild that is," she chuckled, "but they never say it of course. Oh, Ruthie, I'm just so pleased to see you so happy and kind of settled, I know it sounds boring but when I see those beautiful kids… hmmm, wistful note creeps in," she said in light self-parody.

"Yeah, it's great, but I'm in no way complacent, Lou, anything could happen any time to *shatter the dream*," she drew the quote marks in the air with her fingers "and it feels really, well, hard won, I s'pose."

Even as Ruth spoke the words, they were by now in the sitting room having taken their drinks through, she looked around fearfully only too harshly aware that Steve's need to 'atone' could bring the whole carefully constructed edifice tumbling down. This was eating away at her very core, as she thought of it, meaning that she could not even enjoy Louise's visit and their re-acquaintance one tiny bit. She realised this with a sudden sense of almost indefinable, certainly unexpected, loss.

"Will you be all right at the wedding, Lou? You'll be the only one from my murky past." This question was posed with genuine concern; she did not want to, nor could she, retract the invitation now.

"Mark's family are just lovely, so are his friends, so are mine – school gate friends really, Mel and a couple of others, a bit more than that now though. Sarah, my bookshop boss – she's great. Hmmm… Mark's best man, Luke, they know each other from uni… well, he's a bit of all right, as Mim used to say. Easy on the eye definitely. Well, Lou…?"

"I'm not 'seeking', as they say," again Louise's fingers formed the quote marks, "but, well, you never know."

Later on in bed, with Lou safely installed on the sofa, she'd said she'd prefer that because she didn't want to disrupt Emmie's and Matthew's sleeping arrangements for just one night, Ruth lying wakeful, scared, and very sad, thought to herself: is it actually such a carefully constructed edifice, as she had put it to herself earlier? That was one thing it wasn't, if you thought about it. Carefully constructed? No, it was all so random really; the tragic events in her own family – she did not spell them out in her mind now, she had too frequently done that in the past she felt. The randomness of chance – was that tautology? Did it matter? Seeing Matthew that day, taking him; rescuing him, as she had so quickly come to think of it; meeting Mark and Emmie, both needing to be rescued especially little Emmie at that time… how could all this be destroyed by one man with a past suddenly finding the need to atone – for what purpose exactly? His own, or was it some twisted, lingering revenge towards her for escaping? Did that matter? Did the *reason* matter? Did she need to atone for her own two crimes perhaps? Was this her comeuppance? And so the thoughts went on and on tumbling through her mind until she fell into a light, uneasy sleep at about 5.30am, just as dawn was appearing, creeping stealthily forward, red and strangely fierce in its intensity and purpose.

~ *Chapter 26* ~

In the event, Louise did not meet Mark that Sunday as she had to leave too early to get to her parents for lunch; they had by now moved to Godalming. Ruth felt strangely relieved though it was difficult to pinpoint why exactly. Clearly Louise would not be dragging out all the information about Steve in front of Mark yet she felt a need to keep her past separate, at more than arm's length really, compartmentalise her life, as the saying went.

Something had been destroyed for Ruth now, security, happiness, some perception of a future stretching ahead for her and Mark and the children... Of course, gardens could be dug up anytime, she reminded herself, but even if... she actually felt she had a strong defence to *that* crime at least – post-natal whatever it was, depression, psychosis, grief, fear for her mother, controlled by Steve, vulnerable 18 year old, now a mother... she had only been an accessory after the fact of concealing a body after all. What she contemplated now was something quite different, just as, she supposed, was 'taking' Matthew all those months ago – ten months to be precise.

And so it was that in the weeks that should still have been filled with joyful, busy anticipation and planning and excitement about what should be going to be the happiest day of her life, *"that on which"* – as her English teacher had so nit-pickingly insisted all those years ago, ten years, to be precise, (even her thoughts were now echoing in her mind, resounding, as they rampaged through her stricken brain) – she was to be married, Ruth spent most of her time, free or otherwise, plotting to commit her third crime. She needed to be careful now, meticulous in her planning and covering her tracks – she had so much, too much, to lose this time round.

And this time round, again the echo, the key difference – she articulated it clearly to herself – was the premeditation. Unlike her previous two crimes this time round, words rebounding off the bony walls of her skull as she concentrated intensely, there was to be, had to be, meticulous planning yet she was aware too of the element of happenstance... again the lapsing into strange, almost literary, certainly old-fashioned language, as she found herself looking in from the outside at her story, detached almost: the psychologists would have something to say about that, she had no doubt. So happenstance – if she had not met Louise by chance, if Steve had not been taken ill...

What came to her mind as she plotted and planned, knowing she had only this brief window of opportunity whilst he was still vulnerable in hospital, was a vivid memory of her dying grandmother's dry, cracked lips during her last acute hospital admission, her constant thirst, the different nurses hurrying around, none aware seemingly that her beloved and only Mim needed help with drinking and how she had loved that iced grapefruit juice which Ruth lovingly, painstakingly, had chilled and brought in in a thermos flask. This came to mind distressingly but so too did an article she had read recently about the potentially lethal interaction between grapefruit juice and many medications including statins. Had she inadvertently hastened Mim's death perhaps? Was she implicated in *another* crime? If Steve had had a stroke, or a series of mini strokes, as Louise had thought Rachel said, there was a high probability, she realised, that he was at least on statins.

She toyed briefly with the idea of hunting for some type of poisonous mushroom in the local woods, again there had been a recent report, of four people being taking ill and one of them dying, having picked, cooked and eaten them. *Too risky,* was her immediate thought, *plus he may not die, plus getting cooked mushrooms into someone in Steve's state would be very tricky indeed anyway, even if she were to make a tempting mushroom pâté; no that felt ridiculous somehow and easily traceable to her, she may contaminate cooking tools, and she would feel like a mad woman roaming the woods and...*strangely she thought then of the light-hearted salutation to mushrooms sung by Mark on that early autumn day in the garden barely seven months ago and found she had almost physically to shake herself free of that thought. So grapefruit juice it would be.

And what of Mark whilst Ruth was thus preoccupied? How to tell it, how to express it all? How even to write it here? Well, for his part, Mark felt that Ruth, his Ruthie, somehow strong yet vulnerable, somehow resilient yet fragile, had not only rescued his little Emmie she had in fact, he felt, rescued him. Jane had commented that he seemed to be thawing out. This implied of course that he had been strangely frozen during his years of trying to cope with Meg, his suspension from the job he loved, and the accusations, the loss of trust. He knew for certain he had been emotionally frozen, and now, he realised, almost physically too. He had become virtually catatonic until he had met Ruth; he understood that now.

Happily this frozen state had in no way extended towards his little daughter, but the intensity of feeling for her, his sense of powerlessness to help her, to rescue her, had been suffered by him as if in a weird, comatose-like, lower state of awareness.

He had read of a neurological condition associated with severe brain injury called 'locked in syndrome'. Terrifying. Such sufferers felt, felt suffering in fact, the feelings and suffering made more intense by the victims' loss of ability both physically and emotionally to express those feelings and this suffering due to complete loss of all physical function. This sometimes included even breathing itself therefore these people required mechanical ventilation with its associated terrifying, acute discomforts, the endotracheal tube itself, the loss of control.

He realised all this just at odd moments in his busy life but as he watched Ruth during this premeditation phase he simply could not fathom what was eating her, as he put it to himself, and he was worried. Was it pre-wedding cold feet? Was something going wrong with all the balls she was juggling? Was it some slightly mysterious woman's problem? Was she not well? He couldn't call it, nor did he want even to express his fears for fear of giving them substance.

And so he kept his fears to himself and truth to tell it was only his mother who sensed that all was not hundred per cent rosy in the garden. But as she too so wanted to believe in this new beginning for Mark and Emmie and had grown to love Ruth like a daughter and Matthew like a grandson she did not give voice to her misgivings either, for fear, as she thought of it in her own reflective moments, of giving them an identity, letting them out. How true that you never stopped worrying about your children, she shuddered.

Bob kept his own counsel as ever but knew that Anne was his priority now and sought to allay her concerns just by his warm physical presence, gentle, solicitous and ever loving. He watched the new little family carefully and both he and Anne rejoiced to see Emmie and Matthew together, growing stronger in every way. Matthew had a very close bond with Bob, it was noticeable, and the little boy was growing in confidence daily.

There were some occasions that stuck in Ruth's mind though and how she berated herself afterwards, oh how she beat herself up, *what was she thinking, anything could have happened.* It was a sunny afternoon and they had been shopping in Kingston, under sufferance – all of them – for shoes – the one item for which it really was necessary to drag the children round possibly more than one shop. Ruth herself hated shopping and she always felt sorry for children who had no choice but to follow round their parents. Mark and Ruth felt exactly the same way about this chore so they endeavoured never to involve the children unless it was absolutely essential.

On this occasion when they were nearly home Ruth remembered they had run out of baked beans – of all things, she said to herself afterwards – and so pulled up in front of the small *Spar* shop which sold everything it seemed. Rather than unstrap the two children she quickly called over to them – without turning round, *without even turning round,* to see their stricken little faces as she afterwards imagined they would have been,

"Won't be a sec… two ticks that's all."

And so it seemed she was, but that was all it took. On her return, Emmie was actually purple with distress, Matthew was barely holding back the tears but was doing his best to comfort her, just saying "Shh, Emmie, shhh," with his hands tightly clapped to both ears. When Ruth re-appeared his look of relief and his usual quiet joy at seeing her was quickly suppressed to be replaced by one of accusation. "She was frightened, Mimi, really frightened. She thought somebody would *steal* her, steal both of us."

~ *Chapter 27* ~

So how did she do it exactly? It is difficult still to tell it, to lay it out like this for public consumption by you readers. Ruth researched it all meticulously as was her way and with the integrity for which she had become known by those closest to her. And this is what, how, why and when she did what she had to do, and all of it went against the grain…

Ruth plotted to visit Steve in hospital, vulnerable, captive as he was there, and she knew this had to be soon. Nobody stayed for long in an acute hospital bed these days, she knew that well and remembered it from her days of caring for Mim in her last illness. It was an NHS resource issue of course, she understood that. She needed to be incognito – that went without saying; after all it was only just over four years ago and she did not know how many of his mental faculties, she paused over the phrase, Steve retained. She could not risk his recognising her.

Hating herself for the deceit, she approached Pauline. Pauline was known for her small collection of human hair wigs which she had bought during her chemotherapy treatment, preferring them to the synthetic hair wigs supplied by the NHS, good quality though these were – and she kept her carefully chosen wigs as a talisman, she explained, hoping that in so doing the cancer would not return. If she disposed of them in a wild fit of elation at being apparently cancer free, she explained to her family, life being what it is or Sod's law… she did not complete the thought, there was no need. So it was that Ruth asked to borrow one of these, telling, lying to Pauline that she was going to a reunion of her old high school Class of 2011, and that they had decided to go in fancy dress with the aim of heavy disguise to see how long it took to recognise people, just for fun. They had last seen each other over six years ago and a lot can happen in six years of course.

So that was the first deceit. It needs telling in this rather chunky way, laying it bare as a form of confession and it feels important that you readers understand exactly how it was. Whether it is important or not is another matter, but it feels as if you should know this detail.

The next deceit was freeing herself for the hospital visit or more likely visits, whatever it took. She told Sarah that she really needed to meet two crucial editing work deadlines before the ten days she was taking off for the wedding and honeymoon. The precision of the "two", Ruth felt, lent the lie credibility. She asked Sarah if she could take five days off – unpaid of course and – to make it easier for Sarah who really did need another pair of hands – she would offer to replace herself with Paul, Sally's boyfriend, who would work those five days for Sarah on lower pay than Ruth, lifting and shifting, unpacking, sorting, making coffee, whatever needed to be done; he a was a quick learner and completely trustworthy – he could be the "one", Ruth laughingly told Sarah. Why would he do this? Well, the payoff for Paul would be if Sarah would allow him to advise her on a new lighting scheme for the shop – this was already on Sarah's urgent to do list, so no real coercion there – and hopefully receive the commission to fit the scheme at a reduced trainee rate.

Paul was in his last year as an apprentice electrician and needed to gain a certain number of hours of paid work – with testimonials from customers – in order to complete his portfolio of evidence to submit as part of his final coursework, this carrying a large percentage of marks. Sally had met Paul when he was doing temporary holiday work in her office during his course. He had a particular interest in, and flair for, lighting. His aim, once qualified, was to set up his own business which, unfortunately, he was planning to call *A Flair for Lighting* as this is what he had been told he had throughout his course. Sally, her siblings and some of his friends were trying to encourage him to choose something a bit snappier, even suggesting "Flair Lighting.co" but he seemed to be sticking his heels in at the moment for some unaccountable reason.

Sarah seemed to be delighted by this arrangement and exhorted Ruth not to work too hard reassuring her that she totally understood her need to be free to meet these deadlines and unburden herself in this way for her wedding.

"Yes, I will feel unburdened, Sarah," Ruth replied thoughtfully, only too painfully aware of the double meaning, so aware that she hoped it had not somehow revealed itself in her very mien, strange word again, it always happened at such times. "Thank you for understanding. I'm just so pleased there's a benefit for you too." And she was, genuinely she was, it felt like mitigation for this second deceit. "You'll like Paul, I'm sure."

So, disguise nearly sorted, glasses and some uncharacteristic but not too obvious make-up would complete it, part time job sorted, how now to get rid, no, no, no she silently screamed it, free herself of her beloved childcare responsibilities for those five days? Divide and conquer she felt, that's what friends are for but she needed to take care not to overburden either children or friends.

Thus it was, telling the exact same lie (what else would she do after all?) to Mark, to Melanie, to Pauline, to Sally and Paul, Jane and Tim and even Anne and Bob as back up, all those closest to her in fact, she set about organising Paul to take Emmie with him as usual to Sarah's explaining that he needed to be in time to pick Matthew up from school every day but Monday. On Monday, to spread the load, Matthew would be going to Sam's to play, with Melanie picking them both up. This she knew was helpful for Melanie, now heavily pregnant. The boys would be self-sufficient with their own company insofar as 5 going on 6 year olds could be.

This helpfulness towards Melanie once again seemed to mitigate the deceit for Ruth, *'stepp'd in so far'*, she sensed already that *'to return would be as tedious as go o'er'*.[30] Here we go again, she felt resignedly, quoting high literature at such a time yet entirely identifying with the wracked Macbeth at this time. Paul would get the children home each day and Ruth undertook to all of them to be home by 5pm each day; she just needed to maximise this 'freedom' to ensure the deed was done. *'If t'were done then t'were well t'were done quickly'* [31] – or something. Was that Lady Macbeth egging him on? She just could not quite remember.

---

[30] William Shakespeare: (c 1606) *Macbeth* Act 3, Sc 4
[31] William Shakespeare: (c1606) *Macbeth,* Act 1, Sc 7

~ *Chapter 28* ~

So how to tell the next bit exactly? It is getting harder but it has to come out. Ruth decided to drive to Surrey and Guildford University Hospital Trust. She had told Mark, *lied* to Mark, let's tell it as it was, lay it bare in fact, that she needed to be in the office at *Petersons* to get really head down for these deadlines, she could hot-desk there, and she felt it important to remind people in that office, her former employer, of her existence from time to time. She felt the need to be in her own enclosed world, in the car away from CCTV on railway stations, and alone with her premeditations really. She could park up, away from prying eyes, slip the wig, glasses and make-up on surreptitiously inside the car and she could retreat to this haven and her laptop during brief breaks in visiting.

Luck was on her side, as she told it to herself later, again this need to tell her story, to let it out. She found a parking place easily in the overflow car park constructed for the duration of some building works which were to house a new cancer centre she discovered from reading the notices. This was to be a place for patients and families to come during prolonged treatment visits, funded by *Children with Cancer UK* charity, but thankfully at the moment just a rather deserted-looking building site. She felt certain that they would not have extended any CCTV coverage down as far as this hastily constructed, gravelly and pot-holey car park, temporary as it was.

She was quickly able to discover which ward Steve was on by asking at main reception. She received her answer from a bored looking, fifty-something woman who merely clicked her computer mouse a couple of times and made no eye contact whatsoever whilst giving her the one word response. Ruth thought fleetingly of a syndrome she had heard of somewhere, *compassion fatigue,* useful she felt perhaps for people working in such places. *Immune to, immured, closed off from suffering was another way of looking at it*, she mused, *time to get out of that environment perhaps, in that case*, she thought.

More luck was to come her way. As she entered the ward the first person she saw was a very new and nervous looking student nurse, her name badge proclaiming her to be Amy Leverett, a student nurse from the University of Surrey.

"Oh, that's handy I'm just going into his room now – he's in isolation, MRSA – you know, that multi resistant bug thing? So we need to put on the aprons and gloves and masks out here. My mum says they used to call it barrier nursing when she trained, sounds horrible, behind a barrier, but maybe 'in isolation' is no better. I've been reading up all about it, patients can get really isolated but he's a bit beyond that at the moment, he's not well..." She stopped herself suddenly, "Oh help... are you family?" Nervousness, excitement perhaps, was making her garrulous; she was probably about the same age as Ruth.

Ruth, noting her discomfort and anxiety that she had said too much quickly put her at her ease, "No, I'm not, don't worry. He has no family. I got to know him when he..." she lowered her voice rather theatrically pausing, "...you know when he was first taken into police custody before his trial. I'm a volunteer custody visitor in my spare time." She lied easily and had in fact only read about this interesting role a few days previously. "I got to know him well, actually. He talked a lot, you know, I think having nobody else and having confessed all – sort of thing – he just wanted to open up to somebody, anybody really."

Amy listened intently. "Yes, it seems sad... we don't know what he did, just that he's in prison, I never thought I'd be looking after a prisoner on my very first placement, my early experience placement actually. I've only been at uni 5 weeks but I love it and I love coming out on this two week placement so soon into my training. I've chosen Steve as my case study to present – it's so interesting with the liver transplant and everything. I'm just going in to make some notes before my mentor gets back from her break. Oh, and I must see if he wants a drink, we have to encourage fluids but he keeps falling off to sleep so it's difficult. He has to have two prison officers, guarding him at all times," explained Amy, she lowered her voice, conspiratorially, "it seems ridiculous really, waste of resources if nothing else. Steve can't move, he's nearly comatose most of the time, how do they think he's suddenly going to do a runner? The outlook isn't good for him," she continued, "you know, prognosis they call it," she was obviously pleased to be using the medical term. "The prison officers are quite interesting to talk to actually," Amy told Ruth. "Apparently they're paid overtime to do this 24 hour 'guarding' in shifts and it's usually a really cushy number, they just sit and drink tea, do puzzles, play games on their phones. They just have to complete an hourly log, 'no change, no change, no change' kinda thing, easier than normal prison officer work, easier than nursing, that's for sure, the ward's manic at the moment. Steve doesn't really get the level of care he needs to be honest, he's left alone for quite long periods of time, apart from one or other of them," she said, indicating the two prison officers, one obviously nearing retirement, the other a new recruit, much closer in age to Amy and Ruth it seemed, "short-staffed, rushed off our feet...oh, I probably shouldn't have said that," she tailed off, confused for a moment by the burden of new responsibilities, new ways of behaving.

"Come on, I'll show you how to gown up, we have to do that before we go in, bit of a palaver. The older ones," Amy peered through the small glass pane in the door, as she showed Ruth how to tie the fastenings of the plastic apron at the front having brought them round from the back, "you see the one looking out of the window, like him, well, they encourage the younger ones to do it for experience (which it is of course) but then they leave the newbies on their own with the patient for ages whilst they go and have a smoke – or whatever – my mentor explained all this to me. It's not right. But the younger one, Pete, he's good to talk to, just finished a criminology degree at Surrey, walked straight into a full time job with prospects aged 21, that's what he told me. I just cannot imagine anyone wanting to be a prison officer but we're all different I suppose. I hope you won't be too shocked to see Steve compared to when you last saw him; come on in."

It was being handed to her on a plate, Ruth felt. By this time she was safely behind a mask, gloved and aproned up. She approached the bed where Steve was lying, apparently sleeping, and looked down at his emaciated face: grey, receding hair, beginnings of a grey beard, dry looking mouth and felt... well, nothing actually, absolutely nothing. This took her by surprise but it helped her carry off her disguise and continue with her plot.

"Shall I wake him to offer him a drink, Amy? I brought some cold juice; I remembered that was all he ever wanted when he was in custody so I brought plenty along."

"Oh, great, thanks, yes, do."

Ruth stroked his hand, still thankfully feeling nothing. "Hello, Steve, it's Sue, remember me? I've brought you some lovely cold juice." She lifted the cup to his parched, cracked lips and he sipped thirstily without even acknowledging a new presence. She felt she was doing actual good.

"One whole cup downed more or less in one, Amy. Do you need to write it down anywhere?"

"Ooh yes, those cups are 200mls, thanks."

"I'll try him with some more in a minute." Ruth couldn't help remembering how angry and distressed she had been during her grandmother's hospital stays towards the end of her life that no-one ever seemed to have had time to help her drink or eat, always filling in paperwork. Wow! It had made her so mad. But now, still, she felt nothing. She watched Amy writing busily.

"So do you have to know about all those drugs?" she asked, suddenly interested as well as having an eye to the main chance – she went into narrative mode to herself again.

"Yes, I do for this bit of coursework… it doesn't count towards our final grade – that's a long way off anyway," she grinned, but it's what they call 'formative work', I think it's formative," she looked doubtful, "or is it summative, I wonder? All these weird words…"

"Probably formative I should think," said Ruth, "like a formative experience, you know, from childhood or something, it informs… sort of. Summative sounds like something that you would add up, cumulative type thing."

"Yes," replied Amy, "they talk about 'only formative' so that's reassuring. But we have to do a case presentation during this placement, that's really scary, formative presentation, that's it."

"What are all these drugs for anyway?" asked Ruth. "You could explain them to me and that would be good practice for the presentation."

And so it was that Ruth learnt within twenty minutes or so of arriving at the hospital that Steve was indeed on statins following a series of TIA's – "minor strokes or transient ischaemic attacks," Amy explained, obviously pleased with herself, "that he had suffered over the last two years." She heard too from the excited, young, naïve student nurse that he was high on the list for a liver transplant and that they had just heard today that it looked as if a liver would be available in the next forty-eight hours or so from a young boy who had died aged 17 out on his first motor bike ride.

"I'll have masses to write about and present to my group. We have to think about the ethical and legal issues in everything we do and the staff were all talking about this at handover. They were saying it's hard not to be judgemental when we know he's a convicted criminal and his prognosis is so poor because of his TIA's and lifestyle choices, as they say, you know, smoking and drinking and stuff," said Amy happily anticipating getting to grips with this 'interesting patient'.

"Why is he so high on the list, exactly?" asked Ruth also fascinated and simultaneously horrified by all of this and noticed Pete, the young prison officer, was listening in an interested way too, whilst periodically checking his phone.

"Well, I'm not that sure – it's only my early experience placement, don't forget – but they were talking about his liver being nearly completely shot this morning. But the awful thing is there's a little kid upstairs," *presumably on the children's ward,* thought Ruth to herself, "whose liver is in a similar state from some weird sounding congenital problem. He's only 7, but he has some awful infection at the moment so is probably too ill to be transplanted… Anyway, they'll see who's the best match today or tomorrow; the motorcyclist is thought to be brain dead but they'll do the definitive tests soon. He's on ITU here so my mentor says I can go and watch if I like as I may not get another chance and it would be interesting and relevant to my case study. I probably will, though it feels a bit much, a bit morbid…"

She broke off as her mentor was beckoning her from outside the room. "Back in a minute, carry on trying him with drinks if you like. That's great, really helpful."

Ruth couldn't help thinking that if she hadn't been there Steve probably wouldn't have got any drinks for most of that morning – but still she felt nothing – and managed to get two more full cups into him to a muttered, only just audible, "thank you." He seemed to her to be a nasty colour and very ill-looking, and perhaps her journey wasn't really necessary; her grandmother had jokingly used that wartime phrase from time to time just in ordinary chitchat.

"Is your journey really necessary, darling?" she would say as Ruth buzzed around the place, sometimes, especially towards the end when Mim just seemed to want her close. At this stage even rushing down to the local shops for just one thing by way of getting some fresh air, light, freedom, escape, left her feeling guilty. She recalled the sense of guilt even now.

~ *Chapter 29* ~

So it was that by the end of that first day, as she took off her disguise in the car, Ruth felt satisfied with the day's work, feeling she was well on track towards successful accomplishment of the deed, especially as she had by chance, serendipity, she said to herself, gleaned much of Steve's medical condition. She thought briefly of her namesake, Ruth Ellis, and then later, much later, Rosemary West, determined, wicked women, set on a course of action.

She sometimes had to remind herself that she had not in fact killed her own child, only colluded in concealing the death as they buried his tiny body in a roughly dug grave in the garden. She did wonder though if she had contributed inadvertently to her beloved Mim's death. *If that ever came to light,* she pondered, *it would be all about – it would turn on – as they said, knowing what was knowable at the time, that is the toxic link between grapefruit juice, some other juices and various medications, many more coming to light it seemed.*

So it was all about knowing and you readers know all of Ruth's crimes to date though those closest to her do not. She knows them though, you know that she knows them and she knows that you know them; perhaps that is why her narrative voice creeps in persistently, disembodied, remote from the reality of those crimes. Were they heinous crimes? Or are they just crimes in name? Do you know? Does she know? What was known to all though was that at the end of that first day she held Mark, Matthew and Emmie all very, very close indeed at various times that evening and, in Mark's case, during the night too. Those close ones, though, did not, in fact, know why she did this.

And the week continued as planned. The routine worked well. At home the children knew how the week was panning out, seemed busy and content and as ever overjoyed to see Ruth on her return at 5pm everyday just as she had promised. Ruth felt her meticulous planning had paid off, but could not say she felt complacent; she was only too well aware of pride coming before a fall. What she felt throughout was mostly nothing. It would be to overstate it really she felt, to surmise that this was some kind of displacement, denial, whatever. She just felt nothing for Steve, nothing for her planned course of action; it was something that had to be done to complete the course of action set in motion when she had first spied Matthew watching the monkey in the shop window all those months ago.

It was a bonus to have Amy's company and she was genuinely interested in the progress of the case study for Amy's sake actually. She learned that Amy had worked as a health care assistant at weekends whilst she was doing her A levels at a local high school in order to enhance her application for nursing and to ensure this really was what she wished to commit herself to, not only in terms of the course, which was no walkover, Ruth discovered, but as a career for life, she hoped. She discovered Amy was only just 19, having an October birthday, and it was clear to Ruth that Amy would come to see and know a great deal about human suffering before many more months had passed.

She was kept in touch with all the potential liver transplant discussions. It turned out that both Steve and the 7 year old boy on the children's ward were close matches; this was a huge coincidence as the blood samples were matched against a national database. Outcomes for the child were probably statistically better if he recovered from his current infection in time to receive it. Steve, if he recovered from this episode of acute liver failure, would have to make lifestyle changes – that phrase again – if it were to be a success. The chances of outright rejection were similar for both of them. Ruth also learnt that if the liver transplant were successful for the little boy that his life expectancy would return to normal from being currently a matter of weeks at the most.

"So, if Steve was not a match or..." she hesitated, "his condition deteriorated further," she'd nearly said "in time" but stopped herself, "the boy would have a better chance of receiving the liver?"

"Yep, it's a lottery really, isn't it?" said Amy ruefully. Ruth detected her rapidly developing maturity, accelerated really by what she encountered in the realities of health care practice whilst still a teenager.

By the end of the second day Amy was touchingly delighted that Steve's kidney function at least was improving apparently due to his improved fluid intake.

"He's got you to thank for that, Ruth, you're so devoted. I should nominate you for a volunteer's award or something," she giggled. "They've just put this year's award winners in the hospital magazine; I was looking at it during my break."

"Oh no, no need for that, I hate that sort of thing. It's just part of my role." The iced grapefruit juice was still going down well. She had done her research – she knew this was her best chance so she continued to offer him drinks every hour or so having added plenty of sugar to make it palatable. She also helped him with his lunch, again feeling nothing, as she spooned the sustaining nutrients into him. At times he was almost chatty, asking about the weather, and what day it was.

When she arrived on the third morning she saw somebody just outside his door busy divesting herself of the apron and gloves. Ruth noticed the dog collar and she felt her heart literally leap into her mouth, and her knees turn to water.

"You must be Sue, I've heard from the student nurse all about you and your interest. Steve asked to see a chaplain in the early hours of this morning, said he wanted to confess to some different crimes, but now he's unresponsive, he's taken a real turn for the worse. They could have called the service, one of us is always on call but they didn't know, the night staff, you know, the nurses, always rushed off their feet anyway it seems, day and night. I don't blame them, but it looks to me as if it's too late now for any confession to be honest. Whoops, a bit of a pun really, sorry. Well, see what you make of him, I'll pop back later for what it's worth."

Ruth put on the familiar barrier, as she thought of it now, the apron, mask and gloves, like an automaton as she felt the blood return to her heart; in a way her heart was settling back into position, she supposed.

The change in Steve was stark certainly; Ruth felt she was looking at a dying man. Amy breezed in and confirmed what Ruth saw. He had taken a dramatic turn for the worse at about 6.30am; apparently he had been awake a lot in the night, Amy told her, quite chatty and upbeat, the night staff said, was asking to ''fess all' to a chaplain, any flavour would do he said and was actually laughing. "He was drinking and eating well, he loved that flask of iced juice you left him, Sue, but he just went downhill quite suddenly, went a bit vague, then a bit aggressive, confused, and his lips went blue. His blood gases are all over the place – the levels of oxygen and carbon dioxide and stuff in his blood," Amy explained to Ruth, having just been reading up on it for her case study. "Oh and it looks as if I won't get to write about the liver transplant – he's too ill – the little boy's better from his infection and the liver's going to him today, or I think some lobes of it or something and it regenerates, I think but I might have made that bit up, I'll find out."

Throughout the fourth day of Ruth's planned campaign week Steve continued to deteriorate. The prison officers sent to be with him were more in evidence and Ruth made herself scarce for most of the day, just saying to Amy, she would be back later. She managed to get another 400 millilitres of juice down him during that last morning, but by 3pm he was completely unresponsive.

"I think I'll phone before I come in tomorrow," she said to Amy as she left. "What's the ward's extension?"

Amy found it for her and said, "This is my last day of early experience placement as we have a study day at uni tomorrow so I won't be here if you do come in. Mind you, I have a feeling Steve might not be here either…"

"I won't see you then," said Ruth. "Good luck with the rest of your course. I hope it all goes well and thank you for explaining everything to me so clearly. It must have been easier with me not being a relative I suppose, just interested."

So it was that on the fifth day, Ruth phoned in re-identifying herself as the volunteer custody visitor who had been in to see Steve during the week, but keeping her number private by the simple device of putting in 141 at the start, to be told that he had died peacefully at 4am without regaining consciousness. Did she know of any family at all?

"No, he told me he had none. I guess the prison staff will deal with everything?" she asked.

And the footnote is that the liver went to the little boy who was recovering well and there was no reason to believe he would not continue to do so and lead a full, happy and productive life.

~ *Chapter 30* ~

Quite, quite alone now on the night before her wedding day as was her choice, Ruth listened to the torrential rain falling against the bedroom windows, and on next door's conservatory roof, interspersed with sudden, even more alarming, splatterings of hailstones seemingly actually about to break the glass. They had decided, in the traditional way, Ruth and Mark, to spend the night apart and had arranged for Matthew and Emmie to stay with Jane and Tim and their cousins Lucy and Georgie. That way Jane could be responsible in her competent way for dressing them all, the older girl cousins could help Emmie make her daisy chain headdress, pick the wildflowers they were to carry and generally have a fun sleepover. Mark and his best man, Luke, a friend from university who had supported him unconditionally throughout all his more recent ordeals and had rejoiced with him over Ruth's and Matthew's appearance in his life, were staying at Anne and Bob's house, Mark's childhood home of course.

Mark and Ruth had strongly felt the need for some time together just as an engaged couple, not long, just a night and next day together was what they decided. So on the last school day, a Thursday, of the spring half term Anne and Bob happily agreed to collect Matthew from school at 3pm, pick up Emmie from Mel's – who had nobly, enjoying the exercise, she said, in her advanced pregnancy, collected her at lunchtime – and take them both for a sleepover at Grananne's and Granbob's about which both children were nervously excited.

Mark and Ruth had relished this time alone, even managing to include a lovely peaceful lunch at a riverside pub they liked, before Mark headed off to meet Luke at Guildford Station and take him back to his parents' house to meet Matthew and Emmie and re-acquaint himself with Anne and Bob. Mark had easily negotiated time out from his INSET day – Natton primary having closed for the half term holiday the day before Thames Lacey primary – undertaking to do most of the training online. All the staff, including the new head, were only too well-aware of the extra hours Mark put in with all the extracurricular activities he organised for the children and several of his colleagues understood just how momentous this next step in his life was.

As for Mark, he enjoyed catching up with Luke. Whilst his parents did bath and bedtime for the children on their own, they were quite capable, they reassured him laughingly and it was a novelty for the already excited children, Mark and Luke nipped down to Mark's favourite local for a swift half – he used his father's not entirely accurate phrase. Mark felt almost completely relaxed, a rarity for him and they caught up on each other's news, 'developments' as they put it to each other, quickly and light-heartedly. Luke was now engaged to his long-standing girlfriend, Gina, who was Spanish and currently visiting her parents in Spain as her father had had a recent heart attack, now back home recovering.

They chatted on whilst enjoying their pints of real ale, *Adnams'* 'Ghost Ship' for Mark, and 'Surrey Bitter' from a local brewer, *Pilgrim*, for Luke. When the group at the darts board finished their rather noisy game, the two friends decided to play. They had both been quite good at darts in their university days, but were now considerably out of practice. They opted to play 301 as they were aware of needing to get back to Mark's parents and in fact were looking forward to spending a civilised evening with them the night before the wedding. As they played and chatted easily they were both conscious of the familiar competitive edge – you played to win. In the event, needing 19 to win Luke did it nicely with a 3 and a double 8.

Not quite ready to leave the convivial atmosphere of the pub that early summer evening they gravitated towards the recently vacated pool table and again, after a close game, it was Luke who potted the black: "You've got other things on your mind, mate," he laughed putting an arm round his friend's shoulders. They finished their second pints and strolled back to the honey coloured house in the valley now bathed in a golden glow of late evening May sunlight, warm and welcoming, the two friends feeling nicely mellow.

But here, now, alone at home, waking on the morning of her wedding day, Ruth felt, quite suddenly, unexpectedly, bleakly alone, deserted, abandoned, it seemed. Why had she chosen to spend the night alone, she could not fathom it out now? Was she seeking a period of quiet reflection on the next step in her life, a period of quite atonement for her crimes? She just didn't know. This was not how it should be, she whispered to herself. *What fury are the gods unleashing on me? I know that the day itself should not matter so much, but the last weekend in May when everything could be just so beautiful, should be really, everything would be sodden, miserable, chilly, dark.*

Louise had asked her if she wanted her to come to the house before going to the church but Ruth had been adamant that she did not want that at the same time as not wanting to hurt Louise's feelings. The truth was that Louise brought back so many dark memories and it was even she who had brought the latest dark distress to Ruth's life. No, Ruth wanted to reach out to the warm embrace of her new family, her new, her first security, Matthew's too, and lovely Sally was coming round anyway to help her get dressed and do her hair; Ruth had wanted to keep it all simple and quiet.

So, she rather wearily got up – it was still only 6am – and ran herself a deliciously deep, scented bubble bath whilst she made tea – this was in itself quite a luxury of course, no small children to think of first, no rush, she realised, pulling herself together, shaking the blues away – as Mim used to say, and soon, quite soon, she would be seeing all those she loved most in the world.

Sally arrived just after nine as arranged with her home hair dressing kit.

"Hey, Ruth, Ruthie," she called out as she let herself in, hearing no response to her strikes with the huge old-fashioned door knocker which Ruth's grandmother would never replace with a bell. "Coo-ee, where are you?" she sang out merrily but on hearing the steady roar of the hoover she made her way upstairs.

"Sally, oh, Sally it's lovely that you're here."

"Give me that now," demanded Sally, "not on your wedding day... Where else needs doing? I'll do it."

Ruth laughed. "No, it's fine, that's the last. Let's have some coffee. Wow, I'm pleased to see you, I can start being excited now but just look at it," she gestured outside despairingly at the sodden garden, "it was supposed to look so pretty and it's all just, well, yuck, miserable."

Sally hugged her close and said, "Well, as Mum always says, the weather is the one thing we can do nothing about but have a look at this..." she tapped the screen of her phone bringing up the weather app, tapping a few more times then passed it across to Ruth. Ruth looked quickly at the kind of graph showing black clouds and stair rod rain from 1am to 10am, it seemed, then fading miraculously into cloudless blue skies by just after 12 midday in that area.

"Don't believe it," Ruth said flatly but chuckling a bit as it was well known how Sally, the glass half full girl, loved that weather app.

"Oh yes, I've just remembered, this is Paul's present to you. He said he'd prefer you to open it now when it is just us coz he's a bit embarrassed about it – he needn't be, I think it's great," she said excitedly, "Mark won't mind if you open it now."

They sat at the kitchen table and Sally poured the coffee while Ruth turned the envelope over wonderingly. Inside was a handwritten card decorated at the edges with various types of electric light pictures from catalogues and this is what it said:

To Ruth and Mark

As a wedding gift

Consultation on Revamp of Lighting throughout

Supply of all materials

Completion of all work

In return for a glowing (ha ha) testimonial in my portfolio.

Oh, Sal... it's... it's just a wonderful present. Brilliant – whoops, pun by accident." But Ruth was so touched by this present and she relished the idea of that personal touch, somebody taking a real interest in how the lighting would work and making sure any ultra-modern approach would complement the older house rather than fight with it. She was worried though about the generosity of it in terms of time and money.

"Don't be, Ruthie, honestly." Sally was reassuring as she sipped her coffee cupping her hands round the steaming mug. "He has to spend the time for his course anyway, he loves that consultancy side as well as the actual doing, and the money... well to be honest he can get materials at cost price or trade price or something – special rate for apprentices on the course. I know it's fine, I really do otherwise he wouldn't have offered, honestly." She gave Ruth a quick hug. "Just enjoy it, Ruthie."

Ruth turned to look out of the window as she noticed a car pulling up – Anne and Bob and the children.

Ruth's dress was simplicity itself and as she stepped outside gingerly, worrying about mud splashes, the bright, strong, late May sun suddenly appeared and the effect was instantly nothing short of stunning. The wet grass glistered, deeply green (you could almost hear it growing) and with the rain drops so soon to be taken up once more into the atmosphere, Ruth suddenly remembered the book about water on earth that Matthew had so loved when she'd first got him home all those months ago and the page with just 'PITTER PATTER!' on it in very large letters.

The sun was warm on her face as she went to show them where best to park today.

"Oh, darling, my lucky, lucky son… you look just gorgeous." Anne took her face in her hands and kissed her lovingly and naturally. Ruth loved the easy, affectionate way she always called her 'darling'; she called all her children 'darling' with just the same loving ease, no affectation. All part of that belonging, that tumbling into the warm embrace of Mark's family, Ruth often reflected, holding the thoughts close, clutching them tight so aware was she of the outer darkness, "th'encircling gloom",[32] as she thought of it. Bob gave her a light kiss on the cheek; he was to give her away to his own son though of course she was not his, or anybody's for that matter, to give to anyone; it just felt nicely traditional so they all went along with it.

Jane and Tim were the next to arrive in their people-carrier with all the excited children tumbling out, running forwards along the familiar garden path then all stopping suddenly as they caught sight of Ruth. Matthew and Emmie hung back staring, then Matthew took Emmie's hand and said, "Come on it's Mummy – she's a princess!"

Ruth was overjoyed to see them both and bent down to hug them with Jane watching closely ever ready to protect The Dress from whatever havoc the small children might wreak. But all was well, as it turned out.

"Where's Daddy?" asked Emmie reasonably enough, looking round.

"Oh, we'll be seeing him at the church, sweetie, very soon now, he'll be standing at the front and he can't wait to see you properly after the wedding ceremony."

"I like this cenoromy," said Emmie happily, "I'm a bridesmaid."

"You're my bridesmaid, darling," said Ruth putting an arm round her little shoulders as they walked towards the long-established, rose garden, crisscrossed with the mellow brick path, for some preliminary, informal photos. This part of her grandmother's house, now hers of course, was so familiar to the child Ruth, that once lost child, cast into outer darkness, now moving into ever brightening, healing light.

---

[32] John Henry Newman (1833) *Lead Kindly Light Amid Th'encircling Gloom.* Hymn published in 1033 Hymnals

Anne was admiring some just appearing dark pink rosebuds when she suddenly looked thoughtfully at Ruth. "What do you think about putting just a few of these in your beautiful hair, darling? I think they would look lovely, so pretty and natural and well, seasonal, I suppose. What do you think, Jane?" Ruth had still not been able to decide quite what to do about her hair which fell in a lovely natural wave and was a rich, dark brunette, thick and lustrous.

"There. Perfect," as she and Jane skilfully slipped some in. And so they were, even subsequently warranting a mention, in reverent tones, in the brief write up of the wedding in the small, local, free distribution, magazine, *Just Thames Lacey:*

The bride, Ruth Forster, granddaughter of the late Marianne Forster, wore fresh rosebuds in her hair and the bridesmaids carried small posies of garden wildflowers.

As if ordered from some top, specialist florist, Ruth grinned to herself, when she read this much later, on return from honeymoon.

Ruth turned now towards the shouts of the four cousins as they ran down towards the ranks of bluebells which grew along the raised bank at the end of the garden, evoking a haze of purplish blue like a fairy glade. The rain had stopped so recently that the whole vista was glistening slightly, subtly, like the silver lining every cloud has, Ruth thought to herself, as she put her hand up to feel the tiny rosebuds nestling in her hair. But this went so, so far beyond that of course. Her life leading up to this had been more than a cloud, this was way, way more than just a silver lining; it was a deep renewal, rebirth, profound and wholly redemptive.

Ruth watched the children laughing and running; it was all too real to be fey, though there they were collecting wildflowers, dancing around in a fairy glade, dressed like little creatures of the sun-filled meadows. She thought suddenly of the poor outcomes for the LAC's she had read about recently, those so-called 'looked after children' into which pit both Matthew and Emmie could so easily have been tipped. She had seen another horrifying statistic quoted in the press only last week about the number of these so-called LAC's who went missing each year and were literally just forgotten about by the councils looking after them – the article said this even included 19, *nineteen,* babies and a phenomenal percentage of children aged 4 to 7... She glanced again, almost involuntarily, at her little Matthew, shaking herself free of the thoughts, physically propelling herself forward, as it were, into this joyful day.

They had decided just to walk the hundred yards or so to the church with careful explanations to all the children to keep together. Luke was driving Mark to the church in true best man fashion. Ruth realised they had not even thought about what they would have done if it had been raining – if wet under large umbrellas, she supposed; she knew Tim, at least, had a large golfing one.

~ *Chapter 31* ~

Time out of mind, as Ruth was to think of it later, much later. By this time more was known, known by many and, in the case of the children, they were of course to come to know more than they at first understood, like James' Maisie, like so many children, in fact.

Their ten days on Crete passed in a gentle, hedonistic whirl. Early May, the sea was a piercing, sparkling blue and just like iced champagne as you plunged in; it literally stole your breath. Unlike the home shores though you came out onto baking hot, white sand and got warm and dry in no time. Their hotel room was called 'bungalow style' in the brochure; this meant that there was not only delicious privacy but also their own, well-trod path to the beach, again that phrase, Ruth thought to herself, *their* beach as they immediately thought of it.

All the comforts of the hotel were about five minutes' walk away but there was none of the enclosed hotel corridor feel and, certainly in UK hotels at least, rather fusty carpets. Instead their 'room' consisted of a sitting area with a very well set up little kitchen divided off by a substantial breakfast bar, bunk beds which let down from the wall, a double sofa bed, a small double bedroom, really only big enough for the bed, and a small, but lovely, bathroom with shower and bath.

Catering was as easy as the day was long and the days *were* long at that time of year. Lunches were simple cold cuts, and salad, cheeses, yoghurt, fruit all readily bought from the tiny grocery shop strategically placed near the hotel and clearly doing a roaring trade in all holiday necessaries. It was run by an enormous Cretan man, smiling and efficient who played tricks on Matthew and Emmie such as producing a coin from behind one of their ears. They loved it. Ruth had an initial worry that they might run screaming, as Emmie had always done from clowns but no, the grounded reality of the friendly grocer and his shop stuffed full of homely objects was in itself deeply reassuring.

In the evenings they could either have a meal in the hotel, in the nearby taverna, *Nico's,* or cook at 'home'. Even that had novelty as they got to grips with the tiny cooker and rustled up simple pasta dishes on two or three occasions, other times indulging themselves by eating out. It was a very special time for all of them after all... *after all they had all been through* Ruth thought to herself, and she frequently used that justifying phrase for any extra treats during this special week.

The children slept like logs every night, loving the novelty of the bunk beds, loving knowing that Ruth and Mark were with them, either just out on the little veranda which led off the sitting area through French windows wide open to the evening air, or in the sitting area itself. They woke early though as small children do, and Mark took to going for an early morning run on the beach whilst Ruth snuggled as long as she could in bed with the two of them, reading stories from the small selection of books they had brought with them. Mark would bring her tea on his return, juice for the children, and they were all up and dressed by 8.30 at the very latest so none of the day was ever 'wasted'. These were precious times.

They shared a beautiful, figure of eight shaped, aqua blue pool with about half a dozen similar bungalow style rooms. They used the pool mostly to cool off in on return from the beach. As the children were still so young they decided only to inflict one sight-seeing trip on them – to Knossos. Matthew was genuinely fascinated by the ruin, trying in his mind to imagine so many years passing and daily life taking place all that time ago. Emmie was simply and contentedly absorbed by the lizards scurrying behind rocks as they approached. They all enjoyed the taverna lunch thrown in with some token dancing on tables and plate smashing – Emmie's and Matthew's eyes like saucers during this – but were equally delighted to return 'home' to their haven and plunge into the pool for a cool off.

Both children could now swim unaided but Mark and Ruth had, of course, hammered home to them both the safety messages about never going in the pool or the sea without one of them, and not ducking each other. They had explained about sea currents and tides and rip tides doing strange things, they had explained about swimming pool filters, empty swimming pools, cramps; in fact any tragic reporting of a child's drowning was relayed to the children carefully not so as to frighten them, but in the knowledge that forewarned is forearmed. It was only May but, as ever, the summer to come would bring forth such tragedies – August being a wicked month indeed.

Mark found himself in his own rewind mode during his rare quiet moments alone, mostly his runs, and his shopping trips for essentials which he sometimes did on his own when the children were happily absorbed, often in the pool, returning to join them there for a game of beach ball catch and swim rides for Emmie on his back. He returned triumphantly one day from one such trip with a couple of lilos, "for pool use only" he explained in no uncertain terms, explaining about winds and currents again.

This holiday gave him pause enough to reflect on the tumultuous last few years with Meg, Emmie's birth, the case against him, the battle to rescue Emmie before her entire childhood was stolen, his finding Ruth and Matthew on the beach, their growing friendship, love, his new job, the court case for care and custody, Meg's death, his new family, the wedding, – all passed through his mind in a kind of slow motion blurry vision of tortured nights and highly pressured days, causing him to hold tightly onto this present joy. His two main confidantes, apart from Ruth, were his sister, Jane, and his friend Luke, the latter mostly in brief text exchanges, along the lines of:

All good with you mate?

All good. You?

Fine. Pub when you're home? Squash?

Yep. Both. We'll sort out an evening, midweek best for me. You?

Fine. Let me know. Honeymoon on. ☺ ☺ ☺

Cheers. No emoji!

Jane had borne witness to Mark's unhappiness from childhood onwards, from the loss of a much-loved family dog, run over by a speeding driver during a summer walk one August (hit and run), to the bullying and casual cruelty suffered at school, shared with no other family member, considered to be part of boys' boarding school life, to his first tentative relationships, his difficulties with Meg, Emmie's birth and the aftermath, the case against him, and his finding of Ruth and Matthew. Now they occasionally exchanged friendly, solicitous emails each of them ensuring the other's current well-being.

Jane's journey, whilst knowing her own loneliness at times, had been far less tumultuous than Mark's, and she was able to provide comfort and reassurance in her unconditional love for him and little Emmie, now drawing Ruth into this enclosing yet widening circle of strength. He felt a physical opening up towards all those closest to him in the bright, warm, Cretan sun though at times he felt this new-found happiness to be suspended on gossamer thread much as a carefully constructed cobweb, built to entrap nourishment, will catch the dew, the sunlight, withstand summer breezes, shimmer beautifully, yet be destroyed by a single wanton act.

As the languid days proceeded at their own 'sweet nothings' pace, Ruth was put vaguely in mind of the "silken girls bringing sherbet" of Eliot's *Journey of the Magi,*[33] probably only because of the eastern feel of Crete and the association of ideas with 'summer palaces on slopes'. But for them it was not 'silken girls bringing sherbet'; instead old ladies on donkeys bringing lemons, nothing to do, she felt then, with thoughts of a birth and a death.

There were two of them who passed their way unhurriedly every mid-morning, the same patient donkey plodding along, loaded with panniers strung either side of his sturdy body. The deep lines of the cross on his face seemed a more subtle echo of the lines etched by sharp sunlight and hard work out in the open on the two women's faces. These were always now creased into wide smiles revealing several black and broken teeth as they spotted the little family especially the little children. They bought lemons from them every day which Ruth made into big jugs of lemonade, flavoured with the mint growing alongside their path to the beach, and the children were not fazed by the women touching their soft cheeks and clucking maternally, allowing them to stroke the donkey's soft nose.

Ruth and Mark, to their shame, had scarcely any Greek between them, apart from *efharisto, kalimera, kalispera, ne, ohi,* but they were able to ascertain that the two women were sisters and had ten children between them, now grown up… some in Athens. It was not quite possible to understand their grandchildren status; Ruth tried pointing at Matthew and Emmie then at the women but that only produced wild giggles and more stroking of the children's hair.

In the evenings Ruth and Mark would usually sit together on the veranda, once the children were asleep, supping either a gentle fruit punch concocted from a little rum, angostura bitters, peaches and pineapple, these last two also sold by the women with the donkey, or fresh lemonade made with soda water.

Once again, Ruth feeling the need to tell her story, looking from the outside in as it were, felt they resembled Lorenzo and Jessica during their beautiful, lyrical 'in such a night' exchange. [34]

There was a renewed sense of promise, of new beginnings as they sat close,

---

[33] T S Eliot: (1927) *Journey of the Magi,* Faber and Gwyer, London, UK
[34] William Shakespeare: (c 1598)*The Merchant of Venice,* Act 5, Sc 1

touching hands and arms, watching the darting stabs of dragonflies lighting up the velvety dark night sky competing with the flickering electric light of human habitation reassuringly visible around them. Mark had a gentle way of rhythmically stroking Ruth's lower arm where the skin was particularly soft, unsullied, from wrist to elbow crease. It was both soothing and intensely erotic. 'In such a night' they could, and did, make love, actually on every single night of their holiday, truth be told.

Of course it all had to end, they all knew that. Anne had counselled both Mark and Ruth quietly on their wedding day, "Just really enjoy this day and your honeymoon, darlings because we all know as your Grandmother Dawson's daily help used to say, Mark: 'Life gets daily don't it?'"

~ *Chapter 32* ~

The journey home, as it turned out, had been the only downside of the holiday. They had booked a very early flight because their dates were so constrained they had had no choice. Anyway, Ruth had shared her grandmother's philosophy regarding early morning starts with her new family: "Once you're up, you're up". They all liked that approach, Matthew and Emmie, probably, it's true, for its nonsensical sound, rather than for the reality of it at this stage in their young lives.

Aspects of that day were to remain with Ruth for many years to come; perhaps too with Mark, Matthew and Emmie, but only they would know that and only they could tell if they chose to and each would, of course, have their own ways of processing such events, such knowledge, such awareness of ever present threat.

For Ruth though it was the abrupt intrusion of unexpected terror into the elemental beauty of the Cretan dawn during the early trip to the airport that stayed with her. Dawn, full of promise and hope, by definition fleeting yet lingering long enough to have evoked for her visions of ancient gods still striding the hills, languorously, yet purposefully, lighting the hill tops with their fiery touch, ethereal, seductive yet strangely threatening.

This was succeeded first by the gradual appearance of the somehow more worldly beneficence of the whitish, gold sunrise, no less beautiful for its worldliness, and reassuring in its ability, very gently, to dispel the mysterious, brooding light of dawn. The emerging sun warmed the earth once more in its diurnal cycle of renewal, once more filled the day with a surer promise, a stronger hope.

This though was short-lived, shattered to pieces suddenly by the very incarnation of brash worldliness. Ruth would never forget it. The taxi driver was driving fast, cheerfully and erratically along narrow roads riven with potholes, wrenching the steering wheel this way and that, twisting and turning in order to navigate the frequent tortuous bends. But it was not this which produced the terror; it was instead the sudden screeching to a halt as they came across a very rackety-looking single decker bus, strewn right across the road, its front and back wheels straddling a particularly sharp hair pin bend above a steep rocky cliff overlooking a tiny, inaccessible bay, dark, forbidding. No sunlight would ever enter here such was the angle of the overhanging rocks.

This was no accident though. This was a deliberate road blockade by a large group of British tourists, many in rough approximation of clowns' disguise, some with crudely painted red noses, some wearing plastic red noses, some in striped trousers, some in wigs, some with painted arched eyebrows and rakishly applied bright red lipstick, most obviously drunk, shouting, swearing and gesticulating at the occupants of two, much smarter, well-maintained coaches. These were brightly painted, shiny-clean vintage charabancs conveying troupes of real clowns to a much publicised Clowns' Convention.

Ruth and Mark had seen the posters advertising the show which was to open in Heraklion then move to venues around the tourist resorts on the coast. The idea was a deliberate attempt to showcase clown folklore and tradition in as non-threatening a way as possible with a view to promoting alternative cultural heritages and traditions going back centuries in an educational and fun way. The British tourists, in a mindless attack on those following a different way of life – "it was just meant to be a bit of banter" – one of the less inebriated explained to Ruth, shrugging his shoulders – had caused some serious injuries to some of the real clowns during this violent confrontation. They had, too, caused some very expensive damage to both the lovingly restored, vintage vehicles belonging to the real clowns.

Emmie was rigid with fear in the car, holding her arms out towards Mark, sitting in the passenger seat in front of her, whilst Ruth tried to comfort her, stroking her cheek, as Matthew stared straight ahead, eyes wide with terror. The police presence was strong forceful and itself frightening. Scores of them, it seemed, boarded the bus, shouting, clearly armed with guns, and rough-handled the British tourists down the steps, lining them up, arresting the most drunk and abusive, handcuffing them unceremoniously and bundling them into the waiting police vehicles with blacked out windows. It was 40 minutes before the bus was moved by its terrified Cretan driver and the Clowns' Convention vehicles continued with stately progress in their dignified way.

Mark looked at their taxi driver, whose face was set rigid, proud, and somehow scornful of these antics. Sign language combined with subconscious body language between the two men sitting in front spoke volumes: incredulity, disdain and relief to be on their way were the most obvious of these.

The early start, they had had to leave their 'bungalow' at 3.30am to get to the airport in time for a 4.30am check in, even though they had already checked in online, followed by this disruption and subsequent hanging around in the airport, was then further impacted by a delay to their flight. The aircraft had developed a fault; no details were supplied to the waiting passengers, understandably enough perhaps, and most were thankful to wait for a fault-free aircraft to be allocated to them. This situation, though, was exacerbated, made almost immediately ghastly actually, frighteningly quickly, by the fact that the airport catering staff were out on a one day strike and had not replenished the vending machines.

So it was that with an air temperature which had reached 32 degrees Celsius by 9.30am, the waiting, checked-in passengers, corralled, unable to leave the building to replenish stocks of food and water, became seriously 'uncomfortable' as the euphemism had it. Small children and babies had been crying and fretful, parents were indignant, anxious and, in some cases, obviously frightened by these conditions which seemed to have arisen out of a clear blue sky, quite literally.

Mark and Ruth retained their calmness for Matthew's and Emmie's sake. The two children were still mostly silent, eerily subdued, following the ordeal of the drive to the airport, as their parents read stories to them and played paper games: noughts and crosses, hangman, stone/paper/scissors and the like. They had long since finished their small supply of bottled water. Thoughts of *Lord of the Flies* and *Life of Pi* invaded Ruth's apparent calmness even as she folded paper with apparent absorption to make a fortune-teller each for Matthew and Emmie. She remembered all this so vividly afterwards.

Matthew, at length, looking for different distractions, wandered across to a multi-tiered, revolving glass display carousel in a little boutique which proclaimed itself in mock ancient Greek script above the door, to be selling 'Duty-Free Souvenirs from Crete'. He was watching a group of *Murano* glass clowns (*very Cretan* Ruth thought to herself, following his gaze) as they circled slowly, relentlessly, as if demented, trapped in this cyclical, inescapable entertainment for tourists, in a grotesque mime of the tourists' own current imprisonment, dizzying, mesmerising and strangely disquieting – *as clowns are of course,* thought Ruth, again to herself.

This particular set, though, in their garish glass colours, their cavorting, twisted bodies a cruel echo of some inner turmoil, or, at the least, of a struggle with some unseen demonic presence it seemed, twisted and turned madly and maddeningly. Demons, demented. Their painted, tortured, grimacing faces put Ruth in mind suddenly of the Italian glass workers amongst the fiery furnaces strangulating the molten glass into these harsh, twisted images as a cathartic response perhaps to their own enclosed working conditions so tightly regulated, trade secrets closely guarded. The workers found themselves thus forever trapped on the island by the very success of their craft much as these clowns were forever trapped on this dizzying carousel, much as the homeward bound tourists were trapped in this sweltering enclosure – the Departures Lounge so called, suddenly a prison, no less.

For Ruth now the instantaneous association with tragi-comedic enterprise, again out of a clear blue sky, echoing the irony of this hideous glass product being so coveted by so many for so long, served only to perpetuate the irony, the unfairness of the workers' situation in this never-ending re-enactment of tragic farce. And how exactly Matthew's pose now so obviously recalled her first sighting of him went without saying, so much so that it seemed writ somehow, preordained; this thought was, of course, far too disturbing to dwell on.

Mark began to pace the length of the Departures Lounge which further unsettled Ruth; his restless strides seemed to echo the tumult of her feelings as she watched Matthew quietly. Mark, the hunter-gatherer, soon returned to them proudly and productively though with two small paper cups of water for the children.

"It didn't *say* it wasn't drinking water," he explained to Ruth, "and look at Emmie, her lips are actually cracking." He felt her forehead. "She feels burning hot." He looked at Ruth anxiously. Ruth realised simultaneously that the *Calpol* was in the luggage waiting to go in the hold and that there was no pharmacy in the small Departures Lounge. She tried to quell her growing panic by going to the toilet where she too drank from the tepid, slow drizzle of water which emerged from the cold tap. She quite suddenly imagined herself smashing the wretched clown figures in imitation of Harold Fry, distressed, distraught. [35] She would in this way protect Matthew from all memories, all dark thoughts but she it would be who would take responsibility, there would be no tragic Queenie figure to carry the can and suffer the appalling consequences. [36] Those were to be hers and hers alone.

When she returned, Emmie had fallen asleep on Mark's lap, and Matthew who had gone into listless, suffering child mode was sitting still rigidly as one who has once known to wait in silence, it seemed. She sat down quietly and he leant against her, ever trusting, something to be thankful for at least, Ruth felt.

From time to time crackling, almost inaudible announcements were supplied, first in rapid Greek, followed by faltering French, followed by even more hesitant English. These were under-confident predictions as to how much longer it would be for the aircraft to be ready, and half-hearted, rather defeated sounding apologies for the lack of food and drink, with: 'It is matter which is out of our control' being translated into 'It is matter which has escaped from our hands'. This caused Mark and Ruth to catch each other's eye but both took care not to laugh openly at this brave attempt knowing that in UK airports announcements would most probably be in English only, the like it or lump it approach.

Thus it was that they spent their last morning on Cretan soil, determined not to let these experiences taint the memory of their holiday idyll, before they finally boarded their aircraft at 2.30pm whereupon the captain announced that the food ready for the flight would be distributed to them before take-off. They had to wait for a take-off slot anyway and this might only delay them for another forty minutes or so during which time they would be looked after, he explained. Ruth was struck by his caring, professional tone and felt herself and her little family to be at last in safe, competent hands.

Emmie perked up considerably after she had eaten her meal, enjoying inspecting all the little packets and asking Matthew how to open them. Matthew, solicitous as ever towards her, helped her carefully. Ruth felt a huge sense of relief that they were now on their way home; Emmie seemed to be feeling better so Ruth and Mark could sit and relax for the flight. Shortly after take-off both children fell into the deep, abandonment of childhood sleep – 'the land of baby nod', as Ruth called it. She leant against Mark's shoulder and in turn abandoned herself to deep relaxation, stroking the back of his hand in soothing acknowledgement of their immediate troubles being over.

---

[35] Rachel Joyce: (2012) *The Unlikely Pilgrimage of Harold Fry*, Penguin, UK
[36] Rachel Joyce: (2013) *The Love Song of Miss Queenie Hennessy*, Black Swan, UK

They finally found themselves on their own front doorstep at 9pm, *tired but happy*, as Ruth again put it to herself. Sally and Paul had a salad supper ready for them, and were keen to hear about the holiday and show them the new lights. Ruth revelled in the subtlety of the scheme which revealed itself only gradually as twilight slowly slunk in, almost apologetically, after the children were in bed at the end of the bright, long summer's day, the first in June. Sally and Paul left just before midnight – thankfully they all had the next day – Sunday – to unpack and recover from the journey a bit before school/work started on the Monday.

Back on home turf with the last half of the summer term approaching there was not so much a sense of post-holiday renewal, more a sense of the honeymoon having been something other, magical, special and an appetiser for the long summer holidays ahead of them, to be spent at home, relishing all the best aspects of English summer days to come as a newly formed complete little family.

~ *Chapter 33* ~

In the event it was Melanie, with her own new-born daughter, Amy, held close in a sling, at school pick up time in the playground, who first noticed that Emmie was still not quite herself a week on from their return from this idyllic holiday. Ruth berated herself long and hard that it was neither she nor Mark who spotted it first, especially she. This provoked neither hostility nor any strange distortion of jealousy towards her friend; she would be forever grateful that Melanie had cared enough, and known Emmie well enough, to spot this.

But this is what mothers should do, she thought, *notice, know their children so well that they can pick up the slightest change.* Emmie was not her biological child of course but that was no mitigation, nor should it be in Ruth's view. It was unassailable – she so nearly failed Emmie, absolutely failed her and for this reason she often found herself thinking back to the sequence of events during those first few tumultuous weeks following their return from honeymoon.

Uncharacteristically Ruth had had real difficulty summoning the energy to start the day on that first morning back, she remembered. She had felt leaden in body and spirit, as she put it to herself rather dramatically and wonderingly. Emmie, too, had seemed tired, and at times unreasonable, almost baby-like in her routine demands. Matthew, though, was clearly delighted to be home amongst familiar things and helped keep Emmie amused when he could on that Sunday.

Mark attended to lesson preparation for the next day, did a week's food shopping, cut the grass which Paul and Sally seemed not to have noticed growing – that was their only minor failing to be fair – whilst Ruth saw several washes through, sorted out the children's clothes for the next day, and cooked a roast dinner for them all.

Mark and Matthew tucked into this with gusto commenting on the deliciousness of home-cooked, English food once more, but Emmie was uncharacteristically fussy, eating only some of the runner beans and carrots, half a roast potato – which she usually loved – and none of the lamb beautifully carved by Mark. Ruth found the roast lamb disappointing too; it was difficult to explain why exactly. Everything on her plate seemed to taste of a dull sameness so that she could scarcely be bothered to eat; if she had needed to lose weight, which she didn't, this could really work, she thought to herself. "Obviously exhausted by yesterday," Ruth said to Mark. "We women have no stamina you see," she laughed lightly, as she cuddled up to him later on the sofa once Matthew and Emmie were asleep in bed.

The early start for work and school the next morning again required Ruth to dig deep to find her rapidly disappearing energy levels. Mark was up and out by shortly after 7 as usual. She packed the children's lunch boxes; Emmie liked to have her own lunch box to take to Sarah's; she would sometimes carry it importantly, with a pretend school bag like big brother Matthew. Ruth put them ready with their bags by the front door as Mark left with his usual quick kiss, then went to rouse both children.

Matthew, as small children do, awoke immediately and smiled at Ruth with excitement; he was looking forward to the first day back after half term with no qualms whatsoever. Emmie, on the other hand, was whimpery and fretful, complaining of a headache and a tummy ache.

"Oh, sweetheart, let's get you some *Calpol* and we'll take it gently. I'm afraid you're just too little to leave here on your own while I take Matthew to school even though I'd like to." She thought momentarily of ringing Melanie or Pauline and asking if one of them could call by to collect Matthew. She quickly dismissed the idea though as it was out of their way and would involve an unwanted car journey at very short notice for both of them, Melanie with new-born Amy in tow, on a route that was particularly traffic-filled at this time of day. Emmie would soon perk up, she felt, after *Calpol* and some breakfast, and she always enjoyed the walk to school.

Emmie barely touched her favourite cereal and just picked at the blackcurrant jam toast fingers which Ruth made for her. Ruth herself felt a touch queasy, as her grandmother used to say, and she thought fleetingly of the tepid water from the airport toilets they had all drunk so thankfully. *It's probably a bit of a bug*, she thought, watching Matthew tucking in in his usual absorbed way.

Ruth was pleased to catch up with her friends at the school gate. She had not seen Melanie, Pauline or Nicola since the wedding not to mention Amy's arrival on 30th May, and they all gathered to reminisce about the wedding day, admire Amy, check on Melanie's state of new motherhood, ask about the trip to Crete, chat about their own half term breaks and generally catch up. Ruth took the conscious decision not to regale the group with the terrors of their journey home; these she pushed decisively to the back of her mind, where the buried memories lie, she mused, determined neither to give thought nor voice to the end of that sentence: *'in wait'.*

Maureen Pinkerton came beetling over to greet the small group of friends beaming with delight and taking hold of both Ruth's hands telling her what an absolutely stunning sight she had been on her wedding day and just how lovely and happy the whole day had been. She enquired solicitously after Mark: how his new school was treating him, did he like the new head, and how their holiday in Crete had been, that sort of thing. She remembered too to peer in at little Amy: "You forget just how small they are when they first come out, don't you. How are you dear?" this to Melanie in her motherly tones.

"Well, you've really worn this one out, I see," she said, glancing down at Emmie who had fallen fast asleep in the buggy. "All this jet travel and excitement, I don't know," she chuckled. "You look quite worn out yourself, dear," she remarked glancing more closely at Ruth. "That's married life for you. I must go in, now… start the day, the term, no time to take a breath now until the summer holidays," and she scuttled off happily and with purpose to do just that.

"Are you going straight to Sarah's now?" asked Melanie, "or have you time for coffee and a bit more of a proper catch up?" Amy, at just three days old, was usefully transportable, requiring only feeding and changing, still sleeping for most of the time.

"Oh yes, we have actually, because Sarah has a hospital appointment and decided not to open until midday today to give herself a breathing space. That would be great."

With Emmie still sleeping in her buggy, and Amy still fast asleep in the sling, the two friends set off for Melanie's house once the bell had rung for the start of school. Matthew and Sam, it has to be said, had not given either of them a backward glance as they rushed off to do their own catching up which probably did not involve much discussion of the scenery in Crete.

Ruth decided to forego her usual coffee and opted for a cold lemon squash instead – coffee and tea had both tasted, well, odd really, since she got home.

Melanie too, tired out from sleep deprived nights and scarcely recovered from a very long labour, was full of quieter and more reflective memories of the wedding day. "You both just oozed happiness," she said, "I know that sounds cheesy. And Mark's family seem lovely. It was all so pretty too. Your granny would have loved it, wouldn't she?"

Ruth felt Melanie's genuine warmth and interest, envelop her like a comforting coat.

"How are things with you, anyway, Mel? How are nights? How's Sam finding it? And Jess and Liam? Richard coping? Gosh, parents of four."

Melanie laughed. Kids are all fine, so is Richard; it's just so discombobulating though isn't it? But Amy is such a little person already, that always amazes me, She is her own self...you see I'm not making sense still. Nights, hmm. Well, Amy goes down at about 11.30, wakes at 2, then 3.30 ish. But the 3.30 feed is weirdly special Ruth; it's just about getting light then. It's quite beautiful actually, sitting feeding her, watching the dawn come up. That's special but bloody exhausting to be honest," she laughed. "I then zonk out into one of those deep, after dawn, sleeps and when the alarm goes at 7 it's like coming up through a tunnel. Oh well, at least it's light and not freezing cold now. Trouble is she's fast asleep then and I have to get her up for the school run. Now look at her, all fasters, not a care in the world. She'll be waking soon, full of beans. It's all worth it though. The kids love cuddling her and this new baby time goes so quickly doesn't it?"

So comfortable did she feel in Melanie's company, and momentarily distracted as she was by her own searing memories of new motherhood that Ruth only just stopped herself in time from remarking that she wouldn't know would she. Instead she quickly substituted it with, "It does yes; it all seems such a blur now." That at least was true.

Emmie was beginning to stir, and Ruth asked if Melanie had any orange squash for her. While Melanie went to get the drink and check on Amy, Ruth sat quietly watching the little girl wake up, then unstrapped her and lifted her out.

"Ooh, you're hot again, sweetie." She glanced at her watch. It was only just over two hours since she had had the *Calpol*. Melanie returned with the orange squash in a mug in one hand and Amy held securely over her shoulder, her as yet unfocused gaze seemingly taking things in nonetheless. She looked wise, knowing yet, at the same time, unknowing, Ruth reflected, unable herself quite to make sense of this thought.

Emmie, however, was not to be won over by the sight of tiny baby Amy. She sat listlessly on Ruth's lap sipping the orange juice. Ruth told Melanie that she had a temperature and explained about the horrors of the airport food sellers' strike.

"She may have picked up a bug, I suppose, from the water which Mark fetched from the loos. It seemed an absolute life saver at the time."

"Poor kid, horrible to feel yuck and not really to be able to explain how and not to know that it'll pass; we've got all that to come with this one." Melanie turned to look lovingly at Amy who just then looked the absolute picture of health, still protected by Melanie's antibodies passed first through the placenta and then via the rich colostrum of her mother's milk. The fleeting nature of this protection seemed to Ruth symbolic of the abrupt expulsion into worldly dangers and threats, known as birth, which for her still held only terror, and tragedy, no joy.

"Mark and Matthew seem fine and I'm okay, but just 'not quite the thing', as Mim, my granny, used to say," Ruth laughed. "How's Richard taken to new fatherhood?"

"He's great, actually, just reverting to the old roles as if it was only yesterday. Brings me tea and a marmalade sandwich if he wakes at the dawn feed. Now that *is* a life saver, I can tell you. He's very competent with this incredible car seat we've got for her too. If she's asleep you don't have to hoik her out, it just lifts out and you can wheel her off. Brilliant invention, not around for Sam and Matthew were they, nor for Liam and Jess, come to that?"

"They weren't," said Ruth, once again on dangerous ground suddenly. She remembered Mark's collection of wheeling and carrying equipment for Emmie, leading her young life between her two parents; again a deeply unhappy, tormented memory.

"I don't think even Emmie had anything like that. I first met her when she was 20 months and Mark only had ordinary car seats and buggies, I seem to remember."

Emmie, by now, had climbed stiffly off Ruth's lap and was playing desultorily with a tower of coloured rings on Amy's baby rug. Amy, on her tummy, little legs kicking out behind her with excitement, was watching with interest. Emmie had devised a game whereby she slipped the rings quickly over the plinth to build the tower then upended it causing them to tumble down and make Amy seem to follow the bright colours. It was fun to watch. Emmie then amused Amy by pressing and whirling all the parts on a sort of baby mobile fairground toy, making a variety of squeaks, whistles, bleeps and rings. Amy jerked her limbs at the loud noise, her expression uncertain. Emmie soon tired of this though and asked to get back on Ruth's lap leaving Amy suddenly bereft resulting in a piercing new-born wail. Emmie put her hands over her ears and turned her face into Ruth's shoulder.

Melanie chuckled. "That's just how I feel when she squeals, Emmie darling," she muttered as she scooped up her baby for a nappy change.

Ruth asked Emmie if she wanted the toilet before they left – she was out of nappies most days now, only wearing them at night time. In the bathroom Emmie had a sudden distressing outburst of:

"Don't want to go to Sarah's, want to go home," which descended into heart-breaking, gulping sobs.

"You'll have a nice buggy ride to Sarah's, sweetheart, then you can cosy up on her big sofa and have one of her special freezies, which you love."

Sarah had introduced both of them to frozen yoghurts and they now kept their own supply in Sarah's freezer. This seemed to mollify Emmie a little.

"See you later then, Mel and you, you gorgeous thing," said Ruth stroking Amy's soft face. "You give your mummy some rest now won't you? I can collect Sam if you like this afternoon if it's any help, and bring him home or he can come to ours if that suits you?"

"That's kind of you, Ruth but we quite like the routine, getting out, you know how it is. I'll save that offer for a time of more desperate desperation," she laughed. "See you later. Hope you feel a bit better soon, Emmie love."

~ *Chapter 34* ~

Emmie rallied remarkably at Sarah's, as small children do. She enjoyed her lunch of crackers and cheese and baby tomatoes followed by her favourite flavoured freezie – strawberry – and played happily with the boxes and their bubble wrap as Ruth unpacked parcels and catalogued the arrivals, putting some on the shelves and some in the 'Orders to be Collected' section of the shop.

She and Sarah caught up on all their news happily; the hospital had given Sarah the all-clear that morning after a breast lump scare which had necessitated a further scan. Her daughter was visiting at the weekend and she had much enjoyed having Paul's help in Ruth's absence; the new lighting scheme really worked well. She had written a glowing testimonial for him.

So it was that Ruth and Emmie left at 3, in the midst of all this positivity, to collect Matthew, feeling light-hearted, pleased to be heading for home and looking forward to the evening when they would all be together again. Matthew ran out delighted to see them, full of his day and as affectionate as ever towards Emmie.

But little Emmie's improvement turned out to be short-lived. By tea time she was fretful and feverish again, complaining of a headache and tummy ache and not wanting to eat anything much. Mark was solicitous as far as it went but was distracted by the volume of work he needed to get through before the next day. Ruth herself felt leaden with tiredness again and neither did she have much appetite so had sympathy with Emmie.

"Gosh, Emmie, that journey home has knocked us girls for six hasn't it, sweetheart? Early night, I think. We'll soon feel better. I'll take you up now, Matthew you have another half hour or so as you're bursting with energy and it's so lovely having these light evenings. Mark might be able to fit in a quick kick about perhaps?" She looked at him enquiringly and a little beseechingly.

Mark needed no beseeching though.

"Great idea." He jumped up with alacrity. "Come on then, Mat, let's clear this lot and get out while the light's good."

Later, much later, Ruth's flashbacks to that first week back from holiday, like a video on rewind, were vividly to recall such light-hearted moments in those bright early June days interspersed with memories of her own plodding weariness. She saw herself stumbling through the days, bone weary, as her grandmother used to say, both she and Mark up with Emmie at night as the little girl's high fevers produced frightening, hallucinatory images impossible for her burning brain to process, and thus terrifying.

She would cover her ears theatrically when Ruth spoke softly and reassuringly to her, "Too loud, Mumma, too loud. Go away, you're all big, too big," she would say pushing at her. It was the same with Mark.

The video on rewind contained frequent flashes of the pretend and real clowns confrontation on the way to the airport, flashes too of her watching Matthew watching the *Murano* clowns in the airport; her watching Matthew, much younger, watching the swinging monkey; her watching Matthew's blood swirling in the rock pools. Was it Louise who had told her such images were associated with recovering from periods of acute stress?

"We must have picked something up in Crete," Ruth said to Mark, "some Cretan bug; perhaps that water from the airport. I'm feeling pretty yuck most of the time, but at least no temp. like poor Emmie."

Ruth felt they just had to ride it out, let it take its course but it was Melanie, the following Monday, who commented, "Ruthie, she looks terrible. Her skin looks like wax; she looks as if she's wasting away. She needs to see a doctor, honey, she really does. She's just not picking up."

Then it was that the chronology, to Ruth's instant alarm, suddenly added up; it hit her like a physical force it seemed; not only was Emmie not getting better, she was actually getting worse. She felt then that she had been so wrapped up in her own exhaustion, uncharacteristic as it was, her own need to struggle to get through the days, such an alien feeling to her, that she simply had not noticed Emmie's continued decline, and Mark had been guided by her, as mothers do so often guide in these circumstances.

She decided to try for a doctor's appointment as soon as she got home. She was told to bring Emmie in at 5 and the doctor would see her at the end of the day's booked appointments; there may be a bit of a wait, the receptionist warned: the doctors had been very busy all day she admonished Ruth, almost accusingly. She texted Mark quickly explaining and ensuring he would be home by 4.45 at the latest reflecting how natural it was for her to assume the responsibility for taking Emmie to the surgery, not her father. She worried too that the busy doctor would be tired and so keen to finish the day that he or she might overlook something.

As it happened she had no need to worry on that count. The doctor examined Emmie thoroughly and with touching tenderness, asking Ruth to repeat some aspects of the story of this illness. Things then moved very fast indeed. She was to bring Emmie in the next morning for a blood test, but the doctor also instigated a referral to a paediatrician that very evening. Due to her pallor and some breathlessness which he noted when looking at the rapid rise and fall of her tiny chest and then listening with a stethoscope, he believed Emmie could be severely anaemic, and anaemia, he explained, could be associated with many other conditions; therefore he felt an urgent paediatric referral was prudent. He was sorry he could not be more reassuring at this stage.

"Children often bounce back quickly from the more minor bugs but the length of time she has been unwell and probably getting rather worse as you describe, Mrs. Williams," he looked over the top of his glasses at her for what felt like a long time, "means this needs proper investigation." He ensured the surgery had mobile contacts for her and Mark as he thought the appointment would come through soon and he ruffled Emmie's hair,

"We need to get you some energy back don't we, sweetie pie?"

Ruth had a sudden, all too vivid recollection of her momentary loss of calm late last week when Emmie had set up a protest about getting into her car seat. She had clung onto Ruth sobbing, whining,

"It hurts, it hurts, Mumma, no, no, no," the wails rising rapidly to a crescendo of tantrum-like screams. Heads turned. Ruth had then basically man-handled the little girl, as she put it to herself, into the car seat, using more force than she had wanted to, with Emmie arching her back and kicking her legs out. She herself had felt fraught to breaking point, tense with a desperate tiredness, an evening of small children to face, she thought guiltily, everything to be done, until she could sink onto her own pillows. As she had slipped the car into gear and headed home with Emmie still sobbing, passers-by looking accusingly at her, or so she thought, Emmie fell into a defeated sleep.

Ruth had hated this realisation and actual manifestation of her physical power over this tiny child only knowing she had to get her home and knowing too that she had criminal – what was that word – propensities? She had 'previous', after all. She could not talk to Mark about this episode but it stayed with her disturbingly.

As she left the surgery with the familiar advice to keep treating the fever with *Calpol* as she had been doing, Ruth felt her earlier, somewhat paranoid, response to the doctor's reflecting on the progression of Emmie's illness – whatever it was – had been unfounded. She had at least done the right thing with the *Calpol*.

When they got home Ruth explained to Mark about the surgery trip to the doctor for the blood test the next morning, which she could easily factor into her day as Sarah was so understanding, accommodating and quite concerned herself by the change in Emmie. She described his thorough examination of Emmie, his mention of anaemia and that it could be a sign of many things therefore needed investigating, and the referral to the paediatrician. Mark seemed reassured that things seemed to be in hand; Ruth felt she could not share with him her fears that this could be something very serious. She had rescued him and Emmie, just as she had rescued Matthew, how could things not now be safe? How could she inflict such pain and uncertainty on Mark? Uneasily she felt the sands shifting beneath her feet.

~ *Chapter 35* ~

Things moved very quickly following this surgery visit. Ruth received a call to her mobile from the doctor they had seen the day before telling her that the paediatrician would see Emmie that afternoon at 3pm at the hospital; the preliminary blood results were through and they did indeed reveal that Emmie was severely anaemic. He explained that she needed to take Emmie to the children's outpatients department and that she would be directed to the right clinic area from there. Ruth arranged for Melanie to pick Matthew up and asked her to explain to him that she needed to take Emmie for another appointment; he and Sam would have a great time, Melanie reassured Ruth. She also rang Mark, suggesting he meet them there once lessons were finished, he would come on the train to save two lots of parking fees; they could pick the car up from school later.

Making these basic arrangements was comforting and Ruth longed for Mark to be with her to an extent that surprised her. Sarah was of course not just accommodating but deeply empathetic.

"Oh you poor darlings, what a worry it all is for you, just after your happy wedding. You and Emmie have your lunch now then set off. Would you like some of this soup I brought with me as it needs finishing up – I made it on Saturday – leek and potato? I've got a lovely new colouring book that Emmie might like to take with her while you wait – they're usually well set up there but it's my present to her anyway. Take these coloured pencils too."

"Mmm, yes please to both, Sarah, thanks. Hot soup is so comforting somehow…" Ruth had a sudden urge to weep without cease, to bury her face in Sarah's comforting, maternal bosom – that really was the only word that suited – and just to weep, to tell it all, to let it out. She could not do this of course because of Emmie but the urge was such that she quickly took herself off to the toilet and wept silently and desperately there for a good couple of minutes while Sarah set Emmie up with the colouring book and put the soup on to heat up. Ruth returned via the little kitchenette.

"I'll do this, Sarah and bring it through. I wonder if Emmie'll be tempted by some soup. I've got her favourite bowl with me."

Sarah glanced at Ruth and saw immediately that she had been crying. "Be strong, Ruth, you always are, I admire you so much, but just know I'm here for you, darling, and will do anything I can to help."

"Don't be nice to me, Sarah that will just undo me again." She smiled though and made some toast fingers to go with Emmie's soup, whilst defrosting rolls for her and Sarah. As she carefully placed the soup in front of Emmie, the little girl looked up at Ruth, and just stroked her recently wet cheek with her tiny fingers.

"Mumma all right?" she asked with a fearful look. "Mumma hurt?"

"No, darling, Mumma fine, but tired, that's all." She stroked Emmie's soft fringe back from her forehead a little and noted again that she had a fever, despite having had *Calpol* less than two hours earlier. By recent standards though Emmie tucked well into the soup and toast fingers and even had some cut up cheese and apple afterwards. It was as if she was growing used to being feverish, was beginning to tolerate it, a thought which worried and saddened Ruth a great deal, pleased though she was to see Emmie eating with some enjoyment.

The soup was just the thing for Ruth too; she had brought a hastily made ham and tomato sandwich with her but, looking at it now, it somehow just did not appeal. She was getting 'picky' she realised, which was not helpful and she must certainly hide this recent trend from the children, she thought to herself. Last thing they wanted or needed was for the children to pick up fussy fads about food.

She explained gently to Emmie about the hospital trip and that Daddy would meet them there so they would be able to hear what the doctor said together. After a short-lived protest that she had already been to the doctor and the blood lady, Emmie seemed to be interested in Ruth's description of there being lots of doctors and nurses and x ray people in a big, busy building and wanted to know if Matthew would be sharing this exciting sounding trip.

Arrival at the hospital, Surrey and Guildford, sparked an immediate, unwelcome, horrible memory for Ruth, which she quickly dismissed and paradoxically briefly relished the fact that she was a legitimate visitor on this occasion with no evil intent. On arrival at the children's department she was struck by the informal atmosphere of calm, competent solicitude and team work and felt her burden shift a little if not lighten exactly. Melanie had texted her a good luck and told her that she was cooking Matthew's favourite sausages for tea so not to hurry to pick him up.

To Ruth's relief Mark turned up just as they were called; he had left early realising he might otherwise miss the actual appointment leaving his class with two teaching assistants for the last lesson of the day.

And so it was that Mark and Ruth sat together to hear the softly spoken Scottish paediatrician confirm what were, for Ruth at least, her worst fears while a nurse who had skilfully managed to play peekaboo with Emmie in the waiting room as she recorded details from Ruth, took her off for another blood test with no protest.

"Well, I'm sorry to say, Mr. and Mrs. Williams that the most likely cause for Emily's anaemia is a form of childhood leukaemia – I expect you've heard of that." He paused taking in their stricken looks and their held breath.

"Now, I realise this is a shock but we don't yet know which type and it's true that treatments are improving all the time. I'll be referring her to the real experts, world class actually, who are fortunately just down the road at the main specialist cancer hospital, you know the one, in Croydon? The London and District Specialist Centre they call it. They'll need to admit her as an in-patient to confirm the diagnosis, pinpoint the type, and set up a treatment plan for her – obviously the quicker we get to this the better." Again he paused, looking at them both. "I expect you have some questions." He did not look away, or shuffle paper, or turn to his computer screen; he remained looking at them both with what could only be described as a kind of deep, unforced compassion and empathy.

Mark was squeezing Ruth's fingers so hard that they hurt. He turned to her not the doctor and said:

"Jesus, Ruthie, why *her,* why Emmie, what has *she* done to deserve her crap life? Sorry, sorry, sorry," he said now looking at the doctor.

The doctor inclined his head and gave them a sad smile: "I've heard much worse than that I can assure you."

Ruth asked what the treatments were and how different they would be depending on the type of leukaemia. The doctor provided a brief summary and explained that the anaemia needed correcting as a priority so that she had more strength to fight the disease itself, the current infection in her urine, and also to undergo the treatments. Ruth had an impression of blood transfusions, bone marrow transplants, compromised immunity, susceptibility to infection, strong drugs which came under the heading of chemotherapy – this was after all a blood cancer, the doctor had spelt that out in no uncertain terms, not to be cruel but to be clear. Mark held his head in both hands. At that moment the phone on the desk rang.

"Excuse me, I asked my secretary to let me know this: it's to do with Emily. Thank you, Carol, I'll tell them." He turned to Ruth and explained that there would be a bed for Emily at the Croydon hospital tomorrow on McKinley Ward. They needed to bring her in between 9 and 10 – whatever suited them.

"Emmie has an older brother doesn't she?" he asked. "I expect you'll want to get him to school first and make various arrangements. Parents can stay with their children. We'll send this scan result over now to the experts to interpret. I do realise how frightening this all is," he said gently, his kindness and understanding threatening to 'undo' Ruth once again, "but at least I can tell you that she'll be in the best possible hands. I'm sorry," he held both his hands out to his sides, palms open in a gesture of some sort of supplication it seemed.

"Regarding explaining the hospital stay to her, we find it's best to keep it very simple at this stage and definitely at this young age. Obviously try to hide your own fear and distress from her and concentrate on the small details like telling her that there'll be lots of children together, plenty of toys, nurses and such like. There's a good leaflet here," he handed it to them with something like helplessness again. "Once they've worked out the type of leukaemia it is they'll obviously be able to explain about the treatment and outcomes. It's the most common type of cancer in young children I'm afraid, but treatments are getting better and better all the time. In fact if people donated to childhood cancer research instead of donating toys... sorry," he interrupted himself, "you don't need that from me right now, but we do get more toys donated than we know what to do with... still, people want to help, I know."

"Thank you for explaining it all as far as you can," said Ruth quietly, as the nurse returned with Emmie proudly showing off her scan sticker but looking horribly and deathly pale in the harsh hospital light. The nurse stayed with them whilst they got Emmie into the buggy and offered to take them to a more private place where they could ask her any more questions, if they wished, away from the waiting room.

"Let's do that, Mark, while we think about what to do with ourselves this evening."

He nodded and took the buggy while Ruth walked just ahead with the nurse. The tea and biscuits were welcome but the reality was that the nurse could offer little more information given that the type of leukaemia was not yet known. She was able though to explain to them gently that the diagnosis would be made by doing a bone marrow puncture for which Emmie would be anaesthetised.

"We know she has far too many leucocytes in her blood – those are the white blood cells – just from the blood test and this procedure tells us what type of abnormal white cells these actually are." She glanced at Emmie who had fallen asleep during the trip to this private room and looked, like the other waiting room children, very unwell indeed.

~ *Chapter 36* ~

By the time they left the hospital it was 5.30 and the traffic was rush hour heavy, or crawl hour, as her grandmother used to call it. Ruth wished her grandmother was still alive for her wise comfort, for a shoulder to cry on, to lift the burden a little, to feel her unconditional love so instinctively passed down to Ruth who was now suffering as a mother does for her children in distress.

They went for a walk in Nonsuch Park with its calming, sweeping lawns, and secret wooded paths rather than going home or collecting Matthew. Melanie expected him for tea and he was probably having fun with Sam; such times were to be treasured and stored in readiness for the coming months, Ruth felt.

She decided to text her friend anyway though as she hated to leave people wondering; she believed this trait stemmed from her time living with her grandmother and she could never understand how her university friends could be so vague with their parents or friends or flatmates – but she had of course by then seen and known so much hurt.

We're just leaving the hospital but we're thinking of going for a walk in Nonsuch, the traffic's vile. Is all OK?

All fine, don't worry. Amy has two new super heroes in her life, they're sweet with her. How's things?

Not good. It's leukaemia – admitted to the cancer hospital in Croydon tomorrow to confirm which type – explain more when we see you. Obvs don't say anything in front of the boys – little pitchers and all that. We'll work out how to tell Matthew tonight. Sorry about the shock. See you later. Thanks for being you, Mel, having Mat and everything.

Oh hell. Take care of yourself Ruthie as well as everybody else. See you later honey xxx

The bright, early June sunshine with its promise of many more such sun-filled hours before twilight was in stark contrast to the all-pervading darkness that was currently Ruth and Mark's world. Who knew what the sleeping Emmie made of it all?

Mark drove with a fierce concentration. He had nodded numbly in response to Ruth's suggestion of this Nonsuch diversion; they always loved the walks there; it was not that far really from the hospital and on their way home. The rhododendrons and azaleas would be lining the wooded walk they all loved. Here Matthew and Emmie would usually race along the wide open meadows, or play roly-poly down the gentle hills where the land sloped enough. Ruth had consciously to halt these memories now. Emmie sat languidly in her buggy showing little interest in her surroundings and soon fell fast asleep as they walked.

Whilst they were there the traffic would die down a bit at least. Ruth *Googled* 'childhood leukaemia' on the way and discovered that the hope would be for Emmie to have acute lymphoblastic leukaemia (ALL) as opposed to acute myeloid leukaemia (AML), less common, about 80 children diagnosed with this each year in the UK, as opposed to approximately 400 with ALL. Emmie was at the most common age for the diagnosis but was thankfully just out of the poorer prognosis groups: younger toddlers, babies and, surprisingly, 10 to 14 year olds, tended to fare worse. Perhaps it was something to do with rate of growth; she had a layperson's vague understanding of cancer as cells growing fast, uncontrollably and abnormally. She presumed it was no different with blood cancers. And of course, they were just a step away from a world centre of excellence for cancer. *How long had Emmie been brewing it?* Ruth wondered. She thought back to the wedding and to Crete.

Had they been so wrapped up in their own lives moving forward that they had simply not noticed its stealthy onslaught? Mark was clearly fighting his own, similar demons. She put her hand gently on Mark's as he changed gear. They would face it of course but why should Emmie have to? There would be all the telling of family and friends, unloading the distress. They needed this time for the news to be theirs and theirs alone. How long to wait before irrevocably changing other people's lives too?

They took their favourite route and on this beautiful early evening the rhododendrons actually formed a scented, colourful tunnel, their bright blooms dispelling the darkness formed by the huge overhanging branches and their darkly green leaves. There was an air of promise and light in every direction.

Small groups of people were out enjoying the warm sunshine, ordinary routines put on hold as they frequently would be during the forthcoming summer months. Inhibitions would be loosened a little, time out and away planned, hopes of mellowness and relaxation, nature's reward for enduring the winds, rains, fogs, occasional snow and long hours of darkness for so many months.

Deciding to stop for a bite to eat at the pub on the edge of the park with a good children's area, they thought this would be something of a treat for Emmie as they could tempt her with things she usually loved like scampi and chips. It also delayed the inevitable homecoming and the need to make family contacts with this news. It was Anne's birthday on Sunday so that planned trip would be put on hold, or at least Mark would probably go with Matthew while Ruth held the fort at the hospital.

They started together to plan, to think. They planned the next day in detail now, deciding Ruth would take Matthew to school, Emmie had in any case been finding that something of an ordeal lately. Then they would both take Emmie to the hospital and be there with her and for each other whilst the diagnostic tests were performed. Mark knew he could not face his class of lively 9 year olds tomorrow and all that a normal full-on school day entailed. He would ring the head teacher, Joseph, when they got home. After this they would play it by ear. One of them would sleep at the hospital with Emmie each night; they would work it out and endeavour not to neglect Matthew.

Dear Melanie meanwhile had sent another text to Ruth asking if they would like her to have Matthew overnight so they could just concentrate on getting Emmie into hospital in the morning but they both felt strongly that they wanted to be a family at home that evening and night – for Emmie's last night at home – and they needed to explain it to Matthew as best they could. Melanie's text back indicated that she was not at all surprised by this and she would see them later.

Apart from Emmie staying in the car asleep with Mark while Ruth went to the house to collect Matthew all was as normal on the surface. Melanie and Ruth, in mutual but silent recognition that there was just too much to be told, to be gone into then, concentrated determinedly on practicalities, ensuring Matthew had his school bag, his PE kit, his football (which he had taken to school that day) and a pair of wet, muddy socks changed at Melanie's suggestion on arrival – he was wearing a pair of Sam's to go home in.

Matthew was full of news about his afternoon and evening at Sam's, how they had played endless rounds of penalty shoot outs in a goal they had constructed from some chicken wire which Melanie said they could use and how he had had two helpings of ice cream at tea time as well as being allowed to go out to the ice cream van in the street when it had called with its jingle jangle tune shortly after returning from school. Richard had joined in the football game with the two boys when he got home. Puffed out, he'd said it was no weather for football and had found an old cricket bat, small enough for the boys to use, and set up a 10 over cricket game with a tennis ball and only one fielder. Matthew carefully explained the rules of this improvised game.

"We'll play that when Sam comes round to ours, old chap," Mark responded, looking at Matthew in the rear view mirror. "We'll have some fun with that." Emmie slept on.

Ruth explained to Matthew that Emmie needed to go to hospital tomorrow to find out why she'd been feeling so poorly lately and to try to make her better as quickly as possible.

"Will she have an operation?" he asked with a worried frown. "Is she hurting?" Ruth explained it all as best she could and as usual he was asleep virtually as soon as his head touched the pillow.

Emmie had a feverish, restless night, and actually vomited small amounts onto her pillow without seemingly being aware of it. This so worried Mark and Ruth that they took her into their bed. Feeling her hot, restless body between them was more reassuring than worrying whether she would inhale her own vomit, though Ruth lay wakeful, remembering how she had thought to protect her baby close beside her in bed.

Neither of them slept much, in fact, and the feeling of being dog tired never left Ruth as she stumbled through the morning routine, being unreasonably sharp with Matthew when he struggled a little with his new skill of tying shoe laces. He looked briefly stricken with fear but as she knelt to help him and affectionately pushed her head gently into his tummy he stroked her hair gently twirling one of the curlier bits in his fingers as he liked to do.

"I love you, Mummy," he said quietly. "I love Emmie and Mark too and I love school and Sam's my best friend."

"That's all good then, isn't it, sweetie? I'll see you later at pick-up time and we'll see about going to see Emmie in hospital after a snack at home, shall we?"

And so began the dim, long, dark descent into serious childhood illness. The journey of Emmie's illness, with its twists and turns, its despair and hope, its shocks and moments of quiet calm, is too pitiful to relate in detail. Suffice it to say that Emmie herself entered that tunnel in innocence; she was, within that tunnel, that 'illness trajectory', as the professionals put it, to know much, much more than she at first understood, but that knowledge was not, as James noted, to defile her innocence in ways that are easily understood at first.[37] It was a stealthy taking.

---

[37] Henry James: (1897) *What Maisie Knew*, Heinemann, London, Stone, Chicago, Penguin/Random House

~ Chapter 37 ~

The key aspects need to be noted, that is enough, the facts, as the lawyers say. The first shock was that Emmie's leukaemia was of the rarer type with the rather worse prognosis – AML – acute myeloid leukaemia. This meant her bone marrow, the very core of her as Ruth thought of it, was filled with immature myeloid cells which stopped its vital function of making healthy blood cells. In their immaturity they did not know how to work properly, hence the anaemia, the susceptibility to infection and the reason for the bruising all over her body – a physical manifestation of hurt, of bleeding. The sub type of AML also put Emmie into a very high risk category in terms of survival, though her age, just over 2 and under 9 was slightly in her favour. This sub type was important to know as it determined the treatment protocol, as the nurses explained – she fell into one of the commoner sub types – M4 – acute myelomonocytic leukaemia. Though commoner, it is important to note that the better survival rates were not associated with this type.

The consultant oncologist's use of negative constructions in his sentences served paradoxically to soften the blows he rained down on them; needs must. He was gentle and compassionate just as the paediatrician in the local hospital had been. The treatment would be gruelling he explained having introduced himself to them as Dr. Onslow, one of the consultant paediatric oncologists, the person responsible for Emmie's care. The course of treatment though was, surprisingly, of shorter duration than that for ALL. The object was to get her into remission but, and the next shock, she would need to be in hospital for the whole six months of the treatment as she would be so vulnerable to infection and relapses and the treatment itself, mostly chemotherapy and steroid therapy, could make her very unwell whilst it did its damnedest – the ambiguity in that choice of word was not lost on either Ruth or Mark.

"Something you'll need to consider," Dr. Onslow explained, still gentle, "is whether you would like us to extract some eggs from her ovaries before treatment starts. These can be safely frozen for her as sadly the treatment does most often cause subsequent infertility."

This strangely gave Mark and Ruth instant hope, almost a feeling of elation as they said to each other later, for the obvious associations of new life, of Emmie surviving long enough to be a mother. They quickly agreed to it, having checked that it would cause only relatively minor discomfort and that Emmie would be sedated during the procedure. This would be done the next day as they planned to start treatment the day after that. She was to be put on a course of intravenous antibiotics, into the vein for maximum and quick effect, he explained, and given a blood transfusion following which she would probably briefly start to feel better before she got worse from the treatment. He was sorry to have to tell them that. Each child was different of course and it was impossible to predict outcomes at this stage but he had to emphasise to them that she was very, very seriously ill; he was sorry, again.

There was a lot of sorrow about it seemed. Some progress was being made with stem cell transplantation with this type of leukaemia he went on to explain gently. This was experimental but real strides had been made in some of the commoner types of leukaemia, for example, lymphoblastic. A good source of stem cells was cord blood, umbilical cord blood and the NHS did in fact run a cord blood bank but supplies were very limited, cord blood itself was very much a finite resource, like everything in the NHS of course. Any privately run firms were usually not used for altruistic donations of this sort, but for parents as a kind of insurance policy against their own child or children developing diseases as Emmie had done.

"Exploiting new parents' fears, I'm afraid and making a lot of money as a result. Perhaps you have some sympathy with that," he smiled sadly, "if you knew anyone who was pregnant, preferably fairly local and soon to give birth, especially a relative, this might help Emmie."

Mark and Ruth immediately thought of Sue, their sister-in-law. It was worth asking whether she and Simon would consider this, their second baby was due in about a week's time. It might be worth asking Melanie too if she had stored cord blood. Ruth thought she might have known if Mel had been planning to do this, but possibly not. She had been preoccupied in the lead up to the wedding, then the honeymoon of course and had missed her daily chats with her friend. Mark said he would talk to Simon about it first. It was certainly a ray of hope.

"So this would be Emmie's aunt by marriage?" the doctor asked. "That may be something as the cord contains maternal and foetal cells mixed and although a match does not need to be so exact with cord blood intuitively we feel that a closer match may have a better chance of success. We're well placed here as there's already an NHS cord blood bank set up at the S&G but we haven't found a remotely close match there for Emmie so far. Your GP very enterprisingly instigated that search the very evening he saw her, he knows of the good work they do there. There's no scientific evidence to support this point about close matches yet, but, as this is experimental, if the new mother was willing to donate we would have to enrol Emmie into a clinical trial. This could help others. Unfortunately, or maybe thankfully, it's difficult to recruit large numbers to the trial due to the rarity of her particular disease. But this is a multi-centre, international trial which is already underway, ethics approval all sorted some months ago, so that cuts out a lot of delay."

This all sounded positive, or, at the very least, a straw to clutch and hold on to tightly.

And so it was that the hospital ward and its surroundings, the newly built specialist centre full of deeply committed staff, second to none, it seemed, became their unsought after second home. Ruth and Mark often commented to each other that in the midst of all this sadness they felt surrounded by a form of simple goodness and dedication which of itself was life-affirming. Matthew visited most days, short, lively visits when Emmie was up to it. The affection between them remained strong and Matthew would often make little things for his sister: a card, a drawing, and a pipe cleaner doll called Pointy which she loved. Emmie quickly introduced Pointy to Stripey, saying firmly to them that they could play with each other if she was too tired. Ruth found this particularly heart-breaking and wondered how much it echoed her own recent, pathetic, sometimes impatient, responses to Emmie's demands since their return from honeymoon in Crete. Uncharacteristic as those responses were they now filled her with a renewed guilt which simply would not shift.

~ Chapter 38 ~

On the last day of June, only ten days after the longest day, Ruth woke to loudly splashing rain outside her window which she tended to leave open to the night air on these hot, mid-summer nights. She was alone as Mark was staying at the hospital. She lay listening to the rain wetly falling thinking suddenly of the water on earth book again which Matthew had loved so much. She imagined the large drops outside falling lazily, making the green leaves shiny dark; how he had loved the page with just **PITTER PATTER** written on it in huge letters. She thought of her sister-in-law, Sue – how formal and settled that sounded – Simon's wife – asking so many questions about the cord blood, asking almost suspiciously why she had not been told about this in her previous pregnancies. They explained the cost of collection could be prohibitive for the cash strapped NHS so it was not offered routinely and invited the couple to *Google* it for themselves.

Sue and Simon did this and agreed to donate this precious cord blood, a generous gesture, if Mark and Ruth would undertake to organise the collection of it by the S&G blood bank when the time came, when Sue's time came, as biblical texts put it. In the late stages of pregnancy with two other young children Sue felt she just could not cope with that aspect. Ruth leapt at the chance to help in this way – in any way – and had it set up following a brief phone call to the cord blood bank, in no time at all.

Emmie had been fairly well for a week after the blood transfusion and antibiotics, just as the consultant had predicted. The word remission had been briefly mentioned, whispered almost by the nurses, but she had since succumbed to a series of chest infections leaving her fighting to breathe at times and requiring enormous doses of different, stronger, rarer intravenous antibiotics into her tiny veins already made fragile by chemotherapy.

Ruth climbed out of bed slowly still fighting the leaden tiredness that had dogged her since returning from the Cretan idyll. "I am dog tired," she said to herself. She stood looking at Matthew's little boy-shaped dark head for a few moments before gently waking him for the morning routine, feeling the familiar protective, all-encompassing love for him. He beamed at her sleepily, and jumped up to look at the rain, an unfamiliar enough sight lately, laughing delightedly as he spotted an enormous, almost cartoon-like toad, sitting on the brick path grinning with joy it seemed as the refreshing drops continued to plop down languidly.

"He loves it, Mummy. I wish Emmie could see it now."

Ruth had taken to skipping her own breakfast as she seemed to have gone off all the usual breakfast fare. She did rely on a couple of cream crackers and hot lemon squash with honey though to stem any queasiness – the Crete bug, as she thought of it, was certainly in no hurry to leave her.

A text from Mark buzzed through.

Em's about the same. They've had to put a line in her neck for the drugs – about 11pm last night, poor kid. Sue's in labour and they're on their way to the S&G – main reason for this early text. You all right sweetie?

Yep, all fine. I suppose it may be quite quick as it's her second. Think I should get there to make sure all goes ok with the cord blood collection?

Yes, I do. Give the bank a ring too. Will Sarah be OK with that?

For sure. She's with us all the way.

Talk later. Give Mat a high five from me. Love you. Xxx

And you. Kiss Em for me. Lots for you. Xxx

Ruth realised that she suddenly relished the positive action to be taken; it gave her a surge of energy, rare enough, lately. She had been planning to go in to be with Emmie later.

They had in fact taken to leaving Emmie for short periods – there needed to be some sort of normality for all of them. Both their 'works' had been kindness, flexibility and understanding itself but neither of them wanted to abuse that flexibility knowing that they were in it for the long haul and would be likely to need time off at other times. Ruth was able to ask Paul to step in to replace her when Sarah wanted him to. As for the other times she simply insisted on not being paid. Mark was able to take a few days' carer leave here and there but it was definitely beneficial to all of them including Emmie, who, after all, was in very good, very caring hands, to have a break from the enclosed vigil-like hospital visits at times, much as they tried to make them feel as un-vigil-like as possible. Fortunately for Mark the long summer holiday approached and the last two days of term were training days which his helpful Head said he need not attend in the circumstances.

As for Ruth, she certainly felt surrounded by love and understanding from all sides. Her newly acquired family on Mark's side were all helpful in their different ways. Jane and Tim were practical, busy, visiting Emmie, suggesting lines of research, offering time out in the Angmering house whenever they felt they could get away. Sally and Paul had been stunned into a horrified but entirely empathetic, shocked silence and were sweet and generous with offering meals, bringing cooked leftovers for Ruth and Mark's freezer; real practical help which Ruth welcomed wholeheartedly. She was actually so off food herself that it was good for Mark and Matthew to have some delicious homemade food ready made for them, only needing to be heated through.

Simon and Sue too, with their own hands full, were, of course, helping in a very special way. Her own friends, Melanie and Pauline in particular, dear Sarah of course and, surprisingly, Maureen Pinkerton, all proved a valuable source of wise counsel and comfort. The head teacher was clearly very fond of both Ruth and Mark and would ask Ruth in sometimes for quick update chats at drop-off time in the morning, always attentive, always caring. Ruth frequently found herself to be talking through her tears on these occasions whilst Maureen listened quietly. She also asked them both for the odd meal at the weekend while Matthew would go to one of his aunts or to Melanie's for a play; it was clear how much mutual respect she and Mark had for each other and how much they enjoyed each other's company and that of her partner, Sheila, too.

And Anne and Bob in the midst of their own, almost uncomprehending, distress were just like two rocks, standing stoic against the storm and surge of nature at its cruellest. Ruth grew very close indeed to her parents-in-law and they in their turn took the motherless young woman close to their hearts.

Simon and Sue's baby girl, Josephine, arrived quickly as Ruth had predicted; a lovely cause for a family celebration. Ruth was at the hospital when Anne and Bob arrived and Mark had, on his way, already delivered their own welcome gifts to the new baby to their house. These were a suitcase full of scarcely worn baby girl clothes which he had lovingly bought for Emmie's visits to him but which her mother had despised for some unfathomable reason, hence their pristine state and the rather sad memories they invoked. They also gave them a voucher towards a family holiday at a *Center Parcs* of their choosing with two years in which to redeem it – specially designed as a gift for new parents; cunning marketing, Ruth noted.

The cord blood turned out to be a 42% match for Emmie, much stronger than any other, so that would form a part of the next phase of treatment once she was over this latest bout of infection. However, nature was busy sharpening yet another sheave of arrows it seemed. For, in the early hours of the morning, on their first night together since Emmie had been admitted, Mark and Ruth received a call to their landline – unusual these days – from the hospital saying Emmie had taken a turn for the worse and that they should come in.

Though they hated doing it, Mark and Ruth, stricken and scared, quickly decided to ring his parents first. Mark sobbed on the phone but managed to arrange for them to come over and be with Matthew to take him to school the next morning, whilst Ruth quickly sorted his clothes and school bag and wrote a note about breakfast preferences and timings. Mark would go ahead to the hospital, Ruth would wait for his parents to arrive and then join him there.

"Give us half an hour, 40 mins, love. Dad's already dressed. I don't take long. We'll explain it all to Matthew. He's such a sensible boy. I think you're right for him to carry on as normal. Be strong for each other and Emmie. We're with you all in spirit."

This time it really was a vigil. Emmie had been moved to an isolation room in Intensive Care and was being artificially ventilated on a breathing machine, in order to improve her oxygen levels. The latest chest infection was not responding to treatment, she was very weak. They had had to paralyse all her muscles artificially with muscle relaxant drugs to ensure she did not 'fight' the ventilator – that was to try to breathe against it – they explained, and sedate her heavily so she could better tolerate this otherwise terrifying experience.

Thus it was she appeared to them doll-like, unconscious, ready to succumb it seemed. Her hair had been washed and brushed by the intensive care nurses lovingly and skilfully looking after the little girl on a one to one basis. Again, this competent, loving, skilful environment was deeply reassuring at this time. They were encouraged to talk to her and touch her if they wished; it was possible, they were told, that she could hear and feel them beside her. They had induced this coma-like state artificially, she had not become unconscious on her own, they explained carefully. They were waiting for her lungs to start working better and in the meantime giving her vital organs a rest and this was the best way of encouraging that to happen. The doubt was plain to see in their faces and hear in their voices.

~ *Chapter 39* ~

But Emmie did indeed rally, she fought and was well enough to receive the cord blood by the third week in July just when all the school children and their teachers were preparing for their six week break, or longer for some, and her little first cousin, Josephine, named for Sue's grandmother but already known more often as Josie, had regained her birth weight as she was supposed to do, text book fashion, at two weeks and six days old. Ruth discovered that Josephine was from the Hebrew, Yōsēf, meaning to add or increase, a kind of plea or prayer implied in the name, 'may God add/increase' – appropriate, she felt.

A few days after this good news Melanie and Ruth were in Ruth's garden. It was the first day of the summer holidays, the paddling pool was out, Amy was on her rug, and Matthew and Sam were sploshing in and out with Liam egging them on from a safe, dry distance. Mark was at the hospital with Emmie; Ruth would take Matthew in at about 4 or so. Paul was covering for her for 2 weeks at Sarah's. He needed the money, as did she of course, but she also so, so needed to be with Matthew, just at home, taking stock, enjoying the summer as it stretched ahead in that seemingly endless golden haze of childhood summers, a summer that Emmie would not experience in this way. Precious time: her first proper summer with Matthew, now safely hers for a year.

At the end of the two weeks Mark and Ruth would box and cox childcare in their usual way with added help from Anne and Bob and Jane and Tim and their brood when they could. Ruth had picked up some freelance commissions which she worked on in the evenings when not at the hospital; in fact she could do some work there whilst Emmie slept or played with other children on the few occasions she was really well enough to do so.

She was by no means out of the woods yet, that was the hospital staff's well-worn phrase, but back on the children's ward and infection free at least for the time being. Sally and Paul were always happy to babysit in the evenings, there was Melanie and, to some extent, Pauline, but Sam and Matthew were such good friends that it became obvious that this was the arrangement which worked best with the added benefit of giving Melanie almost uninterrupted Amy time as the two boys were such good company for each other.

Ruth and Melanie were sitting on the rug, eating grapes and discussing Ruth's long-lasting 'Cretan bug'; the mood was light-hearted.

"Ruthie, I just can't believe it. Did it never occur to you? Good grief, you will send Emmie to me for those sessions won't you when the time comes – the birds and the bees, you know?" Melanie spluttered with laughter. Ruth sat silent now though, looking, Mel realised, under intense strain suddenly. The atmosphere had unaccountably darkened.

"*If* Emmie gets better and it is a really big if, Mel, as I thought you realised," her voice sounded harsh, strained, unnatural even to her own ears, "she'll be infertile, *infertile*, imagine that. So how can you sit there and laugh about teaching her the facts of life?"

Ruth was sobbing uncontrollably now, great gulping gasps. "I mean, we rescued Em from her horrible life, Mel, from those who hurt and injured her in so many ways every day and now look at her hurting. We brought her to this."

"Ruthie, Ruthie," Mel had her arms round her friend's rigid shoulders now, "I am so, so, so sorry. I am a complete idiot, crass fool… I wasn't thinking. But Emmie knows she's loved and cherished and cared for. She knows that deeply, Ruth, Emmie knows. It's not what Emmie knew, it's what she knows now that you need to hold onto."

At the same time as Melanie was trying hard to make amends for what she realised had been an insensitive comment and trying hard to suppress the thought that was uppermost in her mind, 'hormones', Ruth was trying to banish the unsolicited literary allusion, and thoughts of what Matthew had known once.[38]

Melanie's thought would serve only to belittle both Ruth's grief and Emmie's suffering somehow whilst Ruth's thought was just plain intrusive and maudlin really. Mel handed her friend a tissue, crumpled but clean. Amy was unusually still, stopped in her tracks by the adult grief and confusion surrounding her so suddenly, literally out of a clear blue sky, looking from one woman to the other, trying to work it all out.

"I'll be back in a sec., Mel, I don't want the boys to see me like this." Ruth

---

[38] Henry James: *What Maisie Knew*, Heinemann, London, Stone, Chicago, Penguin/Random House

smiled shakily. She returned looking better and carrying a large, floppy sun hat for herself and one of Emmie's for Amy, rather too big, which Amy immediately shook forward over her face determinedly. "That's clearly that then," said Ruth, laughing more normally now but rather uncertainly still.

"So when are you going to get a test, Ruth? Actually come to think of it I've got a spare box at home, still in date. Don't buy any. They are crazy expensive just for a little stick. I'll bring it over... tomorrow, or do you want to wait?" she asked suddenly more serious and solicitous now.

"I think I hardly need to do a test." Ruth gestured at her tingling breasts. "These are what I most remember being a tell-tale sign the first time round," she confided with perfect honesty. "And it would explain all the queasiness and tiredness, I suppose. Give it to me when I next see you. I kind of like the wondering," Ruth said quietly, hugging her knees with that slightly closed, secretive, somehow inner look that pregnant women have, "and I think I'd like to share that time of wondering with Mark."

"How would you feel if you *were* pregnant?" Melanie asked with interest. Unusually, she could not quite read Ruth at this moment.

"Undeserving," was Ruth's laconic answer.

Melanie looked at her closely, turned to look at Amy intently watching a patch of bright daisies on the grass, and then, rather bemused, asked,

"Why 'undeserving'? We all deserve happiness. Mark would be pleased wouldn't he?"

"Oh yes, we'd even actually talked about it, knowing the facts of life as we do," Ruth laughed lightly and much more normally now. "I don't quite know *what* I mean exactly to be honest, Mel. Maybe something to do with being happy and healthy and forward-looking when Emmie is so ill, in the midst of, and knowing, her own darknesses when we're not even there to try to explain them to her. They say even very young children who are very ill develop incredible insights into their own mortality and she's seen other children on the ward get worse and disappear and crying parents, hushed voices; it's horrible, Mel, I tell you. It's like a stealing of innocence every single day. I reckon she's worked out a lot of things. She knows that we know that she knows... kind of thing, you know? And she's so young still."

"Mmm, yes, I think I do." Melanie rescued Amy from rolling onto the stony path and took her to the edge of the paddling pool so that she could enjoy the dancing, shimmering water. The two boys were now in a hastily built, rather ramshackle, wigwam, Liam having by now joined his own friend, Ben, cycling up and down the quiet cul de sac, so Melanie slipped Amy's nappy off and sat her in the warm water without fear of the boys saying "Oh no, she'll wee everywhere or maybe…" rolling their eyes, pinching their nostrils and collapsing into giggles at the awful thought.

Ruth felt what could only be described as a rather clichéd pang at this innocent, albeit scatological, humour knowing that all too soon it would become less innocent, more salacious and they were only just 6 years old.

The Seven Ages of Man,[39] she thought suddenly, then needed to focus sharply on the matter in hand.

"Actually, Mel, I've just had an amazing idea. I just need to *Google* something quickly. Are you okay for a mo? It won't take long but it's a bit too bright for my screen out here. I need to do this. It feels urgent. Do you want me to bring you a coffee out when I come back?"

"Yes, please. I'll just lie in the sun and play with my bambino, bino, bino," she crooned to Amy as she lay on her back with Amy sprawling comfortably on her tummy, loving the upside down view, closeness and warm smell of her mother.

Ruth quickly put the coffee on to filter, hating the smell that she had once so loved, and just as she switched on her iPad, easier for googling, a text buzzed through to her phone.

Hi Ruth, it's Louise. Hope this is still your number. Got some news. Can we meet?

A familiar feeling of dread washed over Ruth, and she felt suddenly faint. She could just ignore it but she knew Louise would track her down. Bite the bullet. She texted back before she stopped to think:

Sure. Really busy. Lots of reasons. But could do a quick meet up, maybe near John Lewis? That's a treat for me. Hope all well?

Yes. Think you'd want to hear this though.

Fine. Will work out some dates and get back to you. Might bring Matthew as it's school holidays, combine it with a fun trip perhaps instead, he doesn't do shopping!

OK. Get back to me asap. Feels important.

She decided, almost instantaneously it seemed, to turn her negative foreboding about this meeting to positive anticipation. She could feed her need to give Matthew some fun summer holiday time while she still could, (she

---

[39] William Shakespeare (c 1623) *As You Like It*, Act 2 Sc. 7

could not voice her fears even to herself about that 'still could') at the same time as helping Melanie and giving Sam and Matthew a day out at London Zoo as a top holiday treat. She would, in this way, show Louise that her life really had moved on. She would be fine with the two boys on the Tube and she really couldn't ask anyone else to join them as she needed to hear what Louise had to say, whatever bombshell was to be dropped, on her own, whilst the two boys were absorbed in a play area or something in a child friendly eatery somewhere.

Ruth's *Google* search revealed that actual strides were being made in the use of foetal stem cells for stem cell transplantation treatment in childhood leukaemia. These were taken either from living foetuses, crucially without harming them, or from the extra foetal structures, as they called them, such as the amniotic fluid, the amniotic membrane, the umbilical cord blood, or the placenta. She read quickly, her professional skills coming to the fore here, having tracked down some respectable evidence-based research simply through a *Google* scholar search in no time at all, just whilst the coffee filtered in fact.

"This could be it," she said to herself under her breath.

Taking coffee and lemon cake out to Melanie on the mat she explained what her impulsive thought was and how fruitful her *Google* searches had been, leaving her to digest that briefly whilst she took squash and biscuits to the boys in the wigwam. Melanie listened attentively.

"We must move fast, Mel. No more wondering time for me," she laughed excitedly. "I do want to talk to Mark before I do the test though. What I think I'll do is try to make an appointment to see Dr. Onslow – just me – not wanting to raise Mark's hopes pointlessly. He'll be able to check that I haven't missed anything obvious in the articles, for example that they can't do this without destroying the foetus," she looked momentarily stricken as she said this, "then I'll talk to Mark on his own, tell him I think there's a strong possibility that I'm pregnant, do the test tomorrow, get back to Dr. O and get things moving. Protocols and all that – may take time. Caution, ethics, discussions, experimental stuff. But Emmie has nothing to lose, and no time. Gone into negatives mode like Dr. Onslow," she said reflectively. "Just going to ring my contact at the cord blood bank, see what she knows too. She's always so helpful and positive and forward-looking."

"Sounds promising, Ruth. Gosh, you moved quickly on that. We were only discussing the fact that your knowledge of the birds and bees was, erm, shaky a moment ago it seems." Melanie laughed again, trying to lighten the mood.

Chapter 40

Ruth felt that her surge of mental and physical energy, rare as it had been lately, needed acting on before she lost it or events intervened. She did not voice even to herself what those events might be. She rang her cord blood bank contact, Marion, who said cautiously that she had heard about this but honestly didn't know much about it. Good idea and essential of course to discuss it with Dr. Onslow, whom she knew, as soon as possible. She asked after Emmie too and Ruth was able to recount the turmoil of the recent intensive care stint. She listened sympathetically.

"It certainly seems as if you have nothing to lose, Ruth, good luck and, I hope, congratulations. Fingers crossed. Let me know, won't you?"

"Will do. Thanks, Marion."

She and Matthew arrived at the hospital at 4pm as arranged. They had dropped Melanie, Sam and Amy off on the way, the baby tucked between the two boys in her rear-facing car seat and loving the attention from her two super heroes. Melanie returned swiftly to the car with the package in its discreet chemist's bag having deposited the children safely indoors. Ruth planned to use the test tomorrow morning; she and Mark were, with relief, planning a rare night together at home.

Ruth was also busily planning the trip to 'put paid', as she put it to herself, to any ongoing, regular contact with Louise, with no evil intent, she reminded herself. Louise, her long-standing friend, would just innocently be relegated to Christmas card contact and possibly the odd postcard if they ever went anywhere exciting again; unlikely, she felt at the moment.

She decided as well to try and help others she felt that she 'owed' while she could and also give Matthew and Sam this planned, fun, holiday day out at London Zoo; they had never been there. She knew how much Melanie relished undiluted Amy time when she could get it knowing well how quickly that time passed (Jess and Liam were often busy with their own friends these days) and Ruth decided to see if Simon and Sue would like some new baby quality time too. There would be the added benefit of Matthew getting to know his young cousin, Stuart, a bit better.

Simon had a particular work project to finish, which he hoped to complete by the weekend; once done he would take some paternity leave followed by his annual holiday. This meant that he could travel with them to London, three excited small boys on the Tube and escalators plus one buggy for Stuart when he needed it was quite a daunting prospect perhaps. Louise would meet them at the exit where Simon would leave to get his bus so there would always be two adults. Louise could tell her this news in the anonymous surroundings of the zoo whilst the children were gazing at monkeys, something like that perhaps.

She texted Louise back suggesting Thursday, the day after tomorrow for this trip, knowing that Jane and Tim were visiting Emmie that day before leaving for their two week holiday in Portugal. She'd already checked with Melanie and Sue that their children would be up for this. She was gratified to hear a delighted "yess!" coming from Stuart, and she knew that Sam was hoping and hoping that this trip really would happen. Matthew was full of excitement too and busily working out which animals they would see.

Emmie was well enough to take Matthew to the bright, welcoming playroom when they arrived later that afternoon so Ruth and Mark took themselves off to the parents'/visitors' centre, made a cup of tea, lemon squash for Ruth, and took it out to the little patio surrounded by lavender bushes and hydrangeas, for the chance of a chat on their own.

"She seems a bit better today," Ruth commented.

"She perked up incredibly when she saw Matthew," said Mark rubbing his hand across his eyes wearily, "but she's been sleeping most of the day, not eating much. They're worried about her blood count too."

"Mark, I have something I must tell you before they come back," said Ruth quickly, fearing this opportunity would soon be lost. "I think I may be pregnant. I haven't done the test yet but I'm almost certain. I'm doing the test tomorrow – Melanie had a spare one which she's given me."

"Oh, Ruthie darling really? I know we talked about it but what with everything I didn't really think..."

"Me neither," she interrupted with a grin. "I've already had a lecture from Mel about the birds and the bees."

"Gosh, darling love. If you were, just think – our own child, something new and positive to look forward to." He looked closely at her.

"Come to think of it you do look different, around the eyes, something about your skin pigment, hmm, don't know." He stroked her cheek loving the softness of her skin, "Just here," he said, gently tracing the orbits of her eyes.

"Now, there's more," she said briskly, fearful of time passing and interruptions. "I've been looking into the use of foetal stem cells, started to check it out. I've talked to the cord blood bank people, found some solid looking research. Lots of recent advances. Much better outcomes than with cord blood and not such a finite source as repeated samples can be taken. I was going to talk to Dr. Onslow about it for Emmie. What do you think?"

"Well, crikey me, it's a lot to take in. You're pretty sure you're pregnant aren't you? I can tell. Familiar feelings, I suppose?"

"Yes," she responded truthfully enough within the ever present lie.

A nurse appeared then to tell them that Emmie had tired quickly and was back in bed, wanting them. Matthew was looking worried, she said, and wanted them too. "Sorry to interrupt, you look so relaxed, sitting out here," she sounded regretful. She told them that Dr. Onslow was dropping by to see Emmie too and would talk to them about her latest blood results.

They quickly returned to their anxious children to find another nurse unsuccessfully trying to soothe Emmie with Matthew watching stoically, obviously willing Mark and Ruth to return and probably wishing he wasn't there at all at that moment. Matthew too clearly knew more now than he would at first understand;[40] another stealthy assault on childhood innocence.

It was gratifying, but humbling, to see Emmie's sobs cease so suddenly and her little, wasted arms go up to be picked up and cuddled, just like a much younger child. Within less than a minute of being cuddled up close on Ruth's lap she fell fast asleep. After about five minutes Ruth put her gently into bed. She did not stir. Ruth read quietly to Matthew while Mark went off to telephone and update his parents.

He returned more or less at the same time as Dr. Onslow appeared. The doctor, who knew only too well how it was to see very sick children, looked at the flushed, sleeping child, perused the various charts at the end of her bed and asked if he could have a word with them. Would Matthew like to help the orderly collect up the water jugs while he talked to Mum and Dad? That way

---

[40] Henry James: (1897) *What Maisie Knew,* Heinemann, London, Stone, Chicago, Penguin/Random House

he would be there if Emmie woke up and he could tell her where Mum and Dad were. Matthew nodded, pleased to be given a proper job.

"We'll just be in that office, Matthew; you'll be able to see us through the window. All right?" Again, Matthew nodded, almost man to man it seemed.

Ruth smiled at him reassuringly. "We won't be long, sweetie."

Dr. Onslow pulled no punches with them. Although Emmie had responded briefly to the chemotherapy and to the cord blood transfusion the improvement was not maintained, as they'd seen; they had indeed, been impotent witnesses to her rapid declines on more than one occasion and witnesses too, with bated breath, to her tantalisingly brief bounces back. The team were planning further chemotherapy, he explained, but he did not hold out much hope for its success. "She is very, very poorly," he emphasised.

Ruth turned to Mark enquiringly. He nodded at her mutely.

"We were just talking in the little patio area a bit earlier," she said to Dr. Onslow, "about the fact that I'm almost certain I'm pregnant, doing the test tomorrow morning, but more than that," she said quickly wanting to cut to the chase, "I had a thought about foetal stem cell transplantation." Dr. Onslow looked at her with sharp interest suddenly.

"I did find some research through *Google* scholar," she said self-deprecatingly, "but we were wondering what your thoughts on this are?"

He used the word again: "Strides, Ruth. We're making real, big strides with this as a therapy for advanced leukaemias which do not respond to our current armoury. This is after years of very, very tiny, uncertain steps. Time is obviously of the essence with children like Emmie. We already have a protocol set up – that in itself can take a while – but we received final approval for this last Friday – amazingly. WHO have given their seal of approval too for use of this therapy in these last resort cases – sorry. If we were to do this you would have to understand that this is highly experimental." He paused. "I understand you're Emmie's stepmother, Ruth, but the good thing about foetal stem cells is that they derive from paternal genomes too, obviously." He looked briefly towards Mark.

"I'll give you my mobile number and if you could let me know either way tomorrow, Ruth, or one of you, that would be helpful. Also, if the test is positive, it would be helpful to know how many weeks pregnant you are. The cells can be harvested at different stages of gestation. I'll alert the team this evening anyway – we can always do with a bit of hope and some good application of science." He stood up to leave then, smiling uncertainly, but set off with a renewed sense of purpose, it seemed.

~ Chapter 41 ~

Ruth's own sense of urgent purpose persisted. She woke early and lay quietly next to Mark waiting for as long as she possibly could before going to do the test not wanting to disturb the first relatively peaceful night he had had for a very long time. She did not feel any huge sense of trepidation about doing the test because she felt so very definitely pregnant; confirmation was how it felt to her. She started the test then went to boil the kettle for their early morning tea. She made the tea in a particularly leisurely way, letting it brew gently, and took hers into the garden, feeling the damp grass beneath her bare feet and relishing the summer day stretching ahead before pulling herself up sharply remembering Emmie, on the brink, as she thought of it.

Going into the bathroom to read the test stick having left Mark's tea on his bedside table, she could see the blue line from the door, so bright and clear was it. It was unequivocal and, much though she had expected this, the sharp jolt of unadulterated joy took her by surprise. She slipped quietly back into bed to read while sipping her tea. Mark stirred and reached out to her to pull her close for a morning cuddle.

"I've made tea, it's beside you. I've done the test and I am pregnant, Mark."

He pulled her closer.

"I love you, Ruthie," he said stroking any part of her he could reach and letting his hand rest gently on her tummy, "it's wonderful."

"I'll ring Dr. Onslow now then, it's eight o'clock. Should be okay? He's usually on the ward by 8.15 to 8.30, I've noticed."

Once again, things moved very quickly indeed. There was a sense of being taken over by medical events just as the pregnancy itself would naturally take over her body.

So swiftly were things moving now in fact that Ruth had a sudden desperate urge to stem the tide, to turn the clock back a little and have some ordinary summer holiday time with Matthew. The arrangement for the day after tomorrow, the last day of July felt all the more sacrosanct therefore despite Louise's pending news pervading the anticipated fun like a spectre at the feast. Still it had to be done. Thursday, 31st July it would be.

In consultation with Ruth's and Emmie's friendly and interested GP, Dr. Onslow arranged the scan himself. Feeling the cold gel on her tummy and with Mark beside her Ruth was numb with anticipation, excitement and fear. The sonographer empathised in a quiet, professional way, detached yet somehow totally with them. But she seemed to be taking a long time, Ruth felt, trying not to catch Mark's worried gaze.

"I just need to get a colleague in for a moment to check something. Don't worry, I won't be a moment."

"How can we *not* worry?" Ruth hissed to Mark.

She was back soon with an older woman who greeted them both with a motherly smile.

"Let's have a look." She performed the same actions on Ruth's tummy with the paddle shaped scanning device.

"Yes, definitely." She smiled at her younger colleague. "Do you want to explain?"

"Fine."

The younger one turned to Ruth.

"Everything is fine. But I can now tell you that actually there are two babies, you're expecting twins. Congratulations."

Ruth squeezed Mark's hand tightly.

"Twins. Gosh. Can you tell the sex?"

"It's too early for that but at your 20 week scan we'll be able to tell. I *can* tell you though that you're already about 14 weeks pregnant from the measurements I'm able to take now so it's not very long to wait for the 20 week scan."

The older woman sonographer now spoke gently.

"Looking at your notes I understand Dr. Onslow from Croydon actually arranged this scan because of your little daughter's illness and the possibility of foetal stem cell transplant for her. I'm sorry to hear that she's so ill. What a worrying time for you both."

"Yes. She's my stepdaughter actually, Mark's daughter."

Mark was still staring quietly at the picture on the screen.

"I suppose two foetuses might increase the chances of success in some way?" he asked sounding rather vague. "Please don't misunderstand us though. These are much wanted babies; it's just that Emmie's illness has taken over our lives big time." He squeezed Ruth's hand tightly.

"Yes, and double the quantity too, in simple terms. Dr. Onslow asked us to ring him with the gestation details. I'll do that now while you're here if you like. He may want to discuss plans with you; obviously time is of the essence I understand."

"Yes, that's fine," said Mark looking at Ruth who was in turn staring quietly at the screen. She nodded. At that point words failed her utterly because she was all at once consumed by an unexpected and overpowering feeling of intense protectiveness towards these babies. *Two babies to carry safely to term, what a responsibility that was. Weren't twin pregnancies more risky?*

She would do her own meticulous research as she did not yet trust herself to speak, partly because of these feelings overwhelming any rational thought and partly because a strong, irrational thought which horrified her in its intensity was foremost in her mind, unbidden, unwanted, insistent: *My first chance of my own happiness, my babies with the man I love and it's suddenly all about Emmie.*

Yet she knew that she loved Emmie as deeply and unconditionally as a mother, and was confused by her thoughts. This use of foetal stem cells had, after all, been her idea. But these were not now foetuses to her, they were her babies, would they be harmed? They were not, absolutely not, commodities.

She felt the younger sonographer looking closely at her, the older one had gone to ring Dr. Onslow, and Ruth felt the sudden embarrassment of tears coursing down her cheeks without cease. Mark put his arm round her and pulled her head gently towards his shoulder. This enabled her to cry and cry; great gulping, gasping sobs. Mark looked at the woman over Ruth's shoulder.

"It's understandable; discovering there are two babies can be a real shock and what with all the worry of your daughter..." She tailed off. The older woman returned, stopped short at the sight of Ruth's weeping and said quietly that Dr. Onslow was coming over to see them here. She asked if they would like some tea or coffee and suggested that her colleague took them to the quieter meeting room to await Dr. Onslow's arrival.

The coffee for Mark and the cold orange squash for Ruth were welcome and somehow grounding as they waited. Dr. Onslow arrived about twenty minutes later. He outlined to Ruth and Mark the protocol for Emmie's treatment with

foetal stem cells; the team had unanimously approved this clutching at straws –
as he put it to them honestly. It was good news too that there were two
foetuses, he told them, definitely, good news.

"Congratulations, by the way," he smiled at them.

My babies, our babies, thought Ruth furiously to herself at this point when
another bombshell, as she thought of it later, was dropped. In his quiet
measured tones the consultant paediatric oncologist told them that although
they could not tell the sex of the babies yet, from what they could see on the
scan, and this was not that unusual in twin pregnancies, he explained carefully,
was that one foetus, (*baby*, interjected Ruth silently but again furiously) was
very much smaller than the other and in fact very small for dates. The
pregnancy would be monitored very carefully for this reason with frequent
scans according to the protocol for high risk twin pregnancies. These would be
organised through maternity services via her GP, he explained, who would be
in close touch with him and the team at Croydon.

Ruth had a sudden urge to be out in the fresh air with Mark, and with their
twin babies growing safely inside her womb, away from all this medical stuff,
home with Matthew and Mark, her little family almost intact. She stood up
abruptly and spoke to Dr. Onslow in a tightly controlled voice. "Thanks for
coming over and explaining everything so clearly. We need to get home to our
6 year old now, a friend's looking after him but she has to be elsewhere by
midday."

Mark looked at her in some surprise which he hastily disguised.

"Oh, yes, of course she does. I'd forgotten. We must get going."

"Fine," said Dr. Onslow seemingly able to read their innermost thoughts.
"Can we see you here for the first sampling on Monday then, Ruth? What time
would suit you? It needs to be in the morning for the specimen."

"Eleven is good for us. I can come here and you and Matthew go to see
Emmie perhaps." She looked at Mark. "We'll work something out," she said
quickly, "eleven o'clock will be fine."

And it was in this way that July hurtled towards its close, the zoo trip still
planned for the last day of that benign month, before August hit with its
wickedness, as Ruth persisted in thinking of that high summer, holiday month.

~ Chapter 42 ~

The last day of July arrived and it was all systems go for the zoo trip. Looking back later, much, much later, what Ruth remembered most about that day was the bright, warm sunshine, cloudless blue sky, excited children, her own feeling of renewed energy, the sense of summer stretching ahead of them and, indelibly, the image of Matthew watching the monkeys' antics through the protective glass of their enclosure, rhythmical, mesmerising and strangely tantalising – as before. Then the memories blurred, possibly post-traumatic amnesia, she was told.

And the day proceeded gently and uneventfully at first. The two women chatted about this and that in a way which somehow anticipated the distance both geographical and emotional that would soon stretch between them. The two older boys, Matthew and Sam, were sweetly solicitous towards little Stuart, even managing to give him gentle swing jumps between them from time to time as they covered large distances between the animals' enclosures.

For a fleeting moment the innocent sight of the three of them, the smallest in the middle, trusting, vulnerable, briefly recalled for Ruth, other images of incomprehensible takings and, in particular, subsequent murder of a little boy by children only in reality a few years older than Matthew and Sam. What was *wrong* with her, she asked herself under her breath, what on earth was *wrong* with her?

But later, at the Monkey House, Matthew stood apart from the others a little, intensely absorbed by their antics as they swung from branch to branch in their enclosed space. Sam and Stuart soon moved on down to the racoons a bit further along but still in sight of Louise and Ruth, as instructed, leaving Matthew briefly alone, tense, rigid with absorption but seemingly uneasy, repeatedly turning to look back at Louise and Ruth who were sitting on a nearby bench at the entrance to the Monkey House. It was of course an anniversary month for Matthew and Ruth, hard though it was for Ruth to summon this memory: the watching boy, the bright July sunshine previously interspersed with torrential rain, the running away, the pursuit, the taking, the no going back.

Sitting now on the bench in the warm sunshine Louise and Ruth seized the opportunity, the first that day, to exchange their news. Ruth heard with a sense of huge relief, surprising to her in its vehemence (she liked Louise after all) that she was not only shortly to be married to a New Zealander – in September – but also that they were to live in New Zealand and to travel there immediately after the wedding via a honeymoon in the States. This meant that lifestyles would change, distance would be put between the two friends and shared memories would be superseded by their new lives in different hemispheres; in this way the putting paid to, the getting rid of, would be easily accomplished. No stealth, no plotting. Louise, for her part, was genuinely pleased and excited to hear of Ruth's pregnancy but saddened to hear of little Emmie's illness.

Ruth chose not to divulge the information regarding foetal stem transplantation for reasons which she found hard to articulate even to herself. If pushed, and she was in fact pushing *herself* to think why she decided to keep this secret simply because it usually was her way to be reflective, analytical at every turn. She felt it must be something to do with needing to acknowledge the momentousness of this pregnancy just for its own sake, an end in itself not a means to an end, she supposed; but there the analysis came to a faltering halt. She kept to herself, too, the dangerous lack of growth of one of the twins. This was straightforward denial she realised; if she did not tell it, it would not be so.

Louise then told Ruth in hushed tones that Steve, her 'stepfather', in name only of course, had actually died in hospital and so had never returned to prison from that admission to the acute hospital in May. "D'you remember?"

"Erm… yes, vaguely. I think you told me when we met at *John Lewis* that time when I was with my then shortly to be mother-in-law."

"Yes, that's right, I did. I felt I couldn't just text you about it, Ruth, but that you should know. That was the 'news' I mentioned in my text. You're rid of him forever now."

Ruth looked towards Matthew who simultaneously turned to look at her, then came towards her very deliberately, slowly and with purpose it seemed, sat next to her, briefly leaning in close before jumping up to go and join the other two at the racoons.

The surge of relief on hearing the news of Steve's death once again surprised Ruth by its strength. She, of course, knew that she was rid of him, and we know that she knew, but it seemed to her now and to us of course, that yet again she had got away with a crime; extraordinary. She could move forward to whatever the future held, unfettered by any past.

Mark's text interrupted these thoughts:

All well sweetie? Coping in the heat?
All fine here. Emmie?
Much the same really. Sleeping a lot. Lots of doctors around talking about the therapy. I've signed the consent form today.
Fine. We'll be heading for home in an hour or so. Boys are beginning to flag, probably time for an ice cream.
Ok. See you later. I'll stay here tonight. She's fretful when she wakes up.
Ok. Talk later. Love you xxxx
Love you too, don't overdo it xxxxxx

While they enjoyed their ice creams and drinks Ruth texted Simon to arrange the meeting time at the Tube. Louise was explaining that the wedding invitations would be going out this week but that she would completely understand if Mark and Ruth were unable to come given Emmie's situation.

They discussed where to go to next in the zoo, looking at their booklet to see what they might have missed and wanting to extract every ounce of pleasure from this expensive and rare treat as long as their energy levels held up. There were no huge time constraints, Simon was happy to continue working until they were ready; he had already made really good progress today he texted Ruth. The zoo didn't close until 6pm and it was only 3.30 in the afternoon.

Much refreshed they decided to look at one of the listed 'events' by visiting 'Giants and Dragons' where, they were told, they would find out more about the largest living lizards and giant tortoises of the Galapagos. They decided that after this they would return to their top favourite Monkey House as it was fairly close by. Ruth carefully explained to Matthew and Sam where the Galapagos actually were.

Some of the big animals' enclosures had been slightly disappointing as understandably, the animals had been sleeping in the shade of their shelter 'homes' on this hot day. But the monkeys were lively and very appealing in their almost human form, some with babies held close.

The giants and lizards event was nothing short of enthralling and actually very informative and they all returned satisfied to the Monkey House, Stuart having taken to his buggy for this rather long walk. Ruth and Louise sat at their same well-positioned table for another drink – tea for Louise and a banana milk shake for Ruth; they could keep all the children in sight here.

And then it was that on returning from a brief visit to the toilets, having left Louise in charge, Ruth looked towards the Monkey House and could see only Sam. When she reached the table she saw that Stuart was sitting next to Louise enjoying a strawberry milk shake. There was no sign of Matthew.

"Where's Mat?" Ruth asked consciously striving to remain calm.

Louise looked towards the Monkey House.

"He was there a moment ago, just watching the monkeys like before, you know?"

"Well, he's not there now. I'll go and ask Sam." She moved swiftly.

"Where's Mat, Sam?"

Just as Louise had done he turned to look to his right, where Matthew had been watching.

"Don't know. He was there," he said pointing to the spot where Matthew had stood riveted for so long.

Ruth felt a sense of rising panic. Perhaps he had turned to look for her as before, seen her gone and had set out to find her.

"I'm going to check the toilets, Louise," she called across. "Stay with these two. Don't let them out of your sight," she commanded her voice tight with anxiety.

She asked people entering the Gents to tell her if there was a small boy in there and to call out his name in case he was in a cubicle. People were helpful and one grandfatherly type advised her kindly to alert the zoo staff because there was a missing child centre for when children got separated from the adults with them. "It happens all the time, love, don't worry. They'll have him safe and sound there and you'll probably hear an announcement soon."

Ruth thanked him but felt herself to be sweating and wide-eyed with fear. She wanted to see his little head. She wanted his hand in hers right now. She wanted to smell his warm skin. She imagined him alone and fearful, lost, wandering or with somebody who came to the zoo to find children and take them.

She returned to Louise, Sam and Stuart and told them she would find a member of staff to explain that Matthew was not with them; she could not say "report him missing." It felt too final, as if saying the words made it true, irrevocable.

The first zoo official she found directed her to the missing children centre which was staffed by a motherly looking woman wearing a high visibility jacket with stylised pictures of lions and tigers on it. She took his description and spoke into a walkie-talkie, explaining that there were 6 missing children centres dotted around the zoo as it covered such a large area.

"Give it 5 minutes," she said briskly but not unkindly, "and we'll hear if he's at one of them. If he is he'll be safe; don't worry, we keep them until they're claimed. It happens all the time, love. Don't blame yourself." She looked at Ruth and added, "I guess he's your son?"

"Yes, he is." Ruth felt her empathy and briefly appreciated it as it made her feel like a mother for a while longer.

Matthew, however, was not in any of the missing children areas nor had he returned to Louise at the table; Ruth had rung her from the missing children area as instructed by the motherly woman.

"I'll just get our manager to talk to you." Once again she spoke quietly into the walkie-talkie.

"I'm sorry but I think I'm going to be sick," said Ruth quickly. The woman ushered her into her office and to the staff toilets only just in time. Ruth knew that she had been sick from sheer anxiety but felt the need to tell this kind woman, by way of explanation, that she was pregnant with twins. She was acutely conscious of needing care and attention and needing Matthew to be found; there was no other option.

The manager arrived and explained that it would be necessary to report this now to the police. He could do that for her. There was no more talk now of, 'it happens all the time, love.' This was serious.

"Yes. Please do it now." Again, Ruth's voice was tight and higher than usual with anxiety. She could feel her throat constricting. By now approximately 45 minutes had passed since Ruth had looked and not seen Matthew; it already felt much, much longer. Oh, how she wanted to hold him close and not let him go. She willed him to know that they were looking for him and would find him. It was not even wicked August yet, she thought to herself suddenly and even now, already, children were going missing, snatched off the face of the earth in broad daylight.

Her phone rang. It was Louise. "Ruth, listen. Sam has just told me that

Matthew said he wanted a monkey to take home. It's a long shot but has anyone checked the huge souvenir shop at the entrance, you know the one we said was there to get your last few pounds as you left if you still had any? He knew the day was coming to an end so maybe he set out to find one. Shall I take these two and go look? I can put Stuart in the buggy."

"Yes, sure, anything's worth a try. I'll tell these missing children people."

The time now was 5.15pm and there was a tangible sense of the zoo beginning to bed down for the evening and night. Rubbish was being emptied, eateries were putting chairs on tables, cleaning, closing sections off; the number of people milling about was noticeably dwindling. This frightened Ruth even more. She simply could not, would not, leave this place without Matthew. Darkness was encroaching, physical and metaphorical. She would wait as long as possible before letting Simon know because she just wanted Matthew to be found and to be able to tell Simon all about it – in the past tense.

There was a sudden flurry of activity amongst the missing children staff and a walkie-talkie buzz and crackle. At the same moment Louise rang.

"Ruth, Ruth, I can see him, just looking in the shop window, just standing still like he did at the Monkey House. We're walking towards him. I think the shop's just closing, not sure." She was sounding breathless with excitement and because she was walking fast towards him pushing Stuart in the buggy.

"Stay on the line, Lou, I can't believe it. Don't let him out of your sight." Ruth was crying openly.

The motherly woman walked briskly towards her.

"Ruth, we have a sighting of a small boy answering Matthew's description. He's been seen looking in the souvenir shop window. The woman who reported it has been watching him for a while because she wanted to make sure he was all right, as he seemed to be alone, but she wasn't quite sure. She thinks she should have contacted us sooner."

"We need to get there now," said Ruth urgently. "Somebody could take him from there."

"We've asked her to stay there and talk to him without frightening him."

"He may just run though, he'll be scared." The memories were threatening to overwhelm her now.

They set off by motorised buggy towards the shop in time to see Louise reach the woman and the boy, Matthew, just as he turned to see Ruth waving and calling to him from the buggy. He looked bewildered and very tired suddenly, and as he walked rather unsteadily towards Ruth she could see tear tracks on his grubby cheeks. She leant down and pulled him up towards her, clutching him tightly as he leaned in close enough to feel safe but not so close as to lose face in front of strangers. She looked over his little head to thank the woman, noticing that she was much the same age as her and appeared to be on her own.

"That's all right, anyone would have done the same; he just looked to be so lost and alone, just watching at the window. I wondered for a while if his parents were inside the shop so I just waited to make sure he was safe. Anything could have happened really, he's so little."

Ruth was immediately put in mind then of a survey conducted by the NSPCC which she had read about recently. This had found that 64% of those surveyed said they would not help a child who looked lost for fear of being accused of 'something'.

And there began a tacit understanding between Louise and Ruth that they would tell no-one about this. They thus became co-conspirators, complicit in the cover up for reasons they did not, could not, articulate. Yet again, she thought, unreasonably resentful, her friend was there for her in her time of need. Louise should, though, have noticed Matthew going off, Ruth reminded herself. They both realised that Stuart was too young to report this 'adventure'; Ruth knew that Matthew would say nothing and she felt that if Sam were to say anything to Melanie she could easily play the whole thing down along the lines of:

"Oh, yes, you know those terrifying times when you turn round and just can't see them for a moment. I did panic for about three minutes..." (laughing lightly, she imagined) "...but then there he was just ahead of us. Phew!"

Time would move on, nobody need know. She would talk quietly to Matthew, as soon as she got a chance, about never going off on his own like that in big, crowded places but again would not overplay it *so as not to frighten him too much,* she justified the plan to herself.

Was Matthew thus also to be complicit with her somehow? Had the cavorting monkeys triggered a buried memory? Did he once more know something he did not yet understand? Had he once more buried a memory which now stirred in his mind, restless, insistent?

They decided to have a restorative carton of chips and a drink and find some last fun before setting off to meet Simon at the Tube station. Stuart had already declared that he was coming back to the zoo tomorrow and he didn't want to leave yet as "it was too fun here."

The last bit of fun available was a trip to the souvenir shop on the way out where each child could choose a memento to take home provided it cost no more than £3. Stuart chose a 20p pencil with a rubber in the shape of a tiger on top, Sam chose a snow leopard in a little plastic snowflake globe, and Matthew chose a book about racoons in the wild and then they set off happily to meet Simon at the entrance to the Tube station where they all wished Louise a firm and, on Ruth's part, suddenly hating the renewed complicity and shared secret with her, deliberately valedictory, goodbye and good luck.

~ *Chapter 43* ~

So waking alone again the next morning was for Ruth to realise that August had sneaked in quietly, on a Friday, like bad news does at times. The eighth month sounded to her to be so far into the year, yet, paradoxically, it is still mid-summer holidays, peak holiday season and here was August suddenly with all her wickedness and random snatchings.

Outside her window the leaves seemed to have turned a darker green overnight, the lawn's rampant growth slowed, even the heat of the summer day felt still, dead, dull almost, unlike the bright sparkle of the day before.

'*Bored Summer with your prattle and chatter of inconsequential things...*' [41] the first line of Louise's prose poem came to mind. Just perceptions, Ruth thought sleepily.

But then the sorry tally of children not returning for the next school year came to mind. This would be recounted usually in local papers unless sufficiently grisly to make national news: drownings, abductions, illness, natural death, unnatural death, road accidents, children going missing. She urged herself to stop thinking like this and thought instead of Matthew lying safely asleep down the landing, none the worse for yesterday's episode.

But that was odd because though she knew Matthew had gone missing for a time she could recall nothing of the detail, nothing whatsoever. She knew it had been momentous, but she simply could not recall anything about it. Nor, strangely, could she recall anything of the zoo trip after saying goodbye to Simon as he set off for work in the morning entrusting little Stuart to her care. How odd it all was? There was no need for any cover up as it turned out because she could not tell it even had she wanted to. It was, simply, erased from her memory.

---

[41] Unpublished prose poem, see author's citation

She lay in bed a little longer reflecting on the date of the twins' conception. Could it be that their idyllic and relaxed honeymoon lovemaking had not in fact resulted in this pregnancy but instead that which took place during the frantic, fraught few weeks beforehand when she was plotting and then committing her third crime? Lovemaking then had been a release of tension, an affirmation that there was good surrounding her not evil. Could twins be conceived at different times? She would *Google* it. She got up and made herself some green tea, her first tentative step towards enjoying tea again.

The summer stretched ahead still and she stepped out barefoot onto the damp lawn savouring the sights and sounds of that summer morning.

"Banish thoughts of autumn's approach," she said to herself dramatically. "We have this time now." It always annoyed her at this time of year that weather reporters on television seemed to delight in announcing "autumnal weather" pronouncing that three syllable word with great pride and great relish.

"I'll give you autumnal, you idiot," she would say to the screen crossly. "We know how autumn can hit so don't talk it up."

Matthew appeared beside her, tousled in his pyjamas, enjoying the novelty of being in the early morning garden in his bare feet.

"It's dew, isn't it, Mimi?" It had been a while now since he had called her that pet name, wanting no doubt to conform to his school mates' names for their mothers.

"That's right, sweetheart. Are you all right? Did you enjoy the zoo yesterday?"

"Mmm, yes, it was great. Can we go again soon?"

"Maybe." Now was her moment, it needed to be soon after the event or the opportunity would be lost. And there and then she was able to explain gently that he must never go off on his own in crowded public places like that as it was easy for children to get lost. She could say this easily and lightly because, though she knew this had happened, the details had vanished totally. Therefore her light tone was not in any way manufactured so as not to frighten him, it was completely genuine. But she was taken aback completely by his quick response.

"Lost or taken, could be, couldn't they?"

"Yes, that could happen. Let's go and have breakfast in our jammies then get dressed as it's the holidays. What do you think? Pancakes?"

Matthew smiled with quick delight at the combination of pancakes, the dressing chore being postponed and the novelty of having breakfast in pyjamas.

It was not until about three days later, when they were in Melanie's sun-filled garden this time, the two boys playing happily and Amy squiggling around with her toys on the rug between them, that Melanie said quietly,

"Sam loved the zoo trip, Ruth, thanks for taking him. He said Matthew went missing. You never said. What happened?"

Ruth lying on her back, relaxed, almost happy, certainly content, looking up at a cloudless blue sky through the steadily darkening leaves of the huge oak under which they had set up camp in the shade, was thinking how precious gardens were, people's little bits of England, to own and nurture, create and cultivate. She'd been about to share this rather fey thought with her friend but as it was she was quickly able to explain, with complete lack of guile, that it was one of those terrible moments... you know, barely a minute or two, she thought. Sam had obviously picked up on her quick panic even though she had tried to hide it, she told Melanie.

And that was that. Ruth returned to her garden musings and shared her thought with Melanie who then replied with a laugh,

"Well, yes, I see what you mean – sort of – but sadly ours belongs to the building society actually and will do for many years to come."

And so began, in those early August days, a strange waiting period for Ruth. She was an expectant mother of course, but more than that it was a waiting period for her little family. Emmie's illness entailed a seemingly endless waiting: for her blood results, for her to get better, for her to respond to treatment, for her to feel better, for tests, for her to rejoin her family at home, for her to pick up her life. This waiting interrupted the narrative of normal life somehow.

Ruth had heard an interview on the radio with an eminent professor – of psychology, she thought it was, from Lancaster University about the concept of waiting; she had happened on the discussion halfway through whilst driving. The former Archbishop of Canterbury was also interviewed on the same subject. He too made some interesting comments which had put her in mind of biblical garden imagery. Emmie was, to be sure, suffering her own Gethsemane wait, as was her family with her at times. Ruth like Eve, in Eden, had been tempted to sin, to conspire with evil, to take what was not hers, to steal, to kill.

Garden imagery from the English metaphysical poets merged with these random thoughts and she remembered inconsequentially how one of her professors of English at university had referred to Andrew Marvell, probably rightly, as Andrew Marvell, destroying her notion of his marvellous name.

Such was that happy garden state
While man there walk'd without a mate [42]

she remembered out of the blue. She felt a need to 'withdraw into [her own] happiness' as she awaited the birth of her babies and hated the odd, surprisingly overwhelming, feelings of resentment that Emmie's illness provoked simply because it detracted so completely from this happy anticipation, as it were:

'Annihilating all that's made
To a 'green thought in a green shade.' [43]

Melanie had taken Amy in to change her nappy and lying on her back under the tree now, whilst the boys played happily, reflecting on her situation Ruth thought about her Eden and her Gethsemane, The Tree of Knowledge, the Tree of life, the Tree as a crucifix, atonement, suffering and above all knowledge, knowledge of good and evil yes, of course, but the whole concept of knowing too. What is known when, what is knowable, what did Emmie know now, what did she once know, what would she come to know, as with Matthew? What did Matthew know? What would he come to know?

She thought too about the word conscience, 'with knowledge' as she understood its literal meaning, science meaning knowledge, 'scire' in Latin to know, 'con' being the 'with' from Latin, she thought. She must look it up sometime. How did this relate to 'conscious' she wondered. *"Thus conscience doth make cowards of us all."* [44]

Oh, she had a conscience all right, her crimes *were* on her conscience, for sure, and she committed them consciously; perhaps, following Hamlet's logic, she was merely brave to have done what she did. She was certainly conscientious in outlook in all aspects of her life. She didn't know. No *'pale cast of thought'* *'gave her pause;'* [45] that she did know. She thought about what was knowable and she knew that the readers of her story knew what she had done, she knew that they knew, and they knew that she knew that they knew so could she tease them, would she tease them with this? Those closest to her did

---

[42] Andrew Marvell 1681 *The Garden,* Miscellaneous Poems
[43] *ibid*
[44] William Shakespeare: *Hamlet: Prince of Denmark* Act 3, Sc 1
[45] *ibid*

not know; she knew they did not know and the readers knew that they did not know. '*Be all my sins remembered,* '[46] she spoke it silently. In the same way the story teller who dispels darkness with his craft as people gather round fires to listen to tales of good and evil knows what his listeners come to know.

She thought then of the new knowledge now helping Emmie, how not so many years ago this would not even have been knowable. She knew she was ruminating on things, as cows do. What did cows know, she wondered, and knew this should not be a footling thought.

She was getting fanciful, she admonished herself sharply, a word her grandmother had used. This was her reality, it needed to be lived. Thankfully Melanie appeared with drinks then, carrying Amy, chuckling happily, under one arm. Reality restored.

And the hospital visits continued, with Mark and Ruth dividing up the overnight stays, but Mark certainly taking the lion's share. There was a subtle change here since Ruth's pregnancy had declared itself. Whether this was an unconscious recognition that she had her own unborn children to think about now or whether it was recognition that, as her biological father, Mark should be taking the lion's share was not clear, not knowable even.

[46] *ibid*

~ *Chapter 44* ~

August marched on in its languid yet relentless way, the willow herb going winsomely, diaphanously, to seed on the roadside verges. Late roses were making a bold and sometimes almost brash appearance, defiantly braving the cooler nights and the later dawns. Ruth took her turn with hospital visiting, including overnight stays, and she and Mark carefully planned nights when they were both together at home. At these times he was sweetly solicitous towards her, excited about the twins, but complained of being weary to the bone, as he put it. Ruth longed for him to be able to enjoy some summer but knew that this could not be the case whilst Emmie was so ill. She herself felt defeated at times; she had so wanted to heal this shattered family, to protect, to nurture, to grow it, and this illness had flown in the face of that with its harsh sentence and uncertain outcome.

She felt herself trying, at times desperately, at other times merely with a wearying and dogged determination, to keep a hold on normal life and felt a continuing urge to make summer really fun for Matthew; who knew what was coming, what was to be faced?

She and Mel planned another day trip with the children, Jess and Liam as well this time. It was to be a beach trip, just a simple fun trip while Ruth was still off work. Although the Sussex coast would have been the nearest she could not contemplate doing this without Mark, she just couldn't, it was somehow *their* coast therefore unconscionable – *unconscionable* – *one of those knowing words again*, she thought, that she and Matthew should enjoy it without him and Emmie. Melanie understood this completely. So they planned to take the train to the Kent coast, Ramsgate, where there was, apparently, a lovely sandy beach. This would be fun for all of them.

"We could even have a glass of wine or something with our fish and chips as we're not driving, live dangerously," Mel laughed. As Jess would be coming too this would of course be helpful with Amy whom Jess anyway loved to 'mother'. Ruth firmly put to the back of her mind any superstitions regarding August and its wickedness, its sudden takings.

By this time Emmie had been in hospital nearly eight weeks but Ruth and Mark understood all too well that there was still a long way to go. They had been told from the beginning that children with AML would typically spend six months in hospital hoping to achieve remission without relapse. Ruth was able easily to explain to Mark her need to give Matthew a fun summer holiday while she could. The dynamic of the household had changed utterly with Emmie being 'away'. Matthew was clearly puzzled by the long hospital stay. He had seen children at school go to hospital with the odd broken bone and come out very soon afterwards, proudly sporting colourful plaster casts which the children drew pictures on and generally had fun decorating. It was all very different with Emmie.

Ruth could not forget the sight of him one evening in Emmie's bedroom talking to her collection of cuddly toys and the few dolls she had. He sat cross-legged in front of them, unaware that Ruth was watching from the doorway, she'd just happened to notice him on her way to putting clean sheets back in the airing cupboard.

"Emmie *will* come home," he told them firmly. "We just have to wait. She's ill but she will get better if we wait without fussing." Then, out of the blue, both his little hands had gone up to cover his face and, putting Ruth immediately in mind of Milton's *Paradise Lost*, appropriately enough, as she was to think afterwards:

'Tears such as angels weep burst forth
as, at length; 'words interwove with sighs found out their way. [47]

And what words they were. Ruth would never, ever forget them, she felt, and Milton's poetry seemed strangely apt in this incongruous 21st century setting.

From her little boy, her only recently turned 5 year old came, remarkably,

"I knew Emmie would be ill, toys, because she was sad for a long time. She knew she was ill too. I know she knows lots of bad things but I know good

---

[47] John Milton: *Paradise Lost, Book 1* 1667

things can make bad things go away. So all of you must be good toys and not fuss, just be quiet, all of you," he said, looking at them sternly, "and wait to see Emmie. And cheer up," he commanded crossly.

Ruth knew swathes of *Paradise Lost* off by heart because she had studied the first two books at A level and aspects of the angels' suffering had resonated with her deeply at that time. So she wondered as she overheard Matthew then:

> '....*what power of mind*
> *Foreseeing or presaging from the depth*
> *Of knowledge past or present could have fear'd...* '[48]

But these thoughts came to her only later. As she stood watching silently she felt immensely sad for Matthew's current suffering, his own Gethsemane it seemed, fearful for his future suffering and angry for the suffering he had already endured about which she knew, or thought she knew, and yet could do nothing. She had closed the airing cupboard door quietly and gone back downstairs.

The beach trip to Ramsgate though was a joyous day of unalloyed fun. It was perfect beach weather, sunny and warm, with no wind, and a sparkling blue sky reflected in the sparkling blue sea. The train journey was smooth; Matthew particularly was struck by the golden fields as he called them, this was of course the ripening corn. These swathes of dancing, shimmering golden crops were occasionally broken up by the subtly beautiful colours of fields of opium poppies, an effect of pale lilac and white, fairy like, mystical almost. These were used to make medicines to help people in pain, Ruth explained to Matthew.

"Like Emmie," he said flatly as a statement, not a question.

"Yes, like Emmie," Ruth replied. She pointed out then how the tall barley swayed to and fro with any slight breeze moving like gentle darts of changing light across the fields much like waves across an ocean; how the wheat grew straighter and strong and how the oats appeared to dance lightly in the sunlight, all known as corn, Ruth explained, whereas in America only wheat was known as corn. Confusing, she acknowledged. Soon the harvest would be in, she explained, all formed into rolled up bales ready to be transported to factories to be made into food like flour for making bread and cakes.

---

[48] *ibid*

These vast golden acres were occasionally interrupted by smaller fields of hops standing in their serried ranks, greener and spindly looking. And there were occasional glimpses of verges of willow herb, some purple still evident but mostly running raggedly to seed, the bright light glancing through the gossamer seed pods appearing ethereal, dream-like, and fey.

Amy, too, was happy during this journey and happy all day actually; thankfully when she was tired she fell asleep without getting fretful, and when she was hungry she ate. Melanie and Ruth discovered they had exactly the same philosophy about beach days. Make the most. Watch the changing moods. Extract the last ounce of pleasure. And so they lingered as the people dispersed, indulging in some harmless people-watching, amused by how long it took families to pack up and leave.

By the time they decided to leave the beach itself and climb up to the café on the promenade for their fish and chip supper – with wine for the grown-ups – the sand was damp with evening dew and the moon could be seen large on the horizon. The moon was in fact exceptionally big for August, Ruth had read, and so correspondingly there had been some very big tide surges. The patrolling lifeguards had put up warning notices of an exceptionally high tide forecast for 11pm that night and 11am tomorrow morning. Similar notices were posted in the car park on the promenade. Ruth explained the link between the moon and tides as best she could, with Melanie chipping in, uncertainly. Both were on shaky ground and they promised to help Matthew find out more when they got home.

And so the high summer days continued, ostensibly tranquil but the sense of waiting was portentous, almost tangible, its physical manifestation evident in Ruth's developing pregnancy. Ruth returned to do her short days at Sarah's; Matthew enjoyed coming with her sometimes and helping, other times Anne and Bob looked after him, either at Ruth's or at their house, obviously relishing getting to know him even better. He spent time at Melanie's too and Ruth felt the closeness of her new friends and family once more enveloping her in its protective embrace, warm and welcoming, keeping the darkness at bay.

Her 20 week anomaly scan was booked for 6th September, a Tuesday. She feared for this, she feared for her developing babies; she had heard birth described as the most dangerous journey of life itself. Not reassuring. She planned to explain to Matthew *after* this scan that she was expecting twin babies just in case… just in case it revealed things too horrible for him even to have ever known about the babies' existence. He had, after all, already known too much in his short life, she felt.

And it has to be spelt out here clearly that so far in this story it is only Ruth who knows what she has done and she has shared that with the readers of this story. Are the readers thus complicit with Ruth, or is she complicit with them? Can she manipulate them at all, or they her? What power does this give to the readers of this fiction? Is the unfolding story in their hands now?

~ *Chapter 45* ~

But how exactly to tell the waiting? What happens during such waiting? What really happened in Gethsemane? What about the waiting watchers? What betrayal was there? What reality was there in that place? There is an intensity in waiting, an expectation of course; an attentiveness. Ruth thought of the French: *'attendre'*. And then, interesting: *'atteindre'* to reach, attain. But what particular Mount of Olives was there yet to climb?

Once again as the year progressed deep into August, as she always thought of it and as she even now remembered thinking of it this time last year when a new life was just starting for her, she was struck by the month's perennial staleness, always trying to push its wickedness to the back of her mind. Were the wickedness and staleness linked perhaps, just as boredom and fecklessness leads to crime? That is well known, of course. What of that phrase "of course?" What course is set? What place fate? What place chance? Ruth pondered such thoughts during this waiting.

So a whole year had passed and she was conscious of happiness stretching ahead of her, unexpected, unsought. She felt herself clinging to this thought amidst the uncertainty of the outcome for Emmie and the anxiety about her twin pregnancy with its inherent risks. Was this happiness really unsought though, she wondered. She was after all still only 23, very nearly 24, as the end of August approached; finding a way in life was a part of young adulthood surely, and happiness, contentment must be a part of that, it seemed obvious really, she thought, even if unvoiced and unacknowledged.

And Mark, what of Mark? He seems to have drifted now into some hinterland of unknown suffering, the father for his suffering daughter, alone but not quite alone in his own Gethsemane, spending vast swathes of time in bedside vigil.

Ruth had been struck, on one of her quick dashes around one of the smaller local supermarkets, by a conversation she had overheard between a little girl and her mother. Out of the blue the child had said:

"Mummy, am I your daughter?"

The young mother had replied with loving patience, sadly unusual, Ruth reflected, when mothers are shopping with small children,

"Yes, darling I am your mummy. You're my daughter," smiling down at her.

"And Daddy's daughter?"

"Yes, Daddy's daughter too, so Mummy and Daddy's daughter."

"I am Mummy and Daddy's daughter," the little girl said happily.

Ruth was so struck by this, and it was only afterwards she understood why exactly, that she actually stopped to ask the mum how old her little girl was. Almost exactly the same age as Emmie it turned out, 2 and just over a half, going on 3. So Emmie may well ask that question one day soon, as might Matthew, different gender substituted of course.

The little girl was dressed very sweetly in mostly pink. Beguiling, a word her grandmother had often used, but Ruth had also discovered just a week or so ago, that it was only very recently that pink had been the default colour for girls and blue for boys. Up until well into the 20th century, until about 1930, she had read, it had been the other way round, pink being seen as the stronger, more robust colour. And astoundingly there had, until the late 15th century, been no differentiation between the genders as babies; boys were known as knave girls and all babies and children were known as girls which meant any child. She had also read that girl foetuses and babies were generally much more robust than boy foetuses and babies, and even that boys were statistically much more likely to develop childhood cancer of all types. Something vaguely to do with evolution, prolongation of the species perhaps; she wasn't sure but she did long to know the gender of her twins. She would have to wait and she filled some of the quieter periods of waiting with such musings unable to share this time with Mark.

But during this period of waiting, life was of course as busy as ever, working at the bookshop, looking after Matthew, fulfilling her freelance commitments for *Petersons* and others, visiting Emmie, seeing friends for both her own and Matthew's sake, likewise seeing Anne and Bob, Sally and Paul, and Jane and Tim when they could. She also stayed in touch with Simon and Sue at more of a geographical distance, via *Facebook* mainly where they posted happy pictures of themselves and Stuart with little Josie. All was well with Stuart and the new baby Josie, so that was good.

There was the ever present difficulty too, of trying to get some time with Mark as they both awaited the birth of their twin babies. She felt this need to be with him like an acute, almost physical, pain of longing. Being without him she suffered the loss; need and loss, similar she thought, whilst at the same time trying to suppress her unwanted resentment at this intrusion of longing and sadness and loss into what should have been a straightforwardly happy, expectant period of waiting.

There were, too, the visits for foetal sampling. The mixture of emotions here: how to tell it exactly, truthfully? This was her precious cargo, she needed to protect it and yet she was subjecting her twin babies to this unpleasant procedure week after week for the sake of their, to them as yet unknown, half-sister.

And to what did the waiting lead ultimately? Again, how to tell it?

Well, important to relate and interesting to the unfolding story is that Ruth became even closer to her mother-in-law during this period of waiting – again how formal that sounded to describe the loving relationship developing between them; truly it seemed as if Anne had gained a third daughter, and Ruth a mother. In Anne's case the gates keeping secure the love she had for her own children simply opened even wider to let Ruth in as one of their own to the exclusion of no-one. For Ruth, this felt new though similar to her feelings for her grandmother, feelings which had all too quickly been subsumed by the changing levels of dependency, one for the other.

Ruth had not known a mother's unconditional love in this way. She had been told she needed a responsible adult to accompany her on these sampling days because she was to be sedated each time and could not drive afterwards. She asked Anne. Her other thought had been to ask Melanie but this would not have been practically possible because of her own small children and baby. Instead Matthew would happily spend the day at Melanie's on these occasions and sometimes the night too if Ruth felt particularly unwell. Ruth could rest assured that Matthew would be having fun in his home from home with Sam and would be safely and lovingly cared for by her friend.

On these days Anne was the perfect company: gentle, loving, practical and supportive and there felt to be a special closeness between them because of the genetic link to her own vulnerable twins and to the very unwell little Emmie, her granddaughter, for whom Ruth was undergoing this unpleasant, counter-intuitive and fear-inducing procedure.

On one occasion Ruth was very unwell indeed after the procedure, vomiting repeatedly, feeling dizzy and feverish. Anne put her to bed, arranged for Matthew to stay on at Melanie's, explained it all to Mark, and contacted Dr. Onslow to describe Ruth's state. Ruth took two full days to recover and it was thought by the medical team that she had had a reaction to the particular sedative drug used on this occasion, but not on others, by a locum anaesthetist.

Shortly after this urgent *'fin de vacances'* sense of needing to maximise every moment of freedom that the end of August brought, followed rapidly by the shock of the back to school complete change of pace, welcome to some in their state of ennui, dreaded by others, it was time for the long awaited 20 week anomaly scan.

~ *Chapter 46* ~

As ever, literary allusions came unbidden to Ruth, and she remembered Claudius speaking to his wife Gertrude in *Hamlet*:

> *When sorrows come, they come not single spies*
> *But in battalions.*[49]

So how to count these? First, Sarah, quite out of the blue, was diagnosed with recurrence of her breast cancer which had already spread to her lymph nodes and necessitated aggressive treatment despite having been given the earlier all clear. Sarah's practical way of coping was to appoint Paul as manager of the bookshop. This was to be a full time paid job, which he much needed, whilst he built up his own business as an electrical engineer with a specialist interest in lighting, particularly as he and Sally had just announced their engagement. Sarah had grown to be very fond of Paul as she got to know him as Ruth's stand in on many occasions. She liked his commitment to jobs in hand, his work ethic, his sense of humour, and his flexibility, she told Ruth.

Next was the news received on the day of the anomaly scan itself, with Mark by her side, when once again the sonographer went to get a colleague. Ruth gazed at the screen; Mark was silent but gripped her hand tightly. Once again the sonographer returned with an older, obviously more experienced, colleague, who was in fact an obstetric Senior Registrar. He wasted no time.

Looking at Ruth he explained gently enough that the scan showed that the twins were not identical, in other words they did not share a placenta. This in

---

[49] William Shakespeare, (c 1599-1601) *Hamlet, Prince of Denmark*, Act 4, Sc 5

itself usually lessened some of the fairly well known pregnancy risks such as twin to twin transfusion syndrome.

"However," he went on slowly and clearly, still looking at Ruth, "here," and he pointed to an area of the screen with the end of his pen, "we can see that one of the twins is much smaller than the other." He paused before asking, "Did you want to know the gender?"

Ruth looked at Mark for confirmation, and as he nodded, she said,

"Yes, oh yes, we do want to know that."

"Well, the boy twin is much smaller than his sister, much, much smaller. Now, it's not uncommon in twin pregnancies for one baby to be smaller than the other," he explained, "even where there are two separate placentas, but it's the degree of difference, the degree of smallness that's concerning here. The boy twin's very small for dates."

Ruth thought of all she had read about the vulnerability of boy foetuses and babies and felt an overwhelming protectiveness towards her unborn baby boy, her boy child. She remembered too, with battalions of sorrows running through her mind, that of course Gertrude's boy child ultimately broke her heart in two.

As Ruth and Mark took this news in, Ruth asked suddenly:

"Could they have been conceived at different times perhaps, I mean so that he is actually in line with *his* dates?" She tailed off a little, but then carried on bravely: "Is it because his sister is jeopardising his chances of survival anyway?"

"Well," the sonographer started his considered reply, "the first situation would be very, very unusual since you stop producing eggs once you're pregnant. And the second situation... well there is an element of that, less so because of the two placentas of course, but only inasmuch as the twins are surviving off you and human beings are really not that well adapted to multiple births – generally – I mean. Of course, twin, and triplet pregnancies even, can and do have very successful outcomes, don't misunderstand me, it's not all gloom and doom, by any manner of means. What has to happen now is even closer monitoring, watching and waiting."

Waiting, thought Ruth to herself, whilst this already felt like a betrayal, a treachery. A betrayal of what exactly she could not think at that moment but probably something along the lines of a betrayal of hope, a betrayal of trust in any happiness that could dare to be waiting for her and Mark, a betrayal of any sort of redemption, forgiveness. There would be no second Eden for her, she had truly lapsed it seemed, she was indeed beyond the pale. Watching,

watching a slow decline, she felt, a slow decline towards death in utero. No chance at all. *'Manner of means'* – what an odd expression that was, she thought to herself.

And then she asked it, the question, the answer to which had haunted both her waking moments and her dreams as nightmares:

"Could the foetal sampling actually be damaging him? It turns out he's the slightly better match for my stepdaughter."

"Truthfully, I don't know," he replied, "but I do know that if Dr. Onslow has told you that there's no risk of harming the foetus he'll be basing that information on the scientific evidence currently available. I can tell you that for certain."

Knowledge knowable now, thought Ruth to herself.

"Actually he's in the building. I can ask him to come and talk to you, if you like?"

"Yes, that would be good, if you could," as, without any warning or preamble, tears started streaming down her face.

Mark helped her off the trolley bed and pulled her gently to him as they were shown to an office. The younger sonographer offered them a cup of tea or coffee while they waited which they accepted gratefully.

Dr. Onslow reiterated absolutely that foetal sampling would not be causing harm, he could show them the papers based on robust research but he knew they were entirely capable of finding these for themselves. He did not over-egg it, Ruth felt, the strange phrase came to her, particularly strange in the circumstances; instead he spoke calmly and factually. And then came the next barrage when all their defences were at their weakest.

"What I do need to say to you both, and I was planning to come by the ward later today to speak to you anyway, is that Emmie has developed another urinary infection which is resistant to all the usual antibiotics. We're trying one which is new and not licensed for use in children although I have to explain that drug companies often put that caveat on their medicines because research with children is, of course, ethically very difficult to conduct. So, this is a serious setback for her and she is again very unwell indeed, I'm afraid."

Ruth shut her eyes and leant back in her chair wanting to shut out everything albeit only momentarily; she craved respite. She was carrying a struggling baby twin, she needed to be there for Emmie and Mark, she needed to be there for Matthew, her rescued boy, she needed to be there too for the other twin, the girl baby.

"Let's go home for a bit before we see Emmie this afternoon," she said to Mark. "We need to take stock of all this," she explained to Dr. Onslow, unnecessarily, since his empathy with their situation was evident in every gesture. "Thank you for explaining things." As they left they were called over to the reception desk to make a scan appointment for two weeks' time.

~ Chapter 47 ~

And so the story must be told, it must unfold; *the winds must come from somewhere when they blow,*[50] the waiting must be interrupted by the narrative now.

So it was that the year forged on sometimes languidly, sometimes purposefully, onward into October, that golden month of lingering summer, of bright days, of sometimes warm sun, of new beginnings, even new growth – in saplings, in hedgerows, building strength for the winter during this special month, once the eighth month in the old calendar but with no vestige now of that eighth month wickedness which Ruth so feared.

Earlier, on the very last day of the school summer holidays, the second day of September, Melanie, Amy and Sam had spent a glorious, sun-filled afternoon in Ruth's garden, with Matthew of course, picking the sumptuous cultivated blackberries which grew in abundance at the secret end of the garden. Ruth was put in mind of Granny Wallon, from *Cider with Rosie,*[51] stirring her boiling vats of nameless liquid potions gleaned from hedgerow and woodland, as Matthew and Sam ran about with purple stained lips, skin healthily browned during the long summer holidays, clutching baskets of shiny fruit which seemed to set the parotid glands in the neck aflame with anticipatory tasting.

Ruth and Melanie decided to freeze the shiny fruit on trays so that this taste of warm sunshine, rich with vitamins and other goodness no doubt, could be

---

[50] "If I Could Tell You," copyright © 1934 W H Auden: (1934) and renewed 1962 by W H Auden; from W H AUDEN COLLECTED POEMS by W H Auden. Used by permission of Random House, an imprint and division of Penguin Random House, LLC. All rights reserved. Copyright © 1934 by W.H. Auden, renewed Reprinted by permission of Curtis Brown, Ltd.

[51] Laurie Lee: 1959 *Cider with Rosie,* Chatto and Windus, UK

made into pies or put in jam with apples perhaps, as Ruth's grandmother used to do. Ruth briefly recalled Louise's prose poem of summer ennui.

They were later to decide to make the jam together one dark and dull November Saturday, again with Matthew and Sam happily helping by stirring the bubbling mixture whilst Amy was absorbed in her baby gym as the waiting continued. The boys were very happy too to intersperse jam-making activities with playing with baby Amy on this indoorsy day. This was very helpful for enabling Melanie and Ruth to continue the jam-making more or less uninterrupted whilst Amy gurgled away happily on the mat and batting the suspended mobiles in her own little world of swirling colour and light. She was clearly delighted to have other small people to play with, laughing delightedly and gazing at the boys with admiration and something resembling adoration. Matthew hit on the idea of twirling the hoops so they spun in bright circles and Amy reached her tiny hand out to them managing to stop the motion and obviously making the association with her hand doing that. She was entranced.

"It's incredible," Melanie said, "how such young babies seem to be able to differentiate between children and adults."

And it was paradoxically in that dullest and darkest of months too that the battalions started gradually to retreat. First sign was that little Emmie began to make a tentative then sustained recovery in response it seemed to the foetal stem cell treatment. The boy foetus provided a very close match. Next, Ruth's two weekly scan in the middle of November revealed that her boy twin's growth, though still delayed, had begun to pick up a little. And Sarah, dear Sarah, had responded well to the first two rounds of chemotherapy. She would have a break from this aggressive treatment now until after Christmas, to build up her strength ready for the next phase of treatment, radiotherapy, in the New Year.

And, mindful that in any narrative, fiction or otherwise, the characters must be allowed their own momentum, author, director, narrator, reader, audience must all therefore retreat a little leaving them to their own devices. This is the point in this narrative that we are gradually approaching. But we will let you down lightly, there is still more to be told, more audience/reader manipulation, yet more enticements to journey along with the force of the fiction, co-conspirators, partners, passive observers though you may be.

By now Christmas was featuring largely in everyone's consciousness. Dr. Onslow spoke to Mark and Ruth:

"We used to make the mistake," he explained, ever gentle, ever solicitous "of striving officiously,[52] if you like," knowing that Ruth and Mark would pick up the Hippocratic reference, "to get children home for Christmas. The problem is that families visit each other at that time. It's dark and cold outside so people are hugger mugger, cousins sharing beds perhaps, bugs are easily passed around, so this really is not the best time we've discovered. Actually, to be honest if they're well enough, the children have a great time on the ward – spoilt rotten actually." He grinned and continued, "So while we're ready to start thinking about discharge home for Emmie we would be looking for that to be well into the New Year. Emmie will have been with us for just over 6 months by then and this is absolutely par for the course in this type of very aggressive leukaemia with all its setbacks. It really is a hazardous journey, this one, as you've seen. Remind me when your twins are due because we would factor that in too."

"They're due on the 11th February but I know twins can arrive early and what with the growth difficulties of the little one..." Ruth tailed off.

"Yes, well, we'll see. Let's see how well Emmie remains in remission, keep her mentally stimulated as much as you can, possibly even the odd day at home – perhaps, let's just see. We also have to remember it's fairly near the beginning of the new school year still so Matthew could be bringing home all sorts of bugs too. Of course we have to balance that with not actually wrapping her in cotton wool for evermore. We've done that successfully here and she certainly has enough white blood cells now to fight infections."

And so it was that Christmas arrived with all its bright sparkle and cheer, its story of birth and death, its tackiness, its mix of gaudy and subtle, even beautiful, decorations in places and, of course, the delights of the primary school preparations with the teaching and re-enactment of the Christian religious feast. Matthew and Sam, as established Year 1 pupils and proud of that status, were chosen to play two of the three kings, Melchior and Balthasar.

They quickly started calling each other Balt and Melch and delighted in their shining, glittery costumes gleaned from Ruth and Melanie's quick trawl of likely garments in charity shops after dropping the boys off one morning. Anne enjoyed constructing their gifts for the baby Jesus: gold (plain gold wrapping paper around a small empty box) for Sam as Balthasar and myrrh (some malt vinegar in a small, glass vase for Matthew) as Melchior. It was a fun, but also deeply meaningful, time for all of them. And it was not until the day of the Nativity Play that Ruth discovered that myrrh was the symbol of death.

---

[52] Hippocratic Oath (c 5th to 3rd century BC,) probably devised by Hippocrates

On Christmas Day itself the family foregathered at Ruth and Mark's house for lunch, all the children having opened their stocking presents in the morning in their respective homes but enjoying being together for exchanging presents in the afternoon. In this way they would all be near enough, as planned, to visit Emmie at different points throughout the day as well as contributing everything for lunch between them thereby leaving Mark and Ruth, now heavily pregnant, just to provide the welcoming setting.

Ruth was by now having weekly scans and could not help feeling anxious at the thought of the Christmas shutdown. However, her scan on Christmas Eve, a Tuesday, showed that although her little boy was small, there was less talk of such qualifiers as "considerably", "significantly", and "worryingly"– just small for dates was how he was described now. The next scan was booked for the following Tuesday – 31st December. Ruth was relieved that this just avoided the next public holiday shutdown on New Year's Day.

Knowing their genders and Ruth particularly identifying wholeheartedly with the babies inside her, she and Mark put their minds to thinking of names, daring to hope but knowing too that, whatever the outcome, these unborn people needed full identities now. They involved family and friends up to a point in this discussion but in the event their firm choices were Colin Robert and Mary Anne. Both second names were for Mark's parents, and Ruth's grandmother and father, Mim's name had been Mary, her father's name had been Colin. They realised that Colin was not currently 'trending' as a name but knew too that these fashions went in waves and that they might indeed start a trend.

They liked the name and 'Col', they joked, could be 'cool' as a shortening. Ruth had always liked the classic name Mary. While neither she nor Mark wanted their daughter to be known as Mary Anne, just plain Mary, as her maternal grandmother had been, they decided that if the child should choose to use her given second name then that would be her prerogative, just as it would be should baby Colin decide to use Robert, Rob, Bob, Bobby or whatever. Ruth liked names with 'l's' and 'n's' she realised and sharing this idle, footling thought with Mark, discovered that he did too.

The allusion to the rescued children, ultimately rescuers themselves, in *The Secret Garden*[53] was not lost on Ruth of course, nor should it be on the reader, but Ruth did not, of course, share that thought with Mark.

---

[53] Frances Hodgson Burnett 1911 *The Secret Garden*, Frederick A. Stokes, US, Heinemann UK

Mark, it can be seen, was now emerging from the hinterland of suffering and the couple rather bravely decided to host a New Year's Eve gathering for close friends with Melanie's children staying over, allowed to stay up long enough to watch the firework displays around the world, on the understanding that once they had seen the London display it would be bed with no arguments. The evening went very well, and it was good to see Maureen and Sheila in an adult, sociable setting again. Matthew and Sam proudly offered drinks and nibbles to their head teacher, not fazed by seeing her in this different role. This is what grown-ups did, you could almost hear them thinking.

It was bed for the adults too by about 1am as a brisk New Year's Day walk was planned along the towpath. Then it would be back to Melanie's for pancakes for brunch, and on to their respective homes to slump in front of any good New Year's Day films on television ready to enjoy the precious last couple of days of the Christmas holidays factoring in a visit to Emmie in the early evening. Only Melanie and Richard and their children were staying over.

And so the narrative continues with its unstoppable momentum.

One week to the day later, Ruth went into labour spontaneously at 35 weeks and 1 day's gestation, not unusual for twin births, she knew, but how she longed to harbour those tiny ones safely for a little longer. Nature too is its own unstoppable force though and so Mary and Colin began their arduous, hazardous journey into the world, arriving at 8 o'clock and 8.15 respectively on the morning of 9th January. Ruth and Mark heard Mary's full throated cry almost immediately and, as she was placed in Ruth's arms and blinked up at her mother in some primeval recognition, that unconditional love was also born. Ruth lifted her up to smell her wet head and the baby girl snuggled into the warm protection of her mother's neck, as her mother expelled the fused placentas safely with that final, intense and easily forgotten birth pain as the team worked on her boy child.

Mary weighed in at exactly 6lbs, in old money, as the midwife explained, reassuringly. Colin, on the other hand did not cry, or move or breathe until he was given a "bit of a jump start", as the same motherly midwife explained, and rushed to the neonatal intensive care unit.

He weighed in at 3lbs 10oz. Ruth remarkably had the presence of mind to remind the team about saving the cord blood from both babies.

~ *Chapter 48* ~

And so it is that baby Colin joins his half-sister Emmie in that twilight world of childhood illness, albeit that Emmie has maintained her improvement, and Colin is only just beginning the second arduous journey of his life.

Ruth and Mary are allowed home the next morning. The strength of the feeling of separation, desolation, and actual loss as they leave baby Colin behind takes Ruth completely by surprise. She knows that she has to be strong for Mary, she has a new-born to cherish, protect and nurture and poor baby Mary must surely herself be feeling some sense of loss even if unable to articulate it.

Mark has shown Emmie the pictures of her new twin baby brother and sister and she traces their features on the screen of his phone with wonderment and gentleness.

And here, now, the detail of the narrative must be condensed and accelerated a little in preparation for reader/audience withdrawal before it ceases altogether as we leave the family to journey along with no external, controlling force, no rough-hewing of their ends[54] by any clumsy story teller. Apron strings must be loosened and moorings must be slipped as we begin slowly to let them go.

But it is a gentle, gradual casting adrift like a preparation for bereavement, that ultimate betrayal.

Emmie is discharged home on the first day of spring, having suffered the minor setback of a chest infection which, on this occasion, responds quickly and well to routine antibiotic treatment. By this time Ruth and Mark are getting to grips with the overwhelming, yet warm and welcome, befuddlement, the fog

---

[54] William Shakespeare: (c1509-1601) *Hamlet, Prince of Denmark*, Act 5, Sc 2.

of new parenthood, with its strange routines, priorities and sleeplessness. This means that having Emmie home at this time only requires that they take the caring for her, and she is well by now of course, easily in their stride.

Colin, meanwhile, is fighting his own battles alone in his plastic incubator, with tubes attached everywhere. His parents spend as much time as possible by his side, watching and waiting. His only problem, it seems, is that he is small, so all his vital organs are correspondingly small, therefore working less effectively but otherwise neither malformed nor actually diseased in any way. So, it is a question of watching and waiting and he is, of course, intensely vulnerable to setbacks such as infections. Watching and waiting, Ruth continues to feel his absence like a physical pain. Even baby Mary, lying on her mat, or in her Moses basket seems always to turn her head to one side as if seeking, searching for her absent brother, her missing twin, her co-traveller.

So what now can we know, what now can we be told?

Colin rallies and grows and is moved from Neonatal Intensive Care to the Special Care Baby Unit on the 1st day of April and maintains his improvement. There had been talk of his coming home on Good Friday but Ruth becomes acutely fearful suddenly of the Christian symbolic significance of this day. To their credit, but just as it should be, the staff, in their non-judgemental way, completely understand this and are able to comply with her wish that they delay this until Easter Day.

Easter is very late that year, 20th April; again Ruth has a discussion with Matthew about the moon and finds an enchanting book for him, beautifully illustrated, which she is editing, called *Easter and the Moon*. He now understands that complex relationship and is clearly fascinated by it.

So baby Colin is home and Mary now turns to him on the mat and finds him, as he does her. Ruth and Mark enter the challenge of looking after twin babies, with, as ever, support from family and friends. Anne and Bob move in for a couple of weeks to help them establish some patterns and routines. The first week of this fortnight is the second week of the school Easter holidays meaning that Emmie and Matthew have a wonderful time with their grandparents. Ruth cries with tiredness on occasions, she is breast feeding and has quickly to suppress any unreasonable irritation, borne only of tiredness, which fortunately both she and Mark have the insight to recognise.

Mark is a gentle father to these babies; he has one or other on his shoulder while working on his computer, rocking the other if necessary in a little seat on his desk. He takes them for drives to soothe them to sleep and to give Ruth either some pure respite or some Matthew and Emmie time. She reciprocates and enjoys her own trips in the car with them, choosing scenic routes, and putting worries about fuel costs to the back of her mind believing that mental quietude, an unusual but appealing word, is more important at the moment.

She finds it relaxing to dream on and plan ahead as she drives her precious cargo, sheltered, cocooned in their car seats, as she imagines a future of less vigilant watching over these vulnerable children, a time of short holidays together, of fun and rest and relaxation in interesting and beautiful places. Ruth and Mark have together become generally interested in piers around the country and their different, usually precarious, fates. They are ardent supporters now of the Bognor pier project and have become Friends of Bognor Pier. Ruth in particular loves the community zeal aspect required to restore and maintain piers, vulnerable as they are to the elemental forces of wind and sea, whilst at the same time representing a kind of brave human challenge to these forces as well as a celebration of simple fun.

They have been ambitiously planning a short summer holiday, in late July, not August, Ruth is adamant about that, on the Norfolk coast. She thinks about this as she drives along. They have decided on Great Yarmouth, it being the most easily accessible by train from London, but are also contemplating asking Sally and Paul if they want to join them and hire an 8-seater people carrier for the trip. Four adults looking after four very young children on beaches and piers seemed to them sensible, less anxious-making therefore more fun.

Ruth, as we know, is fascinated by the community effort in raising funds for the memorial to the victims of the Suspension Bridge Tragedy which she had been reading about on the day she first saw Matthew and she was keen to visit that to pay her own respects. She had read too about the disaster prone piers in Great Yarmouth.[55] The first of these wooden structures measured 700 feet but within a year of being opened in July 1858 it had been struck by the schooner, *James and Jessie,* losing 50 feet of its length. At the very beginning of the twentieth century, Great Yarmouth was prospering as a seaside resort and the purely wooden structure was replaced with a new wood and steel construction with a 200 seat pavilion being built. The work began in December 1900 and was completed by June 1902, only eighteen months, impressive thought Ruth. However the pavilion was destroyed by fire only 7 years later. A new pavilion was opened just a year later, again impressive given the vagaries of the

---

[55] Historical information obtained from www2.britannia-pier.co.uk, web page accessed on 19th April 2017.

weather, Ruth felt, but was destroyed by fire in 1914, thought to be arson. Following this the 'Floral Hall Ballroom' was opened in 1928 but only survived for 4 years, it was re-built and opened in 1933. Surprisingly both the ballroom and the pavilion survived the Second World War, only to be destroyed by yet another fire in 1954.

The fourth pavilion built in 1958, seemed to Ruth to be a triumph of hope over experience but why wouldn't you rebuild, renew, she reflected. It was the natural, instinctive, human way she felt, to survive against the odds. Ruth and Mark plan to see this symbol of endeavour during this planned trip, all being well. They are also keen to visit the Hippodrome Circus, one of only 3 surviving total circus buildings in the world. Perhaps Sally and Paul would be happy to babysit Mary and Colin whilst Ruth and Mark take Matthew and Emmie to a suitable show there, ensuring clowns would not be featuring, just skilful acrobats, magicians, dancers. They would witness the floor turn to water, one of many of the venue's claims to fame, it seemed. Apart from these outings they would do all the usual fun seaside activities and enjoy the beautiful stretches of golden beaches in the timeless way of such holidays.

But for now the letting go must gather momentum, no more leisurely story telling in chapters, our cast of characters must now be left to their own devices, they deserve their privacy. Our pace quickens whilst theirs slows. We have brought them thus far. But we are allowed one final chapter, one stilled screen shot.

~ *Chapter 49* ~

The setting is Angmering during the first week of June; half term, bright, warm, long days, short nights and, by coincidence, spring tides. Again Ruth explains to Matthew that these occur twice each month and are not related to the season called spring but are so-called because the tides leap or spring higher and lower than usual. Matthew mimics this by leaping high and low on the shore's edge during an evening beach walk, the twins in their double buggy, Emmie holding onto it. He remembers too the role of the moon's pull, impressive for a just about to turn 6 year old.

Ruth and Mark are staying in Jane and Tim's house for the week and this is, of course, their wedding anniversary week, Matthew's 6th birthday on Saturday and just over a year since the twins were conceived.

The next day they plan an outing to Bognor pier again. The Save Bognor Pier Group is hosting a series of fun events in celebration of one of its own week long anniversaries – it is 150 years old and in urgent need of rescue.

Ruth and Mark have met the project manager, Mike, as he is a friend of Jane and Tim's. The group is active and highly committed to the rescue. He suggested they come along but is currently tearing his hair out because the combination of strong Atlantic winds forecast for the next day, a Saturday, and very high, spring tides, has meant that all the stalls and sideshows for this last day of celebration and festivity, expected to be the most lucrative being a Saturday, have had to be put a little way back from the promenade, and off the beach altogether. This has caused much extra work, hassles with sea front businesses also vying for custom, as well as some serious safety worries. Mark and Ruth are determined to support the event as best they can and it certainly sounds to be a really fun afternoon/evening for the last day of their little holiday and a good way of celebrating Matthew's 6th birthday. A birthday party with his friends at home is planned for the following Saturday, the 14th June.

And this is where we leave them the next day. The story teller will withdraw between sunset and moonrise as the darkness deepens, late as those fall at this time of year. The sun will set at about 9.15pm and the moon will rise at about 11.45pm and will shed extraordinary, ethereal light on this tossing, churning, threatening sea demanding due respect, not to be toyed with. All playthings must be kept well back. Benign June heralds July fickleness, itself a harbinger of August wickedness it seems.

The little family of six is on the pier, amongst crowds of people of all ages, smells of toffee apples, candy floss, chips and vinegar pervading the night air. The roaring, relentless sound of the huge waves crashing against the sea wall strikes a mocking contrast to such sweet fripperies serving as a salutary reminder that all human frailty, vulnerability, striving, goodness and wickedness are themselves nothing more than endless, churning, froth and fume, spit and waste.

There are newly revamped slot machines, merry-go rounds, dodgems, hoopla, coconut shies, Splat-the-Rat, roll-a-penny, a shooting range using water pistols and plastic targets, and a newly installed mini train running the length of the pier. Punch and Judy play raucously on the wide pavement, the show having been moved from its beachside space. There are donkey rides along the green, cliff top sward; plenty of fairly contented looking donkeys are being cared for in a shady area. And there are also several groups of clowns laying claim to the vulnerable pier as their performing space.

Emmie is not fazed by these now; holding tightly to Matthew's hand she is laughing bravely at their antics, even as they approach her, she has after all seen so much, and she knows a great deal more than she did. Ruth had discovered in a recent internet search about clowns, whilst following up a newspaper article about their extensive history and lore, that the attributes of clowns are playfulness, irreverence and the freedom of 'not knowing'. No further explanation was given for this last intriguing point. Interestingly too, the article had referred to a study conducted by Professor Penny Curtis and others at the University of Sheffield looking at children's fear of clowns. Some of the older children who responded to the questionnaire survey had felt that their fear stemmed from the fact that clowns were '"unknowable."[56]

---

[56] Curtis, Penny et al (2007) *Space to Care: an ESRC funded project exploring children's perceptions and experiences of hospital space: research briefing.* Sheffield; Swindon: University of Sheffield; ESRC.

The hierarchy of different types of clowns is interesting as well, she discovered: the Whiteface, the type that dates back the furthest and is the bossy leader, comprises the well-known Pierrots, Harlequins, and Columbines. This was fascinating to her; she had known none of this, and had shuddered briefly as she remembered the clowns invading the Christmas boat trip and the horrific stand-off which had blocked their way to the airport in Crete as she read on. Then came the Auguste clown, she learnt, next in the pecking order but the least intelligent and most silly, then the tramp or hobo clown, even further down the pecking order, the most popular and the one for whom things usually turn out all right. These 'hobos' can be any character, she discovered, such as a policeman or a farmer. Ruth had had no idea that the clown tradition went back as far as B.C. Apparently a pygmy clown performed as a jester in the court of Pharaoh Dadkeri-Assi during Egypt's Fifth Dynasty about 2500 B.C. "Amazing," she had commented as she had read out snippets to Mark.

Here now, on their stilts, perilous in the strong winds, strutting along the rickety pier, high above the treacherous, broiling sea, the clowns, faces garishly painted with bright slapped on lips, some outlined in black, some with downward turning eyebrows, some with starkly white faces, weave their way maniacally through the crowds. Groups of teenagers are laughing and snapping photos on their phones, even taking selfies with the clowns until one barks, "Enough of that. Get away now," before roughly pushing aside a young girl, perhaps about 13 years old. Ruth recalls with terrifying vividness suddenly the encounter on the way to the airport in Crete; not just the bizarre facts of the encounter itself but her feelings of visceral terror, her strange sense of all-pervading dread.

The crowd disperses rapidly now, parting the way to let the groups of teenage friends through, recalling Moses bravely parting the Red Sea in defiance of the approaching Egyptian army, turning the sea bed into sand thereby allowing safe passage for the Israelites.

Matthew and Emmie are looking on bewildered by this sudden change in mood but still laughing bravely against the odds, just as people do *'when clowns put on their show'*.[57] In the background the merry-go-round's jingle can be heard on repeat: *"Oh, I do like to be beside the seaside!"*

---

[57] "If I Could Tell You," copyright © 1934 W H Auden: (1934) and renewed 1962 by W H Auden; from W H AUDEN COLLECTED POEMS by W H Auden. Used by permission of Random House, an imprint and division of Penguin Random House, LLC. All rights reserved. Copyright © 1934 by W.H. Auden, renewed Reprinted by permission of Curtis Brown, Ltd.

They move on down the pier onto the promenade. The sun is setting now in a fiery red glow on the horizon, its red streaks illuminating calmer water beyond the crashing waves. It sinks into the sea finally and the anticipated deeper darkness descends, a depth of darkness which the artificial fairground lights are powerless to penetrate so close to the shoreline. The haunting melody of a busker singing *Send in the Clowns*[58] accompanying himself very competently on his guitar, causes Ruth to turn towards the sound and gesture to the others to follow.

They stand listening as a family group; the twins are still sleeping soundly lulled deeper and deeper it seems by the plaintive chords and the short, anguished phrases. When the busker finishes Mark wanders over to ask him a question while Ruth stands back. He tells Ruth he is going off to buy the busker a meal from the mobile fast food van just a step away, a veggie burger and all the trimmings, he says. The busker sings the song a second time in response to the crowd's request. Mark returns placing the meal and drink in their polystyrene containers carefully beside him, the musician, nods a dignified thanks.

The air is still warm as the family then braves the buffeting wind to walk a little way along the promenade towards different, such different, music which insistently draws them closer. Neither this nor the wind wakes the sleeping twins in their enclosing buggy; it is very late and very dark after all. Mark is pushing the buggy finding it necessary to keep a very firm grip on it in this wind. Matthew and Emmie are now ahead of them by some distance though still in clear view of Mark and Ruth. Then the two children stop abruptly.

Ruth is struck by Matthew's pose, his absorption once again and she follows his gaze beyond the straggling groups to a hurdy-gurdy man entertaining a much smaller crowd with his captivating rendition of the eponymous song. It is pitch dark by now and the only light comes from his barrel organ. On his shoulder a tiny monkey, disturbingly dressed in a pink and blue tutu, leaps down from time to time to perform little pirouettes, rather clumsily, to the hurdy-gurdy man's command. Ruth had read recently that wild monkeys could be trained to perform such tasks simply by watching videos of these tasks undertaken by other wild monkeys already trained by scientific researchers to do them. The researchers then videoed the monkeys performing the tasks – disturbing on so many counts.

---

[58] Stephen Sondheim: *Send in the clowns* (1973)

Matthew turns to see where Ruth is; his gaze lingers on her for a minute before he is captivated once more by the revolving monkey. He is laughing as the musician plays on at an ever-increasing speed, electrifying, insistent yet strangely threnodic in its intensity, of discordant sounds.

And there the screen shot stills, the bright clarity of the images gives way suddenly to an unfocused blur which is all that remains as a still deeper darkness settles and the story teller must now quietly, but finally, withdraw.

It is only for the time being that the listeners, or the readers, or the audience, have forgotten it is dark outside. To this they must now return.

~ *Afterword* ~

Loss of innocence in childhood is explored here, how and when this can happen. The stealing of the child is plausible as it is an interesting and documented fact that children can disappear from the gaze of the authorities as we have seen when children 'fall through the net' and are harmed or killed by their parents.

Fear of clowns, *coulrophobia,* is perennial yet they are making a comeback with various Clowns' Conventions scheduled to take place in seaside resorts around the country, not to mention the recent scares involving "pretend" clowns. Clown tradition and folklore provide a threatening backdrop to the action at key moments in the story.

The Great Yarmouth Suspension Bridge Tragedy, referred to in the first chapter of the novel, actually happened although the anniversary event with the troupe of clowns performing the mime of which Ruth reads a fictional account in a fictional glossy magazine, is just that, fiction. The fund-raising efforts of Mrs. Julie Staff and her commitment to the cause are however real and I have duly acknowledged the account of these which I really did read in the *Eastern Daily Press,* our award-winning local daily newspaper, on 29th September 2013. I had not previously heard of this tragedy.

~ *Bored Summer - Andrew aged 17* ~

Bored, Summer, with your prattle and chatter of inconsequential things, full to the brim with your grass cuttings, your constant hum and buzz and heavy heat, gratefully I watch at the window for your passing and with relief feel the touch of the curled and crinkled leaves on my face, tramping homeward listen with joy to autumn's doleful whine in the chimney pots. Not that I am not grateful for your sweet nothings and pleased each morning at your unwrinkled brow but after all this bonhomie and everlasting jollity the sweeping and swirling mists and moods of autumn are something of a diversion.

Dank at the bottom of the garden is the old chicken house, disused now for a good seven years, all overgrown with nettles, eerie in the thick fog and half-strangled by the dying bindweed. Damper and draughtier still is the old dog kennel. That was made out of an old packing case and part of the fence we had to take down. Soon we must turn it around, away from the clinging fog and rain and dead leaves; it has been turned all summer to face the sun.

It is mostly the clothes that are different though: the light cord coat is slung back and draped like a flag on one shoulder, the shirt sleeves are rolled back and it's barefoot all day long. Back now to the heavy shoes and drip, dripping gum boots for the stamp and shuffle of snow is in the air, lurking in the thick fog and falling with the dry leaves.

The house too is different in autumn. You can no longer paint it from a corner of the garden with your shirt as a cushion for your chest on the prickly grass and an apple shoved in your mouth. The apples have all gone, eaten or made by rotten by maggots or in jam with blackberries; the climbing rose is dead and dull green and the chimneys smoke.

This is the season of schools, the season of uniform. Buses are crammed dark blue and deep down in the memory it is warm and tiled and smelling of soap and ink and stew.

And from the train windows, washing lines, once vivid with colour, sag; curtains are drawn, doors, so recently ajar, are sealed. Trees are skeletal, stripped of leaves and fruit. Summer withers as the year settles, folds, prepares for sleep. And hidden in the rows and rows of railway houses and mixed with the clackety-clack of the train are the secrets of the salt and milk of love. But fearful of these, I listen hardest to the whispers of death murmured by the falling leaves. Their breath on my ear has me yearning for spring and the turn of the year when once again I will catch my breath in wonder at the year's passing.

CPSIA information can be obtained
at www.ICGtesting.com
Printed in the USA
BVOW03s1047190617
487268BV00001B/26/P